R.D. BRADY
THE BELIAL SACRIFICE

By R.D. Brady

The Belial Series

The Belial Stone
The Belial Library
The Belial Ring
The Belial Recruit
The Belial Children
The Belial Origins
The Belial Search
The Belial Guard
The Belial Warrior
The Belial Plan
The Belial Witches
The Belial War
The Belial Fall
The Belial Sacrifice

Vinci Books

vinci-books.com

Published by Vinci Books Ltd in 2025

1

Copyright © R.D. Brady 2018

The author has asserted their moral right to be identified as the author of this work in accordance with the Copyright, Designs and Patents Act 1988. This work is a work of fiction. Names, characters, places and incidents are the product of the author's imagination or are used fictitiously. Any resemblance to actual persons, living or dead, places and incidents is entirely coincidental.
All rights reserved. No part of this publication may be copied, reproduced, distributed, stored in any retrieval system, or transmitted in any form or by any means, including photocopying, recording, or other electronic or mechanical methods, nor used as a source for any form of machine learning including AI datasets, without the prior written permission of the publisher.
The publisher and the author have made every effort to obtain permissions for any third party material used in this book and to comply with copyright law. Any queries in this respect should be brought to the attention of the publisher and any omissions will be corrected in future editions.
A CIP catalogue record for this book is available from the British Library.
Paperback ISBN: 9781036702519

All good things must come to an end.

> Proverb derived from Chaucer

How lucky I am to have something that makes saying goodbye so hard.

> Winnie the Pooh (A.A. Milne)

Prologue

LATERNO, ITALY

324 CE

CONSTANTINE STEPPED FROM HIS COACH, his gaze straying to the top of the Basilica Constantiniana. It was the first cathedral he had built, and as such, was a first among many in ensuring the salvation of the souls of the people under his dominion.

Constantine was a late convert to Christianity. A sign in the sky before the battle secured his victory in the Battle of Milvian Bridge, outside Rome. He had not recognized the strange cross in the sky at first. After the battle, he sought out others who could help him learn that God had overseen, no, blessed his victory. He learned of Jesus from the bishops and knew then that the cross was a sign of Jesus's triumph over death.

Just as I triumphed over my adversaries.

From the day of that understanding, he dedicated himself to honoring God. And there was no better way than bringing more people into his church.

But his job was not finished. There was still more he needed to do to rein in the heretical teachings that had sprung up like unrepentant weeds.

A wind whipped along the air, ruffling Constantine's tunic. With an impatient gesture to his guards to remain behind, he strode inside.

His sandals echoed off the marble floor as he crossed through the ornate foyer with its colorful fabrics draping the walls. With a quick sign of the cross, he cut to the right of the main room of the church and headed down the stairs leading to the lower levels. The air was much cooler down here. He made his way along the torch-lined hall, stopping at the large open door on the right.

Father Clementis sat at his desk, writing on a piece of parchment. He dipped his quill in an inkwell, his dark eyes glancing to the doorway. Surprise flashed across his face, and he jumped to his feet. "Emperor. I did not realize you were coming." He bowed deeply.

"Rise, Father."

Clementis did, wringing his hands together. "I am most honored by your presence. I have gathered the writings that many have used." Clementis gestured to the books that covered the tables, piled high.

Constantine walked forward, his eyes scanning the array of books. "So many."

"Yes, sire. I believe your concerns are well founded."

Constantine said nothing for a few moments. He walked along the edge of the room, his fingers running lightly over the ancient books stacked along the walls. He could read few of the titles. Unlike many of his time, he was not well versed in Greek—Latin was his most comfortable language.

But even he could see that these titles were not all in Greek. Some had strange markings of languages he did not think he had ever seen before. He straightened his spine. This was one of the greatest problems facing Christianity today. Too many messages and too many messengers. Christ was the messenger, and there should be no confusion when it came to his words.

"Tell me, Father. How many sects of Christianity are there?"

Clementis's eyebrows rose. "That is difficult to say. Dozens, at least."

Constantine nodded. "And that is the problem. The kingdom is divided. We need to all be under the banner of one religion, one understanding of Christ."

Clementis's hands trailed along his desk, his gaze shifting around the room. "That will be difficult. There are so many books, so many teachers."

"But only the Apostles are the true teachers. All others are false."

"That may be, but they do perhaps provide some wisdom."

Constantine shook his head. "No. We will make one Bible. One orthodoxy that all will follow."

"How will we decide which books are included?"

"I will convene a council. We must deal with the Arian issue. Creating one Bible will help solve it."

Clementis nodded, no doubt being well aware of the Arian issue. The Arians had declared that Jesus was subordinate to God. That he was not in fact divine. If those teachings were allowed to spread, they would destroy Christianity.

"Who are the greatest threats to a unified church?"

"The Gnostics," Clementis said without hesitation.

Constantine nodded. The Gnostics believed that people could have an individual relationship with God. The

Church was not necessary to maintain or initiate this relationship. It argued for a Holy Mother and Father and suggested a blasphemous relationship between Jesus and Mary Magdalene. Most damning of all, it argued that the resurrection of Jesus should be understood symbolically. That the resurrection was speaking of Jesus's spirit, not his actual body.

If Gnosticism was allowed to take hold, it would enable women to be the equal of men in the eyes of the Church, which would lead to demands for equality in all aspects of life. That could not be allowed to happen. Paul's First Epistle to Timothy said it best when he wrote: "Let a woman learn in silence with all submissiveness. I permit no woman to teach or to have authority over men; she is to keep silent."

The Gnostics could not be allowed to flourish. The Church, along with their teachings, would become irrelevant, and humans would give in to their basest natures. No, a strict orthodoxy would be required. Clear guidelines and rules for everyone to follow.

Constantine wandered over to Clementis's worktable, glancing at the text he had been copying. The original pages were stunning, with detailed drawings lining the margins. Flowers, fields, and an image of a stunning woman filled the border. "What is this?"

"It is a copy of a text of an ancient religion. Some copies have been found in recent years. This book was found amongst a group of women years ago. It had been locked down here unexamined. I have been working on translating it for the last year, although I must admit, I do not recognize some of the script."

Constantine's gaze shifted to the priest's translation, which was in Latin:

For I am the first and the last.
I am the honored one and the scorned one.
I am the whore and the holy one.
I am the wife and the virgin.
I am the barren one,
and many are her sons.
I am the silence that is incomprehensible. . .
I am the utterance of my name.
. . .
I am the one whom they call Life,
and you have called Death.
I am the one whom they call Law,
and you have called Lawlessness.
I am the one whom you have pursued,
and I am the one whom you have seized.
I am the one whom you have scattered,
and you have gathered me together.
I am the one before whom you have been ashamed,
and you have been shameless to me.
I am she who does not keep festival,
and I am she whose festivals are many.
I, I am godless,
and I am the one whose God is great.

Constantine's mouth fell open. This was written from the feminine. "What is this blasphemy? Is this about Lilith?"

Clementis took a step back, his voice shaking. "This . . . this passage appears to be."

Reaching for the book, he flipped through the pages quickly, anger rolling through him. The woman was on every page. He turned to Clementis. "*What is this?*"

"It is nothing, just an ancient book. A long-dead cult, that is all."

Grabbing the book, Constantine flung it across the room. "It is sacrilegious! Where are your other translations?"

Clementis hesitated before springing across the room and grabbing a stack of papers. He handed them to Constantine with a shaking hand. "These are all I have managed so far."

Ripping the papers from his hands, Constantine read a few lines on each page. "These are gnostic! Why are you bothering to translate them? They should be burned."

"They . . . they are no threat. No one has seen them but me. I would never reveal them."

Constantine eyed the priest. "And no one will. These will be buried with all the other gnostic tomes, is that understood?"

"Yes, yes, of course, Emperor."

"I will have every last one destroyed." He glared at the offending book.

"Yes, of course, Emperor."

The existence of yet another heretical writing that differed from what he knew to be the true intent of God only strengthened his resolve. He had been given this duty to remove these heretical writings that only pulled people from the true path. He would be the one that brought his kingdom together under the banner of Christianity.

Constantine glared at the offending tome lying facedown across the room. These ideas were the reason the council was necessary. People were straying too far from the original words. The Apostles' words were the only ones that counted. These ideas about women, they needed to be eradicated. And he would see that they were.

"Get me a list of all the writings by the original Apostles."

"Sire, that can't truly be known. There are just—"

"Find the texts that assert Jesus's divinity!" He sneered at the tome. "And nothing that asserts the feminine. *That* is not in God's plan. I only want the true teachings of Jesus."

"Yes, of course, Emperor."

Without another word, Constantine strode from the room. God had chosen him. He'd made that clear by coming to his side for the battles that brought him to power. And now, Constantine would repay God for that great gift. He would make sure everyone knew exactly what God wanted them to think, to do.

After all, who better to make that decision than the greatest emperor who had ever lived?

Chapter One

INVESS, CALEVITNIA

Two Months Ago

THE LAST FEW months had been difficult for Sergei Yanovich. The Russian government had been unyielding in their search for the man who had helped Elisabeta Roccorio launch her attack on the world.

And they had not been alone. The Americans, the British, the French, the Spanish, the Chinese, even the Kenyans had aided the Russians in their attempts to find and kill Yanovich. But Yanovich was no easy mark. He had lived his life facing one nightmare after another, and he had survived because he could and would do things others would shy away from.

And unlike most soldiers raised in a modern world, he listened to his instincts when they told him to move or to stay. He did not doubt them. It was how he had avoided the sniper's scope in his last safe house.

He had stayed hidden on the floor of the house for a full three days, not letting himself move from the room he was in or even straighten above a crawl. He had soiled himself where he was and eaten from a small stash of snacks he had in his pack. He had never granted the sniper a single shot. And when the sniper had finally moved in to check the house, Sergei had killed him with his own weapon. It seemed fitting.

That safe house had been one of dozens he had used since the coronation. As soon as he had seen Delaney McPhearson on the dais, he'd known Elisabeta would lose, and he had quickly slipped out of Calevitnia.

He had known all along that Elisabeta's only chance for success was if McPhearson was not in her way. Elisabeta was strong. She was powerful. But she fought for herself. Delaney McPhearson fought for everyone. She would martyr herself to protect the people around her, stranger or friend. It would make no difference to McPhearson. Winning against someone with that level of conviction required the same level of conviction, and Elisabeta simply did not have it.

Now, the world's governments were still looking for him but not as urgently. He had proven too elusive a quarry. And there were bigger fish to fry. They were now looking for McPhearson. Which meant this was perhaps the best chance for him to slip back into Calevitnia. He was not returning due to some sense of nostalgia or homesickness. No, he'd come back for one simple reason: money. Lots of it.

He'd made his way over the border and traveled on foot, staying off the main roads, not that traffic was very heavy. Calevitnia was not well developed. Invess, his destination, was an old town. There was only one paved road leading to the highway. The rest were still dirt.

The safe house where Elisabeta had holed up sat quietly

across the street. This street had a dozen homes, but only one man was outside. He led a cow down the dirt road. The man's shoulders were hunched, his gaze not looking up or around. Sergei scrutinized the man but got no sense he was anything other than what he appeared to be: an Invess farmer bringing his cow to town to sell.

The man's hands were rough and weathered from years spent outdoors, and his boots were layered in mud and worse. That was what the government agents always got wrong: the hands and shoes.

The man made his way slowly down the street, not looking right or left. When he was a few houses away, Sergei hefted the sledgehammer he had brought with him and slipped across the street and around the back of the house. It was a simple house. Sergei was sure Elisabeta had not been happy with the accommodations.

But Sergei was. The entire home was wired. Any electronic communication devices were automatically cloned, all of their information copied. Cameras were spread throughout the home, recording every movement. Elisabeta thought Sergei was a brute, a war dog, and he was. But what she had missed was that war had changed. It was no longer fought with just brawn. Now information and computers were as large a weapon, if not a more dangerous weapon, than a country's arsenal. Sergei, the old war dog, had learned some new tricks.

Sergei slipped open the back door and stepped inside. Shadows made the dingy kitchen look even older. He moved across the peeling linoleum floor to a door in the hall underneath the stairs. He stepped inside, closing the door behind him. He waited a moment, but there was no movement, no sound.

Satisfied he was alone and unnoticed, he pulled on the

light above his head, sending a dim light downward. Old wooden stairs led down to a basement that had cinder block walls and a dirt floor. Basement wasn't even the right word. It was a root cellar. When he'd bought the place, the former occupants had still been using it to store their vegetables and food.

But now the place looked completely empty, and more importantly, undisturbed. Sergei hurried down the stairs, anticipation rolling through him.

He'd had to wait months to return here, and the entire time he had worried that the safe house would be found. But it never had been. All those governments looking, and they had completely missed it. If Sergei were a religious man, he would have thought someone was looking out for him. But since he wasn't, he knew it was because his people would never dare reveal anything about him. Some out of loyalty, but others kept quiet with the certainty that if they didn't, Sergei would not only kill them but every person they loved.

He reached the bottom of the stairs and crossed the dirt floor to the old stone wall at the back of the room. He leaned the sledgehammer against the wall for a moment as he wiped the dirt away from some of the rocks. Spying the marking he was looking for, he grabbed the hammer and swung.

It took him ten minutes to break through the wall. He was covered in sweat and had stripped down to his undershirt. Dropping the hammer, he pulled the bricks away, leaving a large hole. He stretched his arm into the hole, reaching down until he felt smooth plastic. Sliding his hands along the edges of the rectangular object, he gently removed the cords attached to it.

He pulled it out. It was black and only the size of an iPhone. And it was going to change the world.

When he'd been on the run, he'd been able to review some of the recordings made in the house. That was how he knew Elisabeta had recovered the Omni formula. Once he had access to her computers, that formula had been downloaded onto this external disk drive.

And no one, not even Elisabeta, was the wiser.

Sergei smiled as he held up the drive. *All that power, and I hold the key.* He pulled the protective case from his pack and carefully inserted the disk drive before returning it to the bag. He hefted the pack onto his shoulder and headed to the stairs. *Now let's see how much you are worth.*

Chapter Two

BOGOTÁ, COLOMBIA

Today

THE HONDA'S two wheels lifted up as Delaney McPhearson took the turn too fast. Four yelps sounded from the back seat as the wheels slammed back down.

From the passenger seat, Drake raised an eyebrow at her. "Perhaps we *don't* wreck the car during the car chase?"

"I got this." Laney gripped the steering wheel tighter. *God, please let me have this*, she thought as she glanced in the rearview mirror. The Otero family sat huddled together, their almost identical brown eyes wide as their heads whipped back and forth, watching the side of the road zip past incredibly fast.

Mateo Otero, the father, sat on the right, his arm protectively wrapped around his son, five-year-old Nicolas, while his wife, Mariana, sat with her arm around her eight-year-old daughter, Gabriella. Both parents were Nephilim, but only Nicolas had the faint stirrings of power. Gabriella would never have any abilities.

The Belial Sacrifice

The Oteros had been in hiding from the Colombian government for the last month. Just yesterday, Laney had received word from Susan Jacobs, the head of the American Followers, that someone had leaked the Oteros' location to the government. Laney and Drake had flown into Bogota and tracked the Oteros down. They'd barely gotten the family in the car when the Fallen task force the Colombian government had set up had turned onto the street.

Now that same task force was right on their tail.

Laney whipped around another corner, cringing as a man on a bike screamed before jerking into a flower cart on the side of the road.

"Sorry," Laney muttered. They were in the middle of Bogota. Not exactly an easy place to lose a caravan of four cop cars. Laney jerked the wheel to the left, moving around a slow-moving red sedan. Drake sucked in a breath, and she got around the car, barely missing a milk truck coming in the opposite direction.

Gerard's voice came through Laney's earpiece. "We're in place." They never went on these retrievals without at least four team members. Gerard was making sure their escape route was clear or would be soon.

"Great. We're coming in hot," Laney said.

Drake tapped his mike, joining the conversation. "And by hot, she means on fire. We have four behind us and a bird in the air."

"What?" Laney leaned forward, scanning the sky while not letting up on the speed.

Drake cleared his throat. "Both eyes on the road, if you don't mind. I did not live this long, glorious life to end up a hood ornament courtesy of the Colombian police."

Laney jerked her eyes back to the road but not before she caught sight of the dark helicopter in the sky.

Crap. She had lost count of how many of these rescues she had gone on now. Every government in the world had declared it open season on Fallen and Nephilim. Whole families were being rounded up. Some had turned themselves in willingly to their governments, hoping for compassion. They then spent their days in twenty-four-hour lockdown, although some did have contact with the outside world.

Laney couldn't exactly blame the people who turned themselves in. There were more and more reports of whole swaths of people simply going missing. Not all were Fallen, but even if they weren't, they were somehow connected to a Fallen, through blood or emotions. The rest had gone into hiding, trying to reach Laney through the network Susan Jacobs had set up. Laney and her people had saved as many as they could, but it was getting tougher. Her face was well known because of Elisabeta.

But now Drake, Jen, Henry, Jake, Jordan, Mustafa, Lou, Rolly, Gerard—their faces were almost as well known. Avoiding cameras became critical in all their missions, which meant Danny became critical. He'd been training his own crew to work the cameras, but right now they only had about four people that could handle it.

"Laney, you need to take a right," Gerard said.

"When?"

"Right now!"

Laney jerked the wheel.

Drake sucked in a breath, grabbing the bar above his door.

"That one was not my fault," Laney said.

Drake said nothing.

"Pick up the pace, Laney," Gerard ordered.

Laney crushed the gas pedal to the floor. "This is as

good as it gets." But from the rearview she could see that she was putting a little distance between her and the cars behind her. It would have to be enough.

"Now, don't freak out. Just keep driving," Gerard said.

Laney frowned. "Why would I—"

A dark shadow shifted into view overhead. Mateo yelled from the back seat. Laney gaped but then struggled to push down the gas pedal further to get any extra speed from the car.

Drake sucked in a breath as the tractor-trailer dropped toward them.

"No, no, no, no!" Laney whispered as they sailed under it by mere inches. The back bumper got clipped as it hit, sending them careening across the street.

Laney wrestled with the wheel, yanking it back to the right, and slammed on the brakes.

Shaken, she looked behind her. The tractor-trailer blocked the street, crushing the cars parked along either side. A second dark shadow fell in the distance followed by a thump, feeling like a small earthquake.

"They're boxed in. Meet you at the rendezvous," Gerard said.

Laney took a breath as she started once again to drive. "Okay. See you there."

Drake nodded approvingly. "Gerard is getting more creative with his methods."

Laney stared at him in disbelief. "He dropped two *tractor-trailers* onto a city street."

Drake shrugged. "Like I said, creative."

Mateo leaned forward, speaking quickly in Spanish. "Are we clear?"

Laney glanced back at him, answering him in Spanish. "We're clear of the police. We'll head to our rendezvous and then take a plane. We should have you guys in our hideout in a few hours."

Mariana reached up and squeezed Laney's shoulder. "Thank you, thank you."

"You're welcome." She glanced over at Drake.

He smiled at her in response. "You love this part, the saving people."

She grinned. "Yes, I do."

"I only have one question," Drake said.

"What?" Laney said, turning onto the main intersection and blending in with the traffic.

"How exactly did Gerard get two tractor-trailers up there?"

Laney opened her mouth and then closed it. She shook her head. "I have no idea. And I don't think I want to know."

Chapter Three

THE TRIP from Colombia had been grueling. They'd gotten out of Bogota and headed to a small farm on the outside of town. Two old planes had been waiting for them, which they'd all crammed into, and then they headed over the border to a large farm outside Iquitos, Peru.

The farm was owned by a friend of Susan's. Luiz Huanca was a supporter of the network and allowed them to hide people, planes, and gear there. They stopped for only an hour. Long enough for the Oteros to take showers, eat, and then load back onto the plane, leaving everything they had brought with them behind.

Luiz tapped Laney on the shoulder as she was heading for the airfield. She turned with a smile. "Thank you again, Luiz."

He waved away her words. "It's nothing. My Samantha would have been very disappointed if I hadn't. She smiles on all of you."

Samantha Huanca was Luiz's wife. She had died on the

Day of Reckoning. She'd been a Fallen in Chicago and had protected a family that another Fallen had targeted.

"I'm sure she does."

Luiz handed her a large basket of chirimoya, a custard apple native to Peru. "For your friends."

Laney took it with a smile. "Oh, you have just made a lot of people very happy."

"I am sure you alone returning makes them happy."

She shrugged. "Honestly, I think it might be a toss-up between me and your apples. But seriously, thank you for everything. You have saved a lot of lives."

"It is the least I can do."

"And there have been no problems?"

"No. I am too far away from anyone for there to be concern about an old man. And I have too much money for the government to want to annoy me with raids."

Jordan Witt, the fourth member of their team, walked up carrying his own basket of chirimoyas. "We need to get moving, Laney."

"I know." She paused, looking around. Luiz's ranch was nestled in a valley with large green-covered hills surrounding him. "You really have a beautiful spot here."

"Si. I appreciate it. It has been good to me. Now be careful, my friend, so you can come visit me again. Maybe once all of this has settled down you will come for a longer trip?"

"I would like nothing more." She gave Luiz a quick hug. Only a few minutes later, she was strapped into her seat, and Gerard was taking them into the air.

Laney glanced back at the Oteros. Once again, the kids were between the parents, but both children had fallen asleep, their heads resting in their parents' laps. Mariana leaned her head on Mateo's shoulders, and they spoke quietly, looking more relaxed. Laney turned forward with a smile.

Drake reached over and took her hand. "You did that, you know."

She glanced back behind the Oteros, where Jordan was curled up against the window, his eyes closed. "We did that. It's a team effort."

"That's not what I mean. You brought all these people together. You're the lynchpin between us all."

"That's a little scary."

He squeezed her hand, settling back in his chair and closing his eyes. "It shouldn't be. You were born for this. Not just because of your ability but because of your heart. We are all lucky to have you in our lives."

Laney wasn't sure what to say to that, but she quickly realized she didn't need to say anything because Drake had closed his eyes, already drifting off to sleep.

She unstrapped her seatbelt and walked up to the cockpit, taking a seat in the copilot's chair.

Gerard looked over at her. His blond hair had grown a little longer than he usually wore it, and he'd gotten some color on his skin. With his blue eyes, he was beginning to look like a surfer dude. "Everybody good?" he asked.

"They're good. How about up here?"

"Smooth sailing."

"Good." Laney scanned the sky. "Any word from Jake?"

Jake had been in charge of another rescue in South Africa. A young man—although he was only eighteen—had been gathering Fallen together and keeping them on the move and away from the South African retrieval force. They'd been desperate for help, and unlike Laney's job, that one involved about two dozen people.

"He, Henry, Matt, and Mustafa wrapped up their

mission an hour ago. They're in the air. Everyone's safe. They should be a few hours behind us."

"Good, good." With just these two missions, they had added twenty-six to their numbers. They'd have enough room for them, but that was a lot of extra mouths to feed. Luiz had given them crates of food, which they were most definitely going to need.

"Laney," Gerard said.

She turned her gaze from the sky. "Yeah?"

"It's okay. You can relax for just a little bit. Close your eyes, sleep. Take the break. You're running yourself ragged."

As if he were a hypnotist, she felt the exhaustion that she had been pushing away for days crash down on her like a wave. She barely slept when they went on rescues. The people they were helping generally had no training, no skills beyond a God-given ability that many of them had spent years suppressing. Getting them to safety was often much more difficult than the other situations she went into on behalf of the SIA. For the SIA missions, everyone knew their job, and she could count on them to do it. With these rescues, there were families who were so locked in a shocked state that they froze at the first sign of trouble. To say these missions were stressful was an absolute understatement.

And then there was the constant worry about their hiding spot being discovered. Truth was, even if it was, no one would be able to get in. But food would be an issue if they decided to lay a good old-fashioned siege at the entrance.

Issue upon issue—food shortages; incoming requests for help; worry for her uncle, who she hadn't seen in four months—piled up on her. They were all a constant presence in her life. But as of this moment, there were no other good options available to them. No country would give them safe harbor and protect them from all the other countries of the world. There'd been rumors that Canada was protecting its citizens, but they were not open to being a sanctuary to Fallen from other countries. So for right now, hiding or government custody were the only options for enhanced individuals.

"Laney, let it all go for at least the plane ride," Gerard said, pushing harder. "Get some sleep. Even you need it."

"You'll wake me if there are any problems?"

"Without hesitation." He grinned. "And I will expect you to save my ass with all due haste."

"Well, all right then." She smiled. *Drake is really rubbing off on him.* When she'd met Gerard, he'd been so buttoned up. But apparently switching sides had brought out the relaxed side of him. She closed her eyes, exhaustion pressing down on her. She'd barely finished closing her eyes before she was asleep.

Chapter Four

MANILA, PHILIPPINES

THE STREET WAS CROWDED with both cars and pedestrians. Smells from the *palengke* wafted from around the corner, even through the light rain. It was a mixture of fish, fruits, mud, stale water, and pig's blood. Tourists often found it distasteful, but Sergei liked it. It was real.

This part of Manila was a far cry from the glitz and glamour of Makati. A moped zipped along the side of the stalled traffic. A man carrying a brown paper bag stepped between the cars and jumped back with a yell as the mirror of a moped clipped his arm. He raised an angry fist at the moped driver, who didn't slow down but whose passenger raised her middle finger in response.

Sergei Yanovich smiled. He'd always liked Manila. The congestion, the poverty, the desperation. It was never difficult to find people to do just about anything for a little money. He couldn't trust any of them, of course, but for his tasks up to this point, trust had not been necessary.

That was not the case today.

He was in an alley, standing underneath an awning that

kept him dry even as it produced a constant flow of water behind him. Nothing seemed out of place. In fact, he'd been in the Philippines for two days without any concerns. Of course, he had done his best to make sure that no one knew he was in the country. He had laid low since returning to Calevitnia, making sure no one was watching him. He'd entered the Philippines through Tuy Hoa on the coast of Vietnam, after a trip through Burma and Thailand.

He hadn't arrived at one of the main airports. He'd come through a smuggling route out of the Ilocos region of Luzon. Even with all those precautions, he waited, scanning the street one more time. He had survived this long by being cautious. Changing any of those habits would only result in failure. And failure for him at this point was death.

Finally satisfied no one was paying him any attention, he slipped into the pedestrian traffic before crossing the street and zigzagging through the cars. Without hesitation, he stepped into the alley between the pharmacy and the hair salon and headed down the alley to the back of the pharmacy. It was a straight shot to the next street, a second alley cutting through at the back of the pharmacy.

In the alley to his right, an old woman sat with a bowl in her lap. She yelled back at the door behind her before muttering to herself as she continued to stir the black beans in the bowl. She yelled again, this time at a cat that sat on the garbage can across from her, its tail swishing back and forth.

He could see the traffic on the streets, but no one stepped into the alley or even glanced through. He knocked on the door in front of him, a rusted screen along the top half.

A small peephole slid open. "Not open."

The peephole started to slide closed.

"Manny sent me."

The slide halted before opening again. "You have money?"

"Yes."

"Let me see."

Sergei pulled a brown paper bag from underneath his jacket and unrolled it. He opened it, showing the contents to the voice at the door.

The peephole slid shut. Locks rattled before the door opened. A thin man in his fifties, cigarette dangling from his lips, glasses perched on the end of his nose, waved him in. "Come, come."

Sergei stepped inside. The man quickly locked the door behind him before hustling down the hall, his sandals slapping against the old tile floor.

Sergei followed him. They passed two rooms. One was a bedroom with only a mattress on the floor, and the other was a makeshift kitchen.

The man stopped at the room at the end of the hall. He took a seat at a long table. Old lab equipment dominated one half of the room, including an old china cabinet filled with vials. "What you need?"

Sergei pulled the formula from his pocket and handed it over. "I need you to make this."

The man took the paper and scanned it. "This not easy."

"Can you do it?"

He nodded. "Yes. Complicated. Expensive."

Sergei grabbed half the bills in the paper bag and placed them on the table. "Half now, half when it's done."

The man eyed the stack before nodding. "Come back one hour."

Sergei pulled out a stool and sat down. "I'll wait."

Chapter Five

TARIJI, BOLIVIA

GERARD HAD BEEN RIGHT. The flight to Bolivia was quiet, and they landed at a farm on the southern portion of Bolivia with no issues. The mother of the family that owned the farm was Nephilim, as was one of her daughters. They kept an eye out for law enforcement and kept the plane in their barn.

The farm was only one of five landing locations they had within driving distance of their hideout. They changed locations often; the only thing they had in common was that they were out of the way. As was their procedure, they flew in only at night, further shielding them from anyone who would notice their comings and goings.

From Tariji, it was a twelve-hour car ride. Laney, Drake, and Gerard took turns driving every few hours. There were closer places for them to land, but Laney preferred to leave those locations for the other teams. She'd rather they were closer to getting home if there were any problems.

Dusk was only an hour away when they rolled into the outskirts of La Paz. They made their way to a small farmhouse and bunked for a couple of hours. No one was allowed to go near the entrance of the hideout until midnight.

They got the Oteros settled before Laney stumbled down the hall to one of the other bedrooms. She couldn't understand why sitting in a car always proved to be so exhausting. She crashed almost as soon as her head hit the pillow. It felt like it was only minutes later that Drake was shaking her awake. "Time to go."

Laney blinked her eyes a few times before glancing at her watch. 12:15. "Okay. The Oteros?"

"They're ready. We're just waiting on you."

Laney got to her feet, stumbling. Drake caught her. "When we get home, you are taking a *very* long nap."

Laney wanted to argue, but instead she just nodded her head. She was useless this tired. "Agreed."

Laney followed Drake out to the waiting station wagon and climbed in the front seat. Drake climbed in next to her with Gerard at the wheel and the Oteros in the back. Jordan had taken the motorcycle to scout ahead.

As Gerard pulled away, Laney turned around to the Oteros. "How's everyone doing?"

"Good," Mariana said. "But Nicolas is feeling a little dizzy."

"It's the elevation. We're about three thousand feet higher than you were in Bogota. It will take his body a little time to adjust, and then he will be fine."

Mariana nodded, pulling a pale Nicolas toward her. "Thank you."

Laney nodded, turning back to the front. No one spoke for the twenty-minute drive. And then it was a new voice that rang out through the car.

"You guys there?" Jen Witt called over the radio.

Laney grabbed the radio from the dashboard. "Jen, why are you on duty? You should be—"

"Right where I am. The last tourists left five hours ago. The site is clear. Come on up."

"That's my cue," Drake said.

Gerard slowed the car. Drake opened the door and disappeared. Or at least, he looked like he disappeared if the gasps from the back seat were any indication.

"He's just going ahead to pave the way," Laney assured them.

Gerard drove carefully, slowing next to a long, old brick wall before pulling to a stop. "All right. Here we are."

There were no lights, no buildings. The ancient site of Tiwanaku was completely in darkness. Even in daylight, the site required a great deal of imagination. All that was left were a few walls and two stone arches: the Gate of the Sun and the Gate of the Moon.

Mateo leaned forward. "But there is nowhere to hide out here. Tourists come here every day."

"That they do. But they can't go where we're going."

Mateo and Mariana exchanged a look.

"I promise it's safe. I know it's been a rough trip, but I just ask that you trust me for a little bit longer," Laney said.

Another long look passed between Mateo and Mariana before Mariana spoke. "Okay."

Laney stepped out of the car, stretching her back. She grabbed the basket of fruit, tucking it into her side.

A small hand slipped into hers. She looked down at Gabriella in surprise. "Hey there."

"Hi."

"Would you like to walk with me?"

Gabriella nodded.

Laney led the little girl through the ancient site,

explaining some of the landmarks as she went. "This was the capital of the Tiwanaku empire about two thousand years ago. Back then, their empire stretched from Peru to Bolivia to Chile."

"What happened to them?"

"No one's really sure. But like all great civilizations, they came to an end." Not liking the rather dour turn this tour was going, Laney shifted gears. She pointed to the south. "That is Lake Titicaca."

Gabriella giggled. "That's a funny name."

"Yeah, I guess it is. The lake was once considered the center of the world. Well, there was a god named Viracocha, who according to the legend, created both the sun and the moon from that lake. All around, there are magical places."

Finally she stopped in the front of one structure set off on its own. "This is the Gate of the Sun."

The Gate of the Sun stood roped off behind metal wires. Measuring nearly ten feet tall and thirteen feet wide, it was a single rock facade with an arched top. A doorway was carved into its center, winged figures etched on the rock face. Above the doorway was carved a sun god holding two staves with what looked like tears on his face.

Laney pointed to the central figure. "Some people say that that figure there is Viracocha, the first teacher. Others say he is a sun god, or a weeping god due to the tears on his cheeks."

"Who do you think he is?"

Laney smiled. "I think he is a friend. And that he watches over us and keeps us safe."

Mateo stepped up next to them with Nicolas in his arms. Mariana and Gerard were right behind them. "Where are we headed?"

Laney shone her flashlight on the Gate of the Sun's doorway. The light shone right through to the other side. "We're here. This is the doorway."

"But . . . but there is nothing here," Mateo said, panic beginning to rise in his voice.

Laney smiled. "People have said that about the Gate of the Sun for eons. It's a gate to nowhere. But there are others who argue that this is a star gate that leads to the land of the gods." Laney paused letting her words sink in. "Drake."

As if by magic, Drake appeared through the doorway. Laney handed over the basket of fruit. Drake disappeared through the doorway, returning seconds later.

Mariana stumbled back, making the sign of the cross.

Laney unclipped the metal wires guarding the doorway. "It's all right. It leads to our hiding place. Only Drake and myself can get you through."

The Gate was one of the early hiding places for the Tree. Drake thought it could once again be used as a hideout.

Laney held out a hand to Gabriella, who quickly took it. She extended her other one to Mariana. After a moment's hesitation, Mariana took Laney's hand.

Laney led them to the doorway. She paused in front of it. "Ready?"

Gabriella nodded, bouncing with excitement. Laney looked at Mariana, who stared at the door with apprehension before also nodding.

"Let's go." Gripping their hands, Laney stepped through.

Chapter Six

MANILA, PHILIPPINES

SERGEI DID NOT TAKE his eyes off the man for the entire hour. The man stood up at one point and stretched his back and started to leave the room. Sergei stepped in front of him. "Where are you going?"

"Bathroom."

Sergei shook his head. "Not until you finish."

The man frowned. "What? No, I go."

Sergei pulled the knife from the sheath under his jacket, holding it along his thigh. "Not until you finish."

The man's eyes went wide.

Sergei nodded toward the table. "Back to work, please."

The man grumbled under his breath but went back to his work station. He hunched back over his test tubes, measuring and mixing. Fifty minutes after he started, he pushed back. "Finished. You pay now."

Sergei stood up and walked over. The substance was blue. He wasn't sure why that surprised him. Sergei nodded at one of the test tubes. "Drink it."

The man balked. "What? No."

Sergei grabbed the man's mouth with one hand and the substance with the other. The man squirmed, trying to break Sergei's hold, but he was no match for Sergei's strength. Sergei poured the contents of one of the tubes down his throat. The man gagged, some of the substance dripping from the side of his mouth even as Sergei crushed his mouth shut.

He pushed the man back, and he slammed into the lab table, coughing and spluttering. "You, you crazy! Get out!"

Sergei ignored him, watching the man. He wasn't sure what he expected to see. He only wanted to check and make sure the man hadn't tried to poison him. But he wasn't running for the sink, trying to dilute the substance.

Sergei picked up the other tube, tilting it toward the man. "Sláinte." He drained it in one gulp.

The other man stared at him. "What are you doing?"

Sergei licked his lips. There was the slightest hint of berries. That was unexpected, but he felt nothing else. Perhaps he had not outsmarted Elisabeta after all.

Then the tingle began at the end of his toes before spreading up his body. The man held out his hands, staring at them. "What does this do?"

Sergei smiled, feeling strength surge through him. He grabbed the man and twisted his neck nearly completely around. His eyes bulged, and he went limp. But Sergei knew he wasn't dead.

He dropped the man on the table, pulling out his knife. Killing a Fallen was not an easy task, but removing the heart should do it. Sergei hummed as he worked, picturing exactly what he would do with all the money that would be coming to him.

Thank you, Elisabeta.

Chapter Seven

HAVENVILLE, MASSACHUSETTS

LANEY RELEASED Gabriella's hand as soon as they were through the Gate of the Sun. Next to her, Mariana's knees buckled, and she let out a small groan. Laney wrapped an arm around her to keep her from falling. "It's all right. The dizziness will pass in a minute."

Mariana clutched at Laney's hands. A quick glance at Gabriella showed she was not even slightly bothered by the entrance. Her mouth had dropped open, and she looked around with bright, curious eyes. Adults always struggled with the trip through the portal, but children never did. Drake couldn't explain why, but Laney thought that perhaps it was because kids still believed in magic. For adults, magic was a sleight of hand, but never real. Finding out it was real was too much of a cognitive shock. For kids, though, stepping through a portal was the confirmation of everything they believed and hoped for.

Laney led Mariana forward to the chairs they'd set up for just such an occurrence. They'd just stepped aside when Drake appeared with Nicolas in his arms and his other arm latched around Mateo's bicep. Drake released Mateo, who dropped to his knees.

Drake looked at Laney. "You got this?"

Laney waved him away as she helped Mariana into a chair. "Go get the other two."

Drake placed Nicolas on the ground next to his father. He clapped Mateo on the shoulder before stepping back through the doorway. "You'll be all right in a few minutes."

Mateo stared at the empty spot where Drake had just been. "What? How?"

Laney helped him to his feet. She could see the doorway clearly, but for Mateo, it looked as if Drake had once again disappeared. No one besides Laney and Drake could see the doorways. And they were the only ones who could go through them. Everyone else could walk through the exact same spot and nothing would happen.

Laney gently lowered Mateo into a chair next to his wife. Nicolas snuggled into Mariana's lap. Gabriella hung on the back of Mariana's chair, bouncing up and down.

Laney stepped back so she wasn't blocking their view. "Welcome to Havenville."

The portal rested in the back of a cave, but in front of them was a valley bursting with life. Green grass, trees, and colorful flowers spread across the valley as far as the eye could see. The sun shone up ahead in a bright blue sky dotted with a few clouds. And set at the base of the valley was a little town. Cobblestoned streets with homes lined along them drew the eye. It looked like a quaint English town, minus the rain. Even from here, the people walking the streets in small groups could be seen. Two large farms were on either side of the little village. A bell rang out, and seconds later the sound of children drifted up toward them.

They had named the place their second week here. It

just seemed silly to leave it nameless if they were going to spend a significant amount of time here. Drake had some alternative suggestions: Las Drake, Drake Town, New Drake City. Needless to say, no one supported those names. Laney liked Havenville. It sounded old-fashioned, sweet even. And she thought the people living here, especially if it was for a while, were going to need a little whimsy in their life.

"School's out," Laney said as she spied three young children racing through the streets. Two jaguars kept pace with them.

"How?" Mateo asked again.

"That's a bit of a difficult question to answer. To be honest, I think Danny and Dom are the only ones who truly understand the science of it. But to simplify it to a point that would make Danny roll his eyes: We're in a different dimension a few degrees off the dimension we normally live in."

"It's not a different dimension. We're vibrating at different levels," Danny said as he stepped through the portal with Drake.

"See? Told you I'd botch it. But long story short, no one will be able to find us here."

Major Gina Carstairs walked up the path, clipboard in hand. Her posture, as always, was ramrod straight, an aftereffect of her ten years of military training. That career had come to an abrupt halt when she had the misfortune of being sent to help out Senator Bart Shremp. Now she was hiding out with them until they could figure out a way to get her cleared.

She stopped in front of the Oteros. "You must the Oteros. I'm Gina Carstairs. I'll show you guys where you'll be staying and help you get the lay of the land. This is

Wendy. She'll take you down to your place, and I'll be right behind you." Gina nodded to the small woman with light brown hair and a welcoming smile next to her.

Mateo got to his feet, holding out his hand for Mariana, who took it, but she still looked like she was in shock. Numbly, they followed Wendy. Gabriella looked back at Laney with a giant grin and waved.

Laney waved back.

"So everything go all right?" Gina asked.

Laney shrugged. "The usual."

Gina laughed. "One day I'd like to come see what 'the usual' involves."

"You're welcome anytime, Major. How are things here?"

"Good. We just got a supply shipment before you arrived, so we're stocked up."

"Oh." Laney picked up the basket. "Luiz sent some baskets of chirimoya."

Gina picked a chirimoya from the basket, bringing it to her nose and inhaling deeply. "I have never laid eyes on this man, but I would happily marry him sight unseen if he provides me with these for the rest of my life."

Danny walked up, munching on his own chirimoya. "Hey, Gina. I checked on your case while I was out. You're still being accused. I'm sorry."

Gina blew out a breath. "Can't say I wasn't hoping things had changed. Not that I don't love living in an alternate dimension."

"Hey, I get it."

"Well, thanks for checking."

"No problem."

"Well, I think I'll go see how the Oteros are doing. I think Mariana might need a little help adjusting to her new reality." Gina wiggled her eyebrows before heading down the path.

Laney watched the Marine Corps psychiatrist head down the hill. She hadn't been sure how Gina was going to fit in here, but the woman could organize anyone and anything. She'd slowly become completely indispensable.

Drake appeared through the portal with Jen.

Laney narrowed her eyes, walking over to her. "Why on earth were you on lookout duty?"

"Because I am going stir crazy, and I am past the first trimester. Doc said I'm good."

Laney glanced down at the small bump that held her soon-to-be niece or nephew. "Just be careful. You've got precious cargo there."

"I know. But there is zero chance I'm going to stay bedridden for the next five months." Jen placed her hands over her stomach. "I'm perfectly healthy, and so is she or he. Besides, aren't you the one running off risking life and limb all the time? Shouldn't I be worried about you?"

"Fine, fine. We'll both worry about each other." Laney linked her arm through Jen's. "So tell me, what have I missed?"

"Not much. We got another twelve requests for aid."

"Okay. I'll—"

Drake dropped an arm on her shoulders. "Get some rest. There is always going to be people needing help. And there are plenty of us to help them. You need to sleep. The world will keep turning."

Jen looked at Laney with concern. "He's right. You need to take care of yourself too."

"Fine, fine. I'll sleep for a little bit," Laney said, already fighting back a yawn.

Drake smiled. "Good. After all, what can happen in just a few hours?"

Jen and Laney stopped walking, turning toward him. "I cannot believe you just said that," Laney said.

"Seriously, why not just walk under a ladder or break a mirror?" Jen demanded.

Drake looked between the two of them. "You two can't be serious."

Laney shook her head. "We live in a different dimension—"

"Same dimension, just vibrating differently," Danny yelled over.

Laney rolled her eyes. "Whatever, we live in a magical cave. I'm the ring bearer, you're an archangel, and Jen here is a Nephilim. The world governments are trying to find a formula that will allow them to create enhanced human beings like us. Half the history we learned in school isn't true, and I'm about to go sleep in a house my boyfriend created out of thin air four months ago. And you think jinxing us is impossible?"

Drake put up his hands. "Okay, okay. No more jinxing comments. But seriously, how much damage—"

Laney covered Drake's mouth with her hand. "You need to stop talking."

Chapter Eight

WASHINGTON, D.C.

PRESIDENT MARGARET RIGLEY scanned the report on her desk. It held the latest numbers from the Committee of Enhanced Individuals (CEI) retrieval force. They had twenty-two individuals in custody. Five had abilities, and the remaining seventeen did not, although they were related to enhanced individuals.

After the debacle at the Chandler Estate, the CEI had been the focus of intense media scrutiny. Unpopular as it was, Rigley had followed up her initial executive order on the Fallen with a second allowing the temporary detention of any individuals biologically related to a suspected enhanced individual. Half the country hated her for the act and half the country loved her for it. Politically, she knew if a Fallen attacked someone, the media would be all over her for not enacting stricter reforms.

And as strict as some argued her policies were, they were practically a liberal dream compared to some other countries. More than one country had death squads that targeted Fallen and their families. Mass graves were the only indication that the squads were at work. Of course, the countries in question denied that they sanctioned such violent actions. Intelligence indicated otherwise.

A knock sounded at the Oval's door. "Come in," Margaret called.

The door opened. A man who looked like an accountant stepped in. He smiled, as he made his way to the President's desk, and inclined his head. "Madame President."

Rigley put down her pen and studied Bruce Heller, the deputy director of the CIA. Bruce had already been on the job for close to thirty years when Margaret had taken the oath of office. She'd known him now for six years, and she still did not have any idea what made the man tick. She had never met someone who gave away so little of what he was thinking. It made him excellent at his job but made Margaret's job difficult when it came to figuring out exactly what Bruce's opinion on the Fallen issue was. When asked, he simply said his job was to enact the laws and wishes of the United States of America. A perfectly acceptable answer that told Margaret absolutely nothing.

She gestured to one of the seats in front of her desk. "Take a seat, Bruce."

Bruce smiled as he did so. "Thank you, Madame President."

"Any progress on finding Delaney McPhearson?"

Bruce shook his head. "No. We have video of her indicating she was in Bogota twenty-four hours ago. But law enforcement there was unable to apprehend her."

"How did she avoid them this time?"

"Two semitrucks dropped from about ten stories up."

The President's mouth dropped open. "You're kidding."

"No, I am not."

"Was anyone hurt?"

"Only property damage."

"And I take it whoever she was kidnapping has not been seen since?"

Bruce raised an eyebrow, and she knew it was at her choice of words. "That is true. It was a family: mother, father, son, and daughter."

The President grunted. Yet again, Delaney McPhearson had popped her head out of her hole, grabbed a group of people, and disappeared.

"They were Fallen?"

"Unconfirmed. Neither of the parents, nor either of the children had ever demonstrated any abilities, although they were considered people of interest by the Colombian government."

The President looked out the window. She could admit that Delaney McPhearson had saved her life not that long ago, along with just about everyone on the planet's. And perhaps the President could have played the situation better. But they were where they were. And the truth of the matter was, Delaney McPhearson was a threat to everyone on the planet. If she decided to take power, there would be very few who could stand against her. The governments of the world would have to work in concert to guarantee success. And the likelihood of that was lower than the likelihood of Delaney McPhearson turning herself and everyone she was hiding with in to the U.S. government.

With that much pressure on her, you'd think she'd lay low. But no. A few days ago, she'd been in Norway. Before that, Kenya. Two weeks ago, Japan, followed by California. And each of those sightings was verified. There were dozens of sightings of her all over the world. For a woman who was supposedly in hiding from the governments of the world, she was doing an awful lot of globe-hopping. Which brought Margaret to her next question. "Any luck on figuring out *how* she is managing to find these people?"

"Each of the people was on a government watch list. They were all at least suspected to be Fallen by their respective governments. Each had just been added to the list. The case in Colombia is no different. I suspect either there is spyware inside the computers of the world—"

"Could that genius, Wartowski, could he do that?"

Bruce nodded. "He would be capable of it. But it would require almost an entire legion of hackers to make that work. That seems like a rather big operation. We've found no indications of that so far."

"So what's the other option?"

"I think it's more likely a network of Fallen who have connected somehow. They warn each other, look out for each other—"

"They're organizing?"

"Not the way Samyaza had them organized. Each of the people that McPhearson has disappeared with, they've never been in any trouble. Never shown their abilities. I think it's more analogous to a network that hides domestic-abuse victims than a gathering of individuals to do harm."

Rigley's eyebrows rose. "You think they're *victims*?"

"That's not what I said. I said their network is more analogous to that type of network."

"Do you have any proof of that?"

"Nothing concrete, but there are some similarities in the backgrounds of some of the disappeared. For example, a neighbor of the family that disappeared in California said the father had started attending meetings for single fathers. But when we went to check out the meeting, the entire group had disappeared. All traces of them were gone. There was a similar report about a family in Wisconsin."

"Very well. Let me know as soon as you have something. Now, what about the Omni? Are any countries getting close?"

Bruce shook his head. "No. Everyone is stuck at the same point. It is fair to say that most of the countries of the world currently have a sample of blood from a Fallen. However, none have been able to identify anything different about their blood compared to a non-enhanced individual."

"How sure are you of that?"

Bruce met her gaze. "Very."

The President blew out a breath. While it was good no one had made any gains, it didn't change the fact that they hadn't either. There had to be a way to create these abilities. Elisabeta had told them it was possible and that McPhearson knew how. If Delaney McPhearson were a true American, she would gladly tell them what they wanted to know. Instead, she'd run off, taking that knowledge with her.

Bruce's phone beeped. He stood. "Excuse me, Madame President. I need to take this." Without waiting for a reply, he headed for the other side of the room, keeping his voice low.

Irritation flashed through her, but logic overrode it. Bruce was not a disrespectful man. If he needed to take a call, it was no doubt important. Even knowing that was the case, she flitted a nasty look in his direction.

Bruce disconnected the call and strode over to her. "My apologies, Madame President. I was waiting on confirmation before I brought something to your attention."

"And you have it?"

He nodded, not retaking his seat. "A former Russian general, Sergei Yanovich, has extended an invitation to us. He claims to have the formula for the Omni."

The President straightened in her chair. "Is it true?"

"I cannot say for certain but he was the individual who we believe helped Elisabeta in Calevitnia. We, along with our allies, have been actively trying to find him ever since Elisabeta's death."

"What are the chances he has the formula?"

"I am not a betting man. But if I was, I would bet he has it. Yanovich has a track record of gleaning information from the people he works for. Most people view him as an old war dog, but he is an impressive hacker in his own right. If Elisabeta underestimated him, I believe there is a good chance that he does in fact have the formula."

"What does he want?"

"Money."

The President nodded. "How unoriginal. How much?"

"That is to be determined. You see, he has not extended us the invitation exclusively."

The President narrowed her eyes. "*What* exactly is the invitation for?"

"He has invited us to participate in an auction. The winner gets the formula to the Omni."

Chapter Nine

HAVENVILLE, MASSACHUSETTS

LANEY WALKED SLOWLY through the fog. She knew she was in a dream, and yet it felt so very real.

"Laney."

She turned her gaze, focusing on the figure approaching her through the mist. "Noriko? What's going on?"

Noriko was Jen's half sister. She had a similar ability to Laney's ability to communicate with animals, but she also had one other ability: the gift of prophesy. Or curse, depending on the vision.

Noriko took her hand. "There's something you need to see. I wasn't sure if this would work. It's the first time I've brought someone in."

"This is where you go when you have visions."

"This is usually where they start."

Laney looked around. The fog caused goose bumps to rise along her skin. The air felt damp and cold with a scent of decay in the air. Noriko was quiet, almost shy. But if she faced this place again and again, there was obviously a core of steel underneath that quiet exterior.

Noriko took Laney's hand. "We have to hurry. I'm not sure how long I can keep you here."

Noriko's grip was strong as she led Laney through the fog. At first there was nothing, just fog in all directions. But then a light began to glow ahead. Noriko headed toward it. Through the fog, Laney began to see shapes, people. It looked like daylight. Without hesitating, Noriko aimed for it, stepping from the mist and into a small street.

Laney's mouth fell open. Ahead of her was a church. She would describe it as old, but it looked like it had been constructed within the last few years. On either side of the church were simple wooden buildings, most with long wooden porches and railings where horses were tied up. A dirt street ran along the ground in front of them.

A man stepped from a building next to the church. He glanced along the street. Laney tensed, but his gaze slid right past them. *He can't see us.*

"This way." Noriko tugged Laney to the right. "We need to walk a bit."

"Where are we?"

"Salem."

Laney didn't have time to ask any questions as Noriko picked up her pace. She slipped through an alley, making her way to the stable located just off the end of it. Noriko glanced at Laney and then slipped through the door. Laney hesitated for only a second before following.

Two women were inside. One had a head full of white hair and a plump body hidden beneath a dark black dress. The other woman was much younger, and by the state of her dress, obviously not wealthy.

Sarah Goode. The name slipped into Laney's mind. She was the head of the Followers in Salem. She died during the Salem Witch Trials after . . .

Laney's gaze strayed to the woman's stomach where the beginning of a baby bump could be seen.

Sarah paced across the space, a lazy mare watching her from over the stall door. "Are you sure, Rebecca?"

"Yes. They are sending a magistrate. We must take care."

Sarah nodded. "We will. But it is written. You know that."

"I know, but perhaps if we could— Sarah?"

Laney's gaze flew to Sarah, who had gone still, then her whole body began to shake.

Rebecca hurried forward, catching Sarah as she began to fall. Laney lurched forward, but Noriko held her back. "You cannot help her."

With great difficulty, Rebecca helped Sarah to the floor. Her eyes closed, Sarah shook and trembled for what felt like forever, but it was likely only a minute. And then she went still. Laney knelt down in front of her, wishing she could do something to ease the woman's pain.

Sarah's eyes flew open. Laney reared back at the suddenness of the action. There was no confusion in Sarah's eyes, no sign of pain. She pierced Laney with a look. "You must find the weapon. It is the only way to defeat them."

Rebecca frowned. "Sarah, what are you saying?"

But Laney knew the words weren't for Rebecca.

Noriko said no one could see them in this time, but Sarah was looking right at her. "What weapon?"

"Look to the book. You must look to the book. Sacrifice and death will lead you, and sacrifice and death will follow. Blood will lead the way."

Sarah's body arched, and she cried out. Laney felt herself flung backward into the fog before she slammed down. Her eyes flew open. She was back in her bedroom, sitting upright in her bed. Her breath came out in pants as she looked around wildly.

What was that?

She was tempted to write it off as a highly vivid dream, except she could still feel Noriko's hand in hers. Noriko had wanted her to see that. Sarah had wanted her to hear her words. But what did they mean?

Drake lay sleeping quietly beside her. She placed a hand on his chest, needing his warmth. Cleo lay on the large cushion next to the bed, not stirring either. Sarah Goode—she had been the head of the American Followers. She had been put to death during the Salem Witch Trials, and her daughter had been tortured to try to get Sarah to confess. Her other daughter had died during childbirth. So much pain in one woman's life.

And now she was reaching across the years with a message about a weapon. The book, it had to be the Tome of the Great Mother. There was really no other possibility. Laney sat up, rubbing her arms as a chill ran through her as she remembered the woman's words: *Sacrifice and death will lead you, and sacrifice and death will follow. Blood will lead the way.*

There had already been so much death, so many sacrifices. She pictured Victoria before she gave her own life to keep the world safe. Rocky, Kati, Maddox, Drew—they were all dead. And those were only the people in her inner circle. When she extended out further, the numbers grew and grew.

Sarah's words meant there was still death and sacrifice to come. On some level, Laney knew that. With the state of the world, it was all but a guarantee. But she wished Sarah had given her some clue that maybe there was something else beyond sacrifice and death in their future.

She slid silently from the bed, making her way to the window. It was quiet outside. No one was stirring. Movement sounded from behind her. She turned as Cleo brushed against her.

Okay?

Laney nodded. "Just a bad dream."

Cleo looked into her eyes. *Not a dream. Message.*

Laney stared at her friend. *You saw?*

Cleo nodded. Laney didn't truly understand the bond between the two of them. She could understand the other cats and all other animals she came across, but what she shared with Cleo was different. It was as if Cleo was a part of her.

Cleo's head lifted up. She moved to the window, staring outside intently. Laney followed her gaze, seeing Jordan hurrying down the road toward her cottage.

Without a word, she and Cleo went down the stairs to meet him. Slipping on some shoes that she'd left by the front door and a sweatshirt, Laney opened the door. Jordan was halfway down the path and looked relieved as he caught sight of her. "Good. You're up. I need you to come with me."

Laney fell in step next to him, almost jogging to keep up with his pace. "What's going on? Is it the mission?" She knew Jordan had been on a mission to grab another group from the United States.

"No, it went fine. But there's someone who needs to speak with you."

Laney frowned. "Who?" But even as she said it, she saw the tall woman standing with her arm around a younger woman clutching a child to her chest.

Laney gasped, outpacing Jordan as she hurried forward.

The woman caught sight of her, and after a quick word

to the woman, stepped away from her. Her brown hair was still in its pixie cut, her build still strong, but Susan Jacobs, the leader of the American Followers, Fallen, and mother of the deputy director of the CIA, looked tired.

"Hi, Laney."

Chapter Ten

SUSAN WOULD NOT LEAVE the front entrance until everyone she came with was seen to. The group was large, over thirty. But even with the size of the group, they soon had everyone sorted out, and Laney was able to pull Susan away. She ushered her to the control room, placing some waters on the table along with a plate of cheese and crackers. Susan took both gratefully. She closed her eyes as she took the first few bites with a sigh.

After finishing half a dozen crackers and the glass of water, she finally looked up at Laney. "Sorry to barge in on you."

"It's not a problem. But why are you here? Were you discovered?"

Susan nodded. "Yes. One of my people turned me in."

Laney's face must have said what her mouth did not, because Susan spoke quickly. "No. It was an impossible situation. The CEI knew that there was an underground helping ferret Fallen and their families to safety. They'd been slowly pinning us in. They got to Logan, one of my most trusted Followers. Threatened his family. He told them where to find me, but he managed to get a message to me ahead of them so I could get out."

"What about the underground?"

Susan shook her head, her chin trembling. "It's gone. I was the last holdout. The government's been closing all our escape routes one by one. My people have had to go into hiding themselves. Some are here with you, some are spread out across the globe, hiding with friends and supporters. But I don't think you'll be getting many more people. It's bad out there, Laney."

"What about Bruce? Does he know?"

"I'm sure he does by now. But I don't want to pull him into this. Besides, he can do more good where he is."

"Will they be able to link you two together?"

"With enough investigation, they probably will. But I don't think they know I'm a Fallen. They wanted me because I was helping people escape." She met Laney's gaze. "The government is incarcerating anyone who aids in the escape of a Fallen."

"When did that start? Is that even legal?"

"According to them, we are aiding and abetting. They haven't made any announcements, but slowly the people who have helped or failed to turn people in have been getting locked up themselves. It's happening across the globe."

"They're turning the whole world into us versus them." Frustration rolled through Laney. "It doesn't have to be this way."

"No, but people are scared. And the governments' response to fear isn't education but a crackdown. Instead of explaining the monster in the closet is actually just the shadow of a stuffed bunny, they're blowing up the closet."

Laney ran a hand over her face.

"Hey," Susan said quietly.

Laney looked up.

"You're doing all you can. Actually, you're doing more than I ever thought possible. You've saved a lot of people."

Laney shook her head. "*We've* saved a lot of people. Half these people wouldn't be here without you."

"We all do what we can."

"But is it going to be enough?"

Susan sighed. "I don't know, Laney. I really don't know."

Chapter Eleven

LANEY WAS STRUGGLING with Susan's arrival. If Susan was right, then the avenues of escape for Fallen were closing even as the governments were cracking down harder. There had to be something they could do to change that. But what?

Ahead, she caught sight of Noriko in the cats' pen, the cats all circling around her. They really loved her. She was so good with them. Better than Laney, truth be told. Laney could communicate with them, but she was a friend. Noriko had taken over the role of their mom.

Noriko walked out of the pen. The cats swarmed around her before drifting off in different directions. Even Laney could appreciate the incredibleness of the scene. Noriko, with her slim build and smooth skin, stood smiling in the middle of a pack of giant cats. Each cat touched her gently before taking its leave—their way of saying thank you.

By the time Laney reached Noriko, there was only Snow

by her side. Noriko smiled. "I thought I might see you this morning."

"Do you have time to talk?" Laney reached down and rubbed Snow's side. *Morning, girl.*

Hi, Laney.

"All the cats are fed, so I'm free. I guess this is about last night?"

"So that wasn't a dream?"

"No, but it wasn't a vision either."

Laney frowned. "What do you mean?"

Noriko frowned, her dark eyes looking troubled. "My abilities, they're changing a lot. When I first came into them, they were always in the form of a vision. Something abstract that I had to interpret. But then they became more concrete, more straightforward. And then I began to visit people in different times."

"That's what happened with Samyaza."

Noriko nodded. "That was the first time it happened. But it's happened a few times since." Noriko looked away.

Laney pulled her to a stop, studying Noriko's face. She was paler than normal, and there were dark circles under her eyes. "Is that safe?"

Noriko shrugged.

"Noriko."

Noriko sighed. "Is what you do safe? We all have a role to play, Laney, and this is mine."

Laney wanted to argue with her. Tell her she should be careful, but it would probably be a little hypocritical coming from her. And besides, Noriko had a right to be part of the fight. It was her life and the lives of people she cared about hanging in the balance as well. "So that event, we were actually in the past?"

"Yes. Sarah needed to speak with you."

"So that was real? It wasn't some sort of metaphor?"

"No, it was real. You were in Salem. Sarah, she was speaking directly to you."

Sacrifice and death will lead you, and sacrifice and death will follow. Blood will lead the way. Laney shook off the chill at the long-dead woman's words. "Do you know what she meant about a weapon?"

"I was hoping you did."

"No, not yet." She looked past Noriko, straining to think of anything that might be the weapon she had referred to.

"Do you know what the book is?"

"It's the Tome of the Great Mother," said Laney. "It's an accounting of the lives of the Great Mother since before history."

"Wow."

"Yeah. It's pretty amazing."

"Do you have a copy?"

"No. Samyaza had the copy that was in the U.S., and the other copy is held by the Vatican." Laney paused. "But I do know somebody who has spent a great deal of time studying it. I think I need to go speak with my uncle. Thanks, Noriko."

Laney started to head off, but Noriko called out to her. "Laney."

She turned.

"I don't have a vision or anything to back this up exactly, but I just feel like time is running out. I keep dreaming about a giant wave crashing down on a beach and wiping out everything in its path."

"And you think Havenville is the beach?"

Noriko shook her head. "No. I think the world is the beach."

Chapter Twelve

AFTER SPEAKING WITH NORIKO, Laney went to see how the Oteros were settling in. She had learned in her new reality that dwelling on issues did not help solve them very often, so she pushed the warnings from Sarah aside. History had shown her that she would learn soon enough what the warning was about. After spending some time with the family, Laney stepped out of the Oteros' new home, standing on the doorstep.

"If you need anything," she said, "be sure to let Wendy or Gina know."

Mariana grasped Laney's hands. "We cannot thank you enough. Without you—" Her words cut off, and tears clouded her eyes.

Laney patted her hand. "It's all right. We're all in the same boat. But you're safe now. Focus on that."

Mariana squeezed her hand. "I will."

Laney headed down the path as Cleo slipped from the trees to join her. "Hey, girl. How is everything?"

Good. Quiet. Boring.

Laney laughed. "I'll take boring."

A longing to escape the valley for a little while rolled through Laney. "I know. I wish I could take you. But if something happened to you . . ." Laney shook her head. "I can't take that chance."

Cleo stopped glaring at Laney before turning and heading in the opposite direction. Laney blew out a breath. Great. She knew how much Cleo wanted out. But the countries of the world wanted a cat even more than a Fallen. All the cats were now hiding in Havenville. There were acres and acres of land for them to roam through, but Laney knew they needed more, or at least Cleo did. But while there was a chance Laney or any of the others could blend into a crowd, that was not an option for Cleo. No one was going to believe that Cleo was an oversized housecat.

But she hated Cleo being mad at her. Maybe she could take her out for a run one night when it was quiet.

"Hey, Laney."

Laney looked up as Henry walked down the street toward her. Standing at seven foot two, he towered over everyone in Havenville. With his dark hair and violet eyes, her brother looked nothing like her. But the connection she felt when she saw him cemented his place in her heart. He was her home, her family.

She smiled at his easygoing walk. There was a calmness to her brother these days, as if Jen's pregnancy had put the final piece of his life in place. Laney linked her arm through his as he joined her. "Hey yourself. Where are you coming from?"

"Dom's."

The smile slid from Laney's face. "Yeah. I was there this morning."

Dom was not doing well. Gina had actually moved into

the cottage next door to him so she could watch over him, but he was struggling. Being without his bomb shelter required an adjustment he just couldn't make. Lou, Rolly, and Danny had all moved in with him. Cain and Nyssa were in the cottage on the other side of him. Laney and Drake were in the cottage directly behind him, and Jen and Henry were directly in front of him. He did better when people he knew were around. But anything could set him off. A noise, a scent—it was going to be a long road back.

"Did he have a spell?"

Henry nodded. "Yeah."

Laney closed her eyes. He hadn't had a spell for two weeks. She'd thought maybe they were in the clear. When they'd first arrived, he'd had them daily, sometimes multiple times a day. He'd curl up on the ground, his hands over his ears, crying, screaming, or sometimes just repeating the same phrase over and over again: Nowhere is safe. Nowhere is safe.

It was heartbreaking. Laney didn't know what to do to help him. No one did. Usually it required Gina sedating him to get him to calm down. "Is he okay now?"

"Yeah. He tends to snap about of them pretty quickly. Athena is with him."

Laney nodded. Athena was one of the cats. She had taken to Dom as soon as she met him. That was how it usually worked with the cats: They found their person and were completely loyal to them. "Do you know what set him off?"

Henry shook his head. "No. He was in the house. Lou and Danny had just left. Lou forgot something, went back, and he was already curled up on the floor."

Laney closed her eyes, picturing the scene she'd seen too

many times. Guilt once again weighed her down. She should have taken steps to protect him. They all should have realized he'd been taken. They thought he'd be safe. He wasn't a Fallen. He shouldn't have been taken. He wasn't covered by Rigley's executive order. But the lines of the law seemed to become blurred when it came to anyone related to the Fallen at this point. They had underestimated how far the President would go. Naively, they had thought the protections of the Constitution would protect them. As she glanced around, she knew now that naivety had cost them, but of all the people, it had cost Dom and Molly McAdams the most.

"I saw Molly earlier," Henry said as if reading her mind. "She's doing well. Zaria never leaves her side."

Zaria was Zane's sister. Molly had never met her before she stepped through the portal, but Zaria had been waiting for her. She had broken out of the enclosure they'd kept the cats locked up in when they first arrived, wanting to give everyone a chance to get used to them before allowing them to roam freely. But Zaria wouldn't let herself be contained. She knew where she needed to be.

Molly had taken one look at Zaria and burst into tears. She looked almost identical to Zane, except for one small white patch on her chest. Now Zaria lived with the McAdamses. She wasn't a replacement for Zane. She was someone sharing the loss with Molly.

Laney glanced down the street. The McAdamses lived on the other side of Cain. "You know, maybe I'll go stop by and see—"

"Laney!" Danny hurried down the street toward them.

A few people stopped to watch him go by with alarm. *Damn it, Danny.* They were trying to keep this place calm.

Everyone was unsettled with the move here, with leaving their lives. As a result, there was a concerted effort to keep Havenville as peaceful as they could manage. There was no need to worry everyone with issues that they could not help. That burden was shared by a dozen or so people who had started the journey with Laney.

Annoyed as Laney was, her gut clenched at the look on his face. *Something big must be up*. Danny stepped out of the gate every morning and evening to check his computer feeds. The signal couldn't get through to where they were. Danny was working on the problem but was not hopeful at coming up with a solution.

Henry and Laney met him in the middle of the street. Danny sucked in a breath. "It just came over the—"

Laney grabbed his arm. "Not here."

Danny looked around, realizing they had an audience. He winced. "Sorry. Right."

"Come on. We'll go to Gina's." Her cottage was the closest. Laney made a conscious effort to smile at each person they passed and act like everything was fine, even as she felt Danny all but vibrating with nervous energy next to her.

Gina was just stepping out of her cottage as the three of them turned down her path. Gina's eyebrows rose. "Everything okay?"

Laney kept her voice low. "Not sure. Danny has some news."

Gina opened the door. "Come on in." Laney didn't even wait for the door to close. As soon as everyone was inside, she asked, "What happened?"

Danny spoke in a rush, as if the act of not speaking on the walk over had been like him holding back the tide. "I've been monitoring the dark web. I thought if some secondary group or individual, not a government, found something to do with the Omni, they'd try to sell it there first."

"Someone's found it?" Henry asked.

"I think so. He's a former Russian general. He had ties to Elisabeta." Danny quickly explained about Calevitnia and Yanovich's role in Elisabeta's plan. With each word that fell from his mouth, the sense of forbidding doom that had started at the pit of her stomach when Danny called out to her grew.

"It's an auction. Pretty much any country or individual with money has been invited to participate. It's going to happen tonight," Danny finished.

Laney's mind raced. "Okay. Between Cain's money, what Victoria stashed away, and—"

Danny shook his head. "We can't bid."

"What?"

"It's by invitation only. There's no way to get into the auction. I mean, if I had a few days and we could physically get into some government buildings, we might be able to. But there's not enough time."

"Will we be able to monitor it?" Henry asked.

Danny nodded. "Yes. But we won't be able to participate."

Laney looked at Henry, seeing the fear she held reflected in his face. If this Yanovich really had the formula and sold it to the highest bidder . . .

"Maybe it's a hoax. Maybe the formula's wrong," Gina said.

Laney nodded, knowing that was possible. Elisabeta was not someone who would hand that type of power over to anyone. But if Yanovich had managed to . . .

Laney didn't even want to think about what would happen next. Sarah's words rang through her mind. *Sacrifice and death will lead you, and sacrifice and death will follow. Blood will lead the way.*

It looked like she might learn what Sarah meant sooner rather than later.

Chapter Thirteen

DANNY HEADED TO THE GATE, ready to stand outside to see what information he could glean. They had a small cabin, not more than a shack really, at the back of the site that he could use. Former SIA agents Matt Clark and Mustafa Massari would stay with him and keep him safe.

Laney wanted to do something to help, but there was nothing for her to do. She walked through the door of her and Drake's place. Heading to the bedroom, she lay down on the bed, staring at the ceiling. The idea of anyone selling the Omni for money was terrifying. Didn't Sergei Yanovich realize what he would be unleashing?

The world was already in a brittle place. Adding Omni-powered soldiers? It would be like throwing a match on a huge pile of dead leaves. She closed her eyes, trying to force herself to sleep, but all she saw was massive devastation. The world would never be the same once someone used the Omni for their own gain. She sat up.

I need to run. She needed to lose the nervous tension running through her. She needed to exhaust herself until sleep was a requirement, not a choice. She grabbed her running shoes and was lacing them up when Drake appeared at the doorway.

He arched an eyebrow. "You need shoes to sleep?"

"No, I need to run to sleep. A former Russian general says he has the Omni. He's auctioning it off to the highest bidder."

"Well, that's . . . horrible."

"Yup." Laney leaned down and tied her shoes.

"You okay?" he asked.

"No, not really. This is insane, Drake."

"I know."

She looked up at him. "When Samyaza decided to fall, he changed humanity forever. He introduced greed, avarice, hate."

"In his defense, he didn't introduce it. He merely encouraged it."

"Okay, fair enough. But he started this whole battle between the forces of good and the forces of evil. I thought with Samyaza dead that we were out of the woods. That we would just be fighting the regular battles—a Fallen gets out of line, we step in and neutralize him or her. End of story. But this? We can't neutralize an entire army of Fallen." She stared out the window. She could just see Molly McAdams walking with her friend Theresa. Zaria walked next to them. The girls were smiling.

What kind of a world is this going to be for kids?

She turned and saw that Drake was watching the girls as well. "Did you know Samyaza? Before the fall?"

Drake opened his mouth and then closed it, a frown appearing on his face. "I don't know. I don't remember anything from that time."

"Do you know anything about why Samyaza fell?"

"Not beyond what I've read."

Laney stood, blowing out a breath as she pulled her hair back into a ponytail. "This is going to be really bad, Drake. And I don't know how to make it better."

He stepped into the room, putting his hands on her shoulders. "It's not always up to you."

She shook her head, stepping out of his embrace. "Yes, it is."

———

CLEO MET Laney as she stepped out of the house and ran with her. Neither of them spoke. They just ran for ten miles. It was Laney's form of meditation. She focused on each footfall, on the comforting presence of Cleo by her side. By the time she hit ten miles seventy minutes later, her thighs were burning, but she felt better. More at peace. She slowed to a walk. Cleo did the same.

Better?

"Yes." The anxiety that had been crawling through her since they'd learned of the auction had been reduced. It was still there, but it was no longer trying to choke her.

She glanced at Cleo, who moved with feline grace next to her. Cleo always seemed like an old soul. She was always calm, even in battle. Laney had never seen her lose her cool. "What do you think of us? Of humans?"

Cleo's eyes flicked toward Laney before she returned her eyes forward. *Complicated. Angry. Happy. Kind. Cruel. Humans are all.*

Laney nodded. That was true. You could have two children who grew up in the same home, with the same parents, and yet they could be polar opposites in so many ways. When she'd been in school, it was the complicated nature of humanity that had driven her to study criminology, to see if she could figure out what made some people so cruel while others couldn't even stand the sight of cruelty, never mind commit harsh acts themselves.

Together, Laney and Cleo stepped out of the trees and made their way along the back of the homes there. Tiger appeared from between the second and third house and walked with them. Laney got the sense the two cats wanted to continue on alone. "Go ahead. I'll see you two later."

Cleo licked her hand, and then she and Tiger headed back to the trees. Laney stayed along the tree line. She thought of heading to her place, but she really didn't want to. She felt restless, untethered. Without conscious thought, she found herself heading toward Cain's house. She paused at the back fence. Cain sat in the backyard, his head down, his eyes closed. She didn't want to wake him. She'd started to turn when he called out.

"I see you." He raised his head, stretching his arms above his head with a smile.

She cringed. "Sorry. I didn't mean to wake you."

"That's fine. Just a little morning nap. Nyssa has a tooth coming in, and she was fussy last night."

"I can take her over to my place tonight if you want. Let you get some sleep."

"I can stand a few nights of reduced sleep. I think we'd all feel better if you were well rested."

Great. No pressure there.

Cain tilted his head. "What's that look for?"

"What? Nothing?"

He frowned. "Come on. Take a seat so I don't have to yell across the backyard at you."

Laney walked over toward him, taking a seat on an Adirondack chair.

"What's going on?"

She blew out a breath, dropping her head into her hands. "I don't know. I think all the pressure is getting to me."

"I'm surprised it hasn't sooner. You've been holding up amazingly well. So what's brought on this particular bout of self-doubt?"

"Did you hear about the auction?"

Cain shook his head. Laney recounted what they had learned. When she was finished, she felt a little better. For some reason, sharing burdens with Cain always made them feel lighter. It wasn't the same as speaking with her uncle but it was a close second.

"Well, that's not good."

Laney couldn't help it. She laughed. "That has to be the epitome of an understatement."

He gave her a small grin. "True." He paused. "I'm guessing you'd like to be able to speak to your uncle about it."

He was right, even though she hadn't realized that was exactly what she wanted. After they had gone into hiding, her uncle had stayed in Italy. She had spoken with him a few times, but she wanted to see him. She wanted to talk with him the way she used to. The phone, it just wasn't enough. "I miss him."

"Me too."

Laney stared off into the trees. She knew it was safer for her uncle not to be here. But it didn't make it easier.

"Tell you what," Cain said, interrupting her thoughts, "how about you tell me what's going on in your mind, and I'll do my best to channel Patrick. Begin."

She couldn't help but smile as Cain put his hand on his

chin, rubbing his fingers along his jaw the way she'd seen her uncle do a million times.

But her small moment of levity departed as soon as the gravity of what was facing them crashed back down. "I just don't know what to do. So many people are going to get hurt. So many are going to get killed. I don't know how to stop all of this."

"Are you sure that's your job?"

Her head snapped up. "What?"

"One thing your uncle and I agree on is that you take on too much, Laney. You are not responsible for every life on this planet. Yes, I think unleashing the Omni is horrible. People will die. But that is not your burden."

"Are you saying I shouldn't help stop it?"

"Of course you should. But you shouldn't blame yourself if you can't. We humans are responsible for our own circumstances. You try to help as many people as you can. But that is all of our responsibilities, not just yours. Each person has to make a choice: which side of the battle are they going to be on? The good or the bad?"

"Like the children or the belials," Laney said quietly, recalling her conversation with Drake earlier.

Cain nodded. "This battle has been going on for eons. And it will continue to go on long after this battle is a footnote in history."

"But it feels like the stakes are so high now."

"I can tell you from experience, the stakes always feel like they are at their highest point until the next emergency." Cain glanced back at the house. "You know, as Nyssa lay crying early this morning, her teeth hurting, and there being nothing I could do but sit with her, I thought about all that Nyssa has been through and all she will probably go through. The pain of this morning is nothing compared to the pain she has felt at other points in her life. And I couldn't help but think of when she chose to end humanity's immortality. She must have felt much like you do now. That so much was resting on her shoulders. That her decisions would have worldwide ramifications."

Laney nodded, knowing he was right. "And her decisions also had huge personal costs."

"Yes, they did. But she made those choices for the betterment of mankind. You're in the same position."

"But she knew what to do. I don't have a clue."

"Not yet you don't, but you will figure it out."

"How can you be sure?"

He smiled. "Because you always do. Time and again the world has thrown one difficult problem at you after another. And you have sailed through them."

"I think 'tripped and stumbled my way through them' might be more accurate."

"Perhaps, but the important thing is that you got through it. All of this"—he gestured around at Havenville—"is because of you. All these lives and millions of others. Whatever happens in the future with this auction, it will happen. You can't change that. You can only play your role."

"But what if I'm not enough?"

He took her hand. "You've always been enough. We're all living proof of that. When the time is right, you'll know what to do."

"I hope so."

"I *know* so. So put all the doubts and fears aside. They serve no purpose but to make things more difficult. And I think things are difficult enough, don't you?"

She squeezed his hand back. "Now that I can agree on."

Chapter Fourteen

WAITING for nightfall had been one of the toughest things Laney had done. She'd been tempted to cross through the portal well before nightfall, even though that risked the chance of exposure. But to what end? Then she'd just be twiddling her thumbs in Bolivia and potentially putting everyone inside Havenville at risk.

Finally, the day mercifully ended. Darkness fell, and it was safe to step through the Gate of the Sun. Laney stepped through first with Henry. Drake followed with Gina.

Gina took a deep breath, closing her eyes. "It's weird being back in the real world."

Gina hadn't stepped out of Havenville since first stepping in. She was still wanted in connection with the deaths at the facility Dom had been held at. They were trying to figure out a way to clear her name, but without communications and computers in Havenville, it was a decidedly slower process than any of them liked.

"Thanks for agreeing to go," Laney said.

Gina shrugged, although it wasn't as indifferent as

Laney thought she might be aiming for. "We're all in trouble if this auction turns out to be legit. Anything I can do to help."

Matt, Mustafa, and Danny would be waiting for them by the car.

Drake kissed Laney on the forehead. "I'll keep an eye out for any trouble. Just be back before dawn."

"You got it."

Jordan and Jake walked up, M4s slung over their shoulders. Laney turned to them. There were always two people outside Havenville keeping an eye on the tourist site, making sure no one showed too much interest in the Gate of the Sun or the site in general. Dylan Jenkins and Mark Fricano had already taken their spots for the night shift.

"Hey, guys. Any problems?"

"Nope. Just regular tourists. Everybody good inside?" Jake asked.

Laney smiled. "Same old. And the McAdamses are all good. I even heard Molly laughing at lunch with the other kids."

Jake's shoulders dropped. "Good. That's good."

Jordan yawned. "Well, I don't know about you guys, but I could use a nap. I'll see you guys when you get back."

Laney frowned. "Where's Jen?"

"Here."

They all turned as Jen appeared from the other side of the gate. "I just wanted to do one last inspection. We're clear."

Henry opened his arms, and she walked into them. "I'm good," she said. "The baby and I are both fine."

"I know. I can hug you just because."

"Yes, you can."

Danny's impatient voice came over the radio. "Guys."

Jake answered him over his radio. "They're coming."

"You need to go." Jen stepped back from Henry. "We'll keep an eye on things back home."

"You need to get some rest," Gina said.

"I will, I will." Jen shooed them away. "Now go."

Wasting no more time, they made their way down to the parking lot. Dylan stood by an old truck already running. "Gassed her up for you and everything."

Mustafa hopped in the driver's seat, and the rest of them piled in. No one spoke during the drive to the farmhouse. They needed somewhere private to watch the auction. As soon as the car stopped, Matt zipped out the door to run security checks. Danny climbed out almost as quickly, hurrying to the front door and disappearing inside.

Mustafa stepped out. "I'll help him set up."

Henry, Laney, and Gina didn't move from the car, just scanned the quiet land.

"Is it wrong I'm wishing that if we just stay in the car, we can keep any of this from happening?" Gina asked.

"I am right there with you." Laney sighed, pushing open her door. "But none of us are people who hide from reality."

Gina stepped up next to Laney. "This is going to be bad, Laney."

"Maybe a good country will win the auction," Laney said.

Gina eyed her. "And exactly which country would that be?"

Laney sighed. "Yeah. Let's just hope it's a hoax."

Chapter Fifteen

WASHINGTON, D.C.

THE PRESIDENT PACED the command center underneath the White House. She had emptied the room of everyone except her Secret Service detail, Bruce Heller, Vice President Eric Brisbane, and one computer analyst, Chip Winningham.

Despite the fact that there were eight people in the room, no one spoke. The only sound was Chip typing at his keyboard. The President rolled and unrolled her fists, tension coating her skin. They had to win the auction. Losing was not an option.

She'd had every intelligence resource in the United States government focused on finding Sergei Yanovich in the last twenty-four hours. She had SEAL teams on standby across the globe so that as soon as she had a location, they could go in and grab him.

But they'd never found him. Whatever hole he had climbed into was deep. As a teaser, Yanovich had released a small portion of the formula. It was enough to send the labs she had working on the Omni into a frenzy of excitement.

They did not know the amounts, but they said what he sent looked incredibly promising.

It was not a guarantee, but it was enough for her to get permission to bid an obscene amount of money. If they could spend $2.4 trillion on the wars in Afghanistan and Iraq, spending a couple hundred billion to guarantee that they could win any war, potentially even before it started, seemed a no-brainer. Congress had unanimously agreed in a closed-door meeting.

Now they just had to wait.

"We're logged on."

The President hurried over to the analyst. Chip, who looked more like a teenager than the fifty-year-old man he was, nodded at the screen as he projected the information to it.

"How many are logged on?"

"They're all still in the process. Uh, fifty-six, seventy-two, one hundred eight. Um, one sixty-three. Two hundred and two."

The President jolted. Two hundred and two? There were only 193 countries recognized by the United Nations, along with the two nonmember states of Palestine and the Vatican. "Who else was invited?"

Bruce Heller spoke quietly. "We believe they have extended the invitation to certain terrorist organizations as well as some interested private individuals. Our predictions put the total of interested parties at two hundred twenty-five."

"Login is done. There are two hundred twenty-four bidders."

The President sucked in a breath, not knowing when the last time was that she had been so nervous. Scratch that, she knew exactly when it was. It was the day of the coronation.

The Belial Sacrifice

She'd known that if Elisabeta had been crowned, it would be the end of the United States of America. Today's stakes were no less stark. If someone else won this auction, the United States would be held hostage to the demands of whichever country did win.

They *had* to win.

Quietly, she had spoken with the Treasury about how much money was on hand. She had also spoken with the Treasury Secretary and the head of Homeland to see how they could seize funds of wealthy Americans. As far as she was concerned, seizing those funds was no different than commandeering a car for a police action. Except here, the stakes were much higher. Congress had not been privy to those discussions.

"Bidding starts in one minute," Chip said, a thread of excitement in his voice. The President wanted to slap the back of his head. This was not a time for excitement. Anyone with a shred of common sense knew this was a time for fear.

She flicked a gaze at Bruce. He stood staring at the screen, looking like his usual unflappable self, the beating of a blood vessel in his throat the only indication of the man's concern. Strangely, that small tic made her feel better.

"It's starting," Chip said.

The President's attention snapped back to the monitor.

Bruce stood, pulling up a chair next to Chip and taking a seat. "Okay. No bidding at first. Let's feel this out."

Chip nodded. "Opening bid: one billion dollars."

Numbers flew fast and furiously on the screen. One billion quickly moved to two, then three, five, ten, fifteen, twenty-five.

"Now," Bruce said.

Chip's hands flew over the keyboard, the bid jumping to thirty-two billion.

Then thirty-three. Thirty-four. They were talking billions of dollars here, and yet the number kept going up.

"Seventy-eight bidders have dropped out," Chip said.

The President only nodded, gripping the back of an empty chair.

Onscreen, the bid had jumped to eighty-two billion.

Then it jumped to a hundred fifty.

Then it went back to the previous bid of eighty-two.

"What happened?" the President demanded.

"Someone bid more than they could come up with. Yanovich did his homework. He's keeping everyone honest."

Twenty more bidders dropped out, then another forty-two. The bid reached 212, and there were only three bidders left. The President put her hand to her mouth as the numbers climbed. The bids were happening so fast, she didn't even have a chance to read the number before it was replaced.

Come on. Come on.

Then the screen went black. Everyone went still. A message flashed on the screen: *Thank you for your participation.*

The President stared at the screen in confusion. "What happened? Did we win?"

"Uh…" Chip's hand flew over the screen, replaying the auction. Finally his hands stilled.

"Well? Did we win?" the President demanded.

Chip looked up at her, finally looking his age. "No, we lost."

Chapter Sixteen

TIWANAKU, BOLIVIA

THE FARMHOUSE WAS quiet as the bidding played out on the monitor. Laney sat with her arms wrapped around her middle, trying to keep herself in her chair. Countries were bidding on the formula for the Omni. This was going to change the world, and not for the better. Because Gina was right, there was no country that was "good." There was no country that could be trusted with this kind of power. There was no country who had demonstrated any ability to fairly dole out power.

As Laney sat there watching the numbers ratchet up and up, all she could think about was a quote from John Dalberg-Acton. Most people only remembered part of the quote: absolute power corrupts absolutely. But the full quote was "Power tends to corrupt, and absolute power corrupts absolutely. Great men are almost always bad men."

History had borne out the truth of that claim over and over again. Christopher Columbus, who "discovered" America, was lauded as a hero, but in reality he'd murdered, enslaved, and mistreated the natives of the

Caribbean islands he came in contact with. In fact, he had even been found to have traded children as young as nine as sex slaves. JFK's multiple extramarital affairs were well known and well documented, both during his time in the White House and before. Even Gandhi, who had taken a vow of celibacy, slept at night with young naked girls to "test" his resolve and had a documented history of racist remarks.

And in this day and age, she didn't think any of the "great" men or women were going to be any better. Humanity just kept making the same mistakes over and over again.

When are we going to learn? It almost made Laney understand why God thought the flood was a good idea.

"There are only three bidders left," Danny said.

Laney's gaze flicked to the screen. The bid was at over a hundred billion dollars. How much good could be done with that money? *Damn you, Elisabeta.*

The screen blinked. And then a message in a white box appeared: *Thank you for your participation.*

"It's over?" Laney asked.

Danny nodded. "Yeah."

"What was the final bid?" Gina asked.

"Five hundred ninety-two billion dollars."

Laney's hand flew to her mouth. *Oh my God.*

"Who?" Henry asked. "Who won?"

"It wasn't the U.S.," Matt said quietly.

Laney turned to him. "How do you know?"

"Even with all our resources, we don't have enough for that kind of bid."

"Who does?" Gina asked.

"China, maybe Russia," Matt said.

"What happens now?" Mustafa asked.

"As soon as the winning bid is deposited in an account chosen by Yanovich, the formula will be transferred to the winner," Danny said. "It will probably take a little while to verify if the formula works. But if it is the formula for the Omni, within a week, someone could be mass-producing it."

Laney felt sick to her stomach. These powers, they were not meant for humanity. *Her* powers were not meant for humanity, not en masse. Two hundred angels originally fell. The powers were restricted to those two hundred. But then they had children, and their children had children. Not all had powers, but some did, and slowly two hundred with powers became three, then four. That was bad. But this? This was beyond a nightmare. What would happen when whatever country unleashed hundreds more with abilities? What if those who were given abilities decided they didn't need to follow orders? That they were a god in their own right?

And even if they followed orders, what would those orders be? Laney could think of no scenario where the world benefitted from an enhanced military force.

"So what happens now?" Danny whispered.

Laney couldn't put the horror she envisioned into words.

But Gina could. Her voice was low, her words quiet, but they carried the power of a punch. "What happens now? Now the world goes to war."

Chapter Seventeen

WASHINGTON, D.C.

THE CONTROL ROOM was much fuller this time than the last time the President had been down here. She paced along the back of the room, glancing at the monitors every few seconds.

It had been a week since the auction. No one knew who had won, but all signs pointed to China. They had immediately gone dark at the close of the auction, shutting down communications, closing their borders, and recalling all their diplomats.

Many countries had followed suit. She had herself halted all visa programs and was admitting only U.S. citizens into the country. Citizens who were traveling abroad were warned that they may not be allowed reentry. International travel had plummeted, as had the stock markets, in response. Pockets of unrest were springing up all over the country, along with protests about the Fallen and counter protests decrying the treatment of the Fallen. Everyone seemed to have an opinion, and those opinions often boiled over into violent skirmishes.

She had been toying with the idea of instilling martial law until things calmed down, but she wasn't ready to take that step. A nationwide declaration of martial law had never been declared, not even during the two world wars. The President hoped it would not come to that, but the reports she was receiving from law enforcement across the country were not promising.

"We have him," Chip called out.

The President's head snapped up, pulled from her ruminations. She hustled over to stand behind Chip's chair. The defense secretary stood up, offering his chair, but the President waved him down. She was too keyed up to sit. "Where is he?"

"A mile from the target. He's on foot."

The President nodded, her eyes on the screen, and the scene shifted in shadows of black and green. Former United States Marine Corps Captain Mark Li had been assigned by the CIA to China seven years ago. As far as the Chinese government was concerned, he was a wealthy U.S. businessman who had a factory in the southwest province of Yunnan, making electrical conduits. The factory was real. The CIA had set it up almost ten years ago. The parts were sent all over the world, and Li had used his position to send the United States information on the elite society members he interacted with.

Along with the legitimate business ventures, Li ran an underground gambling ring that catered to the elite. A few years back, he'd widened his clientele to include Chinese government officials. Li had maintained acquaintanceships with the officials, plying them with enough liquor to sink a ship. Or in their cases, loosen their lips.

For years, he'd been receiving intel and passing it on to Bruce Heller. Four days ago, he'd learned about a facility in

Wenshan that was highly classified. The officials he spoke with weren't sure what was happening there, but it had been emptied out of all but essential personnel three days before a large contingent of soldiers had been sent to it. That had been enough to greenlight Li's excursion to the facility.

The movement on the screen stopped.

The President frowned. "What's happening?"

Bruce stepped up to her side, pointing to another screen that depicted a satellite image of the facility along with infrared readings that showed people depicted as orange ghosts. "Security patrol. He'll wait until they're gone."

Two orange figures on the bottom right of the screen moved by a single figure that crouched down, unmoving. Once they were gone, the unmoving figure sprang to life, running.

The President shifted her gaze between the orange figure and Captain Li's night-vision recording.

The next few minutes were tense. Li evaded two other patrols and took refuge behind an army truck just outside the facility. He typed in a message: *Coast clear. Heading in.*

Li would be going in alone. They could not risk sending in air support or any other agents. If China got a whiff of what they were doing, it would spark an international incident. But if they waited, someone else would get there first. They knew at least a dozen other countries had operatives in China looking for this location.

"He won't be seen?" the President asked.

Chip shook his head. "I'm running interference with their surveillance. It's being looped."

Li waited behind a truck. Then he sprinted forward until he was hidden behind another truck right next to the door. A second orange figure appeared from the building. Li burst from his hiding spot. Neither camera angle offered a clear view of what was happening as the two figures merged. Then one dropped.

"Bruce?"

"Not Li. He's heading in now."

The President nodded as the orange figure disappeared through the doorway after shoving the body under the truck.

They had no more satellite imagery to help as Li stepped inside. The President squinted at the night-vision screen before it shifted to regular lighting. He was in a hallway. There were three doors: two on the left and one on the right before the hallway turned. Li quickly made his way down.

As he turned a corner, a man in a white lab coat nearly collided with him. Without hesitating, Li reached his hands around the man's neck and broke it. He caught the man, dragging him around to the other hallway before picking up his pace.

"He's just leaving him?" Vice President Eric Brisbane asked.

"His time has been counting down ever since he stepped inside," Bruce said quietly.

"Oh," the Vice President said, stepping back.

The President had known they were sending Li on a suicide mission. Li had known as well. He was moving faster now, heading toward a large room at the end of the hall. From the little intel they had gathered, they believed it might be a laboratory.

Li paused at the door. He attached a small device to the electronic lock. Seconds later, the door popped open. Li pulled it back just enough to look inside.

It wasn't a lab. Instead, a large gymnasium was spread out in front of him covered in gym equipment, reminding the President of an *American Ninja Warrior* course. But this course was built on a much, much larger scale. Rings were fifty feet up in the air. A man leapt up, grabbing on to the rings and swinging across with ease. Giant ten-feet-tall balls were being rolled up an incredibly steep thirty-foot ramp. In the corner, a dozen soldiers, men and woman, stood around a mat as two combatants fought. The speed with which they moved was dizzying.

The President was unable to tear her gaze from the screen. "It was them. They have the Omni."

Bruce grabbed the mike. "Li, get out now, get out now!"

The President jerked her gaze from the combatants, zeroing in on one woman whose head was tilted to the side as she looked toward the door.

Li flew down the hall, moving incredibly fast. But not fast enough. A grunt was the only sound he made as he flew forward, his face slamming into the concrete tiles. His body was rolled over, and the same woman peered down at the camera. She reached out and yanked it up, her hand closing over it.

The feed went black.

The President sat back, staring at the screen. The Chinese had the Omni. They had already created a group of super soldiers. There were 1.6 million active-duty soldiers in the Chinese army. The U.S. had just over 1.2 million. If the Chinese dosed only half of their troops . . .

She swallowed hard. One soldier would be equal to at least ten non-enhanced individuals. No one would be able to stand up to them.

"Madame President, what are we going to do?" Eric asked.

The President looked back at him, maintaining eye contact, keeping all emotion from her face. "Convene a meeting of the security council and have my cabinet on standby. I want responses developed within the hour."

Bruce nodded. "Yes, Madame President."

The President strode from the room, nodding at her Secret Service detail as she crossed into the hallway. She kept her head up, her eyes clear, but inside she was shaking as she pictured that gymnasium. Eric's question floated back through her mind.

What are we going to do?

But this time, instead of answering with the politically correct response, her mind forced her to answer with the honest one: *I have no idea.*

Chapter Eighteen

HAVENVILLE, MASSACHUSETTS

Two Months After the Auction

GINA'S WORDS had proved sadly prescient. Just after the auction, all countries closed their borders. International travel came to a screeching halt as all countries scrambled to figure out what to do. The public didn't know what had happened. News of the auction had not been made public, so all they knew was that all countries were now nervous and untrusting of one another.

Eventually, though, the truth leaked out.

China had won the bid. When a journalist broke the story, it exploded across the airways. It seemed like every country sent small assault teams into China, raiding their labs, their universities, looking for the formula. They never found it. Finally, they just started dropping bombs.

But China wasn't going down without a fight. They dropped bombs of their own. Most of the damage had been away from highly populated areas, but thousands across the globe were killed, tens of thousands injured. And stories of enhanced Chinese troops rattled the world.

Sadly, that wasn't the worst of the problems. Food shortages were reported worldwide, leading to violence and fear. It hit the cities the worst, and people around the globe were abandoning them in droves.

The only good that came of it was that no one was interested in visiting the Gate of the Sun. As a result, Danny had established a network outside, where he could monitor everything. The downside: They saw everything that was happening.

Now Laney paced the little farmhouse, her nerves on edge. Not because she was worried about her own safety. In this new world, she was the last person who had the right to worry about her personal safety. It was the non-enhanced people who had that worry.

She strode to the window, pushing the curtain back. "Oh, come on. Where are you?" But there was no movement out there. Everything was still.

She resumed her pacing, her skin crawling with tension. *I should have gone myself. What if something's happened?*

Laney's radio blared to life. Mustafa's voice came through clearly. "Laney, the caravan's approaching."

Laney flew to the window. Sure enough, five cars were kicking up dust as they headed for the farmhouse. She got no stirrings of her power. No indication that any of them were Fallen.

She had to force herself to not sprint for the lead car. If anyone was watching the house, they could not see her blur. She yanked her hair back into a ponytail and crushed a hat onto her head. She moved to the door, forcing herself to breathe deeply and count to twenty. By the time she hit twenty, the first car should have reached the farmhouse.

At eighteen, she flung the door open and ran to the lead car, which hit the brakes. Her gaze met a pair of eyes that she knew as well as her own. She ran to the passenger door as it was pushed open. She dropped to her knees next to the car, flinging her arms around the passenger.

"Uncle Patrick."

Chapter Nineteen

WASHINGTON, D.C.

THEY HAD BEEN GOING AROUND and around for forty minutes. The generals were arguing for another coordinated military strike on the facility at Beijing along with the other countries of the world. The State Department was arguing that they needed to make inroads diplomatically and see what it was that China actually wanted. The National Security staff wanted to close down the entire country. No one in and no one out.

The President said nothing, listening to it all, taking it all in and letting it work its way around her mind. But it wasn't the people in this room her mind kept shifting back to. It was Delaney McPhearson. The woman had faced Elisabeta head on to defend all of them. She had never used her powers for her own personal gain, and according to the reports from David Okafur, had often put her own safety behind that of the strangers she was saving.

The President knew the Fallen were a threat, but picking out who amongst them were the good guys and who were the bad guys was beyond even the world's best criminologist. Or at least beyond the time crunch to make the citizens of the United States feel safe. But if Delaney McPhearson and the other enhanced hadn't been targeted, would she be helping her government against this new threat?

The President was pretty sure from what she knew of the woman, she would be. But that door was closed to them now. No one had any idea where she was. She'd been spotted across the globe, usually grabbing a family and whisking them away to God knew where. None of those people had been seen again. Her actions had given her a Robin Hood-esque reputation in certain quarters. Others pointed to her hiding as being proof of her guilt. Of course, what she was guilty of they never really identified, just the fact that she was guilty of something.

Originally, the public had their incident, the smoking gun proving Delaney McPhearson was the evil villain she'd been made out to be with the attack at the U.S. facility in Bluefield, Virginia. But like all the other times McPhearson had been painted as an evildoer, closer inspection revealed the truth.

In this case, the closer inspection was actually the testimony of a CEI agent, Roger Hennessey. In exchange for immunity, Hennessey admitted that while McPhearson had broken into the lab, it was solely to release Dr. Dominic Radcliffe. Guards had been hurt, but none had been killed. The deaths came at the hands of Hennessey's partner, Barbara Frankel, and in consultation with Senator Bart Shremp.

The President had kept Shremp out of the public view, pinning all the blame on Frankel, who had been killed when agents moved in to apprehend her. Shremp had taken an early retirement to spend more time with his family. Putting him in charge had been a mistake. She had underestimated his ambition, and good soldiers had died as a result.

She felt eyes on her and turned her head to see Bruce Heller studying her. He rarely, if ever, spoke at these meetings unless called upon. But she knew how well his mind worked. And right now he was studying her. For a moment, she had the uneasy feeling that he might be able to read her mind. His eyes widened for just a second, a smirk crossing his face before it returned to his normal placid look.

"We need to find out what they want," Nancy Harrigan, the secretary of state, insisted. "We can't assume the worst."

"We can't wait for that," the chairman of the Joint Chiefs of Staff insisted just as strongly. "Their response could be enhanced individuals storming our border."

Nancy shook her head. "That's insane. What does that gain them? They are more likely to use this new power as a threat to initiate financial scenarios that benefit them."

"You are not seeing the threat. It—"

Nancy didn't let him finish. "No, I am acknowledging that threats come in multiple forms, not only physical."

The President put up her hand, raising her voice. "Thank you all for your invaluable input. Let's take a little break, and we'll reconvene in thirty minutes, all right?"

"Of course, Madame President," the Joint Chiefs' chairman said stiffly.

Everyone stood and headed toward the door. Bruce was the last to stand, which did not surprise the President and only further supported her view that the man was the most observant person she had ever met.

"A minute, Bruce."

He changed directions and headed around the table toward her. "Of course, Madame President."

She kicked out the chair next to her. "Take a seat." She

waited until he had before speaking. "You've been awfully quiet."

Bruce shrugged. "I tend to find this portion of the decision-making process to be the least effective. I like to save my input for when I think it will be useful and heard."

"Very well. You have my undivided attention. What do you think China intends?"

Bruce linked his hands together. "I think Nancy is right. They will use their new power as leverage in financial dealings. However, I also think that if they do not feel they are receiving their due, they will not hesitate to send their forces out to ensure we understand the power they hold. Unofficially, of course."

"Of course." The President stared at the tabletop. If Bruce was right, it was not as bad as what Elisabeta had planned, but the U.S. would lose its dominance on the world stage. All other countries would as well.

"There is one other issue that is not being discussed that I believe may be even more pressing."

The President frowned. "About China?"

"No, about Sergei."

"What about him?"

"He held an auction and sold off the Omni to the highest bidder."

"Yes . . ."

"Sergei is a man who looks for opportunities to enrich himself. He has done so through the auction."

"Agreed, so why—"

"Sergei *still* has the formula. We have not been able to find him. I do not think we can rest on the assumption that he will not sell it to anyone else."

The President's jaw dropped. They had all been so

worried about who had won the auction and what they would do that she had never considered that. "And you think he will?"

Bruce shook his head. "No. I think he already has."

Chapter Twenty

TIWANAKU, BOLIVIA

IT HAD BEEN six long months since she'd last seen her uncle. Laney held on to him, breathing him in and not wanting to let him go. He felt thinner than she remembered, and his shoulders shook as he held her to him. Tears were in his voice as he spoke. "Oh, my dear girl."

Laney was content to sit there and just hold him for hours. She'd managed to speak with him only a handful of times in as many months. Not having access to him, it was like part of her was missing.

A throat cleared behind her. "Any extra hugs for an old friend?"

Laney choked off a laugh as she turned, tears streaming down her face. David Okafur stood with his arms open wide. Laney launched herself at him, holding him just as tightly. "Thank you, thank you, thank you."

David wrapped his arms around her. "Anything for you."

She pulled back, smiling at him. "Did everything go okay?"

He nodded. "We had some trouble in Spain, but it turned out all right. Everyone's accounted for."

Laney scanned the cars. Most of the faces were children, the orphans from School of the Holy Mother and Home for Children. "We should get moving."

David nodded, glancing around. "I saw one of your scouts, so I take it we're safe for now."

Laney smiled. "We should be, although you shouldn't have been able to spot them."

David shrugged. "What can I say? Here." He placed a set of keys in her hand. "We'll follow you."

She squeezed his hand. "Thank you."

Within thirty minutes, they had reached the Gate of the Sun and had everyone through it. Laney's people were moving the cars so that no one was the wiser. She held hands with the last of the group as she accompanied them through the gate. Father Sebastian Gante stumbled as he stepped into Havenville. Laney gripped him. "It'll pass."

He looked around in wonder. "No wonder no one's been able to find you."

"We call it Havenville."

Bas nodded. "It was a hiding place for the Tree of Life, wasn't it?"

Surprise flashed through Laney. "How did you—"

Bas grinned at her. "I can't take credit for that. It was your uncle who suggested that's where you might have gone."

Her gaze strayed to where her uncle sat, Nyssa in his lap, Cain smiling next to him. "How has he been?"

"Good."

Laney looked at him.

He patted her hand. "I mean it, Laney. The children, he's really blossomed with them. It's been great. He's been eating well, or at least as well as can be expected with the food shortages. But he does have some things he found out from the Tome."

The Tome. Bas was speaking of the Tome of the Great Mother, the written record of Victoria's incarnations here on Earth. The Followers would document her life as well as they could each time they found her again. Laney couldn't help but watch as Nyssa reached up and placed her hand on her uncle's cheek, talking animatedly.

I wonder who will write her next chapter.

The idea of it made her tired. She didn't want Nyssa to have to grow up to the responsibility of being Lilith or Victoria or any of the other names she'd taken throughout her very long existence. She just wanted her to be Nyssa, a little girl who got to live her life like all other little girls. Who made friends, went to parties, went on dates, went to college, chose a path for herself, not one that was preordained thousands of years ago.

Bas smiled over at Nyssa. "That little girl really seems to love Patrick."

Laney kept her voice neutral. Not many knew who Nyssa really was. And that was exactly how it would remain. "Yes. He really cares for her. I worried that because she's so young that she might not remember him."

"Well, that doesn't seem to have been a problem."

"No, it doesn't."

Her uncle looked happy but tired. All of the group that had come with him looked tired. Sylvia and her husband Rosario sat with half a dozen children surrounding them.

David stood next to a dark-haired man who knelt in front of a little girl, listening as she explained something. That must be his partner, Rahim. Bas's sister Angelica flitted from group to group, making sure each of the kids were all right, gathering them together.

Laney frowned as she looked over the group. "Were all these kids at the school when Drake and I were there? I don't remember there being so many."

"No, there weren't." Sadness laced each of his words. "In the last two months, eighteen children joined the school. Most lost their parents to violence, but some, their parents just left them there."

Laney gasped. "What?"

"You have to understand, food is a problem. With all the borders shut, supplies are really low. I think their parents thought we might be able to better care for them. They were desperate people making desperate choices."

Laney's heart felt heavy. So much pain. "Well let's get everyone settled. Our first crops were actually picked just last week. Foodwise, we're doing all right, so we'll get everyone fed."

Bas nodded. "That would be wonderful. And then I'm sure Patrick will want to explain what he's found."

Laney watched her uncle. Cain rested a hand on his shoulder, a smile on his face. Nyssa was snuggled into his chest. A few of the kids were watching Cleo and Tiger with wide eyes, but most just looked exhausted. "You know what? We can hold off on the debriefs. You guys have all been through enough. Let's let everyone get a good night's sleep. It can wait until tomorrow."

"You sure?"

Laney scanned the group again. They looked like refugees, scared, uncertain. Which was exactly what they were. "Yes. Everything can wait. Let's just help them all feel safe."

Chapter Twenty-One

LANEY HAD HELPED GET ALL the kids settled, then Drake had shown up with a box of stuffed animals. Laney had no idea where he'd managed to find those, but more than one little child had held on to their stuffed animal as if it were their only friend in the world. Even a few of the older kids had clutched stuffed animals to their chests, while Sylvia, Angelica, and Cristela bustled around, making all of the kids feel loved. They really were doing God's work.

Laney stepped out of the cottage they were staying at. For tonight, they'd all sleep in the same one. Angelica thought it would be best to not split them between cottages until they felt a little more secure. Henry had organized it, moving beds and sleeping bags in to accommodate all of them. Rahim, Bas, and David were in the cottage next door, although Laney had a feeling they too would be bunking in with the kids tonight.

Laney had brought Cleo around to meet each of the kids and explain that they didn't have to worry about the cats, that they were the protectors of the camp. Cleo had disappeared for a little while and then reappeared with two other cats in tow—Snow, the all-white leopard who was Lou's companion, and Frisky, an almost completely black leopard like Cleo. Frisky was the youngest leopard in the pack.

Frisky and Snow went around greeting each child and then curled up in the rooms where the kids were. Sister Cristela had made the sign of the cross at the sight of them, but the kids collectively seemed to relax when they realized the cats were staying with them.

Now, Laney and Cleo walked down the street toward Cain's cottage. Laney reached a hand down, running it through Cleo's fur. "That was a good idea, bringing Snow and Frisky."

Kids scared.

"Yeah, they've been through a lot."

Safe now.

Laney let out a breath. "I hope so. I really hope so."

Up ahead, light shone through the window of Cain's cottage. The front door opened, and Drake stepped out. He spied Laney and headed for her. Drake nodded at Cleo as he reached them. "Furball."

Cleo nodded back before walking past him. *Archangel.*

Laney stopped, sliding her arms around Drake's waist and leaning against his chest. "Hey."

Drake wrapped his arms around her, resting his chin on her head. "Hey back. How are you?"

"Good. Better now that they're all here."

"Kids settled in?"

"Yeah. Snow and Frisky are staying with them."

She could feel Drake's grin. "How's Cristela liking that?"

"She's giving them a wide berth, but the kids seem to like them being there." She paused. "How's my uncle?"

"Tired, but he's good. I put ramps in the front and back so he can get in and out easily. And Cain already had the bedroom on the first floor set up for him."

"I think he may have missed him more than me."

"You might be right. Cain has been hovering over him. Can't say I've ever seen the immortal so nervous."

Laney smiled. "My uncle means the world to him. Cain hasn't had that kind of bond with a lot of people."

Drake kissed her on the forehead. "Well, go in. I'm going to do a supply run with Mustafa. Go see your uncle."

Laney took a breath, looking at the little cottage.

Drake frowned. "Why are you hesitating?"

Laney shook her head. She wasn't sure. These six months, she'd wanted nothing more than to see him. And now he was only a few dozen feet away, and she was having trouble getting her own feet to move. "He's okay, right?" she asked quietly.

"Laney, look at me."

Laney looked up into his eyes.

"He is doing well. No worse than the last time you saw him and no better. There will be a time when he is gone. But it is not soon. Now go."

She leaned up and kissed him. "Hurry back."

"I always do." He strode pass her. "Keep the bed warm," he called back over his shoulder.

She rolled her eyes even as she felt her cheeks flame. God, he was incorrigible. *And he's all mine*, she thought with a smile. She turned and headed toward Cain's, all of a sudden desperate to see her uncle. She opened the door, and Patrick was just rolling himself out from his bedroom.

His smile widened, the corner of his eyes crinkling. "There she is."

She flew across the hall, wrapping her arms around him, tears pressing against the back of her eyes. "Here I am."

Chapter Twenty-Two

LANEY SAT with her uncle and Cain for two hours, just catching up. For the first hour, she didn't think she let go of his hand. Cain seemed just as relieved to have him back. Nyssa wandered in and out with Tiger. But after two hours, Laney could tell he was tiring. Nyssa had crawled onto his lap and was struggling to keep her own eyes open.

"I think maybe you need a little sleep," she said.

"No, no, I'm fine," he said even as he swallowed a yawn.

"Patrick, we have plenty of time," Cain said. "We're all together again. That's all that matters. So sleep, and tomorrow we will all spend the day together."

"I suppose." Patrick focused on Laney. "But there are things that I've discovered. We need to speak about them."

"I know. But it can wait until morning."

"Laney, it involves the Tome."

"The stories in the Tome are thousands of years old," she said. "They will keep for another night. Cain's right. You need to sleep, and so do I. I thought I'd bunk in here tonight."

"Drake's all right with that?" Patrick asked.

"I didn't ask his permission. Besides, he'll find me. He always does."

"You look tired, too." He squeezed her hand.

"It's been a long six months," she said lightly.

"Somehow I think you're underselling it. But I am tired, so I'll let it pass. But tomorrow, you tell me how you're *really* doing."

"Agreed."

He looked down at Nyssa. "How about you, little one? Are you ready to sleep?"

She shook her head just before she yawned.

Patrick ran a hand gently over her head. "Of course you're not. Well, how about if I read us both a story, and then you can tuck me in?"

Nyssa nodded her head.

Patrick smiled as he wheeled himself and Nyssa out of the kitchen. Tiger followed them.

"I'll go get her in a few minutes," Cain said.

Laney watched the doorway. "He's okay, right?"

"He's okay, Laney. He's been through an ordeal. But he's all right. And I think helping take care of all the children from the school, it gave him a purpose. And you know how he loves that."

"I definitely know that."

"So what's *really* going on?" Cain asked.

Laney turned back to the table, wrapping her hands around her mug. She paused, giving Cain's question some thought. What *was* going on? Her uncle was here. She should be happy. Yet tension radiated along her spine. She couldn't relax. She couldn't seem to just let herself enjoy the moment.

And she recognized the feeling.

"Laney?" Cain asked quietly.

She looked up into his face, reading the concern there. "I've been doing this a while, the whole ring-bearer thing. And there's this pattern that keeps repeating." She paused.

"What's that?"

"Everything seems to be good, or at least all right. But there's a feeling in the air, just under the surface. It's as if I know everything, these moments, are temporary. That everything is about to change."

"I think the world has already changed a great deal."

"That's true." A chill ran over her, and she shuddered, looking down the hall where her uncle had disappeared. "But I don't think we're done yet. And I have a feeling that as bad as things are now, they're about to get a whole lot worse."

Chapter Twenty-Three

MOUNT HERMON, ON THE BORDER OF MODERN-DAY SYRIA AND LEBANON

NIGHT HAD ARRIVED *as Michael landed on the cliff overlooking the human settlement. Fires were spread throughout the encampment in between the tents. He crouched at the cliff's edge, the smell of roasting meat wafting up toward him. He tilted his head, watching their movements curiously. They were always moving, always together. It was rare to spy one of them alone. Voices rose up to him in song. They had very little, yet the voices were full of joy and laughter. Such strange creatures.*

He watched them through the long night, long after the fires had gone cold and they had climbed into their animal-hide-covered tents.

Shadows shifted above him as the first traces of light hit the horizon. He felt his brother long before he arrived. Samyaza landed lightly next to him, his long hair blowing back in the wind. His strong arms wrapped in metal straps like Michael's, a sign of their high rank, as was the red engraving on their silver breastplates.

Samyaza nodded toward his big brother. "I heard you were looking for me."

Michael's gaze did not shift to his brother, moving between the camp, which had begun to awaken, and the horizon. "I was."

Samyaza sighed. "Michael, what—"

Michael held up his hand. "Not yet."

Grumbling under his breath, Samyaza sat on the rock across from him. "Oh, by all means, take your time."

The sky slowly shifted into color. Michael watched in awe. He would never grow tired of this. The sky bursting to life with the dawning of the sun. Finally, the sun rose above the horizon, the colors fading into a soft blue. He turned to study Samyaza, who was pitching rocks at the hilltop behind them.

Samyaza arched an eyebrow at him. "Are you finished?"

"For today. I do not get to see that often enough."

"Well, if you spent a little less time on duty, perhaps you could. Now why did you want to speak with me? And why of all places here?"

"I've heard this is your favorite spot. That you like to watch the humans as they go about their lives below."

Samyaza smiled. "Do you know I think some of them can sense us? Every once in a while, one looks right at me, almost as if they can see me."

"That's not possible. You know that."

Samyaza shrugged. "Not yet, perhaps."

Michael's tone hardened. "You cannot talk that way, Samyaza. It is causing problems—"

"I cannot talk that way?" He shook his head. "I cannot walk amongst the humans. I cannot eat their bread or feel the touch of their women. Tell me, brother, what exactly can *I do?"*

Michael studied his brother. Samyaza's unease had been growing as of late. And it was spreading to some of the others. "Our lives are ones of service."

"And what else? Where is our *reward?" Samyaza threw his arms wide toward the camp below. "Look at them! They do nothing but are loved. We toil, fight, and yet we gain nothing in return but more of the same."*

"Reward? We are the most high. What other reward is there?"

"Power, riches. Amongst men, we would be gods."

Michael recoiled at his words. "That is not the way."

"And why not? Why can the way not change? When we were created, they did not exist. But once they came into being, our world, our existence changed. Why can we not change it again, but this time in our favor rather than theirs?"

"I don't understand. Where does this come from? Why would you say such things?"

Samyaza's eyes glowed as the morning light hit them. "Oh, I am not alone in saying such things."

"What?" Michael had felt his brothers' unease, but he did not think they had spoken their unhappiness aloud. How could it have gotten this far out of control?

"You think our brothers do not long for more than a life of servitude? Then you are the blind one, Michael. A day is coming soon when you will have to choose."

Michael frowned. "Choose? Choose what?"

"Not a what, a who. Who will you be, Michael? A blind servant or a master of your own destiny?"

Samyaza started to walk past him, but Michael grabbed his shoulder. "That is not the question. If you were to step through the veil, your powers would be well above any human's. Their world would never be the same."

Samyaza shrugged Michael's hand off. "Seems only fair since their existence did the same to us."

"Samyaza, they are peaceful, they are good. You would destroy all of that."

"They are sheep, and they need a strong hand to guide them. It just so happens, I have two."

DRAKE AWOKE WITH A START, his gasp of breath sounding extra loud in the silence of the dark room. Laney shifted on the couch next to him, her hand reaching for him and settling on his bare chest. She hadn't been in their home when he returned. He'd eventually found her sleeping in Cain's living room. Rather than move her, he'd simply shifted her over to make room for himself.

He focused on controlling his breathing. Laney had struggled to sleep for the last few hours, and he didn't want to wake her. But what had that dream been about?

"Drake?" She pushed her hair out of her face, glancing toward the window. "What are you doing up? It's barely dawn. Is something wrong?"

"No, no. I simply had a strange dream."

She closed her eyes, snuggling into him. "Do you want to talk about it?"

No." He kissed her forehead. "Go back to sleep."

She nodded absentmindedly, her lids closing.

He waited until her breathing evened out and he was sure she was asleep before he slipped off the couch. He made his way to the window, staring out into the night. He ran a hand over his face. He'd recognized Samyaza. He knew him. But Michael . . . Why had he dreamed of Michael?

He struggled to figure out if he had ever met him, but like everything about his time before Earth, it was a blank. A feeling of unease slid through him.

I must have known him. But why am I dreaming about him now?

He glanced back at the couch where Laney lay sleeping. He loved her with everything in his being. He had for centuries. And right here, right now, as tumultuous as their life was, he wouldn't trade it for anything in the world.

It was nothing. Just a dream. But even in his own mind, there was more hope than confidence in his words.

He sat there waiting for the sun to rise, his chest easing at the sight of the first few rays along the horizon.

He smiled. He always did love watching the dawn.

Chapter Twenty-Four

LANEY SLEPT LIKE A LOG. She couldn't remember the last time she had slept straight through the night without waking. As she blinked open her eyes, it took her a moment to recognize where she was. Turning her head, she remembered falling asleep as she and Cain sat in his living room. She pushed down the blanket he must have covered her with. Cleo lay sprawled out on the floor. A note sat propped up on the coffee table in front of her.

She opened it, recognizing Drake's handwriting.

You were sleeping when I returned. I didn't want to wake you. Let me know when you are up.

She smiled and placed it back on the table. Nyssa tottered into the room, rubbing her eyes with one hand while holding on to Tiger with the other. Laney held out her arms. "Hey there, love bug."

Nyssa stumbled over, climbing onto the couch. Laney pulled the blanket back over the two of them as Nyssa got comfortable. Tiger curled up on the floor next to Cleo.

Laney knew she should get up. She should go check on the new people, make sure everything was fine.

But Nyssa let out a big yawn and snuggled in closer, closing her eyes. And right at this moment, everything felt right, even with the gnawing sense of change around the corner. Her uncle was back. Everyone was safe, if in hiding. And if there was one thing she was the most thankful for thanks to Drake, it was to appreciate the now. So she rested her hand on Nyssa's back, sucked in by the warmth of her closeness, and let herself drift back to sleep.

An hour later, her eyes opened. Her uncle was sitting in his wheelchair in the entryway to the room. He winced. "Sorry, I didn't mean to wake you."

Laney stretched, realizing Nyssa had disappeared. "No, I need to get moving. I wanted to check in on everyone next door."

"Drake is already doing that."

Laney stretched. "Good. How'd you sleep?"

The circles under his eyes were less pronounced, and he seemed to have a little more spark than yesterday. "Like a baby. I swear I did not even stir for eight straight hours."

"You look . . . rested."

He snorted. "Delicately phrased. I thought maybe we could have some breakfast. There are things we need to speak about."

Dread pooled in the bottom of her stomach. "Great."

CAIN WAS FINISHING up breakfast with Nyssa when Laney and Patrick entered the kitchen. He whipped them up some breakfast, placing the food on four plates. Laney frowned. "Are you guys eating again?"

A knock sounded at the front door, followed by Jake's voice. "Anybody home?"

"Back here," Patrick called.

Cain placed the plates on the table. "Nope. Mary Jane and I are taking Nyssa and the girls for a walk so you guys can chat."

Jake appeared in the doorway, Mary Jane, Henry, and Susie behind him. They all chatted for a few minutes before Cain and Mary Jane took their leave with the girls. The remaining four sat at the table and dug into the food. No one spoke as they all enjoyed the benefits of Cain's long years of culinary practice. Then Henry asked Patrick about the state of Italy.

Patrick shook his head. "It's not good. People are going hungry. It's making them desperate."

"Did you have any problems at the school?"

"A few. But Bas and David were always there. No one ever got beyond the walls."

Laney had of course seen the difficulties during her missions, as had Jake and Henry, but none of them had spent any extensive time outside Havenville. Patrick spoke about families that he'd see one day from his window, and then he'd see them packing up and walking toward the countryside. He wasn't sure what they hoped to find. Disease and sickness were beginning to hit the cities too, and medicines were running short. Laney imagined it was even worse in lesser-developed nations.

"And the trip over?" Jake asked.

Patrick shuddered. "Rough. With a group our size, we needed a larger plane, more cars, which meant more fuel, which is also in short supply. It made the whole trip more difficult. But David had it all mapped out. I think he cashed in just about every favor he was owed to get us here."

Laney said another little prayer of thanks that David had been the one Bruce had assigned to watch over her last year. If someone else had been given the mission, if someone besides Bruce had been the one calling the shots, well, things would have turned out a whole lot worse for all of them.

Her mug ensconced in her hands, Laney sat back as everyone went silent. "So I'm guessing you found some information?"

Patrick nodded. "I was able to read some of the translations of the Tome that Bas was able to copy."

"And?"

"And there were these hints about a weapon that could be used against the Fallen."

You must find the weapon. Sarah Goode's words rang through her mind, stealing her breath. With everything happening, she had practically forgotten the vision Noriko had shown her.

Jake leaned forward, ever the soldier. "What kind of weapon?"

"Something that would remove the powers of the Fallen."

"You mean the Omni," Jake said.

"No, no. I didn't get the impression that it was the Omni. The way it was written about, the writers feared it."

Laney frowned. She hadn't spent much time thinking about the weapon. She supposed it could still be the Omni. But why would the Followers fear it? For humans, the Omni had no negative side effects, besides, of course, giving one the abilities of the Fallen.

"I think maybe the beginning of the Tome might have more information, but Bas didn't have a chance to copy those pages. He hadn't gotten to them yet. And to be honest, I only really understood what it could mean the day before we left. There wasn't time for him to get to the Tome safely."

Laney nodded. It was interesting, but Laney didn't really see how it changed anything. They had the formula for the Omni.

Cain bustled into the kitchen, pulling off his sunglasses as he cast his gaze around the room. "Hey. Sorry to interrupt. I forgot the girls' snacks. Has anyone seen— Oh, wait, there they are."

Cain headed across the room, grabbing two snack cups from next to the fridge. "I will be out of your hair in—"

Laney interrupted him. "Cain, you haven't heard about weapon against the Fallen, have you?"

"Weapon? What kind of weapon?"

Jake gestured to Patrick. "Patrick said there was mention in the Tome of some sort of weapon."

Cain gave them a distracted shake of his head. "Can't really say I have."

Patrick blew out a breath. "Well, maybe it is just the Omni. Maybe I was seeing something that wasn't there."

"I'll give it some thought, but I need to run. I left Mary Jane with two girls on the edge of a full-blown meltdown."

Laney waved him to the door. The girls were normally pretty good, but when they were hungry, look out. "Go, go. Good luck."

After Cain left, Jake refilled everyone's mugs, and Laney doled out the pastries Cain had left for them. They spoke a little about Havenville, explaining to Patrick about some of the people whom they'd brought in. Then Henry told Patrick about his and Jen's plans for their baby.

Laney smiled, watching how animated Henry was at the

idea of his child coming into the world. Laney couldn't help but feel just as excited.

Jake stood up. "Speaking of families, I promised to take Molly out for a little self-defense training."

"How's she doing?"

"All right. The nightmares are still there, but she's strong, not just physically." There was a note of pride in Jake's voice.

The back door flew open. Jake already had his weapon clear of his holster as Laney and Henry whirled around.

Cain flew into the room, his eyes wide, his breathing uneven.

Laney ran across the room, grabbing his arms. "What is it? What's happened?"

Cain shook his head as he tried to catch his breath. "No . . . Nothing's wrong."

Laney frowned. "Then what is—"

Cain clutched her arms before turning to the others in the room. "The weapon. I think I know what it refers to."

"Is it like the Omni?" Henry asked. "Can it remove their abilities?"

Cain nodded, moving to the table. "Yes and no. It's like the Omni in that it can remove their abilities, but it's so much more. The weapon, it won't just remove one Fallen's abilities. It will remove *all* of them."

Henry frowned. "All of them as in . . . ?"

Cain looked at each person in turn, his gaze finally coming to rest on Laney. "All of them. Every Fallen in the world. Every. Single. One."

Chapter Twenty-Five

CAIN STUMBLED INTO A CHAIR, looking shaky. Laney quickly got him a glass of water. He nodded his thanks before gulping it down, wiping his mouth on his sleeve.

Patrick spoke as Laney retook her seat. "What do you mean it will remove the Fallen's abilities?"

"Exactly that. It's supposed to remove the abilities of all the Fallen." Cain ran a hand through his hair. "I didn't even think of it when you asked me earlier because it's been so long since anyone has mentioned it. And even then it was more rumor than fact."

Cain took a breath as if collecting his thoughts before he spoke. "The last time I heard about it was not long after . . ." He gestured at his eyes.

Laney felt her own eyes widen. That would have been tens of thousands of years ago.

Cain caught her gaze and nodded. "Like I said, it was a long time ago. Before Lemuria and Atlantis sank. Before I was cursed, we humans could survive a great deal. We were much less fragile than we are now. And our days, you couldn't count them. They went on, unending. And then Lilith changed all of that."

Patrick nodded, picking up the thread as Cain fell quiet. "She made a deal with two angels. A deal that would make humans mortal."

Laney recalled her conversation with Victoria about that time. "She wanted them to have a chance to live good lives. To achieve a final resting place. Without death, humans couldn't appreciate life."

"As much as I hated to admit it, she was right," said Cain. "There were no consequences for our actions. No need to do good or do right. Then the Fallen came. They exploited this aspect of our nature, and we became even worse. By making that deal, she gave us a chance to truly live." He gave a small grin. "Although a little heads-up would have been appreciated."

Laney smiled back at him.

"But what does that have to do with the weapon?" Jake asked.

Cain frowned. "I can't remember a great deal of it. To be honest, I spent a few centuries roaring drunk. But I remember hearing that she had created a way to remove the abilities of the Fallen, if it ever came to that."

"How?"

"I don't know. I'm not sure I ever knew exactly what the weapon was, just that it existed."

"Would it be in the Tome?" Henry asked.

Cain nodded. "If *any* record of it exists, then that's where it would be. Most likely in the beginning of the Tome."

"Which means we need the Tome," Laney said quietly.

Henry stared at her. "Laney, the only copy of the Tome that we know of is back in Rome, with the Brotherhood."

"And they tried to kill you the last time you had a run-in with them," Jake said.

"True, but they failed."

"Laney . . ." Henry said, his voice full of warning.

She held up her hand. "Look, I get it. It's a long shot and not exactly easy in the current climate to zip over to Italy. But if there is a weapon out there that can remove the Fallen's powers, *all* of their powers, we need to find it. The world is on the edge of World War III. And while Elisabeta may be gone, her plans for the Fallen ruling all are still where we are heading. With the numbers of people who will be enhanced, we cannot fight them one on one. If there's a weapon that can remove all of their powers, we need it."

"But how are you going to get into Italy? Everything's shut down," Patrick said.

Laney gave him a small smile. "I guess I'm going to have to hope that David hasn't called in all of his favors just yet."

Chapter Twenty-Six

MACAU, CHINA

MACAU, the Vegas of China, was bustling as Sergei Yanovich's driver made his way slowly through the crowded streets. With over six hundred thousand people living in an area less than twelve square miles in size, Macau was the most densely populated region in the world. It made the Philippines look like wide open plains. Macau was the fourth richest territory, replacing Switzerland on the list. Seventeen million tourists visited Macau to take advantage of their casinos, high-end resorts, and extensive shopping malls.

While Macau was an independent territory of China, the influences of both China and Portugal, who had controlled the territory until 1999, could still be seen. But so, too, could the influences of the Western world.

Sergei's driver weaved through traffic in the City of Dreams in the Cotai area, populated by luxury resorts. Sergei glanced out the window at the Ritz Carlton, the Venetian, the Atira, and the Hotel Okura—all were lit up, inviting the wealthy to come inside and spend their easily won wealth.

The Maybach pulled up in front of the Wynn Palace. A doorman hurried over to open Sergei's door, and Sergei tipped the man without looking at him. His four-man security team took point around him. Another twelve members of his security team had swept through the hotel that morning, making sure everything was safe.

Sergei didn't worry too much about threats, however, even with the bounty on his head. After all, he had just made China very happy, and they would be making sure *he* stayed very happy to ensure the formula did not slip into other hands.

The Wynn representative was flanked by two women. He bowed as Sergei approached. "Mr. Smith, it is a great pleasure to have you at our hotel. I would be happy to escort you to—"

Sergei held up a hand, cutting the man off. "Not necessary. I'm sure your lovely companions would be able to escort me." Sergei held out his arms.

Each woman slid their arms through his with a smile. Sergei grinned back at them. Yes, tonight was going to be a very enjoyable evening.

Chapter Twenty-Seven

WASHINGTON, D.C.

THE PRESIDENT WATCHED Sergei Yanovich step out of the car and button his jacket before striding up the stairs and disappearing into the casino. The camera remained focused on the entrance. "Is that it? Is that all we have?"

Bruce Heller nodded. "Yes. We have no electronic surveillance inside the casino. We were lucky we were even able to get this shot."

The President whirled on him. "How does this help us? We have a picture of the man. If we can't get to him, I'm not sure what the picture does for us."

"I said we didn't have any electronic *surveillance* inside the casino. I didn't say we didn't have any personnel inside."

The President paused. "You have someone with him?"

Bruce nodded.

"What is the plan?"

"When our team is in place, our asset will let them know when to move."

"And this asset, he can handle this?"

Bruce smiled. "Yes. *She* can."

Chapter Twenty-Eight

MACAU, CHINA

SERGEI YANOVICH SMILED as he rolled the dice down the craps table.

"Seven. We have a winner," the dealer called out.

The girl on his arm squealed, jumping up and down. Sergei smiled as well. It didn't matter if he won or if he lost, he had more money than Midas now. But he still liked to win.

"Again, sir?"

Sergei shook his head, slipping his hand around the waist of the woman next to him. "No, I think I'm done for the night."

She giggled, leaning forward, her breast brushing against his arm.

"How about if we find a place a little more private?"

She leaned over, her lips touching his neck as she spoke. "A suite has been set up for you. I can show you to it."

"Perfect."

She slipped her arm through his and led him from the table. His security fell in around him. The girl pouted as she looked at them. "They won't be joining us in the suite, will they?"

He smiled. "No. I think I can handle anything you throw at me all by myself."

She clutched his arm tighter. "I bet you can."

Ahead, his security chased a group away from the elevator. They held the door open. Sergei stepped inside, nuzzling the woman's neck. "You never did tell me your name."

"Arianna."

"Arianna. A beautiful name for a beautiful woman."

She smiled, sliding her arms along his chest. "This beautiful woman has some plans that I think you are really going to like."

"I do love a woman with a plan." He moved toward her mouth, but the door opened.

She turned her head with a smile. "This way."

He let her lead them down the hallway. She pulled a card from inside her dress and stepped to the double doors at the end of the hall. He plucked the card from her hand and handed it to one of his men. "Let them."

She nodded, stepping back from the doorway. One of the security detail unlocked the door, sliding his jacket back and placing his hand on the gun on his side.

Arianna let out a little gasp.

Sergei chuckled as he stepped inside. "No need to be afraid. You are perfectly safe with me."

"I just— I don't like guns."

He ran his hand down her cheek. "And there's no need for you to. A woman as pretty as you will always have a strong man to protect her."

She batted her lashes at him, leaning into him. "Really?"

"Yes. I could take care of you."

She licked her lips, leaning in until she was just a few inches from his lips. She smiled. "But I can take care of myself." She grabbed him by the lapels and threw him into the room as if he weighed no more than a few pounds.

Chapter Twenty-Nine

WASHINGTON, D.C.

ONSCREEN, it was difficult to see what exactly was happening. If it were a movie, the President would have been annoyed at the camera operator for not focusing on the critical action. But here, the camera operator was also fighting for his life.

As soon as the CIA operative had thrown Sergei into the room, four men from the strike team had burst from a supply closet in the hall. Sergei's guard in the room had already been disabled by two other members of the team.

A shot of the ceiling splashed across the monitor as the soldier was sent flying. For precious seconds, the soldier stayed where he was, the ceiling all that could be seen. But the sounds of the fight continuing could be heard.

The soldier rolled to his side. Across the room, Sergei was trading punches incredibly fast, but he wasn't exchanging them with one of the strike team. No, he was going toe to toe with the woman he had escorted into the room.

And she was giving as good as she was receiving. She

ducked under a punch, slamming her fist into Sergei's stomach. A second punch to his kidney made him cry out before she landed an uppercut to his jaw. The President flinched as his head snapped back at a sickening angle.

But she wasn't done. Before Sergei could respond, she grabbed the gun that had been dropped by Sergei and unloaded the entire magazine into his heart.

"Report," Bruce demanded.

The woman walked over to Sergei, pressing her hands to his throat, checking for a pulse. She waved one of the soldiers over, and he handed her an earpiece and a mike. She put in the earpiece, clipping the mike to the strap of her dress. "He's gone."

Bruce smiled. "Nicely done. Any sign of the Omni?"

"Hold on." Maldonado rummaged through Sergei's pockets. She pulled out a small cylinder that looked like a cigar case. Unscrewing the top, she pulled out a rolled-up piece of paper. She unfurled it and scanned the contents before nodding. "I've got it."

The President let out a breath. Bruce had thought Sergei would have it on him. He wouldn't chance leaving it anywhere it could be uncovered.

"Have the team clean up, and bring Sergei's body back with you," Bruce said.

"Yes, sir." Maldonado lowered the volume, speaking to the other men in the room.

The President smiled. "That was a success. But you didn't tell me everything about this particular mission."

Bruce shrugged. "It's always wise to hold back some details of an op."

The President nodded to the screen where Maldonado had just been. "She's with us?"

Bruce nodded. "Captain Maria Maldonado. Graduated

from Quantico Marine Corps officer training ten years ago. Went into intelligence work. I managed to snag her about four years ago."

"You knew she was enhanced?"

"I did."

"You didn't consider it a risk?"

"I considered it an asset. She is a patriot. Her family emigrated here from Venezuela. She is very proud of her American citizenship and loves this country. I have never for one moment doubted her commitment to the United States."

The President studied him. "I sense a bit of censure in your tone."

Bruce shrugged. "No censure. Just a recognition that one characteristic about an individual does not tell you a whole lot about who they are."

"Deputy Director."

The President looked up at the screen. Maldonado was on screen again.

"What is it?" Bruce asked.

"I just sent you a file through the encrypted channel. You need to look at it ASAP."

Bruce frowned, but without a word, he quickly shifted to a different monitor. The President stepped forward to see what he was looking at. It looked like bank transfers. Bruce cursed softly.

The President frowned. "What is it?"

"Sergei was also holding something back," Bruce said.

"What's that?" the President asked.

"We have confirmation. He didn't just sell the Omni to the Chinese. According to these records, he sold it to at least ten additional sources."

"*What?* Who?"

"I don't know all of them." He pointed to one name on the list. "This is a Russian oligarch. This one is an arms dealer in Asia." He rattled off three more names, all individuals who dealt in the seedier side of life.

"Why? Why would he do that?"

"To make more money. To settle grudges. To change the world."

"Are any of our allies on that list?"

Bruce shook his head. "No."

The President grabbed onto a chair, lowering herself slowly into it. "So our enemies now have the power of the Fallen."

Bruce nodded. "Yes."

"Do we have any way to defeat them?"

"Short of nuclear war? No."

Chapter Thirty

HAVENVILLE, MASSACHUSETTS

CAIN AND PATRICK were going over the copies of the Tome that Patrick had brought with him, so Laney took over Nyssa duty. Mary Jane took Susie home to get changed after an unfortunate incident involving a small creek.

Cleo and Tiger kept Laney and Nyssa company as they walked from the field onto the cobblestone streets toward David and Rahim's cottage. Nyssa kept up a constant stream of chatter, and Laney tried to pay attention, but her mind kept going back to the conversation with Cain. It was possible there was an essential doomsday weapon for all Fallen abilities. But even as she doubted its existence, she knew it was not out of the realm of possibility.

After all, Victoria had, in one fell swoop, made the world mortal. Of course, Laney had never asked how she'd accomplished that. She'd assumed the angels had done something. But what if it was the same means by which she could remove the Fallen abilities?

Laney glanced down at Nyssa. All that knowledge was

trapped somewhere in the mind of the little girl next to her. Not for the first time, she wished she could somehow get Nyssa to tap into it. But at the same time, she recoiled at the idea. Nyssa deserved a childhood as innocent and carefree as they could make it.

Laney smiled as Nyssa babbled away at Tiger. Laney only understood every few words, but Tiger kept his head down, nodding as if he understood every word coming out of Nyssa's mouth. Who knew? Maybe he did.

"Laney." She turned, smiling as David stepped out of the gate, Rahim next to him. She headed for them. "Good morning. How'd you two sleep?"

"Better than either of us have in a long time."

"Laney, this is Rahim. You two haven't officially met yet."

Laney extended her hand. "It's great to meet you."

"Not as great as it is to meet you. Thank you for helping us."

Laney waved away his words. "It's not just me. There're a lot of people who make this place work."

Rahim looked around. "It's just so hard to believe that it even exists. It seems real, yet it's not exactly, is it?"

"It's real enough. And it's safe, and that's the most important thing."

"And who is this little one? Is she yours?" Rahim asked, looking down at Nyssa.

"No, not exactly. This is Nyssa, and this is Cleo and Tiger."

Rahim stared at the cats. "Are they . . . I mean I know they're domesticated, but they seem to understand things."

"Oh, they understand. All the cats here are . . . special."

Rahim shook his head. "This is a lot to take in."

"I know. I've been around it for years, and I still have moments when I look around in disbelief." She glanced at David. "Speaking of which, I was hoping to speak with you for a moment."

"If it's okay with the cats," Rahim said, "I'd be happy to take Nyssa here over to meet the rest of the kids."

"I'm sure she'd love that. We were headed that way anyway. Oh, if you see a family of redheads, introduce yourself. That's the McAdamses. They were all planning on helping you guys get settled."

"Will do." Rahim extended his hand down to Nyssa. "Would you like to walk with me?"

Nyssa didn't hesitate. She put her hand right into Rahim's. With a smile at David, he led her down the street, Tiger and Cleo on either side of them.

"That really is an amazing sight," David said.

Laney watched Rahim as he smiled down at Nyssa as they made their way to the cottage next door. "Your partner is not quite what I expected."

"What did you expect?"

"I don't know. Someone a little flashier, maybe more arrogant."

"Nope. I am the arrogant one in our little relationship. Rahim is the heart."

"Why, David," Laney said, elbowing him playfully, "you sound like an old romantic."

"Don't tell anyone. It will ruin my image."

Laney chuckled. "Your secret is safe with me." She paused.

He crossed his arms over his chest. "All right, out with it."

"How difficult would it be to get back into Italy?"

His eyebrows rose. "Depends. How many people are we talking?"

"Three."

"Small group. Shouldn't be too difficult as long as you don't mind moving fast and being a little crammed. Why?"

"I need to go back to Rome. I need to get the Tome from the Brotherhood."

He stared at her, waiting for a further explanation.

"There may be a weapon mentioned in the Tome. Something that could remove the powers of all the Fallen."

"*All* the Fallen?"

Laney nodded.

David let out a low whistle. "Well, now that information would be well worth the trip. You said three? You, me, and Bas?"

"No, I was thinking you, me, and Drake."

David's gaze cut to her. "Drake?"

"Of course."

"I'm all for you getting the Tome. I think Bas should come, though. He'd know where we need to go and how to get in. That intel will be hard to get without communications."

Laney nodded, seeing the wisdom of the suggestion. "Okay."

"And I don't think Drake should come."

"What? Why?"

"There are some things about Drake you don't know. And I just think—"

"Wait, what don't I know? Because Drake would never do anything to harm me. In fact, he'd do everything in his considerable power to *protect* me. We are safer if he's with us."

"That might not be entirely true." He wouldn't meet her gaze.

"David, what aren't you telling me?"

He looked around before nodding toward his house. "Do you mind? You may trust everyone here, but old habits die hard, and I think maybe a little privacy might be best. And I think it would be best if Bas was part of this conversation."

Laney frowned but didn't argue. "So this isn't a CIA thing?"

"No."

"All right." She and David headed back toward his house. "Speaking of the CIA, though, what exactly are they up to with all of this?"

David cringed. "I'm afraid I'm a bit out of the loop. I've been in Italy for the last month, and we've been traveling here for two weeks. Bruce actually helped arrange the transport for us, but the modes of communication were not secure enough for him to reveal anything."

Laney nodded. "Well, thank you. For taking care of all of them, but especially for my uncle."

David held open the door, his tone light. "I'd like to think you would have done the same for Rahim if necessary."

Laney grabbed his arm. "I would, David. Rahim, you, you're part of us now. We protect one another to the best of our abilities."

David stared into her eyes. "You are an unusual creature, Delaney McPhearson. I am glad you're the one who wields that ring. Some of the others with that power would not be so altruistic."

"He is not wrong," Bas said, stepping out of the kitchen.

"Oh, I don't know. People tend to have a habit of surprising me."

"I told Laney we needed to speak with her." David held Bas's gaze. "She needs to know."

Bas nodded as he stepped back into the kitchen to allow them entrance. "Yes. Let's take a seat."

Laney looked between the two of them as she sat down. "What exactly do I need to know?"

"The Brotherhood—they are still very interested in you."

Laney waved her hands. "They are the absolute last concern on my mind right now."

"I know," Bas said quickly. "But you are not the only one they are interested in. They are interested in Drake as well."

Laney frowned. "They know he's an archangel?"

David nodded. "Yes. But he's more than just an archangel."

Laney flashed back on the conversation she'd had with David at the school as they'd watched Drake play with the children. "You said once that he was different than the other archangels."

"He is. He is the archangel the prophecy speaks of when they mention the end of days. His emergence at this point is what has convinced the Brotherhood that the end of days are near and that you are the one who will bring it about."

Laney shook her head. "I don't care about any of that. I have people to keep safe. That is all I care about right now."

"I understand that. And we wouldn't bring it up if we didn't think there may be reason to worry."

"Worry? About Drake?"

Both men nodded back at her.

"Guys, I appreciate the concern, but Drake would never hurt me. Not in any way. I have no doubts about that."

"Drake probably wouldn't, if given the choice. But he may not always have the choice."

Laney looked between the two of them, identical expressions of concern on each of their faces. "I'm not getting this. Lay it out for me, because to be honest, right now I'm just getting annoyed that you're doubting him after all he's done."

Bas glanced at David, who nodded back at him. He turned to Laney. "You are familiar with the end-of-days concept, right? Well, there are different views on what it will entail, but in broad strokes, it involves the end of humanity's time on Earth. At that point, there will be a judgment. The good will be spared, the bad will not.

"The Book of Daniel speaks about the end of days. It says an archangel will herald in the end of days. He will be the one who judges others for their sins."

Laney was vaguely familiar with the idea of an archangel playing judge, but why on earth would they think it had anything to do with Drake? "Have you met Drake? He's not the judgmental type unless it comes to fashion. And there are plenty of archangels. He may be the first one you've met, but he's the third I've met."

Bas licked his lips, only meeting Laney's gaze for a moment before looking away. "We think that there may be a reason for that. He's forgotten who he really is. The burden of that responsibility is not on him—not yet. But once he realizes who he really is, the Brotherhood believes it will all come back. And he will become the judge they have been waiting for."

A chill ran over Laney. "You keep saying who he really is. *Who* exactly do you think he is?"

"He is God's most loyal soldier."

Laney stared at the two of them before shaking her head, a tremor working through her body. *They can't mean . . .* "No. You're wrong. He's an archangel, but not that one."

Bas reached for her hand. "Laney—"

She stood up, yanking her hands behind her back. "No. It's not possible. He's Drake. Yes, he's a good fighter, an exceptionally good one. But nothing else fits."

"Haven't you noticed that the rules for the archangels don't seem to apply to him? He was allowed to be a human for a lifetime. No other archangel was granted that." Bas extended his hands. "He created this. He was given access to this. Who *else* could have done that? Most archangels are messengers or guardians. But when their mission is over, they do not get to stay. They return to the Father."

Laney stared at them, but it wasn't the two men in front of her she saw. It was Ralph as he lay at Heaven's Gate after Victoria had sacrificed herself. His mission was complete, and he had disappeared as if he had never been. "It can't be."

David stood, taking her arms. "You don't want it to be because you love him. But you are not someone who hides from the truth. No matter how difficult."

Laney looked at Bas, who nodded back at her, his eyes filled with compassion. "I'm sorry, Laney, but it's true. He's there, in the Tome. It explains his role."

Laney shook her head, even as the truth hit her right in the heart. "No."

"Yes," said Bas. "And when the time comes, he will be called. And he will judge all of us."

The truth of his words slammed through her. Drake had been Achilles. He had created Havenville. And then she remembered what Father Ezekiel had said in Rome: *Do not kill God's soldier.* She'd thought he was talking about her. But he had been talking about Drake.

"Say it, Laney. You need to say it," David said quietly.

She looked up at him, her heart breaking, knowing that she and Drake were now on borrowed time. "Drake . . . He's the archangel Michael. He is God's sword."

Chapter Thirty-One

THE ARCHANGEL MICHAEL. *Drake is the archangel Michael.* Laney shook her head. She always pictured Michael as being so serious. But Drake, he found a laugh or a smile in everything.

"No. Look, Drake is a lot of things, but he is not Michael."

Laney knew some about the archangel, the highest ranked among all the angels. He had even spoken through Edgar Cayce at times. Her head popped up. "Drake can't be Michael. Michael spoke though Edgar Cayce on at least three separate occasions. But Drake was alive and well during those times, so it can't be him."

"Drake is alive, but *Michael* is sleeping. He is waiting to wake up."

Laney threw up her hands. "What does that even mean?"

"He is without his responsibilities," Bas said.

"But I don't understand how that's even possible."

Laney looked between the two men. "How is he here? How is he *always* here?"

"It is talked about in the Tome. When Samyaza fell and took the angels with him, Michael was bereft. He was heartbroken. He was given a choice: to serve as he always had or to become the guardian of the tree while his heart healed. He chose the tree."

"But why wouldn't he remember who he is?" Laney asked.

"For a long time, he did. But then he asked to become human. And something about that life made him forget his old life, made him *want* to forget his old life." Bas went quiet, but his gaze spoke volumes.

"Me. I'm the reason he forgot."

Bas nodded. "I think that's true. His love for you overrode all those old memories. His love for you filled the parts of his heart broken by his brothers."

"But what if he never remembers?" Laney asked quietly.

"I suppose it's possible. But Michael does play a role in the end of days. And if that is what is upon us, then something will bring his memories back. I don't know what, but something will."

"Even if he remembers, that's not a danger to us. I mean, Drake would never—"

"No," David said quietly. "*Drake* would never do anything to hurt you. Even if it meant his own death. But Michael is God's most trusted. Duty always came first for him, before all. He fought his brothers, whom he loved with all his heart, at God's request. It nearly broke him, but he did it. If he remembers that duty, he will play the role of judge, jury, and executioner. And when an archangel judges, there are only two options: life or death."

"Can an archangel be stopped?"

Bas and David exchanged a look.

"What?" Laney demanded.

"There is only one person who would stand a chance against an archangel. Only one person who would have the tools at her disposal to put up any resistance."

Laney's gaze snapped to David as his meaning became clear. "No."

"I'm sorry, Laney. But if it becomes necessary, you will be the only one who can defeat him."

Chapter Thirty-Two

LANEY STOOD UP. "No. I don't know why you think Drake is Michael, but he's not. If Michael shows up for some reason, I will handle him, but he's not Drake."

David reached out a hand for her. "Laney, you don't know—"

"No, I don't, and neither do you!" She took a breath. "I appreciate your concern. I do. But this is not helping. I need to get to Italy and get the Tome. Can you help me with that?"

"Yes," David said.

"And Drake will be coming with us."

Bas's voice was pleading. "Laney . . ."

"*That* is not negotiable. If that is a deal breaker for you, then I will find another way."

"It's not a deal breaker," David said quietly. "I just want you to be prepared."

Laney studied the two men before her. She didn't doubt that they were simply looking out for her. But she also knew they were wrong. When she had met Drake, he was the entertainer of the year in Las Vegas. The idea of him being Michael was ludicrous. "I know. I appreciate you two looking out for me, but I don't believe you are correct. So let's just drop this, okay?"

Bas and David exchanged another look before Bas nodded. "All right."

"When do you want to leave?" David asked.

Laney took a breath, trying to tamp down her annoyance and her fear. She understood why they were concerned, but just because Drake was an archangel didn't mean he was Michael. "As soon as possible."

"Okay. Nightfall is in twelve hours. Be ready to go," David said.

"Will do." Laney turned and headed out of the cottage, not wanting to say anything more. She kept her gaze down, her thoughts churning. She pictured Drake's face when he saw the statue of Michael atop the Castel Sant'Angelo in Rome.

No, it's not him.

Her mind churned, trying to remember everything she knew of Michael from the Bible. There wasn't much. He was only mentioned three times in the Old Testament, all in the Book of Daniel. And what David and Bas said was correct: He was mentioned as rising during the end of days.

In the Book of Revelation, he led God's armies against the forces of Satan. But right there, even if he was Michael, he would be on their side, right?

"Ah, there is my beautiful woman."

Laney's head snapped up at Drake's voice as he walked down the street toward her. The sun shone on his hair, highlighting the blond streaks that had developed. His blue eyes lighted on her, and the joy in them warmed her heart. Her pulse ticked up and butterflies rolled through her stomach. God, she loved this man.

He reached her and pulled her into his arms before dipping her low and kissing her like the world was ending. She wrapped her arms around him and kissed him back just as fiercely. Giggles broke into their interlude, and she opened her eyes.

"Get lost, brats," Drake growled good-naturedly against her lips before lifting Laney and scowling at the kids. "No interrupting adult time."

The kids squealed and took off like a shot down the road, their laughter trailing behind them.

Drake turned back to Laney with a grin. "Disrespectful punks."

Laney reached up, cupping his face with her hand. "I love you."

He stilled, his brows quirking. "I love you too. But what brought that declaration on in the middle of the street?"

She shook herself from her thoughts. "Just wanted to make sure you knew. I love seeing you with kids."

He looped his arm over her shoulders. "Well, when all this is over, maybe we should talk about having a few of our own."

A pit opened in her stomach even as joy surged through her at the image. "I think that's a great idea."

He pulled her to a stop, wrapping his arms around her and looking into her eyes. "Whatever has got you thinking about the future, especially a future with me, has my undying thanks."

She smiled up at him. "How would you like to take a little trip?"

He wiggled his eyebrows. "Just you and me?"

"And David and Bas."

He sighed deeply. "So not a romantic getaway."

"No. We need to go get the Tome."

His grin returned. "We're stealing it from the Brotherhood?"

"We're taking it. Technically it would be considered robbery, because I'm planning on them being present when we take it."

"Ahh, every time I think I can't love you more . . ." He leaned down and kissed her again.

Laney focused on kissing him back, shoving all her thoughts of Michael aside. Drake was Drake, and he was hers. Nothing was going to change that.

Chapter Thirty-Three

JEN CROSSED her arms over her chest. "I do *not* like this plan."

Laney sighed. "I know losing your abilities is—"

"I don't care about my damn abilities! I don't like you walking into Rome after they tried to kill you the last time you were there."

"Well, to be fair, everybody's pretty much been trying to kill me every time I've gone anywhere for the last few months."

Jen glared at her, even though she knew Laney was telling the truth. Laney had had a target on her back for months, even longer, really. But right now, Jen just had such a bad feeling about her leaving. She rested a hand on her baby bump. Maybe it was the pregnancy making her more emotional than usual. "I know. It's just . . . I need you here. *We* need you here."

"And I will be." Laney's gaze shifted away.

Jen frowned. "What was that?"

"What?"

"That you-looked-at-me-and-looked-away thing."

"What? Nothing. That's how I look."

Jen studied her friend. They'd been friends since college, long before destiny had come calling for either of them. "Something's wrong. What is it?"

Laney bit her bottom lip, a sure sign that something was up.

"Spill it," Jen ordered.

"It's nothing. Something David and Bas said. But it's nothing."

"Okay, well, if it's nothing, tell me, and I'll confirm it's nothing."

Laney sighed. "It's crazy. They think Drake is the archangel Michael."

Jen listened in growing concern as Laney laid out David and Bas's argument. When Laney finished, she asked. "Why do you think they're wrong?"

"Because it's Drake! Does he seem like someone who takes orders?"

"No, but they said he doesn't remember who he is. That he's forgotten."

"Then why does it matter? If he doesn't remember, then he's not that person. He's just Drake."

Jen frowned, not sure what to think. She didn't know either David or Bas very well. Bas she'd met on the estate when he was pretending to be a Vatican representative. Or he was actually one, but either way, she'd met him under false pretenses as far as she was concerned. That didn't exactly earn him her trust.

But there was something about this tale that rang true. Religion had never been her strong suit, though, so beyond what she'd picked up here and there along the way, she really did not know much about archangels. "But you're still worried, aren't you?"

"Maybe just a small, tiny bit. But it's like seeing a horror movie and checking all the closets in your house when you get home. It's not a rational fear. It's just because someone put the idea in your head." Laney zipped up her bag. "It's nothing. First off, it's not the end of days, so Michael won't be called forth. Second, Drake's not Michael, so it doesn't matter."

Jen wasn't as convinced, but Laney had enough on her plate. "I suppose you're right."

Laney grabbed the bag from the bed. "Oh. Drake figured out a way to allow exit while we're gone. The doorway will remain open. He has two tokens that can be used to allow people to escort people in as well."

"We could have used those a little sooner," Jen grumbled.

Laney kissed her on the forehead. "I suppose. But hey, we have them now. And I need to get moving. As soon as the site closes, we're heading out."

Jen grabbed her hand. "Be careful."

"It will only be three days. We'll be fine." Laney disappeared out the doorway, and Jen watched the empty doorway, thinking about what Laney had said. Was it possible that Drake was Michael? That he would turn on them at some point?

Jen wracked her brain, trying to remember anything she could think of about the archangel, but the truth was, she didn't know much. But she did know someone who would. She headed out the bedroom and down the stairs.

She made her way to the cottage next door and

knocked. A few seconds later, Cain pulled the door open with a smile. "Jen. Come on in." He stepped back to allow her entrance.

She slipped in the doorway. "Hi. Is Patrick around?"

Chapter Thirty-Four

THE KITCHEN of Patrick and Cain's cottage was filled with the smell of Irish soda bread. Before Jen could decline, Cain had her seated at the table with a slice and a cup of milk.

"Need to keep your strength up for the baby," he said.

"Thanks," Jen said.

Patrick rolled into the kitchen with a smile on his face. "Jen."

She stood up and quickly walked over to him, giving him a long hug. She pulled away, tears in her eyes. She wiped at them. "Sorry, I've just been . . . I don't know."

He patted her hand. "You've been pregnant. And I've missed you too."

Patrick rolled up to the table, and Cain brought him over a plate and a mug of tea as well.

"All right. I am going over to Mary Jane's with Nyssa. Will you be all right?" he asked Patrick.

Patrick waved him away. "I'm fine. Go on."

"All right, well, I'll see you two later." He disappeared

down the hall. A minute later, Jen heard the front door close.

"Well, this is a nice surprise. Did you get a chance to say goodbye to Laney?"

Jen nodded. "Do you really think there's a weapon that could remove the Fallen's powers?"

"I don't know. But if there is . . ."

"It's worth the risk." She placed a hand over her belly. "I just hope it's safe."

"I'm sure they'll be fine." He took a bite of his bread. "Now, what's on your mind?"

"What? I can't just come over and visit?"

"Oh, you can. But I can see on your face there's something you want to talk about."

"You can not," Jen grumbled.

"I've known you for years, Jen. You don't worry often, so when you do, it's easier to spot."

Jen shrugged. He was probably right. She was not a big worrier. She figured it was better to face your problems head on. Worrying was just wasted time that could be used to solve the problem. "It's not a worry, exactly. More of a potential concern."

He grinned. "Very carefully phrased. Now spit it out."

She smiled back at him. "I've been doing some reading about the end of days. I know different religions have different views about it. And um, I saw something that I just don't have any background on."

"And what's that?"

"There are some who say that the archangel Michael will appear at the end of days and be the judge and jury for humanity. And I was wondering about Michael. Religion wasn't exactly a big part of my upbringing, so I was hoping maybe you could shed some light on him."

Patrick sat back, his hand on his chin. "Michael. He's actually a part of Judaism, Christianity, and Islam. He is considered the patron saint of righteousness, mercy, and justice."

That's not good.

"But that's not how he was first portrayed," Patrick said.

Jen leaned forward. "What do you mean?"

"When Michael was first revered, it was as a healer. It wasn't until the fourth century that the view shifted to the view we currently have of Michael as a warrior."

"Why the shift?"

"I believe we can thank Constantine for that."

"Emperor Constantine? Wasn't he a convert?" Jen knew Constantine was responsible for calling the Council of Nicaea and creating a structure for Christianity. Declaring Gnostic and other texts as heretical, he gave his stamp of approval to the books that now made up the Bible.

Patrick nodded. "Yes. In fact, even though he converted to Christianity, he did not allow himself to be baptized until he was on his deathbed. He worried that if he sinned once baptized, the kingdom of heaven would be banned for him. So he waited until the last minute."

"*That's* the man the Church trusted to direct them?"

Patrick shrugged. "So it seems. Anyway, after a successful battle at Linzin, Constantine had a statue erected of Michael killing a serpent with a sword. In fact, Constantine believed Michael was looking out for his army and felt that was what led to their victories." Patrick shook his head. "Of course, the individuals on the other side of his battles also thought God was looking out for them. Anyway, the statue became popularized as Constantine's influence grew, and soon Michael was seen as an avenging angel across Europe."

"So there's no truth to the idea that he is a warrior beyond Constantine?"

"When it comes to angels, truth is a bit difficult to pin down. But he is viewed by Jews, Muslims, and Christians as a warrior of God, *the* warrior of God, the ruler of Heaven's armies. He is viewed as the guardian of the Church."

Jen was hoping this conversation would make her feel better, but the more Patrick spoke, the worse she felt.

"Some Protestant groups believe that he is not simply an archangel but actually Christ incarnate."

Jen's head snapped up. "What?"

"They believe he is the son of God, that he became flesh as Jesus. Jehovah Witnesses have the same belief. Mormons, however, believe he was Adam, the first of men. In Islam, he is believed to be the archangel responsible for nature."

Jen was starting to get a headache. "Do any of them agree?"

"A few do, but there seem to be as many interpretations of Michael as there are religions."

Jen sighed. *Well, great.*

"I suppose there is one commonality," Patrick mused.

"What's that?"

"That Michael fights on the side of good. That he is God's justice."

Jen went still. But that meant . . .

"Jen, are you all right?"

Her gaze snapped back to Patrick. "Yes. I'm fine. So are you saying that if Michael is on the other side of a battle, that you are the wrong side?"

Patrick shrugged. "I suppose that's true."

Jen's mouth fell open. That wasn't possible. If he was set against them . . . could they all be wrong?

"But I don't think we have to worry about that. It's clear we are on the right side of this battle."

Jen nodded, taking a sip of milk to avoid talking. "Yup. That's perfectly clear."

Chapter Thirty-Five

ROME, ITALY

THE TRIP to Italy had been relatively easy. They had landed at a small airport outside Rome. No one had been there, and it seemed abandoned. But there were signs of life or at least destruction. David decided to stay back with the plane in case there were any problems.

That left Laney, Drake, and Bas to make the heartbreaking trip into Rome. Some of the neighborhoods they passed through looked as if they were ghost towns. Others had houses that were burned-out husks.

Laney stared at one house as they passed. It had collapsed in on itself, the frame black. A swing set stood in the yard untouched. The two swings moved in the wind. "What happened here?"

Bas's hands tightened on the steering wheel. "There have been roving bands of vigilantes. When someone is accused of being a Fallen, they don't wait for proof—they burn the person out. And their families as well."

"And no one does anything?"

"The mob mentality is so strong that the few people that

tried to defend the accused ended up being accused themselves. The brutal are ruling this particular fight."

Laney couldn't help but think it was like the Salem Witch Trials but on a global scale. Everyone accusing their neighbor and no one willing to help for fear of being hurt themselves.

Even when she'd pictured a world with the Omni, she had never imagined its effects would filter through every aspect of life. And certainly not this quickly. It had been less than a year and the world had been radically transformed.

All the more reason we need the Tome. If there was a weapon out there that would end all of this, they needed it. Now. The world would not survive on its present course.

They left the outskirts of Rome and moved toward the more affluent sections. Even here the damage could be seen. Windows were broken. Cars were turned on their sides.

"It looks like a war zone," Drake said.

"It is," Bas replied, steering around a burned-out car. He pulled over to the side of the road and turned the engine off. "We'll have to go on foot from here. The wealthier areas have set up a perimeter around their neighborhoods and have hired private security to keep them safe."

"Are they taking in any refugees from the rest of the city?"

"No." Bas's single word encapsulated all the anger and disgust he felt at that particular policy.

Drake stepped out and stretched. "How long a walk are we talking?"

"Two blocks. You'll see the barricade. This way." Bas stayed along the edge of the buildings, leading them forward. A half a block away, Laney saw the barricade. She shook her head in disgust. It was a fence erected from wood and barbed wire. There were even sniper nests built along it.

Drake grunted. "Charming. Reminds me of East Berlin, circa 1952."

Bas stopped inside a storefront, peering around at the barrier. "Now, getting through the barrier might be a little tricky. We'll need to wait for the guards to—"

Drake put a hand on Bas's shoulder. He winked at him. "We got this." With a smile at Laney, he nodded toward the barricade. "After you, my lady."

"You got him?"

Drake swept Bas up into his arms. "I do indeed."

"Hey." Bas struggled against Drake's grip.

"Let's go." Laney stepped out onto the street and then blurred toward the boundary. She called on the wind. Shutters flung off houses and battered the guards who cried out. By the time they pulled themselves from underneath the debris, she, Drake, and Bas were safely over and hidden from the guards behind a very large house.

A curtain shifted in the window of the house. Laney tensed, waiting for the alarm to be raised, but it was the face of a little girl no more than five that peered out at them. Laney smiled at the little girl and waved. The girl waved back, then put her hand to her mouth, her eyes lighting up.

Laney looked up at Drake, who'd made his eyes large as he tilted his head and stuck out his tongue.

"We should hurry." Bas hustled down the road. Laney waved goodbye to the girl while Drake blew her a kiss before they followed Bas.

The little girl was the only person they saw. Five minutes later, they were standing across from a beautiful villa.

"Apparently Moretti doesn't take that vow of poverty very seriously."

"Technically, he doesn't fully own it. It belongs to his family's trust."

"How many members in his family?"

"He's the last."

"Of course he is," Laney muttered.

Chapter Thirty-Six

THERE WAS an unobtrusive entrance along the side alley of Moretti's villa that the Council used for meetings. It couldn't be seen from the road. Bas led them there, pausing at the door. "Ready?"

Laney nodded.

Bas keyed in his code, and Laney held her breath. As far as they knew, no one in the Brotherhood suspected Bas was anything but a loyal member. But he hadn't been in contact with them for a few weeks, who knew if things had changed?

The light above the keypad flashed green. Laney let out a breath and exchanged a relieved smile with Bas. Bas was sure Moretti was keeping the Tome at his villa, but if Bas's status had changed, the Tome's location could have as well. He opened the door, quietly stepping through. Laney and Drake were right behind him.

Bas stopped at the door only a few feet away. Laney tapped his shoulder, gesturing for him to step back. She and Drake would go first, just in case there were any problems.

Laney opened the door a crack. The hallway was wide, ten feet across, with pale marble floors. No one was in sight, but voices echoed from down the hall.

"Somebody sounds a little upset," Drake murmured in her ear.

"Yes, someone does." Laney slipped through the doorway, making her way down the hall silently, straining to hear any movement from anywhere else in the house, but there was nothing.

She followed the voices to the end of the hall and a set of double doors.

Drake stopped next to her, speaking low. "Ten bucks they are all sitting around some long dining room table under some ridiculously ornate chandelier."

She shook her head. "Sorry, can't take that bet. That's too easy."

He placed one hand on the door handle nearest him. "Shall we?"

Placing her hand on the other, she nodded, opening the door.

At first, none of the twelve men at the long table under the obscenely ornate chandelier noticed as they stepped into the room. They were too caught up in their conversation.

"The Pope must take a stronger stance. He is not—" The man speaking caught sight of them, his gaze automatically going to the face he most recognized. "Bas. What are you—" The man paled, stumbling to his feet. "Ring Bearer."

The rest of the men at the table looked just as shocked. A few pushed back from the table. Two others stood, but most went still, looking like deer caught in headlights.

Laney ignored them, her gaze focused on the man at the end of the table, slowly sipping from his wine glass. "Cardinal Moretti, I believe you have something that belongs to me."

His eyebrows rose. "And what might that be?"

"The Tome of the Great Mother."

Moretti shrugged. "I'm afraid I've never—"

Wind yanked the glass from his fingers. It crashed into the far wall, shards of glass and wine raining down to the floor. The room darkened as the sunlight was snuffed out by dark rolling clouds. "I am not in the mood to be trifled with. The Tome. Now."

"For God's sake, give it to her!" a priest halfway down the table yelled.

Laney spared him only a glance. "Father Ezekiel. Nice to see there was no lasting damage from our last run-in."

Ezekiel narrowed his eyes. "Bas, are you with them? Did you help them at the Castle?"

Bas stepped forward. "I am, and I did. Where is the Tome?"

Laney kept her gaze on Moretti as Ezekiel spoke. He glanced at a panel near him before shifting his gaze back.

"Saw that," Drake drawled as he crossed the room.

Drake ripped a painting off the wall, revealing a safe.

Moretti crossed his arms over his chest. "I won't give you the combination."

"Oh, no. Whatever will we do?" said Drake. With one hand, he ripped the safe door off. It slammed to the ground with such force that the whole room shuddered.

Drake looked in the safe and then shook his head. "Not here."

A priest with a Spanish accent yelled, "You can't have it anyway. It has been in the Church's possession since before the Council of Nicaea!"

Laney narrowed her eyes. "The Council of Nicaea in 323 C.E.?"

The priest nodded, his lips tight. "Yes, exactly. You have no right."

Laney tried to swallow down her anger, but the priest's self-righteousness was making that difficult. "A group of Followers brought a copy to the New World."

"Yes. We are aware of the other Tome," Moretti said dismissively. "We've followed its progress since the Inquisition."

"Did you know the witch trials were an attempt to discover the location of the Tome?" Laney asked.

"Yes. Those poor women. They were very brave," Moretti said.

"Did the Brotherhood know what was happening in Salem back in the seventeenth century?"

"Yes, of course," the Spanish-accented priest said.

Laney's anger boiled. A wind blew through the room stirring the drapes. "Of course? You let those women die to protect the book. And you had another copy. You could have saved them."

Moretti shrugged. "Perhaps but unlikely."

"And what about me? The Church didn't think this book could have been useful in the battle against Samyaza and her forces?"

"We had to think of the long game. If you had lost, we would have had the book for the next battle."

Laney curled her hands into fists. "Thousands of people lost their lives! They could have been saved if I'd known there was a way to remove the Fallen's powers."

The priests at the table jolted, surprise and alarm flashing across their faces, but Moretti barely moved. Laney focused her glare on him. "You knew."

He shrugged. "So what if I did? It is not your concern."

"We could have ended all of this before people lost their lives! You could have stopped Samyaza in her tracks."

"That was not your call. It was ours. Things are supposed to play out a certain way. We have kept the Tome safe for centuries. And your lack of gratitude is insulting. We will speak again when you are more appreciative of our sacrifice." He stood up as if he was going to leave.

"Stop," Laney commanded as more wind tore through the room, slamming the doors shut. Clouds shifted in the sky, darkening the room. Thunder growled.

She stormed toward the cardinal. "You speak of sacrifice. You know nothing of it. The Followers of the Great Mother have risked their lives for eons to keep that book safe. You could have helped them, offered them and the book refuge, but you didn't."

She stood in front of him now, barely able to keep herself from reaching out and shaking the man. "You talk of being a man of knowledge, but you have known of the Great Mother for thousands of years, and you locked that knowledge away. What scared you the most? That Lilith was the equal of man or that she was the one chosen to protect humanity?"

Lightning flashed, bathing the room in flashes of light. Thunder caused the building to tremble.

Moretti's eyes bulged.

Laney held out her hand. "That book was meant to be shared. It was meant to break the cycle. It was not meant for you. It belongs to the Followers."

"It belongs to me."

"Hand. It. Over."

Moretti backed up until his back hit the door behind

him. Laney followed him, not allowing him any escape. "Now."

He glared at her, and Laney thought for a moment he would refuse. She pictured breaking his fingers one by one to get him to talk. She should probably have been revolted at the idea of using torture to get what she wanted. But she was way past that now. She pulled back her fist and slammed it into the door less than an inch from Moretti's head.

He let out a yelp and stumbled to the side. He hustled over to another painting, swinging it wide to reveal another safe.

"Paranoid bugger," Drake murmured.

Laney followed Moretti over. He keyed in the code, then grabbing the Tome, thrust it at her. "Take it. Take it."

Wind roared through the room, tossing plates and chairs. The men scrambled back from the table. Laney stepped back, releasing her hold on the wind, and immediately it died down. The clouds dissipated from in front of the sun.

Moretti scrounged back into the corner. The rest stayed huddled together on the other side of the room, staying as far from Moretti as possible.

Bas stepped to her side. "That was . . . impressive."

Drake grinned. "You should see her when she's really mad. Do you want to look at it here?"

Laney grimaced. "I think I've had enough of Rome hospitality. I'll look at it when we're on the plane."

Bas nodded. "Of course. But Moretti, he does not represent all of us in the Church. Most of us want to do what is right."

Laney immediately pictured her uncle and the other

priests who had been constants in her young life. "Of that I have no doubt."

"I will go get some rope. We can tie them up so they do not warn anyone we are in the country."

Moretti straightened his shoulders, reclaiming his spot at the head of the table. "We will not be tied up like—"

Drake blurred across the room and was back at Laney's side before she could blink. Moretti was now facedown on the table.

Bas looked stricken. "Is he—"

"Unconscious. Better see to that rope, so I don't have to do the same to the rest." Drake smiled at the men in the corner. They all shrank away from him.

"Um, all right." Bas disappeared out the door.

"Picking up another stray, I see," Drake drawled.

"Bas is not a stray."

"No, he is a man in need of a purpose. And you have given him one. Like you have the rest of us." He extended his arm. "So, General, I'd like to treat you to some gelato before we leave. I think you've earned it."

"Not sure we'll be able to find any."

"Oh, I have my ways."

"Then I think that sounds perfect." But her smile didn't last long. She clutched the book closer to her chest, the weight suddenly seeming greater as she thought of all the women who had given their lives so that the book might land in her arms at this moment.

And she prayed that she was worthy of their sacrifice.

Chapter Thirty-Seven

CARDINAL JOHN MORETTI came to twenty minutes after the ring bearer left. Ezekiel buzzed around him. "Oh, thank God. We thought we'd have to call the doctor. But how would we have explained it?"

Moretti put his hand to the back of his head. There was a tender spot, and it ached like the world's worst headache. "What happened?"

"God's soldier hit you."

Moretti closed his eyes. He did not remember that. "Where is everyone?"

"They thought it best if they head back to the Vatican. It is more secure. But I stayed."

Moretti grunted. *Cowards*. "Bring me the surveillance footage."

"Um, yes, sir. Right away." Ezekiel hustled out of the room.

Moretti got to his feet, swaying for a moment as the room swam. Gripping the edge of the table, he waited for the dizziness to pass before gingerly making his way down the table. He grabbed a wine glass that miraculously had not been destroyed and filled it from a wine bottle that had tipped over but hadn't been completely emptied. *That bitch.*

Ezekiel reappeared, a large tablet in his hand. He set it up on the table as Moretti retook his seat. In silence, he watched the ring bearer storm into the room. He felt his face burn as he remembered the fear that had coursed through him when she'd punched the door. He watched himself pitch forward into the table. Then, after tying up the rest of the men, he watched the woman walk down the hall, God's soldier walking beside her, clear in whose side he was on. He rolled his hands into fists as his anger boiled.

Francisco had slipped in while they watched the recording. Now John met his gaze.

But Ezekiel burst out before he could speak. "We can't let her take the book! If she learns that—"

"Silence!" John roared.

Ezekiel stumbled back, his shaking hand flying to his throat.

No one else spoke for a beat. Then Cardinal Francisco stepped forward. "Are we sure it is wise to follow this course of action? Should we not have brought him to our side?"

John shook his head. "The time is not right. Besides, we do not want to be nearby when he is awoken."

"But without the book, how will we be able to awaken him?" Francisco asked.

John turned toward him, raising an eyebrow. "How foolish do you think I am? Do you not think I took precautions for just this occasion? The woman coming here is not a surprise. Her coming for the book, that was always going to happen."

"And Bas?"

John frowned. "That I will admit I did not foresee. But it makes no difference. He knows nothing that can harm us."

"If he goes to the Pope..."

John smiled. "Our brothers will make sure that never happens."

Francisco nodded toward the front door. "And the ring bearer? What are we to do about her? And about God's soldier?"

John's words lashed out. "She is *not* the ring bearer. Call her by her real title. She is the antichrist."

Francisco inclined his head. "You are right, of course."

John pictured the woman. So arrogant. So full of herself. "We have taken on a solemn oath to protect the Papacy from all threats. There is no greater threat to the Papacy and the world than that woman. And we will defeat her."

"With the aid of God's soldier? Because he did not seem to be on our side," Ezekiel said.

John glared at him. "You dare question the loyalty of God's soldier?"

Ezekiel squirmed under his gaze. He shifted his own gaze to the floor, burying his hands in his pockets. "No, I... it's just, well, he seems to like her a great deal."

John waved away his words. "That matters not. Once he knows who he is, he will do his duty."

"So he will be victorious over her?" Ezekiel asked.

John scoffed. "He will be more than victorious. He is God's greatest soldier. He will destroy her."

Chapter Thirty-Eight

HAVENVILLE, MASSACHUSETTS

LANEY STEPPED INTO HAVENVILLE, the Tome clutched in her hands. Drake slipped in behind her. "Ah, home sweet home," he said sarcastically.

Laney smiled. "Actually, I kind of like this place."

And she meant it. The trip back had taken twenty-two hours. On land, they'd had to constantly keep their guard up. The flight offered little respite from the stress. Every time Laney started to fall asleep, she recalled moments from her last flight with David. Needless to say, she hadn't slept much.

Again.

Drake kissed her forehead. "Then I love it. Ah, the welcoming committee."

Laney looked up, seeing Gina heading toward them. "Hi, guys."

"Hey. How's everything going?" Laney asked.

"Good, good." Gina gave her a distracted smile. "We got about twelve more people on Matt and Jordan's last run."

Laney winced. "That's a lot."

"Yeah. We're going to need to talk resources soon. Food's an issue, and some people are beginning to go a little stir crazy. The withdrawal from modern life is really getting to them."

Laney blew out a breath. She wasn't surprised. People were so used to technology that not having it was an adjustment for everybody. She'd even lugged in a set of encyclopedias to help people with their "Google" searches. But she was just as bad. Whose day wasn't made a little better by a ridiculously cute puppy video?

"Any chance people could maybe step outside for a little technology hit? I could set up a schedule."

Laney clucked her tongue, trying to think of all the potential problems. "Let me run it by Danny. The site's deserted at night, but I just want to make sure that a sudden explosion of online activity from a deserted spot can be hidden."

Gina's shoulders dropped. "That's great. I'm sure he'll be able to come up with something. That boy is scary smart."

"Yes, he is. How's everything else?"

"Good." Gina fell in step with them as they headed toward Laney's home. Gina updated them on the new arrivals, the few sicknesses they had, and a few interpersonal issues that required keeping certain people apart or at least really busy.

Laney listened to it all but became distracted by the sound of Jake's voice somewhere off to her right.

"Ready, aim, fire!" The echo of gunshots rang out through the air.

"What the hell?" Laney whirled around.

Gina winced. "Oh, right. Jake and Jen started a new program."

Drake took the Tome out of Laney's hands. "I think I'll take this to Patrick and Cain while you figure out what he's up to."

Laney released the Tome to him without an argument before striding toward the sound of Jake's voice. These people had been through enough. They did not need to hear gunfire. What the heck were Jen and Jake thinking?

Gina's long-legged stride had no problem keeping up with her. "It's a good idea, Laney. You should hear them out."

She was spared answering Gina because they came to the end of the road. In the field to the right, dozens of people had been separated into groups. Some engaged in hand-to-hand combat. Others were stripping and putting guns back together. Still others were going through an obstacle course. And some were just jogging around the edge of the field.

"What is this?"

Jake looked up and caught sight of Laney. He said something to Fricano and headed toward her. "You're back. I take it it was successful?"

"Yeah. Jake, what are you doing?"

Gina nodded at Jake. "I'm going to let you handle this one." Gina turned on her heel.

"Chicken," Jake said.

"Bok-bok," Gina called over her shoulder.

"Jake." Laney gestured to the field. "These people need peace. They need calm. Why would you set this up?"

"I agree they need both. But right now, it's just an illusion. The governments of the world are still looking for all of them, for their families, for their children. This place is great. But one day, someone is going to find us. These people, they have no training. Some have abilities, but if they go against a Fallen with training, they will lose. Heck, some of them will go against a person without abilities and still lose. They need to learn how to defend themselves."

Laney looked over the group. Jen was showing a group of humans basic self-defense takedowns. Lou was leading a group through an obstacle course. "I was hoping we could keep all of them out of it."

"I know. We're safe for now. But I think you know it's only a matter of time before we're found or before we need to leave."

"You don't know that."

"No, and neither do you. We need to prepare, just in case."

Laney wanted to argue with him. She wanted to tell him it would never come to that. But the truth was, things were not getting better. Susan was telling them of more and more individuals forced to leave their lives and hide. Only a fraction were here. Even here, if Gina was right, people were getting antsy. Maybe in the not-too-distant future they would want to leave.

Laney nodded, looking over the group. "You're right. What can I do to help?"

He nodded toward where Jen was instructing a group of people on an over-the-hip throw. "We could use another hand-to-hand expert."

She saluted him. "All right. I'll do what I can."

LANEY SPENT two hours on the field instructing people on some basic, effective takedowns. Nothing fancy, just stuff they could hopefully commit to muscle memory and use without even thinking. Wrist locks, arm bars, off-balance moves. She had to admit, she could see the determination in each person's face, even though some had equal parts nervousness. Jake was right. They needed this. Not just in case they had to leave but to feel like they had some stand in this fight. To not feel powerless in the face of all that was arrayed against them.

Jake's voice rang out across the field. "Okay, everybody. That's it for today. We'll meet back here tomorrow morning."

Laney smiled as each person passed. More than one said thank you. Molly McAdams had been in Laney's group and waited until everyone left. Laney smiled down at her. "You did really well, especially with the off-balance moves."

"Having brothers has to be good for something, right?"

Laney laughed. "That is true."

Zaria and Cleo appeared from the trees. They'd been checking in on them throughout the training. Now Zaria fell in step next to Molly while Cleo stayed next to Laney. Molly ran a hand through Zaria's fur. "Do you think a fight is coming?"

Laney thought about lying to her. She was so young. And still fragile after what she'd experienced at the hands of the CEI. But there was also a maturity in her eyes now. Molly knew what evil the world held, better than some adults. Preparing her for it would better serve her than letting her be surprised if it came to it. "I think eventually it will. But I'm hoping none of you will be part of it."

"Because you'll fight for us."

"Not just me. It's never just me."

Molly nodded. "Will Jake fight?"

Laney studied her. "I'm sure he will."

Molly took a deep breath. "Will he be okay?"

"Jake's better trained than almost anyone here. And he's gone toe to toe with Fallen before."

Molly looked up at her. "That's not an answer."

"No, I suppose it's not. I won't promise something I can't deliver, but I will tell you to never count Jake out. He's one of the toughest people I know."

Molly's gaze shifted to Jen, who was walking with another group of people. "Yeah, no, Jen's the toughest."

Laney laughed. "Yes, I think you're right on that one."

Drake blurred into view in front of them. "Hello, ladies."

Laney stumbled back. "Geez, Drake, give a girl a heart attack, why don't you?"

Drake reached out a hand to steady her. "Hey, just keeping you on your toes. Hi, Molly."

Molly blushed as Drake smiled at her. "Um, hi."

Laney bit back the smile at Molly's crush. She couldn't blame the girl. She had a rather big crush on the man as well.

Molly shuffled her feet. "I need to get going. I promised to help Mom with dinner."

"I'll see you later," Laney said.

Drake took Molly's hand and bowed deeply, placing a kiss on the back of it. "Until we meet again, mademoiselle."

"Uh, bye." Her face now almost matching her hair, Molly all but fled, Zaria loyally by her side.

Cleo bumped him hard in the thigh.

He glared down at her. "Hey, what was that for?"

Don't tease. Cleo headed for the front entrance.

"She doesn't like you teasing Molly."

"I'm not teasing her. She's been through a lot. I'm just trying to make her smile."

"I know. She seems to be better, right?"

"Yes, she does. Now, what's your plan?"

"I thought I'd swing by Cain's cottage and see how it's going."

He raised an eyebrow. "It's only been a few hours."

"I know, but I . . ." She shrugged.

He threw an arm over her shoulders. "Ah, that's why I love you. You are ridiculously obsessed, focused, and optimistic."

"Um, thanks?"

He kissed her on the forehead. "Let me accompany you, my lady."

She slipped her arm through his. "Thank you, kind sir."

Her smiled faded as they proceeded down the road. She knew it was too soon for Cain to have found anything. But Drake was right, she was obsessed. And focused. But optimistic? She sadly was not suffering from that particular characteristic. In fact, right now she was intensely worried. Because if Cain didn't find something that could help them, she had no idea what to do next.

Chapter Thirty-Nine

WASHINGTON, D.C.

THE PRESIDENT STARED out the Oval Office window. There were fewer crowds walking by the fence these days. Fewer people even stepping outside their homes. Businesses were reporting huge absenteeism for workers. Shops were closing early due to lack of customers. Restaurants were going belly up. Even without doing a thing, China had disrupted the U.S. economy.

No, not China. Elisabeta. She hadn't been able to take down the United States personally. But it looked as if her parting gift was going to finish the job just as effectively as if she had still been alive.

I cannot let that happen. And there was only one way she could think of to possibly prevent it. And even then it was an extremely long shot. But right now, she did not have anything but a long shot.

A knock sounded at the door behind her. She called out without turning. "Come in."

Bruce Heller stepped through, his reflection clear in the glass. She turned. "Bruce, thanks for coming in."

He nodded. "I am at your service, Madame President."

She studied her king of spooks. The CIA director was a political appointee and an astute political animal. But Heller, he was a different type of animal. One that thrived in the shadows. He always seemed to be a few plays ahead of her. Surprise was not an emotion she had ever seen flash across his face, but perhaps today she would witness it. "You have, of course, heard the latest reports?"

Bruce nodded. "A large increase in reports of enhanced incidents. Japan, South Africa, Russia, Germany, and about a dozen other countries, all with ties to criminal networks."

"It seems you were right about Sergei selling the formula."

"I wish I hadn't been."

"I do as well. But as we live in the real world, wishes do not help either of us."

"No, they don't."

"What have you learned about Delaney McPhearson's whereabouts?"

"I just received a report that she was seen in Rome, at the home of Cardinal John Moretti."

The President's mouth fell open as she pictured the cardinal she had met with months ago. "She was at Moretti's? Why?"

"According to the Vatican, she threatened the cardinal's life."

"Why?"

"They said she wasn't happy with the statements they were putting out about her."

The President frowned. "That's ludicrous. Everyone is putting out statements about her. Why would she take exception to the Vatican's?"

"I do not believe that is the reason she was there. I believe she was actually looking for something."

"What?"

"A book."

The President frowned. "Why would she care about a book?"

"I'm not sure exactly. But from what I can tell of her, I would assume it is to help someone or perhaps a lot of someones."

"Do you have any idea what book it was?"

"I believe it was the Tome of the Great Mother."

"I've never heard of it."

"Few have." Bruce explained about the Great Mother, how she had been the first wife of Adam and a source of good in the world. How she had chosen mortality for the human race as a way to save them. How she was then reborn every lifetime and the Tome was a recording of all her lives.

Silence fell heavily when Bruce finished his explanation. The President stared at him, wondering if, for the first time since she'd known him, he was joking. "You can't be serious."

"I am. Very."

"That's . . . that's crazy."

"As crazy as a woman who can control the weather or communicate with animals? Or individuals who run at the speed of a superhero? Or heal in minutes from what would be a mortal wound to a normal human?"

The President shook her head. "These are strange times we are living in."

"I believe that is an extreme understatement."

"I believe you are correct." She smiled, and Bruce returned the smile. "All right. Well, the reason I brought you in is that I have an idea of how we might help protect the United States. Although 'idea' may be overselling it."

"All right. What do you need?"

"I need to speak with Delaney McPhearson."

And the President had been correct about one thing: Today was the first day she saw surprise flash across his face.

Chapter Forty

HAVENVILLE, MASSACHUSETTS

DRAKE LEFT Laney at the beginning of the path to Cain's cottage. Her uncle had the door open before Laney even reached it. He put a hand to his lips and closed the door softly behind him.

Laney lowered her voice. "What's going on?"

"Cain is heading to grab a shower. I'm afraid if he hears you, he will head right back out to speak with you."

"How's he doing?"

Patrick sighed. "He's struggling. He hasn't read that language in eons. It's not coming back to him as quickly as he would like. And he's getting extremely annoyed with himself."

Laney couldn't even imagine the difficulty of the task ahead of him. There were approximately 6,500 languages spoken in the world today. Experts believed that one language died out every fourteen days, which meant that the number of languages Cain had probably been exposed to was exponentially higher. Those same experts put the number of languages that had existed between 64,000 and

140,000. Trying to wade through all of that to recall an ancient language was a mind-numbingly difficult undertaking.

And it wasn't just any ancient language he was trying to understand. He was trying to translate the *first* language. Something he had not seen in tens of thousands of years. There were no written records that still existed from that time period. The first language was the language from which hieroglyphs evolved. But even that early language was centuries removed from its source.

"Have you figured anything out?" Laney asked.

Her uncle opened his mouth to answer, but before he could say anything, the front door opened. Cain stood framed there. "A little."

"I thought you were supposed to be taking a shower," Patrick grumbled.

"This is more important." He waved her in, carrying the Tome in his other hand. He disappeared down the hall toward the kitchen.

Laney followed, now understanding Patrick's concern. She had never seen Cain look so rattled. His hair was wild. His eyes were of course still black, but if they weren't, she was sure they'd be red from how often he rubbed them. And there were dark circles underneath them as well.

"I can't figure it out. I mean, I know it's there. But I can't find it." Cain placed the Tome on the table with a thud. Laney winced. The Tome was so old she worried about damaging it, but Cain looked like he wanted to toss the thing across the room.

Cain rifled through the pages before stopping and pointing. "It all revolves around this. But I can't see it."

Laney leaned forward. Cain was pointing at two intertwined triangles within a circle, what had become known the world over as the Seal of Solomon.

He flipped a page. "It's everywhere."

Patrick put a hand gently on Cain's forearm, stopping him from flipping to another page. "How about if you tell Laney what you've learned? Perhaps a fresh ear will help."

Cain looked between them and nodded before slumping into a chair.

Laney got up and poured Cain a cup of tea, grabbing a plate and piling some fruit on it. He nodded his thanks as she placed it in front of him. Patrick sat leaning forward, staring at the Tome. "It really is beautiful."

Laney scooted her chair closer to his to get a better look. He had flipped back to the original page Cain had been reading. There was a picture of Victoria. She looked to be in maybe her forties.

"That is how she looked when I first knew her," Cain said.

Laney looked up at him and then back at the picture. "You mean when she . . ."

"Made us mortal? Yes. She had been alive for thousands of years. In modern day, she would look around forty, maybe forty-five."

Laney stared at the image of the woman on the page. What strength it must have taken to make the decision she did. Not only to know she would cause pain to herself indefinitely but to know each and every human would suffer from that point forward based on her decision. They would live, but they would all die. They would suffer the death and loss of those they loved. Laney was glad she hadn't been the one to make that choice, although the decision to remove the powers of the Fallen might be just as world-shattering.

"Do you think she made the right choice?" Patrick asked.

"Had you asked me right afterward, I would have said no. I would have said she was cruel, selfish." Cain sighed. "But now? I have seen over my long life the incredible kindness in humanity. And its cruelty. Should we all have been kind, her choice would have been unnecessary. But our long lives only encouraged the cruel. Humanity is better off with shorter lifetimes, with less power."

Laney couldn't help but think of the choice ahead of her now. Removing the abilities of the Fallen from all of them. How many would be hurt by her actions? But how many would be spared? There was no way to know that. In her heart, she knew that such power was not meant to be shared like this. She didn't think it had ever been meant to be shared.

"Removing the abilities of the Fallen, it is also the right decision," Cain said, cutting into Laney's thoughts as if he could read her mind. "Like I said, humanity is better off with less power."

"Cain's right," Patrick said. "Look at all that has happened in just the short time those abilities have become available. The world is on the edge of war. We are *not* ready for these abilities. I don't think we ever will be. I don't think humanity is made better because of them."

Laney ran her thumb over the face of her ring. She didn't wear it very often. She didn't need to. Her abilities had become hardwired into her. But she liked the weight of the ring. It reminded her of her responsibilities. She glanced from the intersecting triangles on her ring to those in the Tome. "So what have you found?"

"It does speak of a weapon. 'The blight of the wicked

will be removed from the earth. But the sacrifice will be great.' The mention of sacrifice is done multiple times."

Laney nodded. She'd known sacrifice would be required. "Does it say what the sacrifice is?"

Annoyance crept into Cain's tone. "No. It mentions the weapon can only be wielded by the one chosen to fight the Fallen. But it doesn't say what the weapon *is*."

"Was the weapon created by Lilith?"

Cain nodded. "It doesn't specifically say that, but reading between the lines, that seems to be a possibility."

She knew her mother had been guiding humanity for thousands of years, but it was still awe inspiring how much she seemed to do. *And how little I know of her accomplishments.*

"Do we know when it was created?" Patrick asked.

"After the destruction of Atlantis."

"After they knew how much damage the Fallen could truly do," Laney said.

After Atlantis, the surviving Atlanteans had scattered. Shortly thereafter, great civilizations began to appear out of nowhere across the globe. In the United States, it was the Mound Builders. In Central America, it was the Mayan civilization created by the god Viracocha. In Sumeria, it was the Anunnaki. And in Egypt, it was the dawn of the pharaohs.

She frowned thinking of that last one. Egypt had always been a bit of a conundrum. Mainstream science argued that the Giza Plateau and its incredible archaeological sites were around four thousand years old. The King's List, the Sumerian stone tablet that listed the Sumerian kings as well as the leaders of neighboring areas, however, depicted Egypt's history as going back over thirty-six thousand years. Moreover, research by Dr. Robert Schoch and others clearly demonstrated that the Sphinx was thousands of years older than mainstream archaeologists believed, dating closer to 11,000 BC when the Giza Plateau was a fertile, and more importantly, *rainy* location.

The Sphinx was also, according to Edgar Cayce, one of the repositories for the lost knowledge of Atlantis. It was reputed to be located under the front left paw of the Sphinx, a creature that, according to Noriko, was not supposed to have the head of a man and the body of a lion. The Sphinx was actually a jackal, representative of Anubis, the god of the underworld. At some point, his face had been reconstructed into that of a man.

So much history. So much unknown. Thousands upon thousands of years had come and gone between when the weapon, whatever it was, had been created and today. Laney flipped through more pages, the sheer enormity of what they were trying to figure out overwhelming her.

Maybe Cain's right. We're never going to be able to figure this out.

Chapter Forty-One

PATRICK HAD FINALLY TALKED Cain into stepping away from the Tome and taking a shower. He needed a break. But Laney now sat at the table, flipping through the pages of the Tome. The margins of the ancient book were covered in incredible drawings. Some animals long extinct. Some creatures she could not identify. Others were buildings or people long gone. But a few she could recognize.

Now Laney stared at an image of the pyramids of Giza. A ship was shown next to the Great Pyramid in one sketch, reminding Laney of another mystery associated with the Great Pyramid. Next to it, two pits were found that contained ancient sea vessels. One was unearthed and was on display at the boat museum on the Plateau. It was a 141-foot-high prow seagoing vessel, similar in design to Viking ships. They were at least 4,500 years old. Some experts argued it was more advanced than the ships in existence at the time of Columbus and had to have been created by a civilization with an extensive seafaring history, which of course was not the Egyptians.

The boats were said to have been created to ferry the souls of the pharaohs to the other world. But where had they gotten the design from?

Her gaze flicked to a sketch of the pyramids, the Great Pyramid rising high above the others. And that was always the problem when it came to the structures of the Giza Plateau: How *were* they built? She traced the outline of the pyramids. Creating the pyramids was beyond the capabilities of builders today. All theories used to explain their creation suffered from major issues. The most accepted theory was that ramps were used to create the pyramids. However, creating a ramp that could hold up multi-ton stones was an undertaking in and of itself. Most of the materials suggested would collapse under the weight.

In fact, whereas most people would expect the largest of the blocks to be on the bottom of the Pyramid and to gradually decrease in size, that was not what had happened. Approximately fifty levels up, the stones actually grew larger. Why create a structure where your heaviest blocks are not on the bottom?

Moreover, the size of the ramps was beyond imagination. If they wrapped around the pyramid, they would require either incredibly tight turns or massive rounded ramps. Mistakes would not be an option. If they were straight ramps, a new one would have to be constructed for each block. The building time for each pyramid would be centuries long.

And yet, according to the experts, the Great Pyramid had been constructed in twenty years with 100,000 men, consisting of 2.3 million stones. That meant thirty-one stones would have to have been placed every hour each year. Of course, due to the rainy season, they would only be able to build nine months out of the year. Which meant four blocks a minute would have to have been placed, or two hundred and forty every hour. Impossible.

Laney flipped to another page, but her mind kept stretching back to the Great Pyramid. Something was tugging at her, at the back of her mind. "Uncle Patrick, the passageways in the Great Pyramid are so odd. Some are incredibly short while others stretch to thirty or more feet. Why would they create them that way?"

"That is one of the perplexing questions about the Great Pyramid. Some have argued that it was created in such a way as to predict the rise and fall of humanity. Each of humanity's greatest events is indicated along the path."

"But the path must end."

"Yes, most scholars who subscribe to the notion that the path is prophetic agree that it ends in the year 2038."

"And what happens then?"

"Then the world either changes for the betterment of mankind or . . ." He shrugged.

Right, death and devastation. Well, whatever was happening with the path, it certainly wasn't something she needed to worry about right now.

Assuming I make it to 2038, I'll worry about it then.

Her uncle sat with his hand on his chin. "Even if you don't believe the prophetic passageways theory, the passageways themselves are confounding. You have this amazingly large structure, yet some of the pathways are incredibly small. There's one that leads to the Queen's Chamber that is only inches wide."

"Well, that can't be intended for a human."

"Perhaps, but there is a metal doorway complete with hinges dozens of feet along it. The only one who could open it would be a mouse."

Laney nodded, familiar with the discovery of that small

tunnel. "There's just so much open space. And then these pathways of differing widths and heights. Honestly, it looks less like a tomb and more like a machine."

Patrick nodded slowly. "The name 'pyramid' actually translates into 'fire in the middle.' There's an engineer by the name of Chris Dunn who argues that the pyramids were actually machines. That they used tectonic vibrations to create electricity."

"Is that possible?"

"I'm not sure. The pyramids themselves don't really work as tombs, even though that is the function mainstream archaeology has attributed to them."

Laney knew what he meant. The Valley of the Kings had been the burial spot for the pharaohs and distinguished nobles for five hundred years. Each unearthed tomb was extravagant in its holdings. Yet the pyramids, which were supposed to be the tombs for the pharaohs Khufu, Khafre, and Menkaure, were completely empty of any wealth or funerary goods. Not even a single broken piece of pottery had ever been found there. Experts claimed that was because of grave robbers who had removed everything of value from the sites.

But that explanation had problems too. For example, the Great Pyramid's passageways shrunk at times to three feet in height, expanding in other areas to twenty. How would they have gotten the great tributes left behind out?

And there would have been large objects buried with a pharaoh of Khufu's status. In King Tut's tomb, which was a relatively small tomb by pharaoh standards, over five thousand items had been found. While some were small items, others included gilded panels, couches, chairs, beds, life-sized statues, and six chariots.

King Tut was a child king who became pharaoh at age

nine and died at age eighteen or nineteen. He was a lesser pharaoh in terms of impact, and due to the stillbirth of his two children, his death signified the end of the Thutmosid line. Yet even he had a tomb filled with immense riches. It stretched the limits of the imagination that a pharaoh of Khufu's stature would have only small items that could be slipped through the narrow passages. Yet nothing had been found in any of the pyramids of the Giza Plateau.

Plus, there were no hieroglyphs inside the pyramids. All other pharaoh tombs were lined from floor to ceiling with hieroglyphs. Of course, they were all buried in the Valley of the Kings. The three pharaohs who allegedly built the pyramids broke this tradition. The pyramids' interiors, in contrast to the other tombs, were decidedly stark. Even the sarcophaguses found were simple unadorned rectangular granite boxes.

There were some, of course, who argued that the pyramids were not created as tombs by the pharaohs Khufu, Khafre, and Menkaure and that they served an entirely different purpose. *Could* they have been machines?

Cain stepped back into the kitchen, his hair still wet from the shower, pulling Laney from her musings. He looked better. There was a little more color to his skin.

"Feel better?" she asked.

"A little. I just . . . I know this is important. And I'm annoyed I can't figure it out."

"You're doing the best you can. That's all any of us can do," Patrick said.

Laney's gaze flicked back to the Tome, taking in the Seal of Solomon, Victoria's image, and the one other image on the page. She pointed to it. "Is that an ankh?"

Cain walked over and noted where she pointed. "Yes. It denotes immortal life."

"The three make a triangle." Patrick traced from each of the images, creating a triangle.

Triangle, triad. Laney sat back. Triangle, triad, immortal life. There was something . . . something playing at the back of her mind. She pushed the Tome toward Cain. "How many pages reference the weapon?"

"Four."

"Can you show me?"

Cain flipped through the pages, pointing to the ones that directly referenced the weapon. On each, there were three images, which, if linked, created a triangle.

"What are you thinking?" Patrick asked.

Laney frowned, her gaze flicking across the images. "I'm not sure. I mean, triangles appear all over the ancient world in the form of pyramids. But what if this is trying to tell us the weapon is associated with a triangle?"

Patrick pointed to a sketch on the book. "Or maybe a pyramid."

"That makes sense," Cain said quickly. "Here." He turned the book around, pointing at symbols she did not recognize.

"I don't know what that means," she said.

"Neither did I. See these three dots? They make these symbols meaningless. Without the dots, it speaks to a time of great suffering and the alleviation of that suffering through a dangerous bargain. But in the first language, each dot means something. With these three here, I couldn't figure out what it meant. And I've seen this in three other places. It was driving me mad."

Patrick pulled over a sheet of paper and drew out the dots, separating it from the noise of the other symbols. As soon as he did, Laney recognized it. "It's the Osiris constellation."

Patrick nodded. "And if it's the Osiris constellation, then there's only one spot in the world where this would be relevant."

"The three pyramids on the Giza Plateau. We'll find the weapon there," Cain said.

Laney shook her head. "No, we'll find it at the Great Pyramid."

Patrick and Cain looked at her. "How do you know that?"

"I just do. It feels right." She paused, her mind whirling. "In fact, I don't think we need to find the weapon. I think humans have been staring at it for thousands of years."

Patrick met her gaze, nodding. "You think that that guy Dunn is right, that the pyramids are a machine."

Laney nodded slowly, becoming more sure the more she stared at the Tome. "It's a machine. And we just need to figure out how to turn it on. We need to find the key." She frowned as she glanced at a large image of the Great Pyramid. "Whatever happened to the capstone, by the way? I don't think I've ever heard anything about it."

"That's because there's nothing to tell," Patrick said.

"What do you mean?" Laney asked.

"No one knows if there ever was a capstone."

Laney looked at Cain, who nodded. "I stayed away from Egypt for a long time. By the time I made my way there, the capstone was absent. I never inquired as to where it had gone."

"But there must be something out there."

"Actually, there isn't," Patrick said. "We know that some individuals who have made it to the Plateau of the Great Pyramid where the capstone should reside have experienced some sort of electrical shock. And, of course, there are those who suggest that, similar to what Tesla proposed, the pyramids actually helped siphon electrical energy from the Earth. But as for a capstone, there's nothing."

"Is it possible there never was one?"

But even as Laney said it, she knew that was absurd. The pyramids were an absolute testimony to the precision that could be achieved with such massive constructions. The northern face of the Great Pyramid was aligned almost perfectly to true north, and the other faces almost perfectly matched their directions as well. The error was less than .0015 percent. Modern-day builders didn't understand the need for such precision. After all, with objects the size of the pyramids, a higher degree of error would have made the job of the builders much easier and would not have been discernible to the naked eye. But if the Pyramid were a machine, then precision would have been necessary.

And in fact, precision seemed to have been the name of the game when it came to constructing the pyramids. For example, there was only a difference of eight inches between the shortest and longest sides of the Great Pyramid, a one-tenth of one percent error. Precision of that accuracy would be close to impossible in the modern day, never mind back then. So why go to all that trouble unless you needed to?

In light of the care taken with their creation, the idea that they would just skip the top thirty feet of the Great Pyramid was insane. The more she thought about it, the more she was coming around to the idea that the capstone was the key, both figuratively and literally. When the capstone was in place, would the Pyramid, in essence, turn on?

She turned to her uncle. "There has to be something out there about it."

"I'm sorry, honey. Whether or not the capstone ever

existed has been completely lost to the sands of time. There's no record of it."

Laney slumped in her chair. "Which probably means any chance we have of using the weapon the Tome speaks of is just as out of reach."

Chapter Forty-Two

AFTER SPEAKING with her uncle and Cain, Laney had spent a few hours outside Havenville searching every online source for anything on the capstone. Danny had done the same. There hadn't been much. Like her uncle said, people couldn't agree whether it had even existed at all. And there were no hints, no witnesses indicating where it might have gone.

Even when she'd lain down to sleep, she could not get the ancient mystery out of her mind. She barely slept. And when she did, she had dreams about pyramids, the capstone, and getting swallowed by the sands. As a result, when she woke up, she felt worse than when she went to sleep.

Drake had already been gone when she'd finally stumbled from bed. With Cleo by her side, Laney went for a long run. She needed to stretch her legs. She needed to clear her mind. But each step she took merely pounded in all the doubt, insecurities, and questions she still had. Were they going down the right road? Or were they grasping at the

Great Pyramid because they needed an answer? And even then, without the capstone, what good was that knowledge? Above all, though, she wondered whether it was truly possible to remove all the abilities of the Fallen.

But if Cain was right—and she really had no reason to doubt him—it wasn't a method where she could pick and choose whose powers were removed. All the powers would disappear. Jen, Henry, Matt, Lou, Rolly—they'd all lose them as well. They'd be as defenseless as any other human. And if it worked, would that be enough? Would it stop all the chaos that had broken out around the world?

What if they removed the powers and it changed nothing? What if the world continued on its march to war? *What if I just make it so good people can't protect themselves?*

She glanced down at Cleo. And what of the cats? They had been created through Amar's blood, the blood of a Fallen. What would happen to them? They didn't really have any Fallen abilities beyond a slightly faster healing rate. Their intelligence wasn't due to the Fallen nature of Amar's blood, but the human genes that had been used in their creation. Would they be all right?

Cleo nudged her. *We'll be all right.*

How can you be sure?

We are not Fallen. We are not human. We are something else. Like you.

Laney slowed to a walk. *I hope so.*

Stop worrying. Cleo licked Laney's leg before trotting toward Tiger, who had appeared at the edge of the field. Laney watched Cleo go. She'd been spending more and more time with Tiger lately. Laney knew it was good, but she had to admit she was a little jealous. With a sigh, she turned for her cottage. Thirty minutes later, she was walking down the stairs in her cottage, towel-drying her hair.

The kettle whistle blew from the kitchen. She should have known. She stepped in as her uncle was turning off the burner. He nodded to the two mugs on the counter next to him. "Thought we could both do with a cup of tea."

"You are not wrong."

He reached for them, but she shooed him away. "I've got it."

He made his way to the small kitchen table. Laney placed a mug in front of him before sitting across from him.

He stirred his tea with a spoon. "Did the run help?"

Laney shrugged, stirring her own tea. "Not really."

"It's not an easy decision."

"No, it's not, especially since we don't know how people will react." She flashed on Agamemnon in the tub. "I don't think anyone will be harmed when their powers are removed, at least not from the powers disappearing. But I can't be sure. They won't be removed by the Omni, which leaves room for doubt."

"And what about you?"

She frowned. "What about me?"

"Your powers, your ring-bearer powers. Will they disappear as well?"

"I don't know." When she'd been hit by the Omni on the day of the coronation, she hadn't paid any attention to her ring-bearer abilities. At that point, the loss of her healing abilities was the foremost in her mind. And then she'd been hit by the Omni again, and her Fallen abilities had been restored. She'd never checked if her ring-bearer abilities had also disappeared during that interlude.

"We know they're connected. I can't control the Fallen when I have the abilities of the Fallen, so there is some link. But until we activate the capstone, there's no way to know exactly how it will affect me."

Her uncle stirred his tea without responding. Laney's gaze narrowed as she watched him. "What?"

"Nothing, nothing."

"Uncle Patrick . . ."

He sighed, his gaze flicking to the hallway.

Laney realized what was bothering him. "You're worried about Cain."

He nodded. "I've probably seen too many movies. I keep picturing him aging all at once."

If that were the case, Cain would be reduced to ash. He was thousands of years old. "We don't know that will happen."

"No, we don't. It's just . . ." He shrugged.

"Did Cain find any more information in there?"

"No. There's no real knowledge. Even the writers of the Tome passages hadn't seen it work. It was just stories handed down."

Laney sighed. "So we have no idea how it will affect people with abilities, Fallen or otherwise. And no mention is made of the impact on humans."

"Are you sure it's worth the risk? Is there another approach you could take?"

Laney had spent her night turning that question over and over again in her mind. Did she even have the right to make this decision? Whether she did or didn't, she had been able to come to this decision more easily than some. It would have perhaps been different if the Omni hadn't been uncovered. But with it out there, there was nothing good in store for the world. She met his gaze. "I wish there was. But these powers, it was bad enough when only a handful had them. But can you imagine the world if only those who want power had them? The haves verse the have nots wouldn't even come close to describing the divisions that would be created. That much power concentrated in the hands of a few, it will be a nightmare."

"I know." He blew out a breath. Silence fell heavily between the two of them. Laney pictured a world with enhanced. They could and would run roughshod over the rest of the world. Apocalyptic was the only word she could think of to describe the aftereffects of the battle to come. No matter what happened, if they succeeded or they didn't, the world would never be the same. As visions of mutilated bodies lining streets ran through her mind, she gave herself a mental shake.

Enough of that. Her uncle looked just as disturbed by his own thoughts.

"Any more ideas about the capstone?" she asked.

He started blinking rapidly. "Um, about finding it? No. There are a few sources I can check, but I won't be able to access it from in here. I'll have to go outside."

"I don't understand how it's possible that there are no reports on it. How can no one have ever seen it? I mean, is it possible it never existed? That the Great Pyramid was never actually finished?"

"Well it is true that there has never been a mention of the capstone in any historical records I've seen." He hesitated.

A dramatic pause. That can't be good. "What is it?"

"It's not a historical record. It's a recounting from the Children of the Law of One."

Laney frowned. "I don't understand."

She knew, of course, of the Children of the Law of One. In the time of Lemuria and Atlantis, the world had been broken into two camps. The Children of the Law of One believed in peace, in kindness toward one another. The other camp, the Sons of Belial, believed in attaining power, of asserting dominance over others. When the angels fell, they ushered in the desire for material goods within humans. They nurtured their darker impulses and created the Sons of Belial.

"There is a group I read up on while I was in Italy. It reminded me of the trances that Edgar Cayce would go into. Except this time, the questioner had a name: Ra."

Laney's eyebrows rose at his words. Ra was the ancient Egyptian god of the sun. He was considered the king of the gods, the creator of all. He was strongly associated with the pharaohs, especially during the fifth dynasty, when the pyramids on the Giza Plateau were created. In fact, at that point the pharaohs were considered to be the sons of Ra.

"What did the readings say?"

"According to Ra, there were two capstones in the Great Pyramid's history. The second was made of gold and did nothing more than complete the Pyramid."

"And the first?"

"It was made of black granite. It allegedly acted as a chimney, purifying the environment."

"What happened to it?"

"It doesn't say. But I have been thinking about that. Words often take on a different meaning when we step back. In today's world, when we think of purifying, we think of it in terms of the environment and pollution. But that would not have been an issue thousands of years ago. So when they say purify, they must mean something else."

Laney frowned. Purifying the spirit? But how would . . . She went still, her gaze snapping to her uncle. "Lilith."

He nodded. "I think they were referring to purifying humanity. By her decision, she allowed humanity's immortality to end. Perhaps the capstone was part of that process."

Laney's mind was spinning. Was it possible? Her mother had brought about the end of immortality to allow humans to become better people. Was it possible the capstone was the mechanism by which that happened? She had never really considered *how* her mother had been able to make that happen. To be honest, being angels had been involved, she had kind of thought it was a bit of bibbidi bobbidi boo and voilà, immortality was gone. But what if it required not magic, but science? What if she had to physically do something to make it come about?

"Does Cain know anything?"

"I've spoken with him, but he was not aware of what she had done until after, to his great detriment."

Cain had been the world's first murderer. He did not know at the time that striking his brother would result in his death. Before Lilith made her deal with the angels, it would not have. "Has he ever seen the capstone or heard any rumors that might point us in the right direction?"

Her uncle shrugged. "It wasn't something he ever wondered about."

"I'm not sure if I should be happy we can't find it or worried. After all, if we can't find it, whatever the effect of the capstone might be is a moot point."

"But do we have any other way to make this all go away?"

"Not unless we make enough Omni to either dose everyone who's been empowered and remove their powers or make enough for everyone to be empowered so at least it's a more even fight."

"You're not really thinking of that, are you?"

"No. Even if we could with so many people having the formula, it would be a constant battle. The world's longest game of whack-a-mole."

"So what is Plan B?"

Normally when people said they felt the weight of the world on them, it was hyperbole. But Laney knew in her case, it was accurate. She sighed. "Honestly? We don't have one."

There was a knock on the back door, and then Mustafa stuck his head in the room. "Hey. Am I interrupting?"

"No. In fact, we're happy for any distraction," Laney said.

Mustafa stepped fully into the room. "Well, my news is certainly distracting."

"What is it?" Patrick asked.

"Danny. He got a message." He focused his attention on Laney. "Someone wants to talk to you."

She frowned. "Who?"

"The President of the United States."

Chapter Forty-Three

LANEY'S MIND whirled as she and Drake headed to the control center. She vacillated between fear and confusion. Fear that somehow the President had tracked them down. But she knew Danny would know if that was the case. And being the alarm wasn't being raised, that seemed unlikely.

Which only left confusion. What on earth would the President want to speak with her about? After all, the woman had targeted her friends and family. She'd denied Laney reentry into her own country. She'd gotten what she wanted: all of the Fallen out of the United States. She hadn't been interested in talking then.

As Laney and Drake stepped into the front hall of the control center, Henry, Jen, David, Jake, Matt, Gina, and Danny, who were all gathered at the large table in the first room to the left, stopped their conversations.

"Well, that's ominous," Laney said into the silence as she stepped into the room. "So what's going on?"

Drake pulled out a chair, and she took a seat as Danny began to speak. "I've been running checks on everyone in the camp's communications. All their social media accounts, emails, just in case a red flag popped up."

"Okay. So, whose account did it pop up on?" Laney asked.

"Mine," David said. "It's a backchannel that only Bruce and I are aware of." He glanced at Danny. "Or so I thought."

Danny ignored the glance.

David continued. "According to Bruce, the President wants to speak with you. She wants to enter into some kind of agreement."

Laney frowned. "Agreement? Like what? We all turn ourselves in?"

David grinned. "No. She's agreed to remove all the restrictions placed on enhanced individuals. Everyone would be given blanket immunity."

Laney frowned again. But Drake was the one who voiced her thoughts. "Why would she do that?"

"Because she needs our help," Henry said.

David nodded. "That is my thought as well."

Laney looked at each of the people gathered around the table. "So you think she's going to ask for help? Help with what?"

"Maybe she wants to create a Fallen army out of the people we have here," Gina said quietly.

Jake crossed his arms over his chest. "Absolutely not. These people are not going to be conscripted into fighting for a country that criminalized them for abilities beyond their control."

"Agreed," Laney said. "Besides, that would be just changing the manner of death. Everyone would be right back where they began."

"If we gave them the Omni, though, they could counteract the effects of those other soldiers' abilities," Matt said.

Everyone stopped and stared at him. He was right. They had it in their power to stop any force that was created through the Omni. But . . .

Laney shook her head. "No, expanding the amount of people that have that formula is a recipe for disaster. We can't trust any of the governments of the world with it."

"But maybe we need to think about weaponizing it," Matt said. "To protect our people."

Laney sighed, not liking the logic underneath Matt's words. Because it *would* keep their people safe. They could make sure only people they fully trusted had access to it.

"This is all a moot point if Dom can't recreate it," Laney said.

"I think he might be able to," Gina said. "It might even be good for him to have something to focus on."

"Okay, well, Gina, can you broach the idea with Dom? I'm not saying we're doing it, but I'd like to at least know if it's an option," Laney said.

She nodded. "I can do that."

"Good," said Jake. "Okay, so let's, for arguments sake, say the President is not calling solely for the Omni. Bruce will no doubt tell her Laney won't hand it over. So why is she calling?"

"There's really only one way to find out," Drake said.

Laney looked at Danny. "Can you make sure the call is completely secure? That they have no way to trace us?"

"For a limited amount of time, yes."

"Okay." Laney looked around the room. "Anyone object to me speaking with the President?"

No one said anything. "Okay, David, set it up."

Chapter Forty-Four

TIWANAKU, BOLIVIA

THE PRESIDENT WASTED NO TIME. Laney sat in the farmhouse with Henry, Matt, David, and Danny only a few short hours later. Drake had put up an argument about wanting to be there as well, but if this was a trap, she needed him to stay and protect the group back at Havenville. He had not been happy.

"Danny, we all good?" Henry asked.

Danny didn't look up from his keyboard. "One more minute."

Laney and Henry had arrived at the house an hour ago but Danny, Matt, and David had gone there as soon as Laney had given the go ahead for the meeting.

Danny hit a few more keys on his keyboard and then nodded. "Okay. You have five minutes. They'll be trying to track us. After five minutes, I cannot guarantee the connection is secure." He pointed at a screen, where 5:00 was frozen. "I'll start the clock as soon as the call goes through."

"Okay." Laney sat down at the table in front of the camera. They'd draped a black sheet behind her so there was no visual indication of where they were. David and Matt had also draped heavy blankets over the windows and door to help muffle any additional sounds.

David turned on a white-noise machine. Laney raised her eyebrows. He winked at her. "A little extra protection never hurts. We're good, Danny."

Danny met her gaze, and she nodded. The screen in front of her, which had been emitting a soft blue light, now showed a desk with the seal of the United States behind it and a man sitting there that Laney recognized.

"Stan," Laney said.

Stanton Calloway smiled, which somehow just made him creepier, as if his lips were not used to moving in an upward direction. "Dr. McPhearson. It is good to see you. I hope you are well."

Laney crossed her arms over her chest. "No thanks to the U.S. government, yes, I am."

"I'm glad to hear it," Stan said, completely ignoring the dig. "I'm not sure if you are aware, there was an auction for the Omni."

"You don't say." They had discussed beforehand that they would give nothing away, not even that they knew of the auction. If they did, the government would know exactly how much monitoring they were able to do. And Laney did not want to give them any help in tracking them down. "What does that have to do with me?"

"The United States did not win the auction."

"Who did?"

Stan hesitated, glancing at whoever was coaching him offscreen before he answered. "China. But we believe that more individuals may have since been given access to the Omni, through additional auctions that we were not aware of."

"You mean invited to."

Stan inclined his head. "That is accurate."

"All right, so what do you want?"

"The President has authorized me to extend a full pardon to you and all the people currently residing with you—"

"A pardon? For what? Preventing the U.S. government from torturing people, one of whom was a child?"

Stan's lips thinned. "It was still a violation of U.S. law. And there is *still* a warrant out for you and your co-conspirators."

"So you create a horrific situation, we protect people from it, you call us criminals, and now you are offering to *stop* calling us criminals?"

"While I cannot agree with your characterization, I believe the sense is accurate, yes. The President is also willing to extend an offer of citizenship to any foreign nationals that you have, um, *acquired* in the last few months."

Laney frowned. "Why is the President doing this? I somehow doubt that she is all of sudden feeling beneficent."

Stan plowed on as if she hadn't spoken. "There would, of course, be some stipulations."

"Such as?"

"You would have to agree to protect the United States against an incursion of Fallen soldiers of any foreign country."

Laney narrowed her eyes. "*Who* exactly would be responsible for that?"

Stan hesitated for the barest of seconds, but Laney felt it like it was an hour. *God damn it.* She knew what Stan was going to say even before the words left his mouth. "All individuals with enhanced abilities would be required to defend the United States. Any enhanced who fails to do their civic duty would be incarcerated for a minimum of twenty years. It would be a military service requirement, like in Israel."

"Except in Israel all able-bodied individuals are required to partake in military service for only two years. You are only requiring it of a fraction of the U.S. population." She frowned. "Wait. You haven't stipulated how long they would be required to defend the U.S. So how long?"

Stanton hesitated. "For life."

"Are you insane?" She paused, narrowing her eyes. "What *age* are you suggesting this military service begins?"

"Fourteen."

Laney blanched. "You are out of your mind. You want to send kids into battle? What the hell is wrong with you people?"

"I assure you, there *is* precedent. In the Civil War, over one thousand Union soldiers were under the age of fifteen."

Laney knew that ugly history. When the war was going badly for each side, recruiters would look the other way when obviously underage boys lied about their age to enlist. One of the youngest on record was Johnny Clem, who'd joined the Union army as a drummer boy at the age of eleven. He saw combat and was still actively serving until 1915, when he retired as a brigadier general.

As difficult as it was to wrap her mind around children volunteering to fight, that was not the plan that the government was offering. "I think we've evolved a little beyond that now. And you're *not* talking about volunteers."

Danny waved his hands at her and then pointed at the clock. One minute left.

Stan's voice was stiff. "Be that as it may, this is the offer the government is placing in front of you. If you accept, you will all be allowed to return to the United States—"

"To be used as a shield. We'd be second-class citizens at best."

"That is not accurate. Now, I realize you may need time to think this over. I have been instructed to give you—"

"Oh, I don't need any time. I can give you my answer right now."

Stanton leaned forward. "And what is it?"

"No." Laney disconnected the feed.

Chapter Forty-Five

THE ROOM WAS quiet as Laney blew out a breath. They wanted the Fallen to fight for them, defend them, without giving them a choice. And hang prison time over their heads if they didn't fulfill their requirements.

David shoved his hands in his pockets, rocking back and forth. "So that went . . . horribly."

Laney pushed away from the table. "Can you believe them?"

"Well, we have been on call to defend against the Fallen for years," Matt said.

"By *choice*. Not because we were forced. I mean, what am I supposed to tell the Oteros? They can come to America, lay their lives on the line, maybe orphan their kids, but hey, at least they'll be able to check their Facebook status regularly? Not everyone with these abilities is a fighter. And going up against trained fighters? They won't last a minute, never mind years."

"That was sloppy," Henry said.

Laney frowned. "What do you mean?"

Henry gestured to the computer screen. "Anyone with a lick of sense would know you would never agree to that. That we would never agree to that. It was a sloppy approach to make."

"I agree," David said. "There have to be some hardliners pushing the President behind the scenes."

"Then she damn well needs to push back. She placed the country in this position, not me. We were working with her. She's the one who put the targets on our backs, not the other way around."

David put up his hands. "Hey, preaching to the choir here."

Laney slumped onto the couch. "I know. I just . . ." She shrugged.

Henry sat down next to her. "You just hoped you'd be able to give everybody some good news."

She nodded. "Yeah."

"Well, you still might," Matt said.

"How?" Laney asked.

"This was the first salvo in the negotiation. They came with what they wanted. Now they'll go back to the drawing board, try to figure out a way to get what they want while giving you what you want, or at least as much as they can stomach us having."

Laney slumped lower into her chair. "Great. A long, drawn-out negotiation. Fun."

"No, not fun. Working through the personalities and demands of all the interested parties is not going to be easy."

Yeah, it would make getting through the tunnels in the Great Pyramid look like child's play.

Her breath caught at the thought, something clicking into place. The Great Pyramid. Laney pictured that winding path, each inch, each foot highlighting a different point in human history. And the concourses fifty feet high that were larger than the ones below, as if it needed the extra support. And beyond that all that space, an idea began to form in her mind. She crossed the room to Danny. "Can you do some sort of scan of the Great Pyramid with this gear?"

He frowned. "Depends. What are you looking for?"

"Something inside the Great Pyramid."

He shook his head. "Inside? I don't have access to anything like that."

"You might not need to," David said slowly as he joined them. "If you can gain access to the Egyptian government records on the Pyramid, that is."

Danny grinned. "Oh. That I can do."

"What are you thinking?" Henry asked David.

"The Egyptian government has held access to the Great Pyramid very close to the chest. They allow very little investigation into it, even though it's safe to say curiosity about the Pyramid brings in the majority of the visitors to their country. More information would only increase that and increase the amount of money flowing into the country."

"You mean how they discovered a cavern underneath the Sphinx yet refuse to allow further investigation," Danny said.

"Not cavern, caverns," Laney said. In 1987, a Japanese team had conducted an electromagnetic sounding survey. They found evidence of at least two cavities in the body of the Sphinx, and an additional two were located underneath the Sphinx. Their research was confirmed by a second research team in 1991. The second team also found evidence of tunnels underneath the Sphinx. For Laney, the findings had taken on greater meaning once she learned that Edgar Cayce said that the Hall of Records of Atlantis was underneath the left paw of the Sphinx.

Laney shook her head. "I never could understand why the Egyptian government wouldn't allow further research."

"Or so we've been led to believe," David said. "I had a . . . let's call her a friend, who was stationed in Egypt. She told me there was a lot more research being conducted on the Pyramid than the public was aware of. The Egyptian government wanted to know everything they could about the Pyramid. They were just very selective about who they let know about that information."

"I'm in the Ministry of State Antiquities," Danny said. "What am I looking for?"

"I thought it was the Supreme Council of Antiquities?" Laney asked.

"It used to be, when it fell under the Egyptian Ministry of Culture," Mustafa said. "It became an independent ministry in 2011. The MSA is responsible for the conservation, protection, and regulation of all antiquities and archaeological excavations in Egypt."

Laney peered at the screen Danny had brought up, scanning the names of files, her heart sinking. There were so many. "Can you limit that to only projects related to the Great Pyramid?"

"Yup." Danny hit a dozen or so keys, and the list shortened, but it was still lengthy. "It has to be related to the capstone. Can you check any tests or anything else that was done around the turn of the century?"

"What are you thinking?"

"I don't know. It's probably crazy, but I just have this feeling—"

Danny peered at the screen. "There were a bunch of scans done of the Plateau."

"That seems normal, given the plan to add the capstone at that time," Mustafa said.

Everyone turned to him. "What?"

Mustafa blinked, apparently surprised by their surprise. "It was the plan for the turn of the century. They were going to create a capstone and place it on the Great Pyramid to complete it. They were all ready to go, but then a few weeks before December 31st, they called it off."

"Why?" Matt asked.

"They claimed terroristic threats."

Or maybe they worried that putting it in place would set off a chain reaction they were not prepared for.

"Anyway, it would make sense if there were lots of scans from that time period. They would need to make sure the Pyramid could support the weight of the capstone," Mustafa said.

Danny frowned. "This is weird."

Laney leaned forward. "What?"

"They did a lot of high-resolution scans as well."

"Of the Plateau?"

"No, of the Pyramid. But they seemed to run dozens of them of this one area."

"Above the fiftieth level?"

Danny looked up at her. "How'd you know that?"

Laney leaned forward, anticipation tingling through her. "Can you bring those up?"

"Hold on a sec." Danny hunched over the keyboard, and then half a dozen scans filled the screen. Laney scanned all of them, pointing to one that seemed to be an image of the top of the Pyramid, right under the plateau. "Can you enlarge this one?"

"Yup." The scan filled up the screen. Her mouth fell open, her brain trying to register what she was seeing.

Henry leaned forward. "Is that what I think it is?"

Laney nodded slowly. "It's the capstone. It's been hidden inside the Pyramid this whole time."

Chapter Forty-Six

WASHINGTON, D.C.

NANCY HARRIGAN SAT in the Oval Office, listening to the replay of the conversation between Stanton Calloway and Delaney McPhearson. She had warned the President that the approach would not work. Choosing Stanton had been the first mistake. He had the personality of a wet sock. But offering Delaney McPhearson an out that required innocents being put in the line of fire? It was a non-starter.

But Nancy had been outvoted. The national security advisor, head of the FBI, and Homeland Security director all pushed for the hardline approach. They balked at the idea of handing Delaney a pardon without requiring something stringent from her in return. Had they made the deal for only Delaney, demanding *she* defend the country while being given pardons for the rest, Nancy was pretty sure she would have taken *that* deal. But requiring that a bunch of innocents be slaughtered? There was no chance Delaney was ever going to agree to that.

While Stanton had been offering the doomed proposal, the President had had people trying to track Delaney down.

The signal had bounced all around the globe. When Delaney cut the feed, it had been in Tokyo. Some in the Cabinet insisted that they immediately sent a contingent to scour the city for any sign of her or her people. Nancy had struggled not to roll her eyes. Tokyo was one of the most populated cities on a planet. And while there were about half a million foreigners staying in Tokyo, 97% of them were from other Asian countries. A large group of non-Asian individuals, some of whom were incredibly tall, slipping in and out of a bustling metropolis, along with two dozen genetically enhanced cats, would stand out a little bit. So Nancy knew there was zero chance they were in Tokyo.

"I still think we should send a team. Make sure they're not hiding out there," the FBI director said.

Nancy ran a hand over her face. God, politicians could be such idiots at times.

"I will take it under advisement," the President said. "Now, I'd like to speak with Nancy alone. We'll reconvene in the dining room in an hour."

Nancy looked up in surprise but said nothing as everyone else filed out. The President waited until the door closed before turning to Nancy. "We botched that, didn't we?"

"Yes."

The President sighed as she stood up and strode over to the fireplace. "Why? It was a reasonable offer."

"Not to her."

"But it's not just her. She might be in charge of that ragtag group, but they all have a say."

"That is correct. But you are missing the bigger point: Delaney McPhearson will never offer someone up as cannon fodder, except maybe herself, if it will spare others. When you mentioned the age limit, I have no doubt she flashed on Molly McAdams, who is only a few months away from the age of fourteen."

The President winced. "That was a horrible situation. But this isn't that."

"Isn't it, though? Aren't you telling the Fallen they have no choice? That if they want to come back, they must offer themselves up on the altar of public service? For *life*?"

The President narrowed her eyes. "Whose side are you on, Nancy?"

Nancy put up her hands. "I am on the side of getting this situation resolved. I am on the side of securing the future of all Americans, enhanced or otherwise. Requiring military service from a group who this country has targeted is a non-starter for McPhearson. She was never going to go for that."

"So what *will* she go for?"

Nancy studied the President. "What do you *actually* want her to do?"

"I want her to make this whole damn thing go away."

"Then offer her that."

The President frowned. "I'm not following."

"You tried to get McPhearson to follow the government's playbook on Samyaza, and let's be honest, it wouldn't have worked. Pushing her to the side, letting the traditional forces take over, would have been a bloodbath. But McPhearson, she ignored the conventional approach. She came up with her own. And she did what we needed her to do: She removed the threat of Samyaza."

"Unleashing this new threat."

"Which would have been unleashed no matter who killed her. But the truth is, as bad a shape as we are in now, it is better than the shape we would have been in if Samyaza had survived."

"So what are you suggesting?"

Nancy paused for a moment. "Delaney McPhearson wants her people safe, but she is not someone who sticks her head in the sand and doesn't see the other problems swirling around her. She no doubt also wants the problem of the manufactured Fallen contained. After all, she did not reveal the contents of the Omni for just that reason. She will want to help."

"But how? If you don't think she'll defend our country, what makes you think she'll tackle the larger problem? And how would she even start? We have the best minds in the country working on it, and we still don't have any good ideas."

Nancy smiled. *No, we have the best minds in the government working on it.* Wisely, she did not share that thought out loud. "Well, that's the thing. She doesn't look at problems the way we do. Instead of telling her what we want her to do for us, why don't we ask her how we can help *her* defeat this problem?"

The President stared at Nancy, slowly nodding her head. Nancy knew the President was thinking of how to spin this. And she would see the upside. Yes, they would be helping McPhearson, but it would be McPhearson's show, which meant if everything went sideways, the U.S. could lay the blame there.

"Do you think she would be receptive to that?" the President asked.

"I'm pretty sure Delaney McPhearson is already trying to figure out a way to stop the spread of the Omni. So I think we have two choices: get out of her way or help her. And this time, I think she could actually use our help."

Chapter Forty-Seven

TIWANAKU, BOLIVIA

THAT NIGHT, Laney was back at the farmhouse. She'd explained what they had found to her main group back at Havenville. Everyone had been shocked. Laney couldn't blame them, although she knew the Great Pyramid often offered amazing little finds long after people thought they knew everything about the ancient monument. In fact, it was one of those discoveries that got her thinking. In 2017, a giant cavern, large enough to hide the entire Statue of Liberty had been discovered inside the Great Pyramid. No one knows its purpose. It seemed to be empty. But yet again, the Great Pyramid was confounding the experts.

The fact that they now knew where the capstone was, though, offered a glimmer of hope that they might have a chance of ending all of this. Of course, getting to the capstone was going to be the issue. Laney had spent hours brainstorming idea after idea with the group. But after hours of getting nowhere, they had come to one glaring conclusion: they were going to need help preferably from the Egyptian government. But being a military coup had occurred weeks ago throwing the whole country into turmoil that seemed increasingly unlikely.

With that dour realization in the front of their minds, news reached them that the government was once again looking to speak. Laney was tempted to ignore the call. But she knew she couldn't overlook a chance to help the people in her care. So now, Laney sat at the same table she'd sat at earlier. She glanced at David, who was out of camera range. "Any chance they're tracking us somehow?"

David shook his head. "Not according to Danny, but they might have figured out that we can only use electronics for a few hours a day."

"Will that tell them anything?"

David shrugged. "In and of itself, no. But if they start drawing up a list of locations, it may help them pin down where we are. Of course, the government is notoriously unimaginative. I don't think hidden in a secondary dimension through an ancient star gate will ever make their list."

Laney smiled. "Probably not."

"I'm ready to go when you are, Laney," Danny said.

Drake stepped into the house then and nodded at her. He'd refused to be left back in the cave to "babysit" again as he put it. Laney had conceded when Danny assured her that while the government had tried to track the signal, they had gotten nowhere close.

When they'd arrived at the farmhouse, Drake had immediately taken off to do a security sweep, extending out farther and farther to make sure no one was encroaching on them. It looked like their little farmhouse was still secure. Matt had done one as well. And Danny had spent the last few hours checking to see if any satellites had been redirected near their location. They hadn't. According to the communications he'd intercepted, the government seemed to believe they were somewhere in Japan.

Cleo was the last member of their little group. It wasn't much of a break in the routine from Havenville, but it was something. She had wandered off while Drake and Matt were running their patrols before returning to curl up contentedly on the couch.

Laney glanced back at Danny's setup, spying the clock that he'd run the last time they'd spoken with the government. It was blank. "Five minutes?"

Danny nodded as the numbers 5:00 appeared on the screen. "Yup. Clock starts as soon as we make the connection. You ready?"

"I'm ready."

Danny hit a few keys, and the clock next him sprung to life. Laney focused on the screen in front of her. This time someone else was waiting.

"Madame Secretary."

Nancy Harrigan nodded. "Hello, Dr. McPhearson. I hope you are well."

"As well as someone who is being hunted by every government on the planet can be, yes."

Nancy raised an eyebrow. "Most people would crumble under that kind of pressure. You don't seem to have faltered. In fact, you seem to be traveling through all different parts of the globe according to our reports."

Laney shrugged. "Well, you know what they say, when you have the chance to travel, you really need to take it."

A small smile appeared on Nancy's lips. "Indeed. It's nice that you've had that chance."

"All right, enough chitchat. What do you want, Nancy?"

"The U.S. would like to extend an offer."

Laney held up her hand. "If this is anything like the last

offer, then let's just save us both some time, and I'll say no now."

"It's not like the last one. I think you might like this one."

Somehow I doubt that, she thought, but she waited for Nancy to continue without speaking.

"The U.S. government is prepared to offer complete immunity to you and all the individuals who are in hiding with you."

"*Complete* immunity?"

"Yes. The incidents in D.C. and West Virginia will be expunged from your records. You will be free citizens."

Laney frowned. "In exchange for what?"

"As you know, China has gotten access to the Omni. We have it from reliable sources that at least six other interested parties have also gotten ahold of the formula."

Laney sucked in a breath. Damn it. It had been bad enough when China had the formula. Stanton had mentioned that others might have access, but Laney was hoping he'd been wrong. This was what she feared: that once one person got it, it would only be a matter of time before everyone had it.

Nancy noted the reaction. "Yes. The United States does not think it is in anyone's interest that the Omni continues its spread. We already have word of troop movements across the globe. The United States itself has moved to Defcon 2."

Defcon 2: all armed forces ready to engage in warfare in less than six hours. The last stage was Defcon 1, which would happen when nuclear war was imminent.

"The world is on the brink of war, Laney. It will touch every facet of this planet."

"What does that have to do with us?"

Nancy settled back in her chair. "I've been reading up on you. Long odds against you never seem to pay off. For all intents and purposes, Samyaza should have succeeded on coronation day. Yet she didn't. And that's because you outplayed her."

Laney shrugged. "Perhaps."

"Not perhaps. You did that. Own it. The world would be in much more dire straits if you had not succeeded."

"More dire than on the edge of nuclear war?"

"If Samyaza had succeeded, I think we would *already* be embroiled in nuclear war. So yes. But the danger now is stark."

"And you want me to advise some committee? Because I have to tell you, that didn't really work well last time."

Nancy smiled for a just a moment. "No, it didn't. Which is why the United States is prepared to offer you and a list of people of your choosing complete immunity in exchange for nullifying the threat of the Fallen."

Laney paused, not sure she had heard the secretary correctly. "Immunity *after* the threat is nullified? Because that *will* make it a little difficult to do anything."

"You will be given temporary immunity until the threat is nullified. And you will have the resources of the entire United States government at your disposal."

Laney's jaw dropped. "What?"

"We believe it is in the United States' best interest to follow your lead. So whatever you need, you will have."

Laney stared at the monitor, her mind whirling. Something was off. "Who exactly will be required to aid me in removing the Fallen threat?"

"Only those you choose."

"So no draft."

"No."

The Belial Sacrifice

Laney drummed her hands on the table, her gaze flicking to Cleo in the corner, who stretched and wandered over to Laney, leaning against her leg. "What about the cats?"

Nancy sighed. "We cannot allow them to exist. Within just a few generations, they could number in the thousands."

"I will not allow them to be killed."

"A compromise, then," Nancy said without pause, letting Laney know she'd anticipated her response. "All cats will be sterilized so they cannot reproduce. When they die, of *natural* causes, that will be the end of their line."

Laney looked into Cleo's eyes, her heart clenching. Thinking of Cleo dying was not something she ever wanted to do. Thinking of this world without them was also not something she wanted to do.

"Laney, they were not supposed to be here. They were created in a lab. They were never supposed to exist."

It is all right, Laney. She is right. We are not supposed to be here.
I can't just let you go.
You don't have to. Not yet. Not for a long time. Make the deal.

Laney recoiled at the idea. But Nancy was right. The cats, like the Fallen, were never meant to be part of this world. The cats had an intelligence on par with humans. But that also meant they had human weaknesses: arrogance, pride, envy. In a few generations, they *could* number in the thousands.

Laney kept her gaze on Cleo before turning back to Nancy. "I will agree to that for the moment. But that is an issue we will be discussing in greater detail in the future."

"Good, good. Now, I'm hoping you have a plan."

"I have a rough idea of what needs to be done. With your intelligence, I should be able to see a way forward."

Nancy let out a breath. "Good. That's good. I think it would be best if we met in person to iron out plans—"

"*After* you've sent the immunity agreement and our lawyers sign off on it."

"I'll need a list of individuals."

"You'll have it within the hour."

She nodded. "Then I'll have the immunity agreement to you within two. Now, we can arrange transport for you to—"

Laney laughed. "Nice try. We'll get to the States on our own, and once we're inside, we'll tell you where to send a plane."

Nancy hesitated. "All right. When?"

"Give us twenty-four hours."

"Very well. We'll await your call." The screen went blank.

Laney sat back and looked at David, Drake, and Matt. "So who's up for sneaking back into the United States?"

Chapter Forty-Eight

IN HAVENVILLE, the discussion of who would be heading back to the United States was heated. Everyone wanted to go. Not because they believed the government but because they didn't. But finally, it was decided that Laney, Matt, David, and Drake would go. Drake because he refused to stay behind. Matt and David, who still had friends in government, would also be useful if things went badly. Everyone else would be preparing for leaving Havenville or preparing to defend it if somehow it was uncovered. Laney and her group left Havenville an hour after they returned from the farmhouse. It was going to be a long trip back to the U.S.

They flew first to Colombia, stopping at Luiz's ranch, and then they headed north, staying in international waters before landing in the northern Canadian province of Nunavut. It might be overkill, but Laney wanted to reduce any chance of them figuring out where everyone else was, including hemispheres.

Getting over the border was a little trickier, due to the

increased border surveillance. But David knew a guy who had a tunnel that went under the border, landing them in North Dakota. Apparently, tunnels under borders weren't just for Mexican cartels.

In North Dakota, David arranged for a car. Once they were in Iowa, they called the number Nancy had given them. If the person on the other end of the line had been surprised they were in the United States, they didn't show it. They promised an escort would meet them within the hour.

The trip had been grueling, and Laney wanted nothing more than to curl up in the back of the plane and nap. But as Laney stood at the airfield waiting for the government transport, she knew she needed to ignore the fatigue trying to weigh her down. The next couple of hours were going to determine not only the lives of the people in Havenville, but the world.

David, who'd been sitting in the car with the door open, stepped out with a police radio in his hand. "Looks like we have company." He nodded to the east, where cop-car lights appeared in the distance. If she strained, she could just make out their sirens.

"Over there." Matt nudged his head toward the sky in the opposite direction.

Laney squinted. "Is that . . ."

"A Blackhawk," said David. "Fully loaded, capable of carrying up to thirty-two Hellfire missiles. Sixteen ready to go and another sixteen inside that can be reloaded in the air."

Drake flexed his fingers. "So, trap?"

"Not necessarily," Matt said. "Could just be precautions."

Laney sighed, raising her hands. "If they go back on

their word, I am leveling whatever place they try to hold us in."

David nudged her shoulder. "But you'll protect those of us without special abilities that may be hiding there with you, right?"

Laney kept her eyes on the chopper. "Sure."

David grunted, raising his hands slowly in the air. "Oh, good. I feel so comforted."

Chapter Forty-Nine

NEWTON, IOWA

NERVOUS. That would be how Laney described the military police who met them at the Newtown Municipal Airport. After a few tense minutes, Laney and the guys agreed to travel in the back of one of the military trucks to Camp Dodge in Johnston, Iowa.

Laney looked at the fence perimeter as they rolled through the camp's gates. "I wonder why they didn't take us to Des Moines."

David grinned. "There's an ammunition plant there. I'm guessing they want to keep you away from that."

Drake scoffed. "We don't need ammunition."

Matt shrugged. "Still a wise precaution."

"I suppose." She looked at the two soldiers who sat with them; both looked too young and too nervous for this detail. "So any idea where we're headed or who's meeting with us?"

One just stared at her, his eyes wide. The other shook his head, a bead of sweat rolling down the side of his face.

Drake puffed out his chest, deepening his voice. "You

should strike them dead with a lightning bolt for failing to answer your questions, Ring Bearer."

Both men blanched.

Laney rolled her eyes, hitting Drake's chest with the back of her hand. "Cut it out." She glared at David, who was trying to hide his smile behind a cough. "You too."

The truck stopped in front of a brick building, which to Laney's eyes looked like a dozen other buildings they'd seen on the base.

"Um, you guys need to get out," one of the soldiers said as the other opened the back door.

"No problem." Laney climbed down from the truck, pretending not to notice the nervous tremor that ran through the dozen soldiers who were lined up, six on either side of the truck. Their nervousness was making her nervous. Not because she was worried about being harmed, but if one of them had a nervous trigger finger, their attempts at working with the government were going to go sideways real quick.

Luckily, a female officer stepped out from the building and walked briskly up to them without a trace of fear. Her eyes scanned Laney's group before meeting Laney's gaze. "Dr. McPhearson, I am Major Candace Park." She extended her hand.

Laney shook it. "Major."

"Your transport will be here shortly. If you would follow me." The major gestured toward the building she'd appeared from. Laney fell in step with her while Drake, David, and Matt followed. Six soldiers peeled off and kept them all company, three on either side.

Laney said nothing about the armed escort. If it made them feel better, that was fine with her.

The major led them through the foyer and to a room at

the end of the hall. There was a door at the back of the room that led directly out to the airfield. A small breakfast buffet had been set up along the wall to the left, and wooden tables with barrel chairs were to the right.

The major gestured to the buffet. "I thought you might be hungry. I'm assuming it was a long trip."

Matt shrugged. "Not too long."

"Thank you," Laney said.

The soldiers lined up along the wall by the door they entered. A quick glance out the back window showed more soldiers, about eight that she could see lined up along the back of the building.

Drake grabbed a pastry. "Whom exactly are we waiting for?"

"Captain Jerome Fielding, United States Marine Corps."

Drake's eyebrows rose. "Why do I know that name?"

"He's the Marine who escorted us to the task force meeting."

Drake gave Laney a sardonic grin. "Oh, well, what a good omen for the outcome of this meeting."

FIELDING SHOWED up forty-five minutes later with his own set of soldiers. From Laney's count, there were two dozen.

Drake stared out the window as the plane's door opened, and soldiers began to pour out. "It's like a clown car."

"Where's the trust?" Laney grouched, spying Captain Fielding as he stepped from the plane and strode toward the building.

He didn't hesitate as two soldiers held open the door that led to the room Laney and her friends were waiting in. Fielding scanned the room, jolting at the sight of Drake, who blew him a kiss before he nodded at Laney. "Dr. McPhearson."

"Captain."

"We will be taking a short flight over to Norfolk. Time is of the essence, so if it's all right, I'd like to answer any questions you may have in flight."

Laney looked at David and Matt, who nodded back at her. Drake grinned. "This is your show. You're the headliner. We'll follow your cues."

"All right, then. Let's go, Captain."

THEY WERE TAXIING DOWN the runway less than five minutes later. David and Matt sat in the row behind Laney and Drake. After they reached their cruising altitude, Captain Fielding appeared from the cockpit. He gestured to the seat on Laney's other side. "May I?"

"By all means."

Fielding sat down, glancing over at Drake, whose eyes were closed.

"He's out," Laney said.

"Not yet," Drake murmured. "But close."

"Well, I think the captain here needs to chat," Laney said.

Drake cracked open one eyelid. "Seriously?"

"Well, you know, trying to avoid World War III here."

Drake gave a highly exaggerated sigh. "Fine." He stood up, smiling at the captain. "Same rules apply as last time. A single hair on her head is disturbed, and you feel my wrath." He kissed Laney on the cheek.

She rolled her eyes in response before swatting him away. "Go to sleep."

"Yes, ma'am." Drake gave her a lazy salute before heading down the aisle and collapsing in a seat.

Fielding glanced back at Drake. "He's . . . unusual."

"You have no idea," Laney muttered.

"I've been told to brief you on the state of the world. I'm not sure how much you are aware of."

Laney wasn't sure if he was fishing to see where she might have been hiding or if this was just his idea of an intro. She shrugged. "Let's assume I've been living under a rock."

Drake snorted from down the aisle.

Fielding either didn't hear it or chose to ignore it. "The borders of every country have been closed. Trade has come to a complete stop. There are reports of food shortages, oil shortages, blackouts, and internal unrest in practically every country across the globe to varying degrees."

"Including the U.S.?"

Fielding nodded. "We import twenty percent of our food supply. Thirty-five percent of our fruit. It's beginning to be a problem." Fielding cleared his throat. "Gang violence has become an issue as well. In various locations, individuals are targeting food warehouses. The National Guard has been called out to protect them. For the first time, the U.S. military has been given permission to actually fight on U.S. soil. Homicide rates have spiked."

"What about the Fallen?"

Fielding let out a breath. "Mixed bag. Some have exploited the situation on the ground to enrich themselves.

The Belial Sacrifice

But some have actually been reported to be defending cities, warehouses, people."

Laney wasn't surprised. She just wished the government was *less* surprised. "What about the Omni? How many countries have soldiers with Fallen abilities?"

"China is the only one confirmed. We do know the Omni was sold to individuals after the government auction. As a result, it is suspected that Russia, Great Britain, Japan, Saudi Arabia, and Iran all have access to the Omni."

"My god." Laney shook her head, trying to imagine that many countries with forces that had enhanced abilities.

"It gets worse. We believe those countries, with the exception of Great Britain, may be working together."

"Well, that's just horrible. What's their goal?"

"So far they have not declared one. But China has moved a number of its forces to the islands it has created in the South China Sea. Russia has moved its warships closer to the U.S., right on the border of the international boundaries, and they have essentially parked there. As for Iran, we have received chatter that they have forces moving on Israel and into Europe."

"And the British?"

"They are playing everything close to the vest. They have troops stationed around the globe. We don't know what their response will be."

"Any *good* news?"

"Sergei Yanovich was killed in Macau, so at least he won't be selling any more Omni."

"True, but being all the animals have already escaped, I'm not sure how closing the barn door at this point helps."

"It doesn't. But it's one player off the board."

Laney sat back, letting the awfulness wash over her. This was why she had never trusted anyone with the formula.

She knew if one person, one country got it, it would easily make its way into other hands. And that's exactly what had happened. Now the world map was going to radically change because the power was concentrated in the hands of a few countries.

And the only way out is to either give it to everybody or take it from everybody.

Fielding glanced at her from the side of his eyes. "I don't know what you've been up to these past few months. I've heard some reports about you protecting Fallen."

"Not just Fallen," Laney said quietly. "Anyone who's been targeted because of their connection to the Fallen."

"When I first learned you had a way to make enhanced soldiers and you were refusing to divulge it to the U.S. government, I was angry. I thought you were unpatriotic at best." He gave her a tight smile. "But you were trying to avoid this, weren't you?"

Laney nodded. "No one should have these powers, not even me."

"The higher-ups, they won't admit it, but they're scared. And they are all hoping you have a plan." He paused. "Do you?"

She nodded. "I do. But I'm going to need a lot of help, especially once the other countries who have the Fallen realize what we're up to."

"Will your plan stop this?"

"Yes."

"Then I can guarantee you will have whatever you need."

Chapter Fifty

WASHINGTON, D.C.

THE GENERAL SLAMMED his fist onto the table. "Absolutely not."

So much for having whatever help I need. General Sam Rockefeller glared at her from across the table. He was a relatively short man but stocky. She could picture him as a younger man, built like Yoni. His pale skin was now blotchy as he stared daggers into Laney. "I am not committing my forces to a battle when I do not know what the end goal is."

After landing at Norfolk, they had been flown to Fort Lesley J. McNair and then been driven directly to the Pentagon. Waiting for them had been the chairman of the Joint Chiefs and the secretaries of the Navy, Marine Corps and Army. General Rockefeller was Army.

Matt crossed his arms over his chest. "You know what the end goal is. We need to allow Laney to get to the Giza Plateau."

Rockefeller didn't look away from Laney as he spoke. "But why? You haven't explained that part."

Laney crossed her arms over her chest. "And I don't plan to. You are just going to have to take my word for it."

They had decided not to let anyone from the government in on the full details of the plan. It increased the risk of what they needed to do leaking out. The last thing they needed was more obstacles to getting the capstone in place. If there was a way to avoid telling them about Giza, Laney would have done it. As soon as she said the location, she knew there was a ticking clock on that information being leaked to the other side. The general was not handling her secrecy so well.

"Your word," the general sneered. "I've been in the service since before you were born. If you think you're going to saunter in here and start giving orders, then you are—"

"Attention!"

All the military brass got to their feet as the soldier by the door's voice rang out. Laney looked over her shoulder tiredly. God, she needed a nap. And a handful of ibuprofen for the headache that was starting to build behind her eyes and maybe some earplugs to drown out the general. She didn't know why she'd thought this meeting would go better than the External Threats Task Force meeting, but she really had. Ah, stupid, stupid optimism.

President Rigley stepped into the room, followed by Nancy. Laney got to her feet grudgingly.

Nancy gave Laney a quick smile. Rigley did not smile. She glanced around the room. "I'm going to need the room for a moment. I'd like to speak with Dr. McPhearson alone."

The general balked. "You cannot stay in here with her. She cannot be—"

"*Now*, General."

The general's lips tightened, and he nodded. The President inclined her head toward her Secret Service agents. "Stay right outside the door, please."

The agent hesitated before nodding. "As you wish, Madame President." The agent waited until everyone left in front of him, the general taking his time, before he closed the door.

Silence descended on the room. The President nodded at the chair Laney had been using. "Please sit."

Laney resumed her seat and waited. The President didn't speak for a full minute. She just studied the screen where foreign troop movements were indicated. It seemed as if every country had troops on the move.

Finally the President turned to Laney. "Quite a dilemma we find ourselves in."

Laney gestured at the empty chairs. "I take it this little show of trust was meant to put me at ease."

"Something like that. I don't believe I have anything to worry about from you."

"You never did."

"I'm beginning to realize you are not quite like other people, even without your powers. Could you imagine if Senator Shremp had been the one chosen to be the ring bearer? He would have crowned himself emperor."

"Like Samyaza tried to do before I stopped her."

"True. Captain Fielding tells me you still refuse to hand over the formula."

Laney crossed her arms over her chest. "I do."

"Even though you know our troops could use those abilities to counter enhanced fighters from other countries?"

Laney shook her head. "You still don't get it. They are not a gift. They are an accelerant. Adding more enhanced is only going to make this fire burn hotter." Laney gestured to the screen filled with colors. "This fire needs to be smothered, not fanned."

"And you have a way to do that?"

"I do."

"But you won't tell us what it is."

"No. All you need to know is that I need to get to the Giza Plateau."

The President studied her for a long moment. "So we're just supposed to take you at your word?"

"No. You're supposed to view my actions and then ask yourself whether I am someone who would try to end this war or keep it going."

"And if I choose not to help you?"

Laney gestured at the screen again. "Then this all gets worse."

"It's going to take years to get the world back to normal, if we ever can."

"All the more reason to end this as quickly as possible. Too many people are dying. Too many people are being displaced. Too many people are hungry. This needs to end."

"And what about you? When all of this is done, what do you want?"

Laney didn't hesitate. "A normal life. For people to forget about me."

"I'm not sure that's possible."

"You can help make it possible by keeping up your side of our bargain."

"You doubt my word?"

"Yes. You authorized the torture of a child. You authorized the abduction of a psychologically fragile intellectual. So yes, I doubt your word."

"That wasn't me. That was Shremp."

Laney met the President's gaze and did not let her look

away. "He was a tool, *your* tool. You wielded him to keep your own hands clean. To have plausible deniability. You could have put anyone in charge of the CEI, but you chose someone with unchecked ambition and loose moral restraints. So I'm sorry, Madame President, but you are responsible, more so than Shremp."

The President studied Laney. "I see you like to shoot straight."

"Shooting crooked is a waste of ammo."

"All right, then. I don't trust you enhanced people. I don't trust your ambitions. So yes, I looked for weaknesses with the tools at my disposal. I don't apologize for protecting my citizens."

"The people you hurt were your citizens, too." Laney took a breath, trying to rein in her temper. While she wanted to take the President to task for all she had done, now wasn't the time. As much as she hated to admit, there were larger concerns. "Will you honor the deal you made?"

"I will. If you succeed in your mission."

"I will. As long as you get your people to fall in line."

"General Rockefeller is at times difficult. But there is no one better. He'll follow your lead."

Laney studied her. "You had him push me to see what I would do."

The President stood. "I needed to make sure you wouldn't lash out when things got difficult."

Laney swallowed down her anger. "You're playing games when lives are at stake."

"No, I am making sure the person I put in charge of saving those lives is up to the task. You will have everything you need. Forty-eight hours, and we will be ready to go."

"All right. I'll need to arrange for my team to join us."

"Give me names, and I'll make sure they are cleared.

Let Nancy know if there is anything else you need." The President moved to the door. Her hand on the doorknob, she stopped and looked back at Laney. "I'd wish you luck, Dr. McPhearson, but I don't believe in it. I hope you succeed, because the world needs you to."

Chapter Fifty-One

ROME, ITALY

CARDINAL JOHN MORETTI disconnected the call, sitting back heavily in his chair and staring out the window. His villa offered a beautiful view of the Tiber. From here, he could even see the top of the Castel Sant'Angelo, and of course, Michael on top of his perch.

Right now, though, Moretti took in none of that as his mind raced. The Americans were backing McPhearson. His informant inside the government had just called with the information. No doubt similar calls were going out to other countries across the globe. There would be a race to stop her. In all likelihood, they would succeed.

But what if they didn't? She had proven to be amazingly resourceful. Each time she had been counted out, she had come back stronger than before.

And this time, this time she was trying to remove all the powers of the Fallen. He shook his head. Who did she think she was, trying to subvert God's plan? The time of judgment was upon them. As the Fallen gained in numbers, the devout would flock to the Church for protection. And the

Church *would* protect them. They would stand as a bastion against this blight, staying true to His words. And God would judge them accordingly.

But if Delaney McPhearson succeeded, if by some miracle she managed to remove the Fallen's powers, then none of that would happen. The glory of the Church would not be revealed. His role in protecting the Church would slip by. He knew his role in this drama. He was a herald of the end of days. He was a soldier on the front lines.

No, not a soldier. A general. And his job was to make the tough calls. To ignore base considerations for the loftier considerations of humanity's soul. Humanity needed to be judged. Humanity needed to be humbled. Humanity needed to turn back to their God. And the rise of the Fallen would usher in that era.

And it was Moretti's job to hold that door open. He turned to his computer, pulling up the file he had drafted a few weeks ago in case this day ever came. He read it over, made a few changes consistent with current events, and then sent it to the Pope. He picked up his phone and dialed the Pope's assistant.

Father Gregory answered. "Yes?"

"I have sent a press release for the Pope to read tomorrow morning."

"He has nothing scheduled."

"I am aware. But I have it on good authority that the countries of the world are mobilizing. It is important that we have his voice heard."

"I have heard nothing of it."

"You will. And when you do, the Pope will need to get in front of it."

Gregory sighed. "Very well. I will review it and have it

ready for the Pope when he awakens. Is there anything else, Your Eminence?"

"No. That is all. Have a good night, Gregory."

"You as well."

Moretti sat back again, his phone resting against his chin. Delaney would face down the countries of the world. A formidable enemy.

But he would make sure that she would face one even more formidable. He smiled.

Your time is at an end, Ms. McPhearson.

Chapter Fifty-Two

WASHINGTON, D.C.

AFTER THE PRESIDENT LEFT, the meeting went much smoother. General Rockefeller became much more agreeable. Within three hours, they had most of the details locked down. The sheer scope of the forces involved was mind-boggling. The military representatives talked about number of boots on the ground as well as air, sea, and satellite-driven drone strikes. It was terrifying. All these people and weapons were being put into play.

Laney could not get a sense of what the military leaders truly felt. They were playing those cards close to the vest, so she couldn't tell if they truly believed she would be able to undo the Omni or if they thought these preparations were for the first true battle of World War III. She'd caught more than one of them looking at her speculatively during the intense conversations.

They were to meet again in the morning to finish things up. Now Laney let out a yawn as David drove through the city toward his townhome. Laney doubted any of them would be getting a good night's sleep. Laney, Matt, and

Drake would all bunk at David's place tonight. It was the closest to the Pentagon, and there was safety in numbers. So far, the government appeared to be working with them in good faith. But Laney was well aware that could change at any moment.

David's townhome was in a quiet section of Georgetown. Trees framed the street where gray stone homes with large wooden doors stood with a stately elegance. The interior was just as impressive as the exterior with a marble entryway leading to dark wood floors throughout the rest of the home. Large doorways and tall ceilings made the space seem larger. The pale gray walls and crisp white trim were a great backdrop for the neutral furniture with blue, white, and black accents. All in all, it was stylish yet comfortable.

The guest room David showed Laney and Drake to had a large, heavy wooden-framed bed with a plush white carpet. A loveseat sat across from the bed, near the windows, imploring someone to curl up and read or nap. Laney was tempted to do just that, but David invited Laney for a run.

Laney was tired but agreed. The idea was simply too appealing to resist. While she'd been able to run in Bolivia, running in a city, around people—she'd missed that.

Matt and Drake elected to stay behind. Matt was getting the communications set up so they could contact Danny tonight and relay the plans. Drake was already taking a nap.

Laney and David had run two miles, getting their breathing under control, enjoying the rhythm of the run, when David spoke. "So, how are you feeling?"

"Glad the details are finally getting ironed out. I think we should be ready."

"That's not what I mean."

Laney flicked a gaze at him, seeing the concern on his

face. "I'm all right. I think somewhere down deep, I knew it had to come to an end. That once the world realized what was happening underneath their noses, it was only a matter of time."

"And the prophecy?"

Laney snorted. "Which one?"

David smiled. "Touché. The one from your dream. The one about the sacrifice."

"How did you know about that?"

"Spy, remember?"

She looked at him incredulously. "No, seriously, how?"

"I might have overheard you two talking."

Sarah's words ran through her mind. *Sacrifice and death will lead you, and sacrifice and death will follow. Blood will lead the way.*

"I've accepted it. It is what it is. There's no need to worry about something that is a certainty. All it does is stress you out."

"Have you figured out what the sacrifice will be?"

Laney shook her head. Like with all prophecies, there seemed so many possible interpretations. Was the writer talking about sacrifice on a global scale? Was the sacrifice the Fallen's powers? Was the sacrifice more personal? It could be anything. "No. But I know it will be painful, whatever it is."

"And if you're asked to do something painful? Will you be able to do it?"

"I've accepted I will in all likelihood not survive this, David."

"But if you do, Laney? What if you're not the sacrifice? What if you're asked to sacrifice someone else?"

"You mean Drake?"

He nodded.

"Drake's fine. He's just himself. He's not Michael."

David was quiet for a moment. "But what if you are asked to sacrifice someone *else*?"

She wanted to say she would do it. After all, the world truly hung in the balance. But she wasn't sure that was truthful. "You mean sacrifice someone I love? I don't know, David. I mean, sacrifice myself for the world? I could do that. But sacrifice someone else? I don't know if I have that in me."

"For all our sakes, we better hope you can."

Laney swallowed, lengthening her stride. *I know.*

Chapter Fifty-Three

LATER THAT NIGHT after a quiet dinner, everyone turned in early. They all needed a good night's sleep. But the images from the meeting earlier kept rolling around and around in Laney's brain. Even as she closed her eyes and tried to block them out, they refused to disappear. The militaries of all the countries of the world seemed to be on the move, some to their borders to strengthen defenses, some moving into parts of the world they would never have dreamed of treading on just a few short weeks ago.

Elisabeta's plan had been to remake the world. And now, after her death, that was exactly what was happening.

Next to Laney, Drake's breath evened out as he slipped into sleep. Laney waited a few more minutes and then silently climbed from the bed. She moved to the loveseat by the window. Turning so she faced the window, she curled up on it, tucking her legs underneath her and resting her arms and chin on the back of the loveseat. Streetlights were on, giving off a faint glow on the street below. A few cars were parked on opposite sides of the street. There was no litter, no vagrants, no foot traffic. It looked like a movie set, no movement, perfectly still, just waiting for the director to call action.

D.C. was under martial law. No one was allowed out after dark except for law enforcement. A few hours ago, the President had declared martial law in all major cities, leaving it up to smaller cities and towns to decide if they wanted to institute a curfew. About half had done so. The President worried that when word got out about the mission in Egypt, the country would react badly.

Or if things went wrong, other countries would react badly and retaliate against the United States. It was a huge gamble. But the President was putting her trust in Laney, hoping she could accomplish the impossible. That she could end this entire global nightmare.

Laney sat back, pulling her legs to her chest as she went over all that they knew. She was looking for something, anything that told her she was on the wrong path. But she didn't think she was.

The Tome spoke of a weapon that could be used against the Fallen. One that only the ring bearer could wield. She did not doubt that translation.

It was the next part she was struggling with. What if they were wrong? What if the capstone was no longer inside the Pyramid? Or what if the mechanism to bring it out no longer worked? What if she broke the Pyramid in her attempts to put the capstone in place? What if she made it impossible for the capstone to work?

The Pyramid was a marvel of engineering. Engineers across centuries had been astounded by the accuracy of the structure. But years of humans defiling it must have made some changes that made any attempts to operate it a foolish dream.

So what if I place the capstone inaccurately? What if I pull it from the Pyramid and it simply doesn't work? Or what if Cain misinterpreted the texts? It does not specifically say the capstone is in the Pyramid. It looks like the capstone is. But what if it's something else? What if I pin everyone's hopes on a plan that is doomed to fail?

"Hey."

Laney's head jerked up as Drake knelt next to her. "Oh, hey. Did I wake you?"

He stretched, showing off a very impressive set of shoulders. "Yup. The worries and doubts wafting off you shoved away the delightful dream I was having about being a sultan with a harem of one hundred women."

Laney raised an eyebrow. "A hundred women?"

"Yes. Strange, though, they all looked exactly like this red-haired, green-eyed woman I know."

"Nice save."

"I thought so . . . So, what are you thinking about?"

Laney rolled her eyes. "What do you think?"

"I think you are sitting here tying yourself in knots about our course of action."

"You would be correct."

He sighed. "You need to stop doubting yourself. Aren't you the woman who faked her own death to take on the woman bent on global domination?"

"Yes, but that was different."

"How?"

"I mean, the plane thing, it was just us."

"I'll try not to take that personally," he said dryly.

She took his hand. "You know what I mean. Our actions over the next few days—there are global consequences. What if we're wrong?"

"What if we are? What if we go through all of this and it doesn't work? What will you do?"

"I don't know."

"Well, I do. You will pick yourself up. You will dust yourself off, and you will jump back into the fight. Things go wrong, Laney. You can't prepare for everything. But you can choose to keep fighting. So even if things go wrong, you won't quit. You'll find another way."

She stared into his eyes. He was right. She wasn't a "curl up in the fetal position and pray her problems went away" kind of girl. She was a "face them head on" kind of girl. They had decided on a course of action. She would see it through. Second-guessing, doubting it, was only going to make it harder. And things were going to be tough enough without her adding extra baggage. She leaned forward and kissed him. "You're right. Thank you."

He smiled. "You know, being we're both awake, maybe I could show you some of the benefits of this humanly existence."

"Oh really? And what might they be?"

He pulled her up. "Let me show you."

———

SUNLIGHT SPEARED THROUGH THE CURTAINS. Laney blinked against it. She'd left the curtain pulled back last night, and now she was paying the price. She rolled over, laying a hand on Drake's chest with a smile. He had well and thoroughly exhausted her. She had slept for the rest of the night without a thought.

But now, with daylight creeping through the windows, what lay ahead of them refused to shift back into the darkness. She looked past Drake to the clock on the side of the bed. Three more hours and they would be in a meeting with joint chiefs. This time the heads of the Atlantic and Pacific Fleet as well as the head of the Marine Corps Ground Combat team would be joining them in a video conference. Some equivalent military leader from the Army would also be joining in, although Laney could not for the life of her remember their title. She was awash in military titles at this point.

The world is on the march. The weight of the responsibility of the battle ahead settled on her, but she shrugged it off. Drake was right. No point making it more difficult than it already was.

Besides, it wasn't like she hadn't faced a world at war before. As Helen, she'd been in the middle of a world gone mad. And she had defeated Samyaza, who'd been trying to gain back his powers.

But she'd lost Drake. She ran a hand over his bare chest. She knew in the battle to come, she would lose people. There was no way they would all survive. She was pretty sure that she herself would not survive. She had come close to dying so many times.

You can only avoid the punches for so long.

She closed her eyes, breathing deeply. Whatever happened would happen. She would do her best to protect all those she could. That was all she could ask of herself.

"Are you done with your morning mental gymnastics routine?"

Laney opened her eyes, smiling into Drake's heavy-lidded eyes. "I am."

"Good. Then let me show you—"

She shook her head, pulling the sheet with her as she sat up. "Nope. The car is coming for us in about an hour. And I want a shower and breakfast."

Drake raised an eyebrow. "So we're in a rush?"

"A bit."

"Well, it would probably be more efficient then to shower together. To save time and all."

Laney smiled. "I was just thinking the same thing."

Chapter Fifty-Four

THE BATHROOM MIRROR was completely steamed over. David wiped it away, glad Rahim wasn't here to yell at him about forgetting to turn on the fan. But that wasn't the only reason he didn't want him here. He wanted him as far away as possible from all this craziness. He wanted him safe.

David walked to his closet, choosing his clothes with care. These last few months he'd had two pairs of pants and three shirts to choose from. To say it was cramping his style was an understatement. He sighed at the feel of silk on his skin. When all this was over, assuming he survived the battle ahead, he was going to live in silk.

His phone beeped, and he glanced at it. Chang Kim had sent him a text. He'd contacted Chang, his executive assistant at the CIA, when he had reemerged, just in case there was anything pressing he needed to address. There hadn't been, or at least nothing more pressing than the matter he was currently dealing with. According to Chang's new text, the Vatican was making an announcement this morning. He frowned and walked over to the TV in the corner of the bedroom and flicked it on, turning it to CNN. The Pope was already speaking.

"—much has been made of the enhanced individuals who have dominated the headlines as of late."

David kept one ear on the TV as he finished getting dressed.

"A great deal of fear, but there is hope as well. With God, all things are possible."

David reached down to tie his shoes.

"I would like to leave you with a little-known verse. In the days when the world is at its darkest, a light for the people will appear. God's soldier will aid in their fight."

David's head snapped up, his attention now focused on the TV. "As it says in Revelation: And when the soldier on high appears, he will defend the good, casting out the wicked and laying waste to those who subvert God's plan."

Then the Pope spoke three words in a language that David knew very few were familiar with. But David was one of them. As the Pope spoke, his mind interpreted his words.

He will rise.

David's mouth fell open. *Oh God, no.* He sprinted for the door just as the room began to shake.

Chapter Fifty-Five

HAVENVILLE

ONE HAND RESTING on her belly, Jen walked down the cobblestoned street next to Mary Jane. The two had become closer in the last few months, Jen's pregnancy encouraging that bond. Jen knew little to nothing about babies, so Mary Jane had been a fount of information. Jen had asked her dozens of questions, and Mary Jane had answered them all patiently, never once making Jen feel stupid for not knowing what was probably common baby knowledge for most people.

But today, it wasn't Jen's baby they were talking about.

"She's good," Mary Jane said. "She and Theresa were actually taking some of the little kids down to the river to catch tadpoles."

"Her nightmares?"

"Fewer. Zaria is always with her, which I think keeps them at bay or maybe calms her down when she wakes. She hasn't woken screaming in about a month."

"Good, that's good."

"It is. I think we may have turned a corner." Mary

Jane's eyes lit up, and Jen didn't have to look far to see the reason why. Jake walked down the street toward them. When he reached them, he kissed Mary Jane lightly on the lips before sliding his arm around her waist. "Hey there."

"Hey." Mary Jane smiled.

They both seemed content to smile into each other's eyes. Jen cleared her throat. "Well, never let it be said I can't take a hint."

Mary Jane's cheeks flushed red. "What? No. Sorry. Was there something—"

Jen laughed. "I'm good. Although Danny printed up a baby furniture catalog for me. Maybe you could give me some advice later?"

Mary Jane clasped her hands together, her smile incredibly wide. "Oh, I would love to."

Jen didn't understand the response, because honestly, it was all a little overwhelming for her. But the fact that Mary Jane wasn't intimidated by the idea was more than a little comforting. "I'm going to check in with Henry. I'll see you guys later."

Jen waved goodbye and headed down the street, thinking of Jake and Mary Jane. She was glad that Jake had found someone. When he and Laney had broken up, she wasn't sure what to think. She had liked them together. Her best friend and Henry's best friend—it made it easy to see the possibilities. But Jake needed someone a little more traditional than Laney, and Laney needed someone a little less traditional, like Drake. So right now, everyone seemed to be right where they were supposed to be.

Ahead, Cleo stepped out of Patrick's cottage. Spying Jen, she started to trot toward her. Before tracking down Henry, Jen was going to stop in and check on Patrick. Laney had asked her to, but even without Laney making the request, Jen would have done so.

Cleo reached Jen and rubbed against her leg. Jen reached down and scratched her behind the ears. "Hey, girl. How's everyone doing today?"

Cleo purred. Jen let out a little laugh. "Well, that sounds—"

A tremor ran through the ground. Jen straightened, looking around with a frown. What was that? There'd never been anything like that the entire time they'd been here. She took a step toward Patrick's cottage. The ground shifted under her feet. Jen stumbled, but Cleo zipped next to her, bracing her and keeping her upright. Jen grabbed on to her fur as the ground began to tremble in earnest. A cracking sounded.

She whirled around as a giant fissure opened, stretching from one side of the street to the other.

Chapter Fifty-Six

GEORGETOWN, WASHINGTON, D.C.

LANEY GRABBED on to the side of the couch as the living room shook. The Pope had just finished speaking when the earthquake hit. It felt like maybe a five or six on the Richter scale. Picture frames crashed from the walls, scattering glass across the floor. Drake stood still, his back to her, then on the TV as the shaking stopped.

She laughed. "Well, that was a little ominous."

Drake didn't move. He didn't say a word. But his body seemed to vibrate with tension. Laney frowned, uncurling her legs. She stood, reaching out a hand for him. "Drake?"

"Laney! Don't!" David barreled into the room, yanking her hand back and pulling her toward the doorway.

Laney yanked her arm from David's grasp. "What are you doing?"

Matt appeared behind him, his face showing his own confusion.

David flicked a gaze to Drake. "We need to go. Now."

She shook her head, turning to Drake. David grabbed

her arm again, his voice coming out in a hiss. "He's not Drake anymore."

Laney went still, then turned slowly to where Drake stood. He hadn't moved an inch. Hadn't turned his head at David's entrance. "Drake?"

Drake's shoulders stiffened, and he looked at her over his shoulder. His eyes held no warmth. There was no kindness or laughter in his face. And the voice that came from his lips . . . it was Drake's, and at the same time, not. "Ring Bearer, you are to cease disobeying God's demands."

A chill ran over Laney as he turned to face her. His whole body radiated power and menace. "Who are you?"

"I am God's soldier most high. I am His shield."

Michael.

He nodded as if she had spoken out loud. "Will you comply?"

Laney couldn't form a sentence. She couldn't form a thought.

"You have been warned," he said, his voice sounded like death. No, like the soldier of God, she realized. Light burst from around him.

Laney let out a cry, covering her eyes. The light dimmed, and she turned back.

Drake was gone. She stared at where he had been. What had just happened?

Chapter Fifty-Seven

HAVENVILLE, MASSACHUSETTS

THE GROUND TREMBLED SO HARD that windows cracked. A chimney tumbled off a roof a few houses away. Jen ran for Patrick's cottage. Cain was stumbling out of the door, pushing Patrick's wheelchair, Nyssa in Patrick's lap.

An alarm rang out. It was the emergency beacon. Everyone was supposed to head to the entrance. Cleo peeled off, heading for Dom's cottage with a roar.

"Take Nyssa. I'll get Patrick. Head to the entrance," Jen ordered as she grabbed the back of Patrick's chair. Cain gathered Nyssa into his arms and ran for the road. Jen shoved Patrick forward just as the ground gave way. She yanked him back before he could topple into the cavern.

"We can't take the chair," she said, picking Patrick up without waiting for a reply. She jumped over the divide and sprinted for the entrance. With her speed, she outpaced Cain. Stopping at the entrance, she handed Patrick to Susan Jacobs, who stood by the exit, ushering people through. "Can you take him?"

Susan nodded, holding him easily. "I'll take him through."

"Be careful, Jen!" Patrick yelled just before Susan disappeared through the portal with him. Cain and Nyssa stepped through right after them. Noriko was running up the street, four children with her, flanked by three cats. Gerard was blurring back and forth at the entrance, depositing people before heading back through the crumbling Havenville to get more. Rahim ran toward the entrance, a dozen kids following him.

Jake appeared, the McAdamses behind him. Jen looked over at him. "Havenville's coming apart."

"Everyone go through the entrance." Jake nodded at Lou and Rolly as they sprinted up with Dom and Gina. "Get a head count when you get through."

Rahim grabbed two children into his arms. "Come on, guys." He led them through the wavering entrance.

Jen glanced back at the town. Buildings were shaking so hard they were shattering apart. The cats were running in between buildings, herding people toward the entryway. Jen sprinted back to help.

"Jen!" Jake yelled. But she was already moving. She grabbed one of the Otero kids as they stumbled from the field with three other children. Mariana Otero blurred into view, her eyes wide.

"Get the kids to the entrance. We're evacuating," Jen said.

Mariana picked up two kids. Jen grabbed the other two, sprinting for the exit. She deposited them and headed back for more. She made four more trips. On the fifth, Jake grabbed her arm. "Jen, get out of here."

A scream split the air. Jen shook Jake off and sprinted in the direction of the scream.

The sound was coming from the back of the village. A little girl stood at the edge of a cliff, reaching into it. Jen blurred toward her. She glanced down. Sister Angelica, Bas's sister, held on to the edge. Jen grabbed her arms, hauling her up.

Lou appeared, her breath coming out in pants. "You're one of the last."

Jen pushed the girl and Angelica toward her. "Get them out of here."

Lou grabbed them both and took off at a run. Jen stepped forward to follow when the ground gave way, and instead of running, she found herself falling.

Chapter Fifty-Eight

JEN SCRAMBLED for something to grab as the ground gave way. But there was nothing. Then her descent stopped with a sudden jolt. She looked up. Cleo had Jen's ponytail locked in her jaws.

Jen tried to reach up, but she still had no purchase.

Henry's face appeared next to Cleo's. "Jen!" He reached down and hauled her up. Cleo released her as soon as she was over the edge.

Henry crushed her in a hug, his heart pounding in his chest. "Are you okay?"

Jen reached out a hand, hauling herself upright, using Cleo for balance. "Yes. Thank you, Cleo." Cleo roared in response before running for the entrance.

Henry swept Jen into his arms.

"I can—" Her words were drowned out as he sprinted toward the exit. Part of a house collapsed as they ran by, throwing debris in the air. It was like running through a war zone. Henry zigged and zagged, trying to avoid the shards of stone and wood that were flying through the air.

Jen felt herself go airborne as they took a hit from the side just as the exit came into view. Jen tucked, rolling, her hands protecting her belly. She rolled to her feet as she hit the ground, Henry doing the same next to her. Jen whirled around to see what had hit them. A dark shape lay half buried under a pile of debris. That would have been Jen and Henry if they hadn't been pushed out of the way. "Cleo!"

The ground trembled even more violently, but Jen fought to get to Cleo. Henry beat her there, shoving the debris off of her. Cleo stumbled to her feet, blood seeping from her side. Henry turned to Jen.

She glared at him. "Don't you *dare* pick me up. Get Cleo."

Henry hesitated for only a moment before picking Cleo up. Jen sprinted for the exit as the tremors increased. A giant fissure opened in front of the exit just as Henry crossed through it, Cleo in his arms. Jen leaped over it, diving through the exit. She took the hit on her shoulder, careful to roll to her back to protect the baby as sunlight and the Gate of the Sun came into view. Jake grabbed her under the arms, pulling her back as the ancient gate cracked and crashed to the ground, sending up plumes of dust.

Coughing, Jen stared at it in horror. She looked up at Jake. "Is everybody out?"

Jake nodded. "You three were the last."

Beyond him, Gina was hunched over Cleo, applying bandages. "Cleo?"

"A few cuts, looks like a broken leg, but nothing life threatening."

Henry crouched down next to Jen, helping her sit up. "You two okay?"

Jen placed her hand on her belly. "Yeah. We're good."

Her gaze drifted back to the ancient doorway. "What just happened?"

"Do you think something happened to Laney?" Jake asked.

Henry shook his head. "No, this isn't about Laney. She didn't create Havenville."

Horror rolled through Jen as she realized he was right. "Drake did. Something happened to Drake."

Chapter Fifty-Nine

GEORGETOWN, WASHINGTON, D.C.

A CHILL SEEMED ENCASED over Laney's bones. Matt had put a blanket around her shoulders, but it didn't help. She couldn't stop shaking. She sat at David's kitchen table as David carried over tea. "I don't understand what just happened."

David placed a mug of tea in front of her before sitting next to her. "Bas and I told you Drake was Michael. Somehow, he cast off his Drake persona and embraced his other role."

Matt studied David. "You were already running down the stairs before he turned around. You knew. How?"

"The words the Pope said. They're Aramaic. They mean 'He will rise.' It's in the Tome. It's a call to action for Michael." He looked at Laney. "You were both watching as he said it."

He will rise. Laney clutched the blanket more tightly around her. She flashed on the look on Drake's face when he'd looked at her. It was as if he did not know her or that he did not care, despite what he knew. Even before she knew their history, he never looked at her like that. It was as if he was a stranger. There was no sign of her Drake anywhere.

She cleared her throat. "But what about Drake? It was as if all his emotions were shut off."

David shrugged, but his eyes were full of concern. "I don't know. In the Tome it mentions Michael being called, but it never really explained what would happen to him."

Laney took a shaky sip from the mug in front of her. She welcomed the warmth down her throat because she felt so very cold. She could accept that it had been Michael that she had seen. But she could not accept that Drake was just gone. Or worse, that he had never truly and fully existed. That he'd been only a small sliver of Michael's personality, which now had been pushed out by the weight of his duty. Fear mixed with grief at the very idea of it.

Matt's voice, low and somber, broke into her thoughts. "I haven't mentioned it, but the last couple of months, some of my memories have been returning."

David frowned. "What memories?"

Laney looked at Matt. The wrinkles in his forehead were more pronounced, and there were dark circles under his eyes. His entire frame radiated tension. Matt was a Fallen and had lived many lives, but he'd never spoken of them. "Do you mean your past lives?"

Matt wrapped his hands around his mug. "More than that. My time before I fell."

Laney sucked in a breath. "I didn't realize that was possible."

"I didn't either." He frowned. "But it was strange. I was me, but all my emotions, my thoughts, they were muted, turned down. I couldn't access them. But when I would watch you humans, your joys, your sorrows, your freedom to express and feel it all, I could feel some of it. It was like a breath of fresh air after being trapped in a windowless room for days. Our lives felt so monotonous in comparison. There were no lows but no highs either. No sadness, no joy. Just a never-ending sameness."

"You think that's who Drake has reverted to," David said.

Matt nodded. "I think so."

"But when you fell, you broke through that," Laney said. "Drake, all his emotions, he'd still have them there. He's still Drake."

"I'm not so sure," Matt spoke quietly. "You have to keep in mind that Drake, or Michael, rather, never fell. Everything he's done, it was part of his duty. Even his sabbaticals were ordained. He has never disobeyed. And now, he has been reminded of his duty."

"But he wouldn't hurt us. He wouldn't hurt me," Laney said.

David and Matt exchanged a look that Laney did not like. "Drake wouldn't hurt you," Matt said. "But he's not running the show right now. Right now, Michael is in charge. And Michael follows orders."

"And those orders seem to put him on the opposite side from us," David said.

Laney shook her head. "No. I can't believe he would let that happen."

"I don't think he has a choice," Matt said. "He is not human. Humans have choices. Humans have free will. Angels don't."

Laney looked at him. "So you're saying one of the enemies we are going up against will be Michael."

"More than that. If he believes it is his duty, he will do

everything within his considerable power to stop us. To stop you."

Chapter Sixty

MATT TOOK the lead in the meeting that morning to finalize the rest of the details. Laney was struggling to focus on anything. All she could picture was Drake's, no, Michael's face before he disappeared. A hole had opened up in her chest, and her skin felt like it no longer fit her. Drake, he gave her strength. Just his presence did something. He never doubted what she could do. He never wavered in his support. But that look—it was tearing her up.

"Is there anything else we need, Dr. McPhearson?"

Laney looked over at General Rockefeller. She could tell he was wondering what was going on with her this morning, but she really didn't think he deserved an explanation. "I sent a list last night of individuals who we will need."

"Yes, they've all been cleared. As soon as we know when and where, we will allow them access."

Laney nodded. It wouldn't be dark for a few hours, so she wouldn't be able to reach them until then to finalize everything. As soon as the thought slipped through her mind, her phone beeped, and she looked down at it. It was

Danny. She stood up quickly. "I need to take this." Not waiting for a reply, she left the room. David followed her.

"Danny? Is everything all right?"

"It's Jen, and no. Everything's not." Jen explained about Havenville collapsing in on itself.

Laney leaned against the wall for support. "Was anyone hurt?"

"Some scrapes, cuts. Cleo broke a leg, but that was the worst of it."

"Oh my God."

Jen paused. "Laney, is Drake okay?"

Laney looked up at David, her heart breaking. He was gone. Havenville had been destroyed. If Havenville was gone, then so was Drake. Her whole world collapsed.

David took the phone gently from her. "Jen, it's David."

Vaguely, Laney could hear David explain what had happened to Drake. But it was like she was in a bubble. She leaned her back against the wall and then slid down. Drake was really gone. He was gone.

David crouched down next to her. "Laney?"

Her head jerked up, and she could tell from his worried expression that he'd been calling her name a few times. He gently touched her shoulder. "What do you want to do?"

She nearly laughed at the question. What did she want to do? She wanted to cry. She wanted to scream. She wanted to run as far from all of this as she could and stick her head in the sand. But what she wanted hadn't been a factor in her decisions in a very long time.

And now was no different.

"Contact Luiz. If he's willing, those who aren't going to be in this fight can wait it out there until everything is over. If he can't take them all, they'll have to come back to the States. The government will have to pave the way for all of them. We have no other options right now. We need to know who is going to fight. They need to be on the first plane here. The rest can follow."

David nodded, conveying everything to Jen before disconnecting the call. "I'll go tell them what we need." He squeezed her shoulder before stepping back into the room.

Laney didn't follow. She needed a minute. Truth be told, she probably needed closer to a year. Everything was coming to a head. The countries were on the march. Her people were scared and without a haven. If she didn't succeed, she had no doubt the U.S. government would turn on the people she'd been protecting. And Drake. Drake was gone.

She dropped her head into her hands. It was too much. The pressure, the expectation. It was all too much.

But it didn't matter if it was all too much. It was happening. And she needed to get her butt up. People were counting on her. And if by some miracle she survived all of this, she and Cleo could disappear and leave everything behind.

She pushed herself from the ground, straightening her shoulders.

One last fight, she thought before she pulled open the door and stepped inside.

Chapter Sixty-One

THE TOWNHOUSE WAS quiet as David sat waiting. Laney had gone to bed hours ago. David prayed she slept. Matt was in the hall outside her room in case she needed them. David had been the one sitting there before. Originally he'd planned on sleeping for a few hours before replacing Matt, but a meeting request had changed all that. His phone beeped. He glanced at the message and then silently slipped out the front door. He jogged down the steps and down the street.

Bruce stepped out of the shadows of a small alley between two townhomes just as he reached the corner.

David nodded at Bruce's trench coat. "I see we're going for old-school spy fashion."

Bruce frowned, looking down as he fell in step with David. "What? They said there was a chance of rain."

David snorted.

They walked in silence for half a block before Bruce spoke. "Where was she hiding you guys?"

"Under a rock. But that spot is now dust. When Drake transformed, the hiding place was destroyed."

"So it's true. He is Michael."

"It's true." David paused. "I met your mother there. She's pretty impressive."

A smile crossed Bruce's face. "Yes, she is. I had a feeling that's where she'd gone."

"Have you spoken with her?"

Bruce shook his head. "For some things, it's best if we keep our distance."

David paused, not sure if he should reveal what he knew. But Bruce saved him the trouble. "She's going to be part of the fight, isn't she?"

"I believe her exact words were: I have not spent my whole life preparing for the final showdown between good and evil to spend my time cheering from the sidelines."

Bruce smiled again. "That sounds like her."

"You going?"

Bruce nodded. "I'll be running intelligence from a secure location. You're welcome to join me."

A year ago, he would have accepted. But now . . . "Actually, I think I'm going to take a more active role in this particular fight."

Bruce's eyebrows rose. "You're joining the team?"

"I think I joined it months ago. Laney, she has a way of making you want to do the right thing. It's kind of annoying at times."

Bruce snorted but then sobered. "You're not alone. Maldonado will be joining the fight as well."

David's eyebrows rose. "Laney's passion *is* contagious."

"So it seems. Be careful."

"I will. But I have a favor to ask."

"Okay."

"If I don't make it back, can you look out for Rahim? Just check in on him from time to time."

"I will."

"Thank you."

They turned another corner, and David breathed in deeply. The air felt good tonight. Clean. Or maybe he was just appreciating what might be one of his last nights.

Bruce's voice cut through his thoughts. "What are her chances?"

David hesitated. Not because he didn't know the "her" Bruce was referring to but partly because he felt like it was a betrayal to Laney to answer the question, which was an unusual feeling for him. And partly because he wasn't sure how to answer it. "She's . . . Laney."

Bruce gave him a disgruntled look. "Not helpful."

David sighed. "Losing Drake—it's devastated her."

"You warned her that was possible."

"Yes, but how exactly does someone accept that the person they love might transform into an unfeeling archangel, never mind prepare for it? I mean, I knew what the Tome said. I've read it with my own eyes, and still I wasn't sure it would happen."

"But will she be able to complete the mission?"

"You mean will she be able to function and save the rest of us?" David asked with more than a touch of bitterness. "Yes. She's hurt. She's wounded. But she's still her. We just need to make sure we give her whatever she needs."

"And what about Michael? Will he interfere?"

"He believes events should play out without any of us trying to stop them, and most especially Laney." David pictured Michael as he stood in the living room.

Ring Bearer, you are to cease disobeying God's demands. A sliver of fear ran up his spine. "So, yes. If Laney gets close, he will most definitely interfere."

The Belial Sacrifice

Chapter Sixty-Two

THE PLANE TOOK OFF SMOOTHLY. Jen closed her eyes as the first stirrings of weightlessness hit her. They were heading back to the United States. Jen was part of the first group that would make contact with the United States government. The rest of the group included Jake, Henry, Mustafa, Gina, Dom, Danny, Lou, and Rolly. Jordan was overseeing the transport of all the people who would not be fighting to Luiz's ranch. Then he'd head to the U.S. with the rest of their group.

Assuming, of course, that this isn't a trap and we don't all get arrested the moment we step off the plane.

It was a risk, but Laney was right. It was end-game time. Jen just hoped the President realized that as well. That worrying about the good Fallen on her soil was a pretty ridiculous concern when other countries were going to start mass-producing their own Fallen.

The plane leveled off. Jen glanced out the window at the clouds. The world looked so peaceful from up here. It was hard to believe that the world was on the edge of war.

Jen undid her seatbelt. Henry looked over. "What are you doing?"

"I'm going to go sit with Cleo."

"I'm not sure—"

Jen gritted her teeth. She was really trying to be understanding of this overprotective phase that Henry was going through now that she was pregnant, but her patience was wearing a little thin. "Henry, you need to cool it. I'm pregnant. I'm not fragile. In fact, I may be one of the least fragile pregnant women ever. So just relax, okay? Take a nap, read a magazine. Just cool it."

He gave her a sheepish smile. "Sorry. I just worry."

She took his hand. "I know. I don't want anything to happen to this child either. But I also don't plan on living in a bubble until she is born."

"I know. I know."

She kissed his cheek. "I love you, Henry. And I love our little one."

He placed a hand on her cheek. "I will try to be less annoying."

"Thank you." She smiled at him before she made her way down the aisle.

Jen stopped at where Gina sat. Dom was curled up on the two seats next to her. "How is he?"

"Out like a light. He won't wake up until we're at the estate."

"That's good. He'll like being home."

"I hope so. Going to check on Cleo?"

Jen nodded.

"She's going to be fine. She heals really fast."

"Yes, she does." Jen continued down the rows, stopping at the last row on the left. The seats had been removed, and a platform and cushions had been added to make a bed for

Cleo. Her right leg was in a splint, and bandages were covering her right side as well.

"Hey, girl," Jen said softly.

Cleo opened her eyes. Sadness wafted over Jen. Jen nodded. "I know. I wish we could be there to help her too." Jen slid into the seat next to Cleo. Cleo started to inch forward.

"No, no, no." Jen moved closer. Cleo lifted up her head, and Jen slid her legs underneath. Cleo placed her head down with a sigh. Jen ran a hand through Cleo's fur. Even in a restful pose, Jen could feel the strength in Cleo's body. She was such a remarkable animal.

Jen leaned her head back, once again closing her eyes. With the movement of the plane and the warmth of Cleo, she felt herself relaxing for the first time since Havenville had been destroyed. She still could not believe how quickly it had fallen apart. Everything felt like it was coming to an end. All the experiences of the last few years felt like they were coming to a head. Jen placed her other hand on her belly. *I'll protect you, little one.*

Cleo leaned her head up and licked the hand covering Jen's belly. Jen smiled. *Oh, Cleo, my little girl is going to love you.*

Cleo rested her head back down. A shudder ran through her. Jen frowned as another tremor ran through Cleo's body. "Cleo?"

Then the tremors increased, each one coming on top of the next. Cleo's whole body was shaking. "Cleo!"

Gina was running down the aisle as Jen slid from underneath Cleo. Her heart raced. Cleo's eyes had rolled back in her head. Her tongue hung from the side of her mouth. Jen crouched next to her, her breaths stuttering. Tears blurred her vision.

Gina grabbed Jen by the shoulders and pulled her back, taking her place next to Cleo. "She's seizing."

Jen watched in horror as Gina checked Cleo's pupils and rummaged in her bag before drawing out a syringe. She pulled off the cap and plunged it into Cleo. Jen stared at Cleo's chest. The seizures had slowed, but so too had her heart rate.

Two arms wrapped around Jen. She looked up into Henry's face. Gina started pushing on Cleo's chest. "Someone get me some oxygen!"

Jake appeared with a small oxygen tank and tubing. Gina muttered under her breath, trying to adjust the mask to fit Cleo as he took over compressions.

The rest of the group was huddled around, watching them work, and each had some version of horror or fear on their faces. Jen studied each of them, looking for one little positive sign. But the emotion of hope was conspicuously absent from those around her. She turned back to Cleo, holding tightly onto Henry, but her mind was focused on Laney. She couldn't lose Cleo. Not now, not just after losing Drake.

Don't go, Cleo. Don't go.

Chapter Sixty-Three

BALTIMORE, MARYLAND

LANEY PACED along the front gates of the Chandler Estate. It was dark. There were no lights on at the estate except back on Sharecroppers Lane, but you couldn't see any of them from the front gates. She had wanted to be at the airfield when everyone landed, but they weren't even sure where they would be landing. The airports were a mess these days. Originally they'd been scheduled to arrive at Reagan, then the plane had been diverted to Arlington. They'd been forced to circle for over an hour due to a storm.

Headlights appeared at the end of the street. She quickly moved to the guardhouse. Matt stepped out, the gates already opening. "It's them."

Laney took a shaky breath, nerves running along her skin. She ran her hands over her arms, suddenly feeling cold. The first car pulled through the gate but didn't stop. It continued right past Laney and Matt, heading for Sharecroppers Lane. Dom had to be in that car. Gina, Lou, and

Rolly were with him. They would get him settled back in his shelter and get everything set up.

The second SUV pulled to a stop. Jen stepped out of the passenger seat. Laney ran over to her, holding her tight. "Are you all right? Is the baby all right?"

"I told you, we're fine."

Laney studied her, looking for any hint of injury.

"I'm fine, really," Jen insisted.

Henry walked over to them, hugging Laney tightly. "Is she really okay?" Laney asked.

"She is."

Three more SUVs filled with recruits drove past without stopping, also heading for Sharecroppers Lane. Henry and Jen stepped to Laney's side as the last vehicle in their caravan arrived: an ambulance.

Laney grabbed on to Jen and Henry's arms, tears pressing against her eyes. The ambulance stopped in front of them. The back doors opened, and Jake appeared. He nodded at Laney before stepping back.

Laney gripped Henry's arm even tighter as Jen slipped her arm around Laney's waist. "We're here, Laney," Jen whispered.

Laney nodded, forcing her legs to move toward the ambulance. The light from inside the ambulance shone out into the dark of the night. Steeling herself, Laney stepped into the light.

She didn't steel herself enough. Her breath left her in rush of air, and her knees buckled. Without Jen and Henry's support, she would have crashed to the ground.

Cleo lay on her side, strapped to a stretcher, machines helping her breathe. After they had gotten out of the cave, she had seemed fine. She had broken her right forearm and a couple of ribs, but other than that, she was fine. But on the plane ride here, something had happened. She had collapsed. Gina thought she might have thrown an embolism or blood clot. Her heart had stopped. On the plane, everyone had taken turns performing CPR, keeping her blood pumping until they landed.

Laney climbed into the ambulance on legs made of water. She sat down heavily on the bench next to the stretcher. "Hey, Cleo."

There was no response. She didn't move. She didn't think anything. Everything was still. Laney stretched out with her sense, trying to get a sense of Cleo somewhere inside the body in front of her, but there was nothing.

Jake climbed in behind her, and the ambulance started to move again. They were heading to Dom's. There was a medical unit in the main house, but Laney didn't want to bring Cleo there. She'd be more comfortable at Dom's. He had a med unit set up in his shelter.

Laney stroked Cleo's fur, resting her head on Cleo's neck. *Hey, girl. I'm here. I'm sorry I wasn't there for you, but I'm here now.*

Cleo's chest moved up and down, but there was no other response. And even that felt artificial. It wasn't Cleo who was forcing the air in and out. A machine was doing it for her.

This can't be happening. I can't lose you too, she thought desperately, even though she knew she had no control over this any more than she did over Drake.

She didn't feel the ambulance stop. Jake put a hand gently on her back. "We're here."

Laney sat up, wiping at her eyes. Henry opened the doors from the outside, tears in his own eyes. Jake helped Laney out of the ambulance. She walked into Jen's waiting arms, tears trailing down her cheeks. Jen and Laney stood with their arms clasped around one another as Jake and Henry pulled the stretcher out of the back of the ambulance, careful to keep all the cords attached to the machines helping her breathe.

Danny stood at the door of Dom's shelter, tears running down his cheeks as he held the door open. Laney and Jen followed behind the stretcher as they rolled her through doorways, each one open and waiting for them. Lou stood at the second one, her lips trembling. Rolly was in the same condition at the last one.

Laney could barely see them, her own tears blocking her view. She shuddered with sobs, trying to figure out how she was supposed to get through this. Henry and Jake wheeled Cleo through the main room and into Dom's lab. Through a haze of tears, she saw Dom and Gina waiting for her. Dom looked devastated, but he was holding it together.

They immediately got to work, checking Cleo over with an array of instruments. Henry stepped back, slipping his arm around Laney's shoulders. She buried her face into his chest.

No one said anything as Dom and Gina worked. Laney held on to Jen and Henry, wanting to know but not wanting to at the same time. It was Schrödinger's cat all over again. Right now, Cleo could be alive or not. Until Dom and Gina spoke, Laney could choose to believe she was alive. But once they finished, that choice would be ripped from her.

So she prayed Gina and Dom examined Cleo forever. But of course, that was impossible. Henry leaned down. "Laney."

She shook her head, not wanting to hear it.

His voice was gentle, but at the same time, the cruelty of his words was world-shattering. "Laney, you need to say goodbye."

The breath burst from her lungs in a gasp. Say goodbye? How could she say goodbye to *Cleo*? Cleo wasn't some friend, some pet. She was the other part of Laney. How could this be happening?

Gina stopped in front of her. Laney looked up at her, wanting to hear something different. Something that would not shatter her world. "I'm sorry, Laney. There is no brain activity. Sometimes when someone breaks a bone, a small piece of the bone can fracture off and cause an embolism, a blockage of the blood. I think that's what happened, but there's no way to know for sure."

Laney gripped Jen's hand. If she'd been a normal human, Laney would have crushed it. But Jen said nothing, just held her tightly. "What happens now?"

"The machines are keeping her body functioning. We can continue that, but eventually her body will break down and the machines won't be able to compensate. I'm sorry, Laney, but she's already gone."

Laney swallowed hard. "Everybody . . ." She swallowed. "Let everyone else say goodbye first."

Gina squeezed her forearm. "Okay."

Henry and Jen helped Laney over to the side as Lou, Rolly, and Danny made their way to the table. Each of them placed a hand on Cleo, bowing their heads, their tears dripping onto the table and into Cleo's fur. The three of them moved to the side as Jake stepped up. He kissed Cleo's cheek, resting his hand above her eyes for a moment before wiping his own eyes and moving to the side. Dom shuffled up to Cleo's side, tears raining down his cheeks as sobs wracked his frame.

Henry walked up then, saying his goodbye quietly before joining Jake. Jen and Laney walked to the table together. Laney angrily wiped away the tears that were running as if from a faucet. She needed to see Cleo.

She laid a hand on her friend, her whole body shaking. *I love you, Cleo. Thank you for being my friend. Thank you for being in my life. I will miss you forever.*

Jen kept a tight grip on Laney as Gina spoke. "Are you ready?"

Laney took a shuddering breath. She grabbed Cleo's paw and nodded even as her heart threatened to crack in two.

Gina hit a switch on the heart monitor, and the beeps slowed, coming further and further apart until they went silent. And that was it. Laney's legs gave out. Jen gripped her, keeping her from falling, and then it was Jake who pulled her into his arms, carrying her from the room. He carried her to the couch, curling her up in his lap.

She sobbed for Cleo. She sobbed for Drake. She sobbed for herself and everything she'd lost.

Chapter Sixty-Four

THE HEART MONITOR SLOWED. Her throat tight, Jen tightened her grip around Laney, feeling her friend's strength leave as Cleo's did. Jen could not believe this was happening. Cleo had been fine. Hurt, yes. But not badly. How could it have resulted in this?

Laney's legs gave out, but Jen gripped her to her to keep her from falling. And then Jake was there, pulling Laney into his arms and striding from the room. Jen walked to the threshold of the door, her heart breaking as she watched Laney sob. Grief threatening to overwhelm her, she looked back at Cleo, who was so still. Henry stepped next to her, wrapping his arms around her. She looked back at her best friend, whose heart had been shattered twice in as many days.

Jen leaned into Henry, tears rolling down her own cheeks as she shared her friend's pain.

Laney stood up suddenly, her face pale, tears overflowing her lashes, her eyes wild. "I need to go. I need to run."

Jake reached out a hand for her. "Laney."

She shook her head, stepping out of his reach.

Henry stepped forward. "I'll go with—"

Laney just shook her head and blurred out the door. Jen grabbed Henry's arm before he could follow. "Let her go."

"But she needs—"

"She needs to cry. She needs to run. And the only people she needs right now aren't here." Jen's eyes filled with tears. When she had lost her baby, in the immediate aftermath, the only one she wanted near her was Henry. Drake was the only one Laney would want right now. But he was the other part of her tears. "We can't help her right now. We need to be there for her when we can."

A crash had everyone whirling. Jake had slammed a chair into the wall, anger and grief slashed across his face.

Jen's own anger began to rise. It was too much pain for one person. Jen felt like doing exactly the same thing. Henry tried to hug her, but she pushed him away. "It's not fair! Cleo, Drake, and now what? We're just supposed to ask her to save the world one more time while her whole world crashes down around her? How much more can we ask of her?"

"She's strong, Jen."

"She's strong, yes, but she's human, Henry. Even she has a breaking point. Cleo, she wasn't just her pet, her friend. She was *part* of her. And with Drake gone . . ." Jen's words choked off, the pain her friend was facing robbing her of words.

Jake started for the door. "I'll go see—"

"I need everyone to be quiet!" Gina yelled as she stood hunched over Cleo's body, a stethoscope to her chest. Jen's gaze flew to the heart monitor, but it was still flatlined. What was Gina doing?

Gina frowned as she shifted the stethoscope around Cleo's chest, moving lower and lower down her torso. Her eyes grew large. She all but shoved Henry out of the way as she started CPR.

"Get the oxygen mask on her!"

Jen was too stunned to move, but Danny sprang into action, grabbing the mask and securing it over Cleo's mouth.

"Henry, take over compressions," Gina ordered.

Henry placed his hands over hers and began compressions as soon as Gina slipped hers out. Gina hustled over to the defibrillator and rolled it to the table.

"What's going on?" Jen asked. "Is Cleo alive?"

Gina shook her head but didn't answer her question as she placed the paddles on Cleo's chest. "Clear!"

Henry raised his hands. Cleo's whole body shook as electricity passed through her. A blip appeared on the monitor. Gina nodded. "You guys need to get out. I need room."

Henry turned Jen around. Jen glanced over her shoulder at Gina frantically working on Cleo. What on earth was going on?

Chapter Sixty-Five

LANEY SPRINTED UP THE STAIRS, away from Dom's shelter. Thank God someone had left all the blast doors open, because if she had had to open them, she would have lost her mind.

She blew through the last door, bursting out into the fresh air. She sprinted away from the shelter, away from Sharecroppers Lane. She didn't think. She just ran. Without conscious thought, she vaulted over the fence. A car braked as she landed in the street, but Laney didn't stop. She kept going. She ran as her heart shattered inside her chest. Her legs felt like they'd been weighed down, and as her mind ran with so many thoughts, she wanted more than anything to yank it out.

The world around her was a blur as she sprinted down streets and across fields. She wondered if maybe she could just do this, run, and keep running until there was nothing left of her. She pictured Drake, the lack of emotion in his eyes. He was gone too. There had been nothing of the Drake she knew in the body of the archangel she had seen in David's living room. Her Drake, the man who somehow, despite his arrogance, his flippancy, his ego, had not only slipped into her heart but plunked down roots and declared he would be the last one who did.

Ahead, the tall concrete walls of the cats' old preserve came into view. With a giant leap, Laney's fingertips reached the top. She hauled herself up and rolled over the side. She didn't even try to get her feet under her. She slammed into the ground on her side.

She stumbled to her knees, sucking in a lungful of air. *Cleo*.

The animal preserve was a skeleton of its former self. Dead, scarred trees covered the area. No signs of life burst from the ground.

Laney crashed onto her hands, sobs wracking her body. *No, Cleo, no*. She pictured Cleo when she'd first met her. Yoni had thought she was crazy. Laney hadn't been sure he wasn't right. But the minute she had connected with Cleo, everything had changed. Laney had changed. A whole new world had opened up to her. From that point on, she'd never been alone. Cleo had always been with her, even if she hadn't physically been there. The bond between them, it was beyond friends, beyond family.

And now she's gone. Laney struggled to breathe as the hole in her chest grew even wider. She panted on her hands and knees, desperate for air but part of her wondering if maybe, just maybe, it wouldn't be better, or at least easier, if she was never able to get any.

She fell to her side, taking small panting breaths as the panic attack receded. She lay there, feeling as weak as a kitten.

All this power, all these abilities, and I can't save the ones I love. Visions of Cleo, Drake, Drew, Kati, Maddox, Rocky, Zac floated through her mind. How many more would be added to that list in the days to come?

It was too much. Too much pain, too much death, too much loss. How much more was she supposed to take? How much more could be asked of her?

She knew the answer to that even as she thought it. Everything. Everything would be asked of her. And everything she had would be needed for the fight ahead. But right now, she knew that everything she had wasn't very much. The Delaney McPhearson who had taken on Samyaza, the Delaney McPhearson who as Helen of Troy had defied the armies of the world, was a shell of her former self. She curled her legs to her chest, wrapping her arms around herself.

The Delaney McPhearson who existed right now was broken. And she wasn't sure if she would ever be whole again.

Chapter Sixty-Six

LANEY DIDN'T AWAKEN until noon the next day. She had lain in the cats' preserve for hours before stumbling back to the estate. She had avoided everyone, not wanting to talk. She'd collapsed in bed, seeking the oblivion of sleep. Now she pried her eyes against the brightness. But the sunlight wouldn't give her any peace. As soon as she opened her eyes, she remembered saying goodbye to Cleo. She rolled over, buried her face in her pillow, and sobbed.

Two hours later, she managed to force herself from her bed. She wanted to pull the blankets over her head and just let the world burn. Or at least, she did for a moment. But the faces of all those counting on her played on a carousel through her mind. She needed to get up. She needed to see what the government had arranged. So even though she wanted nothing more than to go back to sleep, she forced herself to her feet and into the shower.

The shower woke her up a little, but the blanket of grief she was wearing didn't get any lighter. She opened the door to her bedroom, smelling food from the kitchen. She frowned, not getting a read on anyone.

Must be Jake.

She headed down the stairs and stepped into the kitchen.

Yoni turned from the stove, an apron tied around his waist. "Hey, kid."

Laney flew across the room and hugged him tightly.

Yoni's arms crushed her to him. "I am so damn sorry, Laney, about all of it."

The tears she'd thought she'd run out of ran down her cheeks yet again. Finally, she pulled away, wiping at her cheeks, noticing Yoni do the same. "What are you doing here? How's Sascha and the baby?"

Yoni smiled, even as he used the apron to mop his face. "They're both good. And Noel, she's beautiful. Dov and Max can't seem to get enough of her."

Laney smiled. "I can't wait to meet her."

Yoni's smile dimmed a little. "You will. When this is all over." He handed her a plate. "Here. Go eat."

"You joining me?"

He grunted. "Of course I am."

Laney headed to the table. She took a seat and poured herself a cup of coffee from the pot already on the table. Yoni joined her a few seconds later with his own plate. Laney hadn't been hungry when she'd gotten up, but after the first bite, she realized she was starving. Focused on her food, she didn't say a word to Yoni until she'd done everything but lick her plate clean. She pushed back from the table. "Thanks. I needed that."

"Apparently you did. When's the last time you ate?"

"Um." She frowned, trying to remember. "Maybe yesterday morning?"

"Well, let me get you more, then." He grabbed her plate and refilled it. Laney wanted to say no, but her stomach had other ideas. After a few bites, she asked, "What are you doing here? You're supposed to be in Arizona with that beautiful family of yours."

"Did you really think I'd miss this?"

She paused, eyeing him. "What do you know?"

"I told Danny to contact me whenever the final battle came."

"You knew there'd be one?"

He nodded. "As soon as we learned Elisabeta had left the Omni behind, I knew it would come to this. Jake told me the plan. I'm in."

Laney shook her head. "No. You have a family to think of."

"That's exactly why I'm here. I need to make sure I do everything in my power to secure their future. And that means making sure that enhanced abilities are gone. Nothing good comes from battles between mortals and the gods. I need to be part of this."

She squeezed his hand. "I'd rather you stayed behind."

He gave her a sad smile. "I think we'd all rather sit this one out if we could. But that's not an option, not if we're going to ensure your success. All of us need to do our part. You can't do it alone."

"No, I can't." Her lips trembled as she thought about Cleo and Drake. Right now, she felt alone.

"You're not, you know."

"Not what?"

"Alone. Cleo's with you. And I don't know what exactly happened with Drake or Michael or whoever he is, but I do know that he loved you. You need to hold on to that, Laney. At the end of the day, who we love, how we love, it's what pushes us forward. It's why I'm here, and it's why even though your heart is shattered right now, you'll do what needs to be done. It's kind of the people we are."

She sniffed. "Is it wrong that I really wish we weren't those kind of people right now?"

"It's not wrong. It's just not us." He stood up and kissed her forehead. "Now finish your food. I'm getting seconds too."

Laney watched Yoni head back to the stove. He had a family he adored, and yet he was still here. If Cleo was here, she'd be pushing her forward. And Drake, if he were still here, would be standing by her side. She took a breath, closing her eyes. One foot in front of the other. She could do this. She opened her eyes, and Yoni smiled at her. She could do this because even if her world had collapsed, there were others who still had love to fight for.

She picked up her fork. *And they need me to fight for them as well.*

Chapter Sixty-Seven

A SHORT WHILE LATER, Laney, Matt, and David headed to the Pentagon for one last briefing. It seemed there was some troop activity around the globe that was worrying the analysts. But by the time she left the Pentagon, there was no indication that their plan to go to Egypt had been uncovered. They would leave tomorrow at noon.

That night, Henry hosted a dinner for all the fighters at the main house. Laney passed on the dinner, not up to chatting with a large group of people, but Jen and Yoni had shown up with some food. The three of them had had a quiet meal before turning in for an early night.

At first, Laney had tried to sleep in her cottage. But she couldn't. Memories of Cleo and Drake were everywhere. Her chest felt like it had been ripped open. After struggling for hours, she walked down to her uncle and Cain's cottage. Letting herself in, she curled up in her uncle's bed and sobbed.

All day she had been focused on the task at hand, locking her grief away. But at night, in the dark, there was nothing to distract her from it. And it came roaring over her in a tidal wave of pain and anguish.

It was wrong. It was all wrong for Cleo to be gone by something so simple. How was that possible? She hadn't wanted Cleo to go with her into this final battle. She had planned on making *sure* she did not go with them. But it wasn't supposed to be like this. Cleo was supposed to stay here, with Dom. She was supposed to be safe. How could she be gone?

Laney clutched a pillow to her chest. And Drake. Where was he? What was he doing? Was he still inside Michael, trying to get out? Or had Michael erased everything that had made him Drake?

She had pictured him being right by her side as she climbed the Great Pyramid. She didn't want to endanger anyone, but Drake, he would never have listened to her if she tried to keep him away. He would have stubbornly stayed at her side, no matter the cost to himself. And part of her had been counting on that. They were a team. Could she even do this on her own? Right now she felt like she was half of who she normally was. Drake and Cleo—they were the other pieces of her. It was like someone had cut an arm and leg off and then expected her to step into a boxing ring.

Tears trailed down her cheeks. She couldn't do this. It hurt too much. Drake's face floated through her mind, his blue eyes intense as his words came back to her. *You will dust yourself off and you will jump back into the fight. Things go wrong, Laney. You can't prepare for everything. But you can choose to keep fighting.*

She wasn't sure that she could this time. Everything hurt. And at the same time, she felt like she was completely cut off from her other emotions. Did she really care if the world fell apart? Hadn't she already done her part?

But even as she thought it, she knew that wasn't her speaking. That was the grief. Because she hadn't done everything. Others had given their lives, and here she was, still living. They deserved for her to give her best. Kati and Maddox had lost their lives protecting Max. Max deserved a future. Jen and Henry's little one deserved a future. She just needed to get through this one last battle. She just needed to see it to its end. She didn't need to live through it. Truth be told, she wasn't sure she wanted to live through it. But she needed the people she loved to make it through, to have a chance at a better future.

But I can grieve now. Tomorrow, I'll be strong. Tonight, I don't have to be. She turned her head into the pillow and cried for all those who had been lost to this stupid quest for power. And somewhere in the middle, God took pity on her and let her sleep.

A HAND SHAKING her shoulder cut through the darkness. "Laney."

She opened her eyes, seeing Yoni highlighted by the dim hallway light. She frowned. "Yoni? What's going on?"

"You need to get up, Laney." Her mind was working slowly. She couldn't piece together what Yoni was saying or why he was saying it. She glanced at the window in confusion. It was still pitch black out. The clock confirmed that dawn was hours away. "Why? We don't have to leave for hours."

"The convoy's on its way. Plans have changed." He paused. "It's started."

"What's started?"

"The war."

Chapter Sixty-Eight

YONI ALL BUT shoved Laney into the shower to wake her up. She put the water on ice cold and stepped in. In less than five minutes, she was still shivering as she pulled open the bathroom door. Pulling her wet hair back into a ponytail, she strode across the bedroom to where Yoni waited in the doorway. "What the heck happened?"

Yoni handed her a thermos of coffee. "Someone tipped them off. Chinese communications were intercepted, which shows they know we're heading to Giza, and they have put out an order for all available forces to head there as well."

"What's the timetable?"

"They'll be there in seven hours. But some of their troops were a lot closer, along with their allies."

"What about us?"

"We'll be there in seven and a half hours. The media has already picked up the story. They're calling it 'the showdown in Egypt.'"

"Damn it."

Brakes squealed as Laney pulled open the front door.

Tingles ran over her skin, making it feel alive. A large military truck pulled to a stop across the end of Sharecroppers Lane. People were heading for it in droves. Laney stopped, staring at the crowds of people. "Where'd they all come from?"

"We had some volunteers in the last few hours as the news broke."

Laney caught sight of a man who looked familiar. He turned and nodded at Laney but kept heading for the truck.

"Is that . . ."

"It's Charlie Garner. You saved his family a few years back. He was one of the first to show up."

Laney watched the procession of people walk by. She knew a lot of the faces. People she had saved in one way or another over the years. Her heart felt heavy at the sight of them.

"Why are they doing this?"

"The same reason you are. The same reason I am. They want to fight for a better future."

"This is really happening."

"It is. Now come on. It's time to get this show on the road."

Laney followed Yoni into the crowd. Her heart squeezed a little as she walked. These people were all fighting for people they loved. And yet she knew not all of them would be able to come back to those loved ones.

How many more would they lose in the fight to come?

Chapter Sixty-Nine

NORFOLK, VIRGINIA

LANEY HAD JUST ROUNDED the hangar when she spied Henry and Jen squared off against each other. They'd traveled by convoy to Norfolk and had been getting set up for close to an hour. Now, the first of the planes had been loaded.

"Absolutely not." Henry glared down at Jen.

Jen glared right back up at him, her hands on her hips, which only served to accentuate her belly. "I did *not* ask your permission."

Henry looked over at Jordan and Mike, who were watching the discussion with rapt attention. "You guys agree with me, right?"

Jordan took a step back. "You know, I think I forgot to pack my toothbrush. I'm going to go see if anyone has an extra." Jordan turned and headed for the group of soldiers milling outside the hangar.

Mike pointed at Jordan's retreating back. "I think I'll go help him." He hightailed it after his twin.

Henry glared at them before he spied Laney. "Laney, you'll agree with me."

Jen rolled her eyes, a look of disgust on her face.

Laney stopped next to them. "Somehow I doubt that. But go ahead."

"Jen thinks she's coming with us." Henry crossed his arms over his chest.

"And?" Laney asked.

Henry's mouth fell open. "And? *And?* She's pregnant!"

Laney's mouth fell open. "Holy crap! When were you guys going to tell me?"

Henry glared at her. "Not funny."

"Henry, they're loading people onto planes. Why don't you go see if you can help?" Jen said.

Henry pursed his lips. "We are not done with this conversation." Henry stormed toward the group of people being shepherded toward the planes.

Laney shrugged. "He means well."

Jen smiled as she watched him go. "I know." She looked at Laney. "You know why I'm going, right?"

Laney nodded. "Yeah. But I wouldn't mind if you kind of stayed at the back a little bit."

"I will. I'm not planning on getting into the thick of things unless it becomes absolutely necessary."

"Excellent," said Gina, who walked over carrying a giant bag. She smiled at Laney. "Thanks for getting my situation squared away."

"Least I could do." Laney eyed Gina's camouflage uniform. "Are you coming to see us off?"

"Nope, I'm going with you. It seems to be an all-hands-on-deck kind of moment." Gina knelt down, unzipping the bag. She pulled out a large bulletproof vest. Standing, she handed it to Jen. "Here. I stopped by the base. This is the biggest size I could find. It should cover that little baby bump of yours."

Jen took it, holding it up to herself. "Thanks, Gina."

Gina looked beyond her, nodding. "First plane's taking off."

Laney and Jen turned. The giant military plane took flight at the end of the runway. "How many people in that one?"

"Two hundred." Gina nodded to the plane taxiing down the runway. "Another two hundred."

Laney swallowed. This was it. They were actually going to war.

Jen looked at Gina. "You've done this before, right?"

Gina's voice was soft, her gaze locked on the plane as it took off into the air. "Yeah, but each time it's different. Each time it feels like the stakes are a little higher."

"How do you handle it?" Laney asked.

"Same way we've been handling everything the last few months. One day at a time, one hour at a time, one minute at a time. You break it down into increments you can deal with."

Jake strode from the other hangar, scanning the tarmac before his gaze came to rest on Laney. He waved her toward him before disappearing back inside the hangar.

Laney stepped away from her friends. "I think I'm needed." She walked toward Jake, Gina's advice playing in her mind with a slight change.

One step at a time, one breath at a time, one second at a time.

Chapter Seventy

THE HANGAR WAS a mix of military folks in fatigues and non military people in regular clothes, the latter being the enhanced people who'd come with Laney and did not have any official training. Everyone was checking gear and getting ready. Laney stopped just inside the entrance, her hands on her hips. The regular folks looked nervous as they glanced at the soldiers who looked battle ready. The enhanced might have a natural advantage, but without training, Laney wasn't sure how helpful that was going to be.

The soldiers looked nervous as well, but due to their continued glances at the enhanced, she was pretty sure their fear had less to do with the coming battle and more to do with trusting the people about to fight next to them.

She spied Jake over by the weapons crates and made her way toward him. "Hey."

"Hey yourself. Got something for you." He reached into the crate behind him and pulled out a handgun, along with an extra magazine. He handed them over to Laney. "Special ammo."

"Oh." She slid the magazine in the gun out. It was full. The bullets were a silvery blue. Omni. "Who's got these?"

"Most of our people, at least the ones I think can be trusted."

"You don't trust all of them?"

He dropped his chin, staring at her. "Do you know me at all?"

Laney chuckled, placing the handgun in the holster on her left hip. Omni on the left. Real bullets on the right. *Please let me not screw that up.* She slid the extra magazine into her vest.

Jake grabbed the clipboard next to the crate and made a notation. "All right. You were the last one."

Laney's gaze roamed back over the group in front of them. "Think they're ready?"

Jake scanned the group. "I don't know. The soldiers' training will kick in, but when going against enhanced, that might not be enough."

"And our enhanced aren't soldiers, so their abilities might not be enough."

"Yup."

"Speaking of which." Laney's fingers drifted over the handle of the Omni weapon. "Have you thought of taking the Omni? It will probably give you an edge."

Jake placed the clipboard down. "I won't lie. It is tempting."

"But . . .?"

"But when you succeed—"

"*If.*"

He shook his head, his eyes locking on her. "*When* you

succeed, all the enhanced will lose their abilities. We don't know what that will look like. The enhanced could be stopped in their tracks, unable to move, unable to fight. If that's the case, I think we need some people around who will still be able to fight."

She nodded. "You're right. That's the big unknown, isn't it? *How* this is all going to work."

"Yeah. But it will." Jake closed the crate behind him.

"How can you be so sure?"

He shrugged. "You haven't let me down yet. This will be no different."

Laney looked away, the emotion, the grief that was just under the surface choosing that moment to try to rise. "I'm not exactly in fighting shape right now."

"Hey, look at me."

Laney faced him.

"You *will* do this. I know you. You won't let people be hurt, not if you can help it. So I have no doubt you will succeed. But I also know how much you are already hurting. Mary Jane, the kids, they are a blessing. But I want you to know, you are my family too, Laney. And when this is all over, whatever you need, I'll be there."

Laney swallowed hard, the lump in her throat making it difficult to talk. "Thanks, Jake."

Captain Fielding chose that moment to walk up. "How's it going?"

Laney looked away, taking a breath and giving herself a moment to pull her emotions back.

"We're good," Jake said.

"Last of the planes are ready. We need to start getting the rest of your group on board. You guys ready?"

Laney looked at Jake, who nodded back at her. She squared her shoulders. "Let's get this show on the road."

Chapter Seventy-One

LANEY'S PEOPLE had been split up amongst three of the planes. She tried not to think that was done so the government could keep an eye on them, but it was difficult not to. She was on the last plane. She saw everyone else into their seats and made sure gear was double-checked before she stepped onto the Lockheed Martin C-5M Super Galaxy. It seemed that all of the two hundred soldiers inside watched as she climbed up the ramp.

Well, this isn't awkward, she thought as she ignored the prying eyes. Jake stood up and waved her over to an empty seat next to him. Henry was on the other side. Laney made her way over to them. Across from them, Jen sat with Gina and Jen's brothers. Matt and Hanz, one of the SIA agents, sat next to Henry. Mustafa, Gina, and Yoni were in one of the other planes with Lou, Rolly, and Danny. She wasn't sure which plane exactly David had disappeared into. But she saw him speaking with Maldonado and Susan so she figured they were together in one of the other planes.

We're just getting started and I'm already having trouble keeping track of my people.

She took a seat between Jake and Henry and quickly strapped herself in. The ramp started to close. Fielding walked down the fuselage, nodding at Laney as he passed on his way to his seat toward the front. In what seemed like only seconds, they were taxiing down the runway and taking off into the sky.

Laney settled back into her seat, letting out a breath. Minutes later, they had started to level out. An image of Drake's smile floated through her mind.

Where you go, I go, Ring Bearer. Pain, sharp and deep, cut through her chest. She sucked in a breath.

He had left. He was gone. He was leaving her to fight this battle on her own.

Henry looked down at her, concern etched into his face. "Laney? You okay?"

She nodded, trying to keep back the tears that wanted to fall. She could feel the eyes of the soldiers on her. The last thing she needed was to burst into tears in front of them. It wouldn't exactly instill confidence in her abilities.

But the image of Drake had been the first crack in her defenses. One by one, as memories of Drake and Cleo rolled through her mind, the defense against her grief began to crumble.

She gripped the edge of her seat, trying to hold back the tide, but she didn't think she'd be able to do it this time. Since Yoni had woken her up, she'd kept herself busy, checking on people, speaking with Fielding, handling a million last-minute details. But now, like last night, all those distractions were gone. Now, all she had was time and nothing else to think about.

"We're going to need these seats, gentlemen," Jen said.

Laney looked up. Jen and Gina stood in front of her, shooing Jake and Henry out of their seats. Hanz and Matt now stood in the middle of the fuselage, blocking her from the view of the other soldiers.

Jake frowned. "What are you—"

Jen placed her hands on her hips. "I love you, Jake, but you need to move, or I'm going to move you."

Jake glanced over at Laney, understanding flashing across his face. He quickly undid his straps. Henry was already up and standing with Matt and Hanz, offering more cover.

Jen slipped into Henry's seat, and Gina took Jake's as soon as he left it. Each of them took one of Laney's hands. Jen squeezed Laney's hand gently. "We're here, Lanes."

She just nodded as the tears rolled down her face.

Gina leaned over, speaking quietly. "Cry, Laney. Let it out. You have nothing to prove to us."

Laney's chest shuddered. "I don't know if I can do this."

Gina squeezed her hand. "You can. We all can. Everyone's carrying invisible wounds into this fight. But we'll get through."

Laney stared at her, reading the pain in the Marine Corps major's eyes. "What happened?"

Gina tried to give her a smile, but it was too sad to truly be considered that. "I learned yesterday that my mom passed away. She had a stroke shortly after the charges against me were manufactured. She lasted a month, but . . ." Gina shrugged.

Now it was Laney's turn to offer comfort. "I'm sorry."

"My sisters are blaming me. Saying the stress of my situation is what caused the stroke."

"That's crazy," Jen said.

"That's grief," Gina said. "But feeling that pain, it's a

reminder of what can be good in this world. You had two people you loved with all your heart. Never doubt they loved you back just as fiercely." Gina wiped away a tear at the corner of her eyes before it could fall, and Laney knew her words were not directed just at her.

"Drake and Cleo loved you, Laney," Jen said. "There are a lot of things in this world we can doubt. But you can't doubt that."

Laney looked over at Jen, who had her other hand resting on top of her baby bump. It hadn't been that long ago that Jen had lost her first child to this madness. And now she was going into this fight not knowing what the days ahead would hold for this child.

"We'll get through this. Together." Jen laid her head on Laney's shoulder. Laney leaned her head into her friend's and squeezed Gina's hand. They were right. They'd all been through a lot. They were all walking into this fight with open wounds. But they'd do what needed to be done. Because to do any less would be to ensure the pain they felt now was dwarfed by the pain to come. Not just for them but for people everywhere.

She shuddered, glancing up at her shield keeping her hidden from the prying eyes of strangers. It meant that for right now, she could let herself feel the pain, the loss. Because if she didn't let some of it out now, she would explode. So she let the memories of Drake and Cleo run through her mind, an unending loop as the tears rolled down her cheeks.

And her two friends held her hands, giving her their love and support.

Chapter Seventy-Two

THEY WERE an hour outside of Cairo when Fielding made his way to the back of the plane. Jen tapped Laney's shoulder, rousing her from sleep. "Heads up, Lanes. Military man on approach."

Laney blinked her eyes a few times, bringing her surroundings into focus. Gina was asleep on her other side. The guys were dozing across from her. Laney wiped at her eyes, feeling the crustiness there from her earlier cry. But Gina was right. She did feel better letting it out. Her heart still ached. She knew that wasn't going to go away for a long time, but sharing it had made it a little more bearable.

"I need to speak with you," Fielding said quietly. He looked over at Jake. "You too."

Laney undid her straps, following Fielding to the front of the plane, Jake right behind her. Fielding didn't speak as they passed the mostly sleeping soldiers. The few that were awake watched their passage with curiosity. Fielding opened the door at the end of the fuselage. There was a small hallway and then another door leading to the cockpit. A soldier was waiting for them, a laptop open on top of a stack of two crates.

"This is Lieutenant Vigo Schmidt. He's one of our intelligence operatives. Schmidt, show them what you showed me."

Schmidt hit a few keys and then turned the laptop screen around so Laney and Jake could view it. "This is our latest drone imagery."

Immediately Laney's eyes were drawn to the Great Pyramid before shifting to the two lesser pyramids beside it. The Sphinx also came into view as the drone continued on its flight.

Then the drone was past them. All Laney could see was sand. But then a darker spot appeared along the horizon. She frowned, leaning forward trying to get a better picture. Was that—

Static flashed across the screen. Laney straightened. "What happened?"

"The drone was shot down," Fielding said.

"By who?" Jake asked.

"We're not sure. We have some of our military in place. They went to go check. Communication with them died almost as soon as they reached the same spot. We haven't heard any word from them since. But we did manage to clean up that image in the background." He nodded to Schmidt, who hit a few keys on the computer. The image they'd seen before was now shown in a much higher resolution. The image was still blurry, but they could make out one thing. "Those are troops."

"Yes. And the drone and our reconnaissance attempts have been rebuffed. It seems safe to assume they are not on our side."

"How far from the Great Pyramid are they?"

"Less than two miles," Fielding said.

"They know," Laney said quietly. "They know we're going to the pyramids." They all knew that the Chinese knew they were heading for Egypt. But they had been holding out hope that they did not know their specific destination.

"That seems to be true," Fielding said.

"What about the Egyptian military? Where do they stand in all this?" Jake asked.

"They sent troops to intercept as well." Fielding shook his head. "None of them returned. And their bases were bombed by the Russians ten minutes ago. Even if they wanted to help, they won't have the manpower or machinery to do so. And we've had confirmation that the full scope of the Chinese and now Russian forces will actually arrive sooner than we estimated."

"Can we make up the time?" Jake asked.

"The pilots are pushing as far as they dare. We'll make up a little, but they will reach Giza before us."

LANEY WAS STANDING on the ramp as soon as the wheels touched down. Henry, Matt, Hanz, and Jake were with her along with seven other enhanced individuals from Havenville.

Jake tapped Laney's shoulder. "The first team is at the rendezvous."

Laney nodded. The first plane had landed five minutes ahead of them. The enhanced individuals had bolted from the plane as soon as it touched down, heading for the Plateau.

"We'll be right behind you," Jake said.

Laney looked over her shoulder at Jen and Gina. Gina gave her a tight smile, but Jen grinned broadly, giving her a thumbs-up. "Go kick some ass," Jen yelled, making more than a few other people smile.

Laney nodded, turning toward the door as it started to open. As soon as she could pass through, Laney sprinted, blurring over the ground. She would meet up with the other enhanced and get a read on the situation—numbers, weapons—and communicate it back to the others as they raced toward them.

Jen would stay behind with Gina at the command center, much to her chagrin.

In mere minutes, she was slamming to a stop as tingles ran over her skin. Matt stopped next to her, nodding at the group in front of them. "Good to see you guys."

Laney said nothing, just walked past them and up a dune to look over the area.

Henry followed her. "Laney?"

So many tingles ran over her skin it felt like a small voltage charge. "Oh my God."

Matt was at her side in seconds. "What's wrong?"

"They're Fallen. All of them."

"How many?"

Laney cast her gaze across the sand. She still couldn't see them. But she could feel them. Every. Single. One.

"Hundreds."

Chapter Seventy-Three

AFTER LANEY SPOKE, Matt immediately relayed the information back to Jake, but Laney stayed where she was. When Matt got off the phone, he said, "They're fifteen minutes away."

"We need more information. We need to get closer."

Henry shook his head. "No one's been able to get close."

Laney smiled. "Well, I'm not no one."

Henry's eyes nearly leapt out of his skull. "Laney, you can't be serious. We need to keep you at the back of the pack. You have a very important job to fulfill."

"I know. But they can't sense me. They can sense you guys, and they can see humans coming from a mile away. I'm the only one who stands a chance."

"Matt, tell her she's crazy."

Matt looked at her speculatively. "If we send another drone to feed us back images and maybe distract them, it would allow you a chance to get closer."

Laney slapped him on the back. "See? Let's do that."

Henry glared at Matt. "I'd like to speak with Laney alone for a minute."

Laney blew out a breath. Henry's overprotectiveness was now apparently extending to her. "Matt, arrange for the drone."

"Will do." He hustled down the dune.

Laney turned to Henry, holding up her hand as he began to speak. "Henry, whatever you are going to say, save it. We need to know what they are doing. Keeping me in the dugout for the last play is not going to work if they've already run up the score."

"I'm not sure that analogy works."

"I'm not a sports fan. But you know what I mean. We need to see what's happening. Matt will distract them and I will be very careful."

Henry looked down at her. "I'm not ready to lose you."

But you're going to have to. The words were on the tip of her tongue but she couldn't say them. She knew how much her death was going to hurt Henry because she knew how much his would hurt her. "I know. But we each have a role to play here."

Laney glanced down at Matt, who gave her a nod. "The drone will be in position in five minutes," he said.

"I've got this. Okay?"

Henry pulled her into a hug, his voice gruff. "Just be careful, okay?"

"I promise." She held him close, taking comfort in his warmth. *I love you, big brother.* The words once again were on the edge of her tongue, but she couldn't say them.

Because she knew he would interpret them as goodbye.

———

The Belial Sacrifice

LANEY STAYED low on the dune. The drone had done its trick, distracting the group she'd snuck up on long enough for her to get past them. Her destination was just ahead: a military truck. Tingles ran over her skin, so she knew there were two Fallen inside.

She waited by the side of the road and tapped her wrist unit. Seconds later, the drone exploded. The soldier in the back of the truck leaned out to get a better look while the driver leaned out his window. Laney burst from her hiding place.

She grabbed the front of the uniform of the soldier in the back of the truck and slammed him into the ground face first. He didn't even have time to yell. And then, with his jaw now at the back of his skull, he didn't have the ability.

Laney blurred around the side of the truck. She yanked open the passenger door. Grabbing on to the edge of the doorframe, she leaped in, her feet flying toward the driver's face.

He jolted back at the last second, so Laney only caught him in the chin and nose. She slammed her elbow into his nose, and before he could react, she slipped both hands around his head and with a vicious yank, broke his neck.

Heart pounding, Laney scanned the area. She sensed no additional movement, Fallen or otherwise. The keys were in the ignition. Letting herself out the passenger door, she walked around and pulled the driver out. Hoisting him over her shoulder, she carried him to the back of the truck. She rolled the other soldier onto his back. The man's wounds were already healing. He'd come to in a few minutes.

She pulled her gun, aiming it at him but could not pull the trigger. She had killed before. And she knew this was war, but she just couldn't do it. It felt too much like cold-blooded murder. She holstered her weapon, her gaze straying to the back of the truck. Crates were loaded in there, a few of them open.

She climbed into the back of the truck. Inspecting the open truck, she found padding inside with rectangles cut into them four inches deep and about nine inches long. A quick check of the other open crates showed the same setup.

Words were written on the side, but being they were in Chinese, that was of no help.

She tapped the mike at her throat. "Are you guys getting this?"

"We are," Jake replied. "I don't like the look of it."

"Can someone translate this?"

"Hold on."

Laney moved back to the end of the truck as Jake came back with a reply. "Those crates held explosives."

Laney cursed softly. That had been her guess.

"The military thinks they may have created IEDs to slow us down."

A reasonable guess, Laney thought as her gaze strayed ahead to where she could make out the peak of the Great Pyramid. A cold feeling rolled over her. "I need to check something out."

"What?"

"I— Just give me a minute, okay?" Laney hopped out the back of the truck. One of the soldiers was almost fully healed. The other's neck had realigned. Laney pulled out her Omni bullets and fired one into each of their legs, careful to make sure she didn't hit anything critical.

Then she hustled to the front of the truck and hopped into the driver's seat. "Laney, what are you doing?" Jake asked.

Laney put the truck in gear, struggling a little with the old shifter. "Taking a little drive."

Laney headed down the road, grabbing a cap from the floor of the cab and placing it on her head. Not much of a disguise, but hopefully no one would get too close.

There was a bag on the floor of the passenger side. Laney grabbed it, rummaging through. *Yes.* She pulled out a pair of binoculars. A mile down the road, she still hadn't seen anyone else, but she didn't want to push her luck. She pulled over to the side of the road, hopped out, and headed for the nearest dune before turning back to the truck and propping up the hood. It might give her a few extra seconds before someone realized she didn't belong there.

Laney hustled up the dune, army-crawling the last few feet to the top. Glancing around, she saw two soldiers on another dune about three hundred yards to her right. Being she got no read from them, she knew they were not enhanced. But they could still pose a problem. Careful to keep her movements slow and not draw attention, she pulled the binoculars up and scanned the area across from her. There were hundreds of troops creating a perimeter around the Giza Plateau.

She squinted, trying to make out what they were doing. There were dark spots on the Pyramid and more spots being added. *What are you—*

Her breath caught as she realized what she was looking at.

Please let me be wrong, please let me be wrong. She increased the magnification. But as the image became clearer, she knew she was not wrong.

Oh my God. With a shaky hand, she tapped the mike, her fear spiking. "They're going to blow up the Pyramid."

Chapter Seventy-Four

IT WAS SMART. Crazy, but smart. If the Pyramid was what stood in the way of them having an undefeatable army, well, they'd simply take it off the playing field.

At the same time, it was hard to wrap her mind around it. The Great Pyramid had stood as the world's greatest mystery for thousands of years, and now some people had decided that all that history, all that wonder the Pyramid evoked, didn't count next to their plans.

It wasn't the first time history had been trodden over during war. The most recent attacks came in one of the oldest regions of the world: Iraq and Syria. Spearheaded by ISIS, the latest attacks involved taking bulldozers and explosives to archaeological sites, some thousands of years old. In 2015, ISIL destroyed multiple sites in the ancient city of Palmyra, including a temple to the ancient god Baal and the 1,900-year-old Temple of Baalshamin. Other attacks included the destruction of, with pickaxes and sledgehammers, the Mosul Museum, home of the artifacts from the ancient city of Nineveh, which flourished from 900 BC–600

BC. And who could forget the destruction of the 1,700-year-old Buddhas in Afghanistan destroyed by the Taliban?

Of course, those weren't in the course of a war. Those were intentionally destroyed for other reasons. But in the course of war, intentional acts of destruction had destroyed incredible sites. The Library of Alexandria was destroyed by troops of Julius Caesar in 48 BCE. But more modern wars had also destroyed incredible sites. During World War II, the 14th-century cathedral of St. Michael's in England was razed. During Libya's civil war, Cyrene, the Athens of Africa, which dated to 630 BC, was all but destroyed. In 2005, the upper part of the Great Mosque of Samarra, Iraq, dating to the ninth century, was devastated by air raids. During the Bosnian War, Croatians intentionally shelled the Stari Most, a bridge create by 16th-century Ottoman ruler Suleiman the Magnificent. And the list went on.

She supposed she shouldn't be surprised by the planned destruction in front of her, and yet somehow she had hoped humanity had learned from its past. Of course, if it kept destroying its past, it never would.

She scanned the area, trying to figure out the best way in. *Maybe I could—*

"Do not even think about going in there on your own," Jake ordered through her earpiece. "Get back here, and let's figure out a plan."

For a split second, Laney was tempted to ignore him. But then reality hit: They needed to make sure that the Pyramid was safe. And going in alone would only serve to probably get herself killed and the Pyramid would still be destroyed. "Fine. I'm on my way."

Laney dropped the binoculars. She didn't need them anymore. She started to crawl back when a yell sounded from her right. One of the soldiers on the other dune was pointing at her. The other one was talking into his radio. *Time to go*.

Giving up stealth, she ran down the dune as shots rang out. But she was already a blur, disappearing through the sands before they were anywhere near her.

Chapter Seventy-Five

IQUITOS, PERU

LUIZ'S RANCH WAS BEAUTIFUL. With the mountains in the background, it was like a little slice of paradise. It seemed so far removed from the rest of the world. There were no neighbors in view. Luiz said his closest were miles and miles away. And yet Patrick could not just let himself enjoy the peace, because as ideal as the setting appeared, it was a mirage.

Tiger leaned into Patrick, placing his head on Patrick's lap. Patrick wiped a tear from his cheek. "I miss her too, boy."

Jen had called them a short while ago with the news about Cleo. Patrick still could not wrap his mind around it. A blood clot? An embolism? Something so mundane? With everything surrounding them, it was a stark reminder that death could come in many forms.

Tiger had been muted since the news. He hadn't left Patrick's side either, except for right after he heard the news. He'd disappeared, and minutes later the cats all let out a cry that echoed through the valley. Everyone went still. The hair on Patrick's arms had stood on end as their cries rose and then cut off. The cats' pain was a visceral thing. Cleo had been one of them. She had led them. She had taken on the role of elder in their group and shown them the ropes. She had let them know that these humans they found themselves with now could be trusted.

It could have easily gone the other way. With the torture they experienced at the hands of Ruggio in his lab, they could have rejected any attempts to link up with humans. They could have rightly seen humans as a threat and responded accordingly. But Cleo, she helped them understand. How different their world would be if she had not been there.

The sun was getting low in the sky. Patrick knew he should get back. He needed to see that Nyssa's dinner was taken care of. Cain had locked himself in his room with the Tome. He didn't want to miss anything that might help Laney and her team.

His heart felt heavy at the thought of her. Losing Drake, then Cleo—he wanted to talk to her. He wanted to see how she was doing. But she would only lie to him. Not out of spite or anything like that, but ever since he'd lost the use of his legs, she'd been careful about what she said to him. He knew she was worried about him. That she didn't want to add to his stress. But worrying about her—he was always going to do that. Even if they had never started down this belial path, he would have worried about her. That's what you did when you loved someone.

He knew how strong she was. He wasn't sure she even realized how strong she was. But these two losses . . .

He'd seen her with Drake. Seen how Drake had looked at her. To be honest, the irreverent archangel was not who Patrick would have chosen for her. But he also knew Drake would have stopped the world to protect her. And that had given Patrick comfort. But now Drake was gone too. He didn't really understand that part. Drake being Michael? He couldn't see that. Michael was God's sword, the ultimate warrior. He'd seen no indication of that in Drake. But could he turn completely against Laney? Wouldn't a part of him still hold on to the love he had for her?

He laid a hand on Tiger's. "Come on, boy. We need to get back." Tiger lifted his head, moving slowly. Patrick leaned down and pushed against the wheels of his chair. They squeaked. He managed to turn himself around, but the trip back was a rocky one. Luiz's ranch was not exactly wheelchair accessible. Bas had taken it upon himself, with the aid of a few others, to create some wooden paths and ramps through the ranch to allow Patrick to get around on his own. Patrick appreciated it. He did not want to be a burden people had to help get from point A to point B. But wooden paths were not the smoothest.

Ahead, three of the cats were lying down in the shade of a tree. Tiger stopped, looking up at Patrick. Patrick nodded. "Go on."

Tiger held his gaze for a moment before heading toward the cats. He had the gait of a much older cat now.

Patrick stopped twenty feet from the entrance ramp to Luiz's main house. He took a breath, flexed his fingers, and then headed forward, trying to pick up speed. He crested the ramp, feeling the small thrill of victory. The main ramp was a little steeper than most. Pulling the long shoehorn from the back of his wheelchair, he hooked the door handle and pulled it open. Pushing himself inside, he replaced the shoehorn, wondering why he hadn't been carrying one around before. It had been Luiz's idea, and it had made some things a lot easier. He rolled down the long hallway, the smell of food making his stomach rumble.

"Ah, Señor Patrick!" Luiz smiled from behind the large colorful island. "Perfect timing. We are about to eat. I thought we could all eat outside tonight. It is beautiful, yes?"

"It sure is."

Mary Jane washed her hands, then dried them on a towel. "Do you think Cain will be able to join us?"

Patrick shook his head. "I'll ask, but I doubt it. He's in research mode."

"I thought that might be the case." She walked over to the island and picked up a bamboo tray with plates loaded with food and a thermos. "I'll go take this to him."

Patrick reached up his hands. "You know, I think I'd like to take that. I want to check on him anyway."

Mary Jane eyed his chair. "Are you sure?"

"Yes."

Mary Jane handed him the tray. Patrick looked down at it with a little concern. Perhaps he'd spoken a little too soon.

"I have just the thing." Luiz rounded the island, pulling two small bungee cords from his pockets. He wound one through one handle on the wheelchair and then the other through the handle on the tray. He did the same for the other side before stepping back with a grin. The tray was now secured to Patrick's chair. "What do you think?"

Patrick smiled. "Luiz, we are going to have to talk about your ideas. I think I need you to make me a little bag with things you think I can use."

"I would love to." Luiz headed back to the island.

Mary Jane stepped a little closer, dropping her voice. "How are you doing?"

Patrick shrugged. "I guess as good as any of us."

"Yeah. I tried to call Jake, but I couldn't reach him."

"Don't read into that. Knowing him, he's turned his phone off or he's in a spot with bad reception. Don't worry until you have to."

"That's not so easy."

"No, it's not."

Mary Jane seemed to shake herself into action. "Well, let me start getting this food out. Will you be joining us?"

"Yes. Nyssa is . . ."

"With Molly and Susie. She's fine."

"Okay. I'll drop this off, make sure he eats a little, and come join you."

She smiled before heading back to the platters of food. Patrick turned around and headed down the hall. He turned at the first hallway. Luiz had handed over his study to Cain. Patrick made his way to the door at the end of the hall. It was closed. He knocked.

"Cain, it's me." Patrick turned the handle and started pushing himself in.

Cain's head jolted upright from the desk, his eyes wild. "I need a phone."

"What's wrong?"

Cain ran a hand through his hair. "I need to warn her."

Patrick's heart started to pound. "Warn her about what?"

"The sacrifice. I know what the sacrifice is."

"What?"

Cain's bloodshot eyes met Patrick's. "It's her."

Chapter Seventy-Six

GIZA, EGYPT

LANEY HAD MANAGED to avoid the snipers on the other dune, but she sensed a dozen Fallen between her and her people. She diverted east to avoid them, then paused on a dune. Four trucks were barreling down the road. They were identical to the truck with the explosives. She pictured the explosives already placed on the Pyramid. They would need a lot more to take it down, and it looked like they had come to the same consensus.

She sensed four Fallen per truck. Sixteen versus one: not great odds. But then she smiled. *Of course, I don't have to fight them directly*. Laney knelt on one knee, casting a glance at the bright blue sky above her. Clouds rolled in across the sun, darkening as they grew.

Lightning lashed out, striking each of the trucks.

"Laney, is that you?" Jake asked, but she didn't answer, needing to focus on her targets.

A few soldiers stumbled from the back of the trucks. Wind yanked them from their feet, tossing them into the sky before flinging them across the dunes. Laney crept toward the nearest truck, sensing only two Fallen left. She peered into the first cab. The two occupants were crispy. She blanched.

"Laney, what's going on?" Jake demanded.

"Do you have my location?" Laney asked.

"Yeah."

"They're bringing in more explosives. I've stopped them for now, but we can't let them get through to the pyramids. Can you take out the trucks?"

"It will take a few minutes to arrange."

Tingles rolled over her skin, and her head snapped up, her gaze narrowing as she looked toward the east. "And I'm going to need some reinforcements. I've got incoming."

She dropped the radio. The first dozen soldiers crested the dune and swept down toward her in a wave.

One soldier broke free, his gaze locked on Laney. She intercepted him as he threw a punch at her face. She slipped the punch, catching him with a hook to his stomach as she moved to his side. A second blow had him screaming as it landed on his kidney. An uppercut from underneath his arm sent him flying off his feet.

Laney had no time to appreciate the arc of his flight as the rest reached her. She back-kicked the first guy near her before lashing out with side kicks to two soldiers flanking her. Someone grabbed her shoulder, and she reached back, contorting his wrist. Turning, she kneed him in the face.

A side kick to her ribs sent her flying. She managed to roll as she hit. As she did, she heard the first truck start up and head down the road. But there was nothing she could do as a soldier charged her. She got to her knees and, lunging forward, she buried her shoulder into his knee. She hit so hard she heard the kneecap dislodge. He screamed, and she crawled up him and whipped her elbow across his chin.

A bullet crashed into her shoulder. The bulletproof vest stopped it, but it still hurt like heck. She rolled, pain charging through her as she jolted her shoulder and grabbed the man she'd taken down, using him as a shield. She crouched down, wincing at the thuds against the man's body.

Gunfire sounded from a different position. "That you guys?" Laney yelled into her earpiece.

"Yes," came Jake's terse response.

She peered out and saw muzzle flashes from a nearby dune. The bullets aimed at her stopped. Laney peered out as Henry blurred to a stop in front of her. He hauled her up.

"One of the trucks got away. We need to—"

Henry's face paled.

Laney whirled around. Half a dozen armored vehicles were heading toward them from the same direction the truck had disappeared. Another three gunships were behind them. A whistling noise sounded. Henry grabbed Laney and dove to the side as an explosion erupted thirty feet away from them.

Laney spit out sand as explosion after explosion rang out. She grabbed Henry. "We need to find where that's coming from."

"I've got it," Matt yelled from somewhere to her right.

Matt blurred toward a truck with a large missile attachment along its back. Without stopping, he leaped for the bed of the truck. He grabbed the front of the missile launcher just as the trigger was pulled. Instead of going airborne, the missile slammed into the bed, sending shrapnel spiraling out in a giant ball of fire.

Laney ducked down as shards of metal littered the ground around her. She looked back in shock at the remains of the trucks as the gunships opened fire. Matt was gone.

The dying had officially begun.

THE NEXT HOUR felt like it lasted years. Part of the U.S. forces converged on Laney's spot while the rest initiated their assault on the perimeter around the plateau. Each time they seemed to gain an inch, another group of enhanced soldiers appeared out of nowhere. The U.S.'s intelligence had been correct: So far, she'd come across Chinese and Russian soldiers who seemed to be working in tandem. Even worse, they had created Omni bullets as well.

Laney tried to keep track of her people, but it soon proved impossible. She had also used almost all her Omni bullets. She crouched down low. "We need a better plan."

The one silver lining was that a U.S. gunship had managed to intercept the truck that had gotten away. The engine was destroyed, so it wasn't going anywhere, so at least they were getting no closer to destroying the Pyramid. Of course, they could just decide to go with what they had and detonate what they already had strung around the Pyramid. Or they could just launch missiles at the damn thing. Laney was wondering why they hadn't already done that. But she was betting they were holding off on that. She had to assume blowing up the Pyramid was a last resort.

"Got a problem," Danny's voice came through the radio.

"What?" Laney yelled as she jerked back just as gunfire tagged the truck she was hiding behind.

"A second truck has reached the first. They're transferring the explosives to the other truck."

"Is there anybody in front of us that can intercept?" Jake asked.

"Fielding here. Someone's moving on it."

Laney frowned. "What? Who?"

Jake's voice came back heavy. "It's Lou and Rolly."

Chapter Seventy-Seven

THE BATTLE HAD BEGUN. Jen could hear the fighting in the distance. She rolled her hands into fists, hating being on the outside but also knowing that she needed to protect her little one for as long as she could.

Jen slipped into the back of the control center and watched footage in real time. She managed to pick out Susan Jacobs on one camera. That woman had guts. But soon Susan became lost in the blur as the group she was with clashed with a group of soldiers who appeared as if by magic. The sound was off, but Jen imagined the screams and yells. She kept trying to figure out who the figures were on screen, and it was making her nuts. She slipped out of the tent just as quickly as she had slipped in.

She made her way over to the intelligence tent and peeked in. Danny was in the corner, an array of monitors around him, his focus shifting from the keyboard in front of him to each of the monitors on his sides. Another half dozen people were scattered around the tent with similar setups. An additional four moved from analyst to analyst, checking something off on a tablet.

Jen didn't step in. Danny didn't need the distraction. She walked toward the edge of the camp, passing two soldiers standing at a jeep.

"I don't know how we can trust them," one of the soldiers said. "I mean, what is Fielding thinking?"

"That we can use all the help we can get?" the other offered.

"I guess, but I still think when this is all over, we need to lock them all up."

Jen blew out a breath, trying not to yell at the idiot soldier. She'd heard more than a few similar comments since they'd linked forces with the government. Some ranged from basic curiosity to downright hate. None of the soldiers ever stopped talking when Jen was near. She figured her belly was throwing them off from figuring out she was also enhanced. But it angered her that the enhanced got no credit for laying their lives on the line, just like the regular soldiers were doing.

Jen climbed a sand dune at the edge of camp, looking toward the fight. She could see flashes of gunfire and occasionally a bigger explosion. *Please let them be all right.*

"Dr. Witt?"

Jen turned as a young soldier stood at the base of the dune, panting a little. She looked down at her. "Yes?"

"Um, Danny sent me. He said you have a phone call."

Jen's eyebrows raised. A phone call? Who would be calling her in the middle of all this? Everyone she knew was aware of what was going on. Most of them were in the middle of it. "Who is it?"

"Some man. He says his name is Cain?"

The Tome. Jen blurred toward the soldier. Her eyes went wide, and she stumbled back. "Where?"

"The-the intelligence tent."

Jen blurred back to the tent, scaring the heck out of a soldier carrying a tray of coffees toward it. He dropped all of them on the ground when she appeared almost right next to him. Jen ignored the poor soldier, striding into the tent. Danny glanced up as she entered. "Take my headset."

Jen grabbed the headset from his outstretched hand and settled it on her head. "Cain?"

Cain's voice had a desperate edge. "Jen, thank God."

"What is it? What's going on?"

"I've learned more about the sacrifice. I— You need to help her." Cain spoke quickly, and Jen listened in increasing horror. She told herself she'd known Laney would be at risk. But this, this guaranteed she would die.

"You have to help her."

"I will." She disconnected the call. Ripping off the headset, she tossed it at Danny before running out of the tent. She stopped in the middle of the camp, her eyes scanning the space.

Come on, think. The red cross on the white backdrop caught her attention. An idea began to form. Would that work?

She wasn't sure. To be honest, she wasn't sure anything would. But she had to try.

She headed for the tent, knowing she was going to need help. She ran through the list of people she knew, discounting all of them one by one. Henry, Jake, her brothers—they would never agree to what she had planned.

But she knew one person who would. She stepped into the med tent, spying Gina sitting at a desk. Gina looked up from checking supplies off on a checklist. She looked up.

One glance at Jen's face, and she placed the checklist on top of the cart and hurried over to her. "Jen? What's wrong?"

"I need to reach someone on the battlefield."

Gina didn't bother asking Jen any questions. She tugged her outside and two tents over. Pulling back the tent flap, Gina waved Jen in. Jen stepped in, her eyes taking a second to adjust to the dimmer light. Two rows of consoles were set up, a dozen people with headsets sitting in front of them. Jen made her way to the first one. "I need you to reach someone for me."

The man looked up at her. "Uh . . . ?"

Gina stepped next to Jen. "Do it."

With a quick glance at her rank, he nodded. "Yes, Major. Um, ma'am, who do you need to reach?"

"Someone with the Chandler Group. His name's Yoni Benjamin."

Chapter Seventy-Eight

A NEW WAVE of enhanced had broken over Laney and her group right after Jake's announcement. She had barely time to process it before she was fighting again. But as soon as she cleared the soldiers around her, taking one bullet to the thigh, she grabbed her mike. "Fielding, clear me a path to that truck!"

"We can't! All our resources are committed elsewhere."

Laney grit her teeth. "I'm going. So if you want me alive for the end game, I suggest you change some commitments."

Throughout the fight, Laney had been asking Fielding and central command for air support for five minutes, and they had refused. She didn't know if it was because they were telling her the truth, because they didn't want to risk her, or because they were just a-holes. But Lou had let out an ear-piercing scream two minutes ago, saying Rolly had been shot and she was out of Omni bullets.

Mustafa sprinted up the dune, panting heavily as he landed next to her. He had a large bandage wrapped around his right upper arm. Dirt and blood were sprayed across his face. She glanced past him. Jordan and Mike Witt were supposed to be with him. But it was David who looked back at her, a bandage on his arm seeping blood. She didn't ask where the Witt brothers were. She wasn't sure she wanted to know.

"What do you need?" he asked.

"I need to get to Lou and Rolly."

Mustafa nodded, grabbing his radio. "Danny, Laney needs a path to Lou and Rolly."

Of course. Why the hell hadn't she thought of Danny?

"On it," Danny said. "Follow the drones."

Laney crouched low, spying the three drones heading for her. One was blasted out of the sky, but the other two evaded the enemy fire.

Laney tensed, ready to move. Mustafa gripped her forearm. "Take care, Laney." She looked into his eyes, seeing the grief and commitment there. She nodded as the first explosion sounded. Then she was running flat out, praying she wasn't too late.

Laney's feet pounded down on the ground. She sensed Lou and Rolly ahead. But she also sensed someone right behind her.

"Laney, there's a gunship aiming for you!" Jake yelled through her earpiece.

She slowed as she shifted some of her focus to the sky above her. Turning to glance over her shoulder, she spotted the gunship barreling down on her. Laney sent a bolt of lightning through the ship, but not before it released a single missile.

Laney sensed Henry a second before he put on a burst of speed, yanking Laney to the side as she thrust a gust of wind at the missile. It shifted the missile so it landed farther to their left, but the blowback still sent the two of them flying. Laney rolled onto her hands and knees, her ears ringing. As she got to her feet, the ringing stopped.

Lou's terrified voice came over her earpiece. "He's bleeding out!"

"Don't move him!" Jake yelled.

Laney looked at Henry. Shrapnel covered his back, but she knew he'd heal in a few minutes. Minutes Lou and Rolly might not have.

He shook his head at her. "Laney—"

She took off before he could say any more. Sprinting across the ground, a bullet clipped her arm. She stumbled but recovered, barely slowing. She could hear the gunfire ahead. The truck had been stopped. She could just make out two figures huddled behind a wheel well. A soldier had his back to her, his attention completely focused on Lou and Rolly.

Growling with anger, Laney put on a burst of speed. She yanked the man back by the shirt, stomping him in the lower back. He screamed. Turning him, she grabbed his legs and then slammed his lower back into her knee, breaking it.

He passed out, his back broken, his body at an unnatural angle as he hit the ground.

Laney rushed past him. The kids were hidden behind the truck. Laney whipped around the side.

"Hold on, Rolly. Please hold on," Lou begged. Her head jolted up as Laney came to a stop.

Blood soaked the area around Rolly. His face was pale, his eyes closed. Without a word, Laney pulled out the Omni gun and fired into him.

The bullet tore into his leg. Laney dropped to the ground, ripping her sleeve off and pressing it to the wound.

Lou rocked back and forth, blood and dirt sprayed across her face, her eyes glossy with shock.

"Stay with me, Lou," said Laney.

Lou nodded but kept up her rocking. "He can't die. He can't die." She kept repeating the words over and over again.

The wound on his leg stopped bleeding. Not sure if it was because he'd lost all his blood volume or because the Omni had started to work, Laney reached down and ripped his pants further to see. The wound was starting to knit closed. Relief poured over her. "It's okay, Lou. He's going to be fine."

Lou didn't seem to hear her. Laney gripped her shoulders. "Lou, he's going to be fine. Okay?"

Lou stared at him before her gaze shifted to Laney. "He's okay?"

"He will be. Give him a few more minutes. Henry's right behind me. He'll help you get Rolly out of here. Head right back to base, okay?"

Lou nodded. "Base."

"Yes."

Laney stood up, wiping her hands on her pants to remove the blood and sand.

Laney inspected the truck. By some miracle, the tires were okay. And the engine didn't look like it had been touched. *Well, okay then.*

Laney opened the driver's door and pulled out the driver, letting him drop to the ground. He groaned. She reached down and snapped his neck.

Straightening, she had one foot on the running board when Lou's voice stopped her. She stood leaning against the side of the truck. "What are you doing?"

"I'm heading to the Pyramid."

"I'll go with you."

"No. You get Rolly safe."

"You're going to need help."

"No. You guys have all done your part. The next part is up to me."

"You're coming back, right?"

Laney just gave her a small smile and climbed into the cab. Starting the engine, she put the truck into gear. In the rearview mirror, she saw Lou pull Rolly away. Rolly's eyes were open. They'd be okay.

She turned her attention to the road ahead of her and pulled away.

I'm just not so sure about me.

Chapter Seventy-Nine

AS SOON AS Jake heard Lou's voice over the radio, he cursed softly and started packing up his gear as quickly as he could.

"What are you doing?" Dylan Jenkins asked from next to him.

"Laney's changing the plan." Jake started down the dune.

"How do you—"

Henry's voice cut through his earpiece, cutting off Dylan's words. "I'm with Lou and Rolly. Laney took off."

"Get them to safety, then wait for me. Do *not* go off on your own."

God damn it, Laney. Jake ran to a nearby Jeep that was already running. "I need this," he told the soldier standing next to it.

"Um, I'm not supposed to—"

"Don't care." Jake jumped in the driver's seat and pulled out.

"Henry, where are you?"

Henry's voice was breathless. "At the first-aid station."

"I'll meet you where you got Lou and Rolly."

Sand flew everywhere as he raced toward Henry's location. He'd barely tapped the brakes when Henry, his shirt shredded and stained with blood, flung open the driver's door. "I'm driving."

Jake didn't waste any time arguing. He just shifted over. Henry jumped in.

"Go, go, go," Jake said.

Henry needed no further urging. He barreled down the road, his knuckles white as they gripped the steering wheel. "You thinking what I'm thinking?" Henry asked.

Jake nodded, his gaze focused on the peak of the Great Pyramid ahead. "She's going to go for the Pyramid. Alone."

Chapter Eighty

LANEY PRESSED down on the gas pedal. She could hear the gunfire, the explosions. A jet flew overhead. She tensed but relaxed only slightly at seeing the American flag on the tail. She prayed they stayed on her side until at least after this battle.

Ahead, the Great Pyramid of Giza loomed. Two guards snapped to attention, pulling their weapons into their shoulders.

"Sorry, guys."

Wind slammed into the soldiers, throwing them into the air and landing them fifty feet away. They would not be waking up anytime soon.

Everything else was deserted. All other resources seemed to have been directed at the battle surrounding them. Laney frowned. That wasn't right. Even with the battle, protecting the Giza Plateau would be a priority. So where was everybody?

She slammed on the brakes as the answer came into view. A pile of twenty bodies lay at the side of the Queen's tomb. Laney scanned the area, looking for who had created the pile, but there was no one. Her gaze snapped back to the Pyramid. The black spots on the Pyramid were gone. She scanned the area, seeing a pile of explosives, wires trailing from them strewn around the Pyramid. What was going on?

She pressed down on the gas pedal, driving more cautiously, waiting for a Fallen to sprint out from behind one of the pyramids.

But he didn't come from the side. He came from the air like an avenging angel.

Laney slammed on the brakes as he dropped to the ground thirty feet in front of her. His head snapped up, and his gaze latched onto hers.

Everything inside of her went cold. *No.*

Laney put the truck in park, never pulling her gaze from the man in front of her. She stepped out of the truck, her pulse pounding. "Drake?"

Chapter Eighty-One

EVER SINCE SHE had stepped on the plane back in Virginia, she'd known Drake would be here somewhere. She had hoped he would be helping her, shaking off whatever had happened in David's townhouse. But if not, she hoped, he would at most watch. She flicked a glance at the bodies and explosives. Did that mean he was helping her?

The man in front of her smiled, but nothing in his face or body conveyed Drake's spirit. "I am Michael."

Laney swallowed hard. "What are you doing? Are you here to help me?"

He shook his head. "God's will *will* be done."

Laney shook her head as well. "No, he can't want this. He can't want the world to devolve into this. People will die. People will suffer. Good people, children."

Michael shrugged. "That is not my concern."

"Not your concern? What is wrong with you? Where is Drake?"

"Drake does not exist. He never did."

Laney's heart clenched. "No. That's not true. He was real. He is real. You *are* Drake."

Michael's lip curled. "When I chose to become human, I forgot my duty. I forgot where my loyalty lies. Because of you."

He spit the words at her. And each one hit her like a blow. She pictured Drake the last morning they'd been together, before the Pope had uttered those words. She held on to that image of Drake as she stared into the cold, unfeeling eyes of the man in front of her.

"Because you loved me. Because you love me still."

He shook his head. "No. The human part of me is dead. I am an archangel. I am not human. And you must leave this place. I know what you intend to do, and I cannot allow it."

"Allow it? Who are you to—"

Michael strode forward. "I am the soldier most high. I am undefeatable. I am God's sword."

Laney held her ground, but inside she was shaking. "This can't be what he wants. This can't be what you want. You've seen the destruction that has already happened. The abilities of the Fallen must be removed. They were never meant for mankind."

He glared at her. "That is not your choice to make."

Anger began to burn inside of her. "It damn well is! I was chosen to hold back the Fallen. I am *mankind's* shield. And I *choose* to end the reign of the Fallen."

"You will have to go through me to accomplish your task."

Laney's heart ached as she stared at him, looking for any inkling of Drake in the heartless being in front of her. But there was nothing. No light, no sparkle of wit, nothing to tell her that Drake still resided in that body she knew so well. But still she hesitated. "There has to be another way."

"You still intend to end the reign of the Fallen?"

Laney nodded.

"Then you have sealed your fate."

Michael moved so fast, Laney could barely register his movement. But years of fighting had ingrained within her instinctual responses. His fist flew past her face as she shifted to the side. She wrapped her hand around his forearm, pulling him off balance before slamming her other hand into his back then slamming her palm underneath his chin, forcing his head over his shoulders.

He crashed into the ground on his back, then brought his feet up. Laney jumped back before he could up kick her. He jumped to his feet instead, circling to his right.

"Don't do this," Laney begged, circling as well, keeping her hands in front of her. "Please, there has to be another way."

Michael didn't answer her in words. He feinted to the left, then threw a side kick at her ribs. Laney slammed her hands down on his kick, forcing it to the ground and snapping her own kick at his knee, buckling it. He swung out with a back fist, catching her in the chin. She flew backward, the side of her face throbbing. But she had no time to worry about that as Michael vaulted over to her. She ducked, rolling to the side and getting back on her feet. He threw a kick at her knees. She stepped to a forty-degree angle toward him, avoiding the kick but slamming her fist into his ribs. An elbow to his chin followed by an uppercut, and now he was the one flying backward before righting himself just as quickly.

She wasn't surprised. Her punches, though devastating to a human, were not her full power. She was pulling them.

She knew she shouldn't, but a small piece of hope clung to the inside of her heart, telling her Drake was still in there somewhere. "Drake, please. We can fix this."

"Drake is gone." Michael jumped at her, his fist aiming at her face, but he shifted at the last second and tackled her at the waist.

She had no way to avoid the move even as she brought her knee up, connecting with his nose before she crashed onto her back.

Michael wrapped his arms around her, but Laney managed to wriggle her right arm out, pressing her forearm against his throat to keep him from squeezing her to death. "Drake! Drake! I know you're in there!"

Michael glared down at her, but his grip weakened. "Laney," he whispered, sweat on his brow, his teeth gritted.

"Drake!" She started to release her grip.

"No, no." His words came out tortured, as if each word was pushed through a vice. "I'm not in control. You have to kill me."

Tears pricked at her eyes. "No, no, I can't."

"He will kill you, Laney. You need to live."

She stared up at him, remembering meeting him, the fight at the biker bar in Vegas with Ralph, him tearing through the back wall at Drew's cabin and saving her. Waking up after reliving her life as Helen and realizing who he was. Moment after moment flew through her mind, each one more precious than the last. She stroked his cheek. "Come back to me."

"I can't. He's too strong." He opened his eyes, and Drake looked back at her. Love, pride, and fear all mingled together in his eyes. "Kill me, Laney, it's the only way. Michael won't stop. I won't stop."

She shook her head, her heart breaking. "No. Don't ask me to do this."

"Love . . .you . . ." His eyes flickered, his gaze narrowing as his grip tightened. "Goodbye, Ring Bearer."

Chapter Eighty-Two

HENRY TORE down the path toward the Great Pyramid. Jake could not tear his eyes off of Michael and Laney. When he'd first seen Drake, he'd been relieved. Then Drake had sprung for her. And now he knew what Matt and David had meant when they said Drake was no longer Drake.

Jake's whole body was tense. He had worried about whether or not the capstone would rise, whether it would do what they hoped it would do. He had never worried about Laney getting to the Pyramid and releasing the capstone. But now as he watched the man she loved try to kill her, he knew she was in trouble. And if she was in trouble, they were all in trouble.

Jake grabbed his M4. Ahead, Drake tackled Laney at the waist. Henry sucked in a breath.

"Henry, turn the car!"

Henry swiveled the wheel to the right as Jake brought his weapon up to his shoulder, flipping to automatic as he took aim. He unleashed twenty shots, all into Michael's back.

Michael flung himself away. Laney flipped onto her stomach and crawled away.

Jake knew some of the shots had gone through Michael and into her, but he didn't have a choice. Henry blurred out of the car, reaching Laney's side. He dropped down, pulling her into his lap.

Jake sprinted toward them, cursing the sand, cursing his refusal to take the Omni. Cursing every stupid thing that had led them to this moment. He scanned the area, looking for signs of Drake. He knew he would need time to heal. But he wasn't sure how much time. Archangels seemed to get a little more of everything than regular Fallen, so he guessed they probably healed quicker too.

Movement flashed behind Laney and Henry. "Behind you!" Jake yelled.

Henry vaulted to his feet as Laney rolled to the side. Henry slipped the first punch and the second, managing to catch Michael on the side of the head with a hook. Laney stumbled to her feet, then launched a jumping side kick that caught Michael in the ribs and sent him sprawling.

"Get back!" Laney yelled at Henry, shoving him aside.

Michael caught her with a fist right in the stomach that doubled her over. Then he brought his knee up, slamming it in to her face so hard blood sprayed across the sand.

Henry yelled, launching a side kick at the back of Michael before sliding his arm around Michael's neck. Michael released Laney with his right hand only long enough to elbow Henry in the cheek. Then he turned, his hand grabbing Henry's face.

Jake opened fire, but Michael acted as if he didn't even feel the bullets. He twisted Henry's head violently that Jake's breath slammed to a stop as he pictured Henry's head snapping from his shoulders.

But he needn't have worried about that. Like a magician, that was the distraction. It was the other hand Jake should have been watching. Because before he realized his intent, Michael plunged his hand through Henry's chest and yanked out his heart.

Chapter Eighty-Three

LANEY ROLLED TO HER SIDE, her face on fire. Time slowed to a snail's pace as she watched Michael grip Henry's face before his hand went through his chest. In slow motion, she saw Henry's heart drop to the ground. Vaguely, she heard Jake yelling, even over the sound of gunfire. But a buzzing had started in her ears that seemed to be drowning everything else out. She stared at Henry's face, all life in it gone.

He killed Henry. He killed Henry. Drake killed Henry.

It didn't seem real. It was like she was in a dream. An incredibly horrible dream.

"*Laney!*" Jake yelled.

His voice cut through the haze around her. She snapped back into the present, her gaze narrowing on the archangel. He strode toward Jake, arrogance in his step.

No. He's not Drake. Drake didn't kill him. Michael did.

She surged forward, power rolling through her. Lightning strikes slammed into Michael over and over again. Wind picked him up, slamming him into the side of the

Pyramid, leaving a crater. He tumbled down the side, landing in a heap at its base.

She stalked toward him even as she had the wind pin him against the Pyramid. He smiled as she approached. "You can't stop—"

She didn't give him a chance to finish as she silenced the wind. She slammed a hook into his chin. Then she couldn't tell what she threw. She just didn't stop. Every death, every injury, every injustice that had led to this moment, she took out on the body of the archangel who had thrown Drake away and who had taken the life of Henry. His blood sprayed, his bones broke, but she did not care. She was shaking from anger, from grief, from it all, but she continued to wail away.

Finally, she stopped. The face in front of her was unrecognizable. His eyes were closed, his cheekbones shattered, blood dribbled down his chin. She grabbed him by the hair. "Look at me!"

He managed to open one eyelid halfway.

"You are not from Heaven. You are from Hell. Now go back there." She plunged her hand through his chest and ripped out *his* heart.

Chapter Eighty-Four

JAKE DIDN'T KNOW what to do. Laney was hitting Michael so hard and so fast she was creating a crater behind him in the Pyramid. He only took his gaze from her once to glance over at Henry before he shifted right back to her. He could not focus on Henry right now. It wasn't over, and if he acknowledged what had just happened, he would be useless to everyone. So he kept his weapon trained on Laney and Michael.

Finally, she grabbed him by the hair and plunged her hand through this chest.

A gasp of air shot out of Jake. He didn't think she would be able to bring herself to kill him. Laney stepped back, releasing Michael, and he slid down the side of the Pyramid.

And all the anger, all the rage that had been fueling Laney dropped out of her. She stumbled back, Michael's heart rolling from her hand as she collapsed to the ground. Sobs tore from her chest as she crawled along the ground toward Henry's body. Jake ran over to her, keeping an eye on Michael even though he'd seen what she'd done. He knew he would not be getting back up.

Laney reached out a trembling hand, closing Henry's eyes from view. She dropped her head, her shoulders shaking.

Jake stared at her. Her pain was etched across every inch of her body. Jake sucked in a breath, her heartache a tangible thing.

Laney started to stand. Jake reached a hand toward her to help.

"No." Laney stumbled back, landing on her butt.

Jake stopped, his hand suspended in midair for a second before he let it drop back to his side.

"I can't," she whispered as if even speaking was painful. "I'm not done yet."

He nodded, understanding she couldn't accept comfort right now or even help. That she was barely holding it together. He was struggling to hold back his own grief and horror. He hadn't even looked at Henry's face yet. He couldn't make himself look at him. If he did . . .

"Laney?" His voice was hoarse even to his own ears. She didn't respond. Jake wasn't even sure she'd heard him. "Laney? What do you need?"

She looked up, tears making trails through the blood and dirt on her face. "I had to."

"I know, Laney. I know."

She took a shuddering breath and started to stand. Jake grabbed her elbow and helped her up. She glanced over at Michael.

"It's over. He's gone," Jake said.

She shook her head. "It's not over. Not yet." She met his gaze as she started to hover above the ground. "I need to finish this."

"I can come with you."

She shook her head, her eyes shining with unshed tears. "Stay with Henry." She took another shuddering breath, regaining her control. "This part is on me."

She nodded to Michael's body. "And keep an eye on him. Make sure he's really gone."

Jake glanced where Michael lay, a huge gaping hole in his chest. "He *is* gone. He doesn't have a heart."

She shook her head, speaking so quietly that Jake wasn't even sure if the words were meant for him. "No. He still has mine."

Chapter Eighty-Five

USING THE WIND, Laney flew up the side of the Great Pyramid. Sobs choked her throat, but she refused to allow them to pass. When this was over, she would deal with everything that had just happened. But right now, she could not.

She came abreast of the plateau and cut off the wind as she placed herself over it. Her control was shaky, and she crashed to her knees, rock cutting into both of them as well as her palms. But after what she had just been through, she was practically numb to the physical pain. The emotional pain rolling through her was so great right now, it drowned everything else out.

Bowing her head, she gave herself a moment, just a moment, to feel all the anguish. It covered her like a blanket, weighing her down. She wanted nothing more than to curl up and sob until she wasted away. She pictured Henry's face, and pain pierced through her. Her breathing became heavy.

He's gone. How can he be gone?

Then she pictured Drake that last time he had been Drake. His smile, the feel of his hand on her lower back. She crushed her eyes closed as that memory was replaced with the feel of her hand crushing through his chest.

She bowed her head even lower, not sure she would be able to stand. But then the faces of all those counting on her flashed through her mind. Jen and the baby she would now be raising alone. Jake and the family he had finally found for himself. Cain and Nyssa both, who if she succeeded would finally have a normal life after lifetimes of duty and loss. Her uncle, Yoni, the kids, the faces of all of them and so many more looped through her mind. But it wasn't any of them that finally urged her to her feet. It was the memory of the last time she had seen Victoria.

Each time we meet, I am amazed by your strength and your desire to fight the good fight, no matter the odds. Your heart is your strongest weapon. Never forget that.

Her mother's words echoed through her mind. Her mother, who had sacrificed herself even when she wanted nothing more than to stay. And Laney did not want to let her down. She stood.

Taking in a few shaky breaths to center herself, she looked around for some sign of where she needed to begin. The plateau was about thirty feet across by thirty feet. A tall metal pole on a small rising of square blocks extended thirty feet high from the very center. It had been erected to show the height of the capstone or at least what they believed it to be.

As she stared up at it, she began to doubt. From pictures, all taken at a distance, the capstone appeared relatively manageable. But now as she stood on the precipice, she realized how large and unwieldy it actually was. Like the blocks that made up the Pyramid itself, it would be too large for humans in this day and age to move. Made of granite and standing thirty feet tall, it would outweigh even the largest stones within the Pyramid.

The dimensions lent credence to the idea that moving it would have been incredibly difficult. But those very dimensions seemed to belie the possibility that it had been hidden within the Pyramid all this time. *What if, after all this, I'm wrong?*

She banished the thought as soon as it flitted across her brain. She could not go down that road. Not after all the losses that had been suffered. She refocused her attention on the plateau, looking for a sign that would indicate what she was supposed to do or where she was supposed to begin. The space was covered in a thin sheet of sand and dirt. The winds that buffeted Laney as she stood there no doubt kept too much from settling on it.

She inspected the plateau, knowing she didn't have much time. She moved to the edge of the outcropping in the middle. She got down on her hands and knees, pushing sand and dirt away when she couldn't see the blocks below. She moved in circles out from that center point looking for some sign. But the longer she looked, the more her anxiety increased. She could not find anything that told her what to do. She'd expected there to be something, a sign that showed her where to look. Of course, it had been thousands of years—what were the chances it hadn't been rubbed off?

It was taking too long. Already she could see the fight moving closer. *This is too slow.* She stood up, dusting off her hands, blanching at the sand that had dried there into the blood.

Well, at least I can take care of that. She called on the rain, and it poured down onto the plateau. She directed the wind to push the rain off. The water soaked through her hair and clothes, rinsing the dirt and blood from her body and onto the plateau.

And that's when she saw it. She stopped the rain and wind abruptly as the first faint lines of red appeared on the plateau's surface and spread out. She looked at the palm of her hand, still covered in Michael's blood.

Blood will lead the way.

She followed the trail laid out to the eastern corner of the plateau. The red lines coalesced in a symbol she should have expected: the Star of David. She knelt down and ran her finger over it. It had been carved eons ago, just in case it was needed one day.

Laney pushed against it, but nothing happened. The stone didn't budge. Nothing on the plateau moved. She pushed again, but there was no movement. She sat back. What was she missing? This had to be the spot. There was no way this was here by chance.

Her mother had put this here. Her mother, who had sacrificed herself for—

Laney stopped in mid-thought.

Oh no.

In the Tome, it said that at the time of judgment there would be a choice of sacrifice or death. Her mother had been the judge. And this time, Laney was the judge. If she did not offer a sacrifice, the world would devolve into death.

She held up her hand, seeing the vein pulsing away with blood at her wrists.

Which means this time I'm the sacrifice.

Chapter Eighty-Six

LANEY STARTED TO LAUGH. It was all too much. She fell onto her back, laughter rocking her whole body. She had sacrificed everything for this moment, and now she was being asked to sacrifice just one more piece: her life. Some people went through their whole lives without doing a thing to help anyone but themselves. And here she had spent years doing what was asked of her, helping people. And what was her reward? An early death.

But soon her laughter quieted as the tears rolled down her cheeks. As crazy as it might sound, she had always thought she would come through this. She had faced so much already, starting with Azazyel coming for her before she had any abilities. She had managed to avoid being blown to bits by Elisabeta, had faced down Samyaza, had managed to avoid being killed by the entire United States government. No matter what anyone threw at her, she had always lived to fight on another day.

But today was the last day. Because as with her mother, for this to work, every last piece of her blood needed to be drained from her. And if that worked, then all the Fallen would lose their abilities.

Which included her. Which meant she would not heal. If she did this, she would die.

Laney reached over the side of the Pyramid and punched a hole into the face. Then she pulled up a shard of rock. Part of her rebelled at what was about to happen, but she had to admit a small part of her welcomed it. She did not want to live with the memories of Henry and Drake's deaths. Maybe it was the cowardly way out, but right now, oblivion and not thinking sounded pretty good to her.

She raised the rock above her right wrist but then paused as she pictured her uncle. He would be beyond devastated. He might not even believe it. After all, she'd come back from death before.

I love you, Uncle Patrick. Thank you for everything.

But he was the only one she let herself say goodbye to. If she started thinking of everyone else, she would never be able to do what needed to be done.

With two quick slashes, she cut each of her wrists. Blood bloomed instantly as if it had just been waiting to be released. It dripped onto the Star of David, and she could just make out the faint screech of rock against rock somewhere deep inside the Pyramid.

It's working.

But then the flow of blood stopped. A glance at her wrists showed the wounds she had created had closed.

Her mouth fell open. Her healing ability. It was making this impossible. She reached for the Omni gun at her waist, but the holster was empty. She had lost it somewhere along the way.

She reached underneath her boot and pulled off the

heel, then pulled out the vial that she had hidden there months ago.

She had kept a vial of Omni on her all this time. No one had known, not even Drake. She thought there might be a time when she would need it, but she thought she would be willingly giving up her immortality because the world had calmed. This was not how she had pictured it. With only a moment's hesitation, she uncorked the vial and quickly drank it before she could second-guess herself.

Closing her eyes, she held the back of her forearm to her mouth as she swallowed it down. Once again, the faint taste of blueberries filled her mouth and slid down her throat. She pictured Drake, his eyes filled with concern the first time she'd drank it. Then she pictured Michael's eyes filled with nothing. She thrust her own eyes open.

Before she could think, she sliced her wrists again. The blood once again began to drip to the ground. Slow at first and then picking up speed. She watched as it fell into the lines of the plateau, crossing it and creating a crisscross pattern. A chill started at her fingers and worked its way down through her body. She lay back, closing her eyes, feeling the power leave her along with her blood.

The sun beat down on her, but none of its warmth was able to break through the chill crawling over her. Her thoughts grew tired. Her eyelids closed of their own accord.

So tired.

The plateau shifted beneath her, and she felt herself moving. But she didn't have the energy to lift her head. She did manage to open her eyes, though. She was being pushed toward the edge. The antenna at the center crashed, and the rocks on which it had stood started to tumble over each other. An opening three feet by three feet stood now at the very center of the plateau. She watched as a dark granite point emerged from the hole. It grew in size as the capstone emerged.

Even in her exhausted state, she couldn't help but marvel at its appearance. Hidden away for all these millennium, it rose to take its rightful place atop the greatest structure ever built by mankind.

Her thoughts became slow, her whole body feeling heavier than it ever had. Keeping her eyelids open to watch the capstone rise seemed to take too much energy, so she closed them. Still, she could feel herself shifting along the plateau. Part of her brain was still aware enough to realize she was getting close to the edge. But she also knew there was simply nothing she could do about that.

Then, for a second, she was suspended in space before she began the long plunge down.

Chapter Eighty-Seven

THE ROVER BUCKED up and down as Yoni tore across the sand toward the Great Pyramid. "How you doing?" he yelled over at Jen.

Jen said nothing, just stared straight ahead. She knew if she opened her mouth she would start screaming. Her brothers Jordan and Mike, had been killed. Jordan had jumped on a grenade that had been thrown at Mustafa. There wouldn't even be a body to bury. She didn't know yet what had happened to Mike, only that he was gone too.

The deaths were mounting on both sides of the fight. They had lost over three dozen people from the Chandler Group alone. But the numbers of losses on both sides were going to be in the hundreds.

And then there was Henry. No one had said anything, but she had felt it when he died. She had no doubt. She laid her hand over her stomach, grief making her breathing ragged.

She shifted in her seat, trying to hold her feelings back.

The battle was still going full tilt, but when Cain had called, she knew she needed to get to the Pyramid.

"I can't believe you talked me into this."

Jen shoved all her grief, anger, and pain aside. Denial was now her best friend. "I didn't talk you into it. I merely told you my plan and asked if you wanted to join me."

"You mean your whole 'I'm six months pregnant, I'm going to rush into a battlefield, and if you don't agree to help me, I'm going alone' plan?"

"Yeah, that one," Jen said.

"Oh my God." Yoni leaned forward onto the steering wheel, staring at the top of the Pyramid. "She did it! Laney did it!"

Jen stared as the black granite capstone emerged from its ancient hiding place. Sun glinted off of it. It was beautiful . . . and terrifying. She would lose her abilities. She would be normal. She hadn't been normal since she was a child. And it had not been a good time for her.

Who will I be now? And what about my baby? Will she be all right?

Yoni peered up. "What is that?"

Jen followed his gaze to see the small object on the edge of the plateau. Then the object tumbled over the side, arms flying out wildly. Her heart slammed to a stop inside her chest.

"Oh my God. That's Laney." Jen tore out the door as Yoni slammed on the brakes.

"Jen!"

But Jen ignored him as she blurred toward the falling figure of her best friend. *God, please, I cannot lose her too.* She raced up the side of the Pyramid, dive-catching Laney around the waist.

She twirled Laney around her so she was in front of her,

covering the baby, and then as soon as she hit the ground, she rolled, careful to keep the two of them from hitting too hard.

She stopped, rolling Laney to the side and blinking up at the sky.

Jake ran over. "Jen!"

Jen sat up, staring at the wounds in Laney's arms, still slowly trickling blood. She grabbed on to each of them. "Help me!"

The Range Rover slammed to a stop next to them, sending sand spraying up in a wave. Yoni leaped from the Rover, a metal suitcase in his hand. He dropped to his knees, opening the case and thrusting a needle attached to a blood bag at Jake.

Jake didn't even wait for a command. He quickly inserted the needle into a vein in Laney's arm. Yoni attached another needle into a vein on her other arm and attached another blood bag. Then he sliced open the leg of her pants and attached a third to her thigh, attaching the other end to himself.

"What are you doing?" Jen asked.

"I'm a universal donor." Yoni grabbed gauze and started to wrap one of Laney's wrists tightly while Jen kept pressure on the other one.

"I've got it." Jake gently moved Jen to the side and applied a pressure bandage.

"Why isn't she healing?" Jake asked.

"She took the Omni," Jen said quietly.

"What?" Jake asked.

Jen kept her gaze on Laney, not liking how pale she was, even for her. "Cain told us that this would happen. Laney needed to use her blood to activate the capstone. That's why we brought the supplies."

"Will it work?" Jake asked, eyeing Laney, who looked way too lifeless.

Jen shook her head. "I don't know."

A screeching sounded from the top of the Great Pyramid. Jen gasped as it was followed by a giant thud, the capstone locking into place. Her gaze shot to the top of the Pyramid, finally complete after all these millennia.

Time's up.

Yoni walked behind Jen, wrapping his arms around her. "We're here, Jen."

She nodded, staring up at the capstone as a low hum filled the air which felt electrified. The hairs on her arms rose. Then some of her long hair started to drift upward. A blue transparent light began to cover the capstone, working its way from the base to the top. It moved quickly. Within a minute, the entire pyramid was encased in a pale blue light. The Pyramid began to hum louder.

Jen swallowed hard as fear raced through her. A burst of light thirty feet wide shot from the apex of the Pyramid into the sky. She could feel the static electricity in the air building up and up. Her ears clogged, needing to pop, but they wouldn't.

Pressure pushed against Jen's head. She placed her hands on either side, feeling like her brain was being crushed. In a burst of bright light, the blue exploded outward, slamming like a wave into Jen, Yoni, Jake, and Laney and throwing them all into the air.

Chapter Eighty-Eight

ROME, ITALY

MORETTI STARED at the TV screen. The reports were all about the battle in Egypt yesterday. For hours, they had recounted the opening skirmishes, and then of course, the explosion of blue light that burst from the Great Pyramid and raced across the entire globe. It looked like a giant blue tidal wave spreading to every corner of the Earth.

But this morning, the reports were focused on the effect of that wave. The fighting had stopped immediately. The blue wave had slammed into everyone near the Pyramid with the force of a hurricane wind. Equipment had been lost. Everyone immediately retreated to their sides, trying to figure out what happened. And then it became clear: the enhanced had lost their abilities. No one knew if it was temporary or permanent, but all abilities seemed to have disappeared.

And who was being hailed as the hero who ushered in this new era of equality? Delaney McPhearson.

On the muted set, the news channel was once again playing the footage of Delaney McPhearson plunging from the Great Pyramid, her body lifeless. There were no reports on her condition. Another Fallen had grabbed her before she hit the ground, and then there had been that blast, the one everyone assumed had done something to remove the powers.

Moretti's hands went still as the blue light overcame the Pyramid and then burst outward. Where was Michael? He had heard reports of a fight between Michael and McPhearson, but it had not been recorded. Or if it had, it had not yet been released. She couldn't have beaten him. It was not possible. And yet she had made it to the top of the Pyramid. And Michael had not been seen since.

Moretti shook himself from his thoughts. He grabbed his planner, shoving it into his briefcase. He was heading to his family's home at Lake Como. He needed a little time away while things settled down. He'd been trying to reach the other members of the High Council all morning with no luck. They had no doubt gone quiet too.

Not that anyone knew of their connection, but still, his inability to reach them made him uneasy. The door to his office opened behind him. He didn't turn around. "Evan, I need you to get my bags from the bedroom."

"I'm afraid Evan is a little busy helping with something else at the moment."

Moretti whirled around, surprise and fear flashing through him at the person standing there. He bowed his head. "Your Holiness. This is a surprise. You honor me by this visit."

Pope Innocent stepped farther into the room, no smile on his face. "I assume you've been watching the events unfold in Egypt?"

"Of-of course. I believe the whole world is watching."

"Indeed. Many of our flock have been worried that it was the beginning of the end of times."

"Yes, I'm sure."

"Did you know, John, that the third secret of Fatima, the one released to the public, was not the correct translation?"

"Uh, yes, Your Holiness. I am aware of that."

The Pope nodded. "The real translation warned of a wicked council that would change the Church."

Moretti could not tell where the Pope was going with this line of thought, so he kept silent, his head bowed.

"You are part of that council."

Moretti's head snapped up. "What?"

"You are part of the wicked council that will lead to the downfall of the Church if left unfettered."

"No, Your Holiness. My only aim has been to protect the Church, to protect the Papacy. Everything I have done has been with that goal in mind."

"You called Michael into service."

"What? Why would you say such a thing?"

The Pope glared at him. "I had a very interesting evening last night with Father Ezekiel. He has had much to say and much to show me. Do you deny it?"

Moretti's mind whirled, looking for the right angle, the right words to use to get the Pope to understand. "No. But I did it for the Church, to defeat the antichrist. She could not be allowed to—"

"To what, John? What was she attempting to do that you found so threatening? She was trying to save people. She was trying to stop the world from going to war. And she risked everything, including her own life, to do so."

"But, but, that is not God's plan!"

"Who are you to think you know God's plan? Who are you to act in His name?" The Pope shook his head, no anger on his face, only disappointment. "The antichrist was created to keep people on the path. It is not set in stone that there will ever be one. You looked for something, someone, to justify your claims to greatness. You wanted to be the one they turned to in their time of need."

"That's not true."

"Isn't it? The antichrist believes he is doing what is right up until the moment he is recognized for who he is. Delaney McPhearson defied the world to save it. You sat back and unleashed God's soldier to stop her. She risked everything to protect people, sacrificing those she loved, sacrificing herself. You risked nothing. You sat back, waiting for the glory. Tell me, John, who in this story would be cast as the villain?"

"But, but . . ."

The Pope straightened his shoulders. "You will be charged with crimes against humanity." Two Swiss Guards walked into the office.

Moretti scrambled around the desk. "No, no. You have to listen to me. She is the antichrist. I was defending the Church. I did what needed to be done."

The Pope shook his head. "No, John. You did what you wanted. You went searching for glory, and you did not care about the millions who would suffer."

"You can't do this. You don't have the authority."

"No, but we will turn you over to the authorities at the International Criminal Court at the Hague. They will judge you."

One of the guards reached him and pulled his arm behind his back, snapping a cuff over his wrist. "I don't regret what I did. History will vindicate me. And removing McPhearson from the world will be my greatest legacy."

The Pope stopped, looking over his shoulder at Moretti. "McPhearson is not dead. She survived, John. Although she lost many, and I have no doubt she will blame herself for that. Her conscience, though, is clear. Yours may never be."

John's mouth fell open as the Pope disappeared out the doorway. One of the guards yanked on his arm, pulling him forward.

No, no. This can't be happening. It wasn't supposed to be like this.

He struggled against the strong grip holding him. "McPhearson is the one who should be in cuffs. She's the antichrist!"

The guards' only reaction was to tighten their grip on him as they dragged him down the hall.

Chapter Eighty-Nine

CAMP LEMONNIER, DJIBOUTI

THE SOFT BEEPING of the heart monitor woke Laney. She blinked, not recognizing where she was. It was a hospital room, she knew that much. A TV was on, but muted. She stared at the images displayed on the screen. The images shifted from location to location, scene to scene: people celebrating in the street, troops heading for a plane, a shot of children crying, an image of some sort of tactical force kicking down a door in a warehouse. Laney couldn't figure out what was happening.

"Ah, good, you're awake."

She turned her head, just now realizing she wasn't alone. Her skin tightened at the move, and she knew she had a world-class sunburn.

Nancy Harrigan, the United States Secretary of State, unfolded herself from the chair next to the bed.

"Where—" Her raspy voice cut off, her mouth was so dry. Her tongue felt like sandpaper.

Nancy moved to the table next to her bed and poured her a glass of water. She held the straw to Laney's mouth.

Laney drank, nodding when she was done and then leaning back against the pillows, that little effort seeming like it was the equivalent of running a marathon.

"I'm guessing you were asking where you are?"

Laney nodded.

"You are at Camp Lemonnier in Djibouti."

Laney glanced down at her wrists to check for cuffs and then at the door, spying a guard.

Nancy didn't miss the action. "He is there for your protection. You are not under arrest."

She tried to speak but had to swallow a few times to get enough moisture to form words. "How long?"

"It's been three days. They had to pump you full of blood. Your friends saved your life by getting that blood to you as quickly as they did."

Everything that happened at the plateau came back to her: the battle, the losses, Henry, Drake. *No, not Drake. Michael.* She pushed away the image of Michael and focused on the image of the capstone rising from the Pyramid. "Did it work?"

Nancy nodded with a smile. "Yes. From what we can tell, everyone with enhanced abilities no longer has them."

"War?" she asked.

"Averted, for now. All countries have gone back to their corners. They're not sure if this is permanent or a temporary suspension of abilities." She paused. "It is permanent, isn't it?"

Laney nodded.

"Good. Then I am cautiously optimistic that we will not see a replay of the past few months. The President is calling for a NATO meeting next week followed by a G20 meeting next month to see how we all move forward."

Laney was glad the world was in a better place, but right

now she wanted to know about her friends. She wanted to ask more questions. But her eyelids were already closing. She struggled to try and stay awake but gave up quickly, the effort to keep her eyes open more than she could manage at the moment.

She felt the covers being pulled up to her chin. "That's good. Sleep, Delaney. If anyone has earned it, you have. I'm having you transferred back to the States. I will be accompanying you along with my handpicked guards. And your friend Jake. He has refused to leave without you. He's sleeping in the room next door. You'll be safe. So sleep."

Laney didn't want to sleep. She wanted to find out what had happened to everyone. She wanted to tell Jen she was so sorry that she hadn't been able to save Henry. But her body had other ideas.

And before she could even think to form more questions, she was already drifting back into the dark.

Chapter Ninety

BALTIMORE, MARYLAND

LANEY BARELY REMEMBERED the flight back to the States. She remembered seeing Jake next to her on the plane, his presence steady and strong. But then the next thing she remembered was being wheeled into Johns Hopkins. She was taken to a private room, and she slept the entire first day she was there. When she woke, she knew there was someone in the chair next to her. She rolled over, expecting to see Jake, but it wasn't.

"Hey," Jen said softly.

Laney didn't say anything for a few moments, just studied her friend. Her dark hair was pulled back in a ponytail. She wore no makeup, which made the dark circles under her bloodshot eyes stand out more. So much had changed for both her and Jen since they'd first met. But what hadn't changed was how much she loved her. Jen was her sister.

And right now, her sister was hurting. She looked pale, fragile. And fragile was not a word Laney had ever associated with Jen.

Laney fumbled for the bed controls to raise the back so she could sit up. Jen stood and picked the control up, pressing the button. She placed the control where Laney could reach it easily before kissing Laney's cheek and then leaning her forehead into Laney's. Neither spoke as tears trailed down both their cheeks. Finally, Jen stepped back, wiping her cheeks and grabbing the box of tissues from the side table. She handed Laney some before grabbing some for herself.

Jen pushed the chair closer to the bed and sat down.

"Is the baby okay?"

"She's good."

"What happened after the capstone rose?"

"You don't remember?"

Laney shook her head. Jen explained about the blue light and the power burst.

Laney gasped. "You're sure the baby's okay?"

"We've been checked out. And besides, I landed on Yoni."

A laugh burst out of Laney at the image, and Jen gave her a watery smile in response.

"Did it work? Are your powers gone?"

Jen nodded. "It's taken some getting used to. I feel so . . . normal." She paused. "We almost lost you."

"I thought I was gone." Grief stabbed through her. "I'm sorry about Henry. If I had killed Michael sooner—"

Jen grabbed her hand. "Hey, hey, don't do that. Jake told me everything. Laney, you did everything you could. If that had been Henry, if he had suddenly changed into someone else, I don't know if I ever would have been able to do it. Henry, he died a hero. His little girl will know that. She'll know her uncles did too."

Disbelief shook through Laney. "Her uncles?"

Jen nodded. "Jordan and Mike. They both died in Egypt."

Laney's mind flashed on the twins. Neither had abilities, but both had been Navy SEALs and both had helped her throughout the craziness of her life these last few years. Their loss, it was unimaginable. And the Witt family was so close that this would be world-shattering. "How many did we lose?"

"For the entire battle, the death toll stands at four hundred and seventy-eight. From the Chandler Group, fifty-four."

Laney closed her eyes. *My God.*

"I'm glad you woke up today, because there's something I need to tell you." Jen looked away. "I'm going to stay with my parents for a little while. They're struggling, and I need to just get away from everything."

Laney nodded. She understood wanting to get away.

Jen wiped at the fresh tears breaking over her lashes. "And Henry left me everything. I don't know what he was thinking. I don't want all that."

"No, but maybe one day your daughter will."

"Maybe." Jen took a deep breath. "I'm taking Danny with me. He's just . . . I think it might do him some good to get away as well."

"Yeah, I get that. What about everyone else?"

"Yoni's helping get everyone settled back in. The government's given everyone immunity, so he moved everyone back to the estate."

"Dom?"

"He's settling in. Lou and Rolly, they're staying with him. Gina also moved onto the estate to keep an eye on him."

"That's good."

They fell silent. Laney couldn't think of anything to say, even though the space between them was filled with so much. Finally, Jen stood. "Move over."

"What?"

Jen lowered the bed rail. "Scoot."

Laney inched over, and Jen heaved herself up on the bed, kicking off her shoes before sliding under the blanket. She wrapped her arms around Laney. "I'm sorry about Drake too."

Laney couldn't say anything. Her throat was too tight. So she just leaned her head on Jen's shoulder.

"I liked who you were around him. He could always make you smile, even when everything was falling apart. And let's be honest, it was always falling apart."

Laney let out a watery laugh.

"Drake was real, Laney. Whatever switch went off, whatever change happened, the Drake you knew, the Drake you loved, he was real. He wasn't the one who killed—" Jen's words choked off. "He wasn't the one who did those things in Egypt. Your Drake, you can mourn him. You should. He loved you through lifetimes."

Jen's words broke down the dam that had been holding back Laney's grief. She sobbed, her whole body shaking with the power of her grief. Jen held her, her tears mingling with Laney's as they shared the loss of the loves of their lives.

Chapter Ninety-One

THE SCENES REPLAYED in Jake's head yet again. Drake, the cold look in his eyes; Henry, the light disappearing from his. Laney plunging off the side of the Pyramid and there being absolutely nothing he could do to help. Laney lying in the hospital bed, her skin almost as white as the sheets.

"Jake, we're home," Yoni said quietly.

Jake looked up, surprised to see they were on Sharecroppers Lane. He didn't remember the drive back from the hospital. He'd flown with Laney and the Secretary of State back from Egypt. Laney was now resting at Johns Hopkins Hospital. He'd stayed with her for a full day, but she had stubbornly refused to wake up. He had kept himself busy, distracted by arranging for everyone to be returned home. But an hour ago Jen had arrived and chased him out. She said Patrick and Cain were on their way and Jake should go home and get some sleep.

But Jake didn't want to sleep. He didn't want to come back to the estate. There was a hole threatening to swallow him, a hole that was only growing bigger. Henry was gone. How could he be gone?

The door to the cottage opened. Mary Jane stepped out, looking uncertainly at the SUV. Yoni got out and walked up to her. She hugged him, and they talked with a few glances back at the car, but still Jake sat. He'd lost people before, but this loss . . . he couldn't wrap his head around this one.

The door next to him opened. Yoni stood there. "How about if we head inside?"

Jake shook himself from his thoughts, registering the concern on his friend's face. "Yeah. I've got it. I'm good."

"Of course you are," Yoni said even as he reached out a supporting hand, holding on to Jake as he stepped from the car.

Jake's knees buckled for a moment before he straightened. "I got it. I'll call you later."

Yoni hesitated before nodding. "Okay. Sure. I'll be at Dom's."

Jake didn't reply, just focused on moving one foot in front of the other. Mary Jane met him halfway down the path. She reached for him but something on his face must have stopped her, because she pulled her hand back and walked by his side, opening the door for him.

Jake stepped inside, looking around, but nothing really registered. It was quiet. It wasn't usually quiet, was it? He sank onto the bottom step of the staircase. "Where are the kids?"

Mary Jane crouched down in front of him. "At Dom's. They have Nyssa and Susie with them."

Jake nodded. He couldn't seem to stop nodding, but he didn't say anything. An image of Henry's eyes flashed across his mind again, the gaping hole in his chest. His heart squeezed. A tear rolled over the corner of his eye.

Mary Jane wiped the tear away before cupping his face in her hand. "Jake."

He met her eyes, the love there undoing him. Tears streamed down his cheeks. "He's gone."

She squeezed his hand. "I know."

"I don't understand how he's gone. He had the strength, the power—" He wiped angrily at the tears on his cheeks. "How am I still here and he's gone? Laney's in the hospital, Henry's dead, and I'm what? Fine? None of this makes sense."

"It wasn't your time, Jake."

"It wasn't his either! He has a baby on the way. He has —" His words choked off, looking away, his breathing ragged. He looked back at her. "He shouldn't have died."

"I know." Tears shone in her eyes.

Jake slunk down to the floor. The sobs he'd been holding back since Egypt came out in a mad rush. Henry was gone. He was gone. His friend, his brother . . . nothing would ever be the same again.

Chapter Ninety-Two

JEN AND DANNY left for her parents' the next day. Henry's body had been cremated, but Jen didn't want to hold a ceremony until after her daughter was born. She wanted to hold their daughter as she said goodbye. No one argued with her. No one was quite ready to say goodbye yet anyway. Besides, there were enough other funerals to attend.

Laney managed to make it to Matt's funeral two days later. Mustafa had been there, along with the other members of the SIA. Laney wasn't surprised to see Nancy there, but she was surprised to see the single tear escape from underneath her dark glasses. She hadn't realized they were that close.

She sat with Jake and Mustafa. When Jake went to get the car after the ceremony, Laney had turned to Mustafa. "What are you going to do now?"

Mustafa shrugged. "Not sure. I'm going back to Egypt for a little while. Stay with my family."

Laney nodded. She thought he might do that. "We'll miss you."

"Jake offered me a job with the Chandler Group. I might take him up on it, after a little time."

"I think we all need time."

Jake pulled up, and Mustafa opened the door for Laney. She hugged him tight. "Be well, Mustafa."

Mustafa held her just a little longer than necessary. "You too, Laney." He hurried away, his shoulders shaking.

Laney slid on her seatbelt, watching him go. Everyone had been scarred by this fight. No one would ever be the same.

Jake pulled out into traffic. "You sure you don't want to stop back at the estate? Speak with your uncle and Cain?"

Laney shook her head. "No, I said goodbye before I left."

"Okay." They drove in silence for the next forty minutes. Laney's whole body felt heavy. She wanted nothing more than to close her eyes and sleep. But she'd been sleeping ever since Egypt. How could she still be tired?

Jake pulled through the gates at the airport and drove right onto the tarmac, parking next to the Chandler jet. He put the car into park, popping the trunk. He got out and handed the bag to the flight attendant. Laney just sat in the passenger seat, staring at the plane. It was the same one she had first taken all those years ago when Azazyel, the first Fallen she had ever seen, had been trying to kill her. She and her uncle Patrick had flown to Baltimore in it, not having a clue as to what was happening or why. She had thought at the time that her world had gone insane. But that incident had been downright tame compared to some of the others she'd faced since then. Now it felt like it had all happened a lifetime ago and to someone else.

Jake opened her door, extending his hand to her. She let him help her up. She wasn't fully healed yet. Losing practically all your blood volume apparently weakened you for a while. Jake escorted her to the stairs, stopping at the base of them. "You sure you want to do this?"

"I need some time. I need to be alone."

Jake ran a hand through his hair. "I know. I would just feel better if there was someone nearby, just in case."

She leaned forward and kissed him on the cheek. "I'll be fine. And you know where I am if you need me."

He took her hands. "And you know where I am if you need me. It's okay to ask for help, Laney."

"I know. But this, this is something I need to get through on my own, at least right now. I don't even know who I am anymore, Jake."

"You're Delaney McPhearson. You are brave, you are strong, you are loved. And right now, you are hurting."

Fresh tears sprang to her eyes. They seemed to always be just a breath away. He hugged her tight. "Go heal, Laney. And when you're ready, we'll be here waiting for you."

Chapter Ninety-Three

LANEY SLEPT for most of the flight, not waking until the landing gear started to lower. She sat up and stretched, staring out and seeing the mountains in the background. For the first time in days, she felt a little jolt of energy.

Okay. Let's go.

An hour later, Laney pulled up in front of Drew's cabin. She turned the engine off and just sat staring at the log cabin that had been in Drew's family for generations. The last time she had been here, the FBI was closing in, and Drake had busted through the back door and helped her escape. This was where their most recent story had truly begun. And so this was where she wanted to be. Henry had bought the place and had all the damage done by the FBI fixed. She smiled, thinking of him. Even after death, he was taking care of her.

Her throat started to tighten, and she shook her head. *No, not yet.*

She grabbed her bags from the back and dropped them next to the front door before opening all the windows to air out the place. It had been a while since anyone had been there. She went back to the jeep for the groceries she had picked up and stocked the cabinets. Then she pulled the cleaning supplies from under the sink and got to work.

Laney cleaned the cabin from top to bottom. It wasn't a big place, but it was still three hours until she felt like it was clean. After a shower, she made herself a bowl of pasta and then sat out on the deck to enjoy the sunset and to let herself breathe for the first time in a very long time.

ABOVE LANEY, the sky shifted from blue to pink to darker reds. Every night for the past two months, she'd sat on the porch and watched the sunset. Every morning, she sat in the same spot and watched the sun rise. The fact that every day ended only to be followed by a new beginning reminded her that darkness ended and life began again.

She sipped some red wine, letting the warmth coat her throat. It had been hard to leave everyone, but right now as she sat here, with no one for miles, she felt a peace she hadn't felt in a long time. The pain was still there, the grief, but now she knew that one day she would be able to get past it.

Laney let her head fall back against the Adirondack chair. She pictured Cleo. For some reason, Cleo always came to her at these times. She thought of her friendship, her love. Losing her was maybe even harder than losing Drake. But when she closed her eyes, she could still see her friend. And she felt gratitude for the fact that she was still in her life in this small way.

Laney shifted, letting out a breath. The night was quiet, just as she liked it. She hadn't talked to anyone besides the clerk at the grocery store in the two months she'd been here. She'd sent texts, assuring everyone she was fine. But she just didn't want to talk. Not yet. She closed her eyes, thinking she might sleep out here tonight.

"Hello, Laney."

Chapter Ninety-Four

LANEY JOLTED upright at the sound of the voice. A man stood on the other side of the porch, leaning his hip against the railing. He had dark hair and eyes. And she knew him.

"Ralph?"

He smiled. "I'm going by Uriel these days."

Ralph/Uriel had been the archangel who had guarded Victoria. He had been by her side when she took her last breaths, and Laney had watched him disappear as the sun fell on him the next day.

"How?"

He raised an eyebrow. "Is that really what you want to know?"

She realized he was right. She had long ago gotten past the hows of her whole situation. Angels, arch or otherwise, popping in and out of her life, she accepted. No, there was a different question she wanted answered. "Why are you here?"

"It's time we spoke."

Laney shook her head. "I don't want to hear about destinies or something you need me to do. I am done."

"I know how you feel. I know the pain the events in Egypt and before caused you. When Victoria had to make her choice, to end the long lives of humans, it came at a cost as well."

Bitterness swept through her as she thought of Nyssa taking up her duty one day. "And she's still paying that cost."

"Yes. But you should know, that bill has now been almost paid, thanks to your actions."

Laney frowned. "What does that mean?"

"She will live, she will die. But this will be the last lifetime she will remember who she is. In the next, she will be just like everyone else."

"She will never be just like everyone else."

Uriel's face softened. "Yes, you are right about that."

Laney studied the archangel in front of her. He had been with Victoria in lifetime after lifetime, a constant presence. "Have you seen her?"

"Yes. I have watched her."

"Will you return to her?"

"That is not clear. In each lifetime, she has needed me. There has been no one to guide her, to make sense of all the memories when they return." His gaze met hers. "But you have given her someone who can do that. Who would lay down his life for her."

"Cain."

"You saw good where the rest of the world saw evil. You are an unusual human."

Laney grunted. After all, what did you say to that? "Is that why you came? To tell me about Victoria?"

"No. I have come for a different reason." He paused. "When Victoria made her decision, two of us tried to talk her out of it. She thought she knew better. She thought humankind would be better served by their mortality."

"Was she right?"

"Yes. Humanity over the years has become more and more attuned with its true goals. There are moments of violence and anger, but they never last. The good always outweighs the bad." He paused. "You had to make a similar decision, a similar sacrifice."

Laney turned away, Drake's face flashing through her mind, followed by Henry's. "You mean sacrific*es*."

"Yes. You have done well."

Anger roared through Laney. "*Well?* I've done *well?* I had to kill Drake! Henry died! Do you know all the good he has done? After everything, he deserved to see his child be born!"

Pain flashed across Uriel's face. His voice was quiet when he spoke. "Yes, he did."

And Laney remembered that Uriel hadn't only been close to Victoria. He had helped raise Henry. "How come you feel the pain of his loss, and Michael felt nothing?"

Uriel sighed. "Michael has always been about duty. For longer than humans can comprehend, duty was his world. When his brothers fell, he took it to heart. He could not understand how they could turn their backs. In his grief, he asked to guard the tree, and his request was granted. But centuries passed, and he grew no closer to understanding how his brothers could turn their backs on all they knew. So he asked to be able to live one lifetime as a human."

"Achilles." She knew this story, but hearing it in Uriel's deep voice made it richer somehow.

The Belial Sacrifice

Uriel nodded. "Yes. He was arrogant, he was selfish, he was human. But then, he met you. The love he felt for you changed who he was on a fundamental level. Duty was no longer the driving force in his life. Finding you, protecting you, became that force."

Laney's breath shuddered as she inhaled.

"You made him a better man, Laney."

Laney pictured Michael plunging his hand through Henry's chest. "But then, how? How did he become that monster?"

"His role in that drama was determined a long time ago. There was no avoiding Michael being called."

"But why? You said I did well, which means I made the right choices. So why did *he* have to be called?"

"Because you loved him."

That stopped her short. "What?"

"Sacrificing yourself, you have proven over and over you were willing to do that. But there needed to be one last test. You needed to face the greatest soldier. You needed to prove how committed you were to saving humanity. You needed to demonstrate that you were willing to make the ultimate sacrifice to protect the world. For you, that was not sacrificing yourself. It was sacrificing someone you loved."

"But why? Why did I have to be the one to do any of this? Why did I have to lose all these people?"

"You chose this path, Laney, long before you were born. You chose to take on the pain to spare others from it."

Laney looked away from him, gripping the railing. A kaleidoscope of all those lost in this fight looped through her mind. "It's too much. It's just too much."

"How much you would lose was not foreseen. But you prevailed. And because of that, you are to be rewarded."

Laney scoffed. "Rewarded? There is no reward that would make up for all that we have lost."

"But I think there might be. You see, I have been allowed to offer to you the return of one of the ones you have loved and lost."

Chapter Ninety-Five

RALPH'S WORDS hung in the air between them before the meaning of them truly registered. *You see, I have been allowed to offer to you the return of one of the ones you have loved and lost.* Laney's jaw dropped. "What?"

"Because of your courage and sacrifice, one of those you have loved and lost will be returned to you. You only have to choose who."

Joy pierced through Laney. Drake. She could have him back. She could—

But her joy dimmed as she pictured Jen, the heartache in her face. She had lost both her brothers and Henry. Now she would raise their child on her own.

And then there was Cleo. Half her soul felt like it was missing without her. And Matt, Jordan, all the others they had lost. How could she choose just one?

"I should tell you Cleo is out of your grasp now. She has already been reborn."

Laney's head jolted up. "What? Already?"

"Yes."

"Where? Will I see her again?"

"I cannot tell you that."

Resentment rolled through Laney. Of course not. Why make any of this pain easier to bear?

Tears pressed against the back of her eyes. Cleo was gone, then. There was a chance she would come across her. But would she even know her? The research on reincarnation indicated that while very young, some souls remembered their past lives and the people in them. Would Cleo remember her? Or would she end up across the world, any memories she had of Laney slipping away as she aged?

"Who will you choose, Laney?"

Laney stared at him. How could she do this? She wanted Drake back more than anything. Without him, all her senses felt dull. The world felt dull. But how could she choose him? He had lived for thousands of years. They had had their chances at happiness at one time, short though it may have been. Could she choose him above the others?

She pictured Jen, her hands protectively cradling her belly.

She had suffered through her childhood, finding a home with the Witts, but she had never let her guard down, not until Henry. And Henry himself had finally found his home in Jen. And now their child would never truly get to know what an amazing man he was. They could tell her stories, but she would never feel it the way the rest of them did. And Henry's little girl deserved to feel his love. Plus, look at all the good Henry did. He took care of thousands through his companies and charities.

Tears rolled down her cheeks. She loved Henry, but if she said his name, she was closing the door on any chance of seeing Drake again. He would be lost to her forever.

She took a shuddering breath.

"You have chosen?"

Laney nodded, gripping the railing of the porch for strength.

"Who?"

She stared up at the sky, tears clouding her vision. "Henry."

Chapter Ninety-Six

SCOTTSDALE, ARIZONA

THE LAST OF the dishes disappeared into the dishwasher as Jen wiped the table.

"You shouldn't be doing that," Alice Witt, Jen's mother, said.

"Mom, I'm pregnant, not deathly ill. I don't think wiping the kitchen table will prove too strenuous."

"I know, I just want to make sure . . ." Her words drifted off and she shrugged. But Jen knew what she meant. It had been a difficult two months. Losing the twins, the Witt family felt different, wrong. But slowly, they were learning to live with the new normal.

The hole Henry's loss had created, however, hadn't shrunk in size at all or even shifted. It was always there, just beneath the surface. Jen tried to keep it from her mom, but she knew her mom saw more than she let on.

"Does Danny have everything packed?"

"I think so. The technicians will be arriving in the morning to pack up his computer systems."

Her mom shook her head. "I swear, I do not understand

a thing he does on those computers. But it has been nice having him here."

"Yeah. I think it's been good for him."

By the time Jen and Danny had arrived in Scottsdale, Danny was one step above comatose. He barely talked, barely ate. Jen had worried they'd have to hospitalize him if he didn't start eating. But soon, he began to eat a little, talk a little. Leaving the estate had been a good idea. They both needed to get away. Go somewhere where the memories of Henry weren't staring them in the face every single moment.

But tomorrow they would head back. It was right to get away, but Jen wanted to bring their baby home to her and Henry's house. And she wanted to give herself a little time to adjust to being back there. She wasn't sure how she was going to react to seeing all of his things. Her parents would follow them in a few days. They were actually selling their house and moving to the estate. They wanted to be there to help Jen and the baby. And Jen was more than grateful for that.

"I'm going to go take a walk, okay?"

Her mother glanced out the window. "Maybe you should bring an umbrella. It looks like it might rain."

Jen looked up at the bright blue sky with only a few light clouds in the background and furrowed her brow mockingly. "I think we might need to get your eyes checked, Mom."

Smiling, her mother swatted a towel at her. "I swear I don't know who's cheekier, you or Jordan." Her smile faltered, and her face crumbled for just a moment. She turned her back to Jen, her hand flying to her mouth.

Jen walked over and wrapped her arms around her, shifting a little to the side so her belly wasn't in the way.

"Jordan was always the cheekiest. But I've always been a close second. Mike was always the peacekeeper."

Her mother patted her hand as she struggled to hold back her tears. "That's probably true. Now go on with your walk. I'll be all right. These moments, they just hit out of nowhere sometimes, you know?"

Jen hugged her, leaning her head into her mom's for a moment. "I know."

Her mother shooed her outside. Jen stopped in at Danny's room, but he was engrossed in something on his computers and wasn't interested in a walk. Moxy, however, was happy to join. Clipping the leash on Moxy's collar, Jen stepped out the back door, turning her face up to the sun and letting it warm up the chill that had settled inside her at her mother's words. She hated her brothers being gone. The day the Witts had found her had been the best day of her life. The day she lost her brothers and Henry had been the worst.

Moxy gave a small whine. Jen opened her eyes and looked down. Moxy sat next to her, her mouth open, her tail wagging. "Okay, okay. Let's go."

Moxy jumped a little, prancing in place before settling next to Jen as they headed down the sidewalk. Without her abilities, Jen made sure she stayed active. Every day, she and Moxy took a three-mile walk. Weight training at the local gym and working on the bag in her parents' garage kept her nice and healthy and gave her something to look forward to each day.

But she had never realized how much she had relied on her abilities. It was strange to struggle to run or to lift something. The pregnancy made her feel even more unwieldy, although she tried not to think of it that way. However, when you had to plan how to roll over in bed, it was hard to think of yourself any other way.

Jen put her hand on her stomach. But it was worth it. Just another month, and she'd get to meet her daughter.

Jen pulled out her cellphone and checked her text messages. Laney had sent her one last night. She was tempted to call her, but Laney never picked up. She only communicated by text. But she had promised to be back in time for the baby's birth. Jen slid her phone back into her pocket. She knew she needed to respect Laney's privacy right now. She was dealing with a lot. Henry's death was hard for Jen, but Laney had been the one who had taken Drake's life. What Laney was going through . . . Jen wasn't sure how someone got over something like that.

Ahead, Jen spied the large man-made lake in her parents' development. Moxy became more alert, looking for the ducks that always rested along its shores.

A squirrel darted from one tree to another ahead of them. Moxy let out a whine and looked up at Jen. Jen glanced around. There was no one around. She reached down and removed the leash. "All right, girl, go run."

Moxy did not need to be told twice. She took off like a bolt, sprinting for the squirrel. Of course, the squirrel saw her and immediately scampered up a tree. Undeterred, Moxy pranced around the bottom of the tree, barking and jumping.

Jen smiled. She was never going to catch those squirrels, but she tried every single time they came here. Jen continued on the path, and Moxy caught up with her only a few minutes later. Jen reattached the leash. Straightening, she caught sight of a man sitting on a bench a couple hundred yards away with his back to her. Her heart leaped as the sun touched his dark hair. She took in a shuddering breath.

It's not Henry, she reminded herself, turning away from the man and heading the other way around the lake.

It wasn't the first time she'd caught sight of someone out of the corner of her eye and thought it was Henry. The first few weeks, it happened almost daily, then weekly. But it still shook her each time.

She focused on her breathing, trying to stop her racing heart. *It's not Henry. He just looked like him. There are lots of big guys with dark hair. That guy probably had a hook nose and fleshy jowls.* She smiled at the image, conjuring up the man's face in her mind's eye. *Yup, definitely not Henry.*

She and Moxy crossed the halfway mark of the lake, and she glanced over. The man was still sitting on the bench. His shape, it seemed so familiar.

Not Henry, but her heart gave a little tug nonetheless. She picked up the pace, wanting to see the man's face, knowing it would crush her, knowing it would be like losing him all over again, but also knowing she'd rather get it over with than let this stupid illogical hope fester in her chest. By the time she had reached the other side of the lake, she was practically running. She forced herself to slow down. She'd consciously kept from looking over at the bench. She glanced there now. It was empty.

Despair crushed through her. She shook her head, coming to a stop and running a hand over her face. *It was never Henry. You don't need to see his face to know that. You already saw Henry's.* She flashed back on seeing Henry at the base of the Great Pyramid. He was gone. She knew that. But she still had wanted to see the man's face.

"Okay, Moxy, let's head back, okay?" She started heading back toward her parents' place, but Moxy pulled her in the opposite direction. Jen turned around, looking at her. "What are you doing?"

Moxy whined, pulling again toward the dock.

"It's time to go, Mox. Let's—"

With a large tug, Moxy ripped the leash from Jen's hands and sprinted toward the dock.

"Moxy!" Jen hustled after her. What on earth had gotten into her? She'd never done that before.

Jen spied the end of the leash disappearing down the dock ramp. She stepped on the ramp, scanning the thirty-foot dock. Moxy was at the far end, her tail wagging excitedly as she jumped and pranced around the man who had been sitting on the bench. He was crouching down, rubbing Moxy behind the ears. His hands, they looked so very large as they ran over Moxy's dark fur.

On autopilot, Jen stumbled forward, her hand gripping the handrail to keep from falling. The man stood with his back still to her. He was tall, so very, very tall. And his shoulders were so broad. And that shirt, she knew that shirt. She'd given him that shirt.

No, no. It's not possible. It's not possible. Jen's feet touched the dock, but she didn't move forward. There was no railing along the dock, and she knew her grip on that railing was the only thing keeping her upright.

Moxy spied her and sprinted over, but Jen ignored her as the man turned. Violet eyes locked on to hers. Jen's breath left her in a swoosh. And then the man was running, and Jen was falling. He caught her before she could crash fully to the ground. He stared down at her, confusion on his face. Jen reached up and traced the lines of his cheek. "Henry?"

He smiled. "Hi."

Chapter Ninety-Seven

JEN STARED UP AT HENRY, not knowing what to say. Reality seemed to be splitting apart. "I'm going crazy."

"No, you're not," the hallucination that looked so real said. She had to curl her hands into fists and place them behind her back to keep from reaching out to him.

No. Jen pushed herself up, stumbling away from him.

"No, you're dead. I saw your body. I mourned you." She ran her hands through her hair. "I've lost it. I'm hallucinating." She rummaged in her pocket, pulling out her phone. She needed her mom. Something was wrong. She needed—

Her phone slipped from her fingers, crashing to the deck. She crouched down to get it. Henry's large hand covered hers. "Jen, it's me. I promise."

Jen shook her head, struggling to stand. Henry gripped her elbow, pulling her up. She shook him off, backing away and sitting down hard on the bench. She punched in a number. "Answer, please answer."

Danny's voice cut through the line. "Jen, I'm in the middle of—"

"Danny, I need you."

Danny's voice immediately shifted from distracted to focused. "Is it the baby? Should I call an ambulance?"

"No, no, it's something else. I'm at the dock. Come quick, okay?" She disconnected the call, not waiting for his reply.

Henry knelt down, running a hand through Moxy's fur. "You're not going crazy, Jen. I'm really here."

She shook her head but didn't respond. You didn't talk to hallucinations. She put a hand over her belly. *Please let this be temporary. My baby needs at least one parent.*

It was only two minutes later when Jen heard a car's brakes. Seconds later, Danny's voice called out, "Jen!"

"Down—" She cleared her throat. "Down here!" she called, her gaze shifting from the hallucination in front of her to the top of the ramp as Danny appeared.

His gaze locked on to her, scanning her as he sprinted down the ramp. "Jen, are you all—" Danny stumbled, managing to grab a hold of the railing before he pitched forward. "Henry?"

"You can *see* him?" Jen asked.

Danny nodded, his mouth hanging open, his eyes wide. "Henry?"

Henry covered the distance between them in two quick strides, engulfing Danny in a hug.

Breath burst out of Jen, and tears welled in her eyes as she stared at the two of them. Henry released Danny, who had tears streaming down his cheeks but a giant smile on his face.

"How?" Jen asked.

Henry walked over toward her slowly as if he was afraid he would spook her. "I'm not exactly sure. The last thing I remember was Michael. He was attacking Laney at the Great Pyramid. I grabbed onto him, and then nothing."

"You died, Henry," Danny said.

"That's what Ralph said."

"Ralph?" Danny asked. "You saw Ralph?"

He frowned. "I think so. He said I needed to go back. It wasn't my time. That Laney had paved the way for me to return."

Shock flooded Jen. "Laney got you back?"

"That's what Ralph said. And the next thing I knew, I was sitting on a bench staring at that lake." Henry looked around. "Where are we? Is Laney here?"

Jen shook her head. "No, she's . . . she's been having a tough time. Drake . . . he's gone. He killed you."

Henry blanched. "I need to call her. Tell her I'm back."

Jen reached out her hands, and Henry pulled her up. He stared at her belly, his mouth dropping. "How long was I gone?"

"Two months."

"That means . . ."

Jen nodded. "She's healthy, and she'll be swinging by to meet us in a month." Then Jen grimaced as pain swept through her stomach.

Henry gripped her arms. "Jen?"

Wetness slid down her legs. "Oh no."

"What?"

"I think your daughter is going to be swinging by a little sooner than expected."

Chapter Ninety-Eight

BALTIMORE, MARYLAND

THE ESTATE WAS TEEMING with life. Flowers were unfolding their petals to the sun. Construction sounded from the far side of the estate. Laney walked down the path from Henry's house to Sharecroppers Lane.

She had flown in this morning. Jen had had a little girl last night. And she had had her on the estate. When her water broke, Jen demanded she be taken back to Baltimore. Henry had tried to talk her out of it, but there was no swaying her. So they packed up Jen, Danny, her parents, and a full medical team and made the cross-country flight.

Jen gave birth an hour after touching down in Baltimore to a six-pound-five-ounce little girl. Jordan Victoria Chandler came roaring into the world with a cry and then promptly settled down with her mother. Jen and Henry had barely taken their eyes off their daughter since. Laney could practically see cartoon hearts floating above the three of them as they nestled together.

Warmth spread through Laney at the picture of her

brother looking so happy. Jen looking so happy. She had made the right decision.

Then why does it still hurt so much?

"Laney."

She turned as Jake jogged down the path toward her. She forced a smile to her face. "Hey."

"Hey back." Jake fell in step with her, and they walked along in companionable silence for a while before Jake broke it. "So Henry's back."

"I noticed."

"In all the hubbub, I never really did get an explanation of how that happened. Henry said you were the reason."

Laney shrugged.

Jake pulled her to a stop. "Could you have brought back Drake?"

She hadn't told anyone about the choice she'd been given. Everyone was so happy to have Henry back that she didn't want to spoil any of that joy. But she wanted to. She needed to. It was eating her up inside. She kept imagining how her life would be right now if Drake were here. She looked up at him and nodded.

He sucked in a breath. "Oh God, Laney." He pulled her into him. Tears sprang to her eyes. She loved her brother. She was glad he was back. His daughter deserved to get to know him. But she still felt like she'd had a part of her carved out. And she couldn't show that to them because she didn't want to dim their happiness.

But right now she let herself cry, let herself feel the loss of Drake and the compassion of Jake. Finally, she pushed herself back and wiped at her eyes. "Thanks."

"I'm here for you, Laney. Anything you need."

"I know. Um, how are the McAdamses? I haven't had a chance to stop by and see them yet."

"They're good. Molly losing her powers, it lifted a weight off of her. I think she's going to be all right."

"I'm glad."

"Do you want to join us for dinner? Mary Jane said something about grilling out."

Laney shook her head. "Another time. I'm going to stop in and see my uncle and Cain."

They'd reached the end of the path. "Well, if you change your mind, just follow the smell of barbeque."

"I will."

Jake leaned down and kissed her cheek. "You will always be my hero, Laney." He headed toward his cottage.

Laney turned toward her uncle's cottage. She pushed open the back gate, then paused. She wasn't sure she was ready for this. She turned around.

"Planning to run away?"

She turned around, spying her uncle's face in the window. "Of course not." She let the gate swing shut behind her. She could hear his chuckles as he headed for the back door. It slid open. He rolled himself through and down the ramp toward her.

She met him halfway down the path and threw her arms around him. "I've missed you."

He rested his hand against the back of her head. "And I've missed you."

She pulled back, smiling down at him. "Cain inside?"

"Yup, taking care of a package Dom had brought up here for you."

Laney tensed. It couldn't be the Omni. Had he figured out it still worked? Had he—

Her uncle gripped her hand. "Hey, hey, sorry. It's not anything bad. Those days are behind us."

"Sorry, old habits."

"Well, it will take a little time for all of us to adjust to this new reality."

"Laney!" Nyssa appeared in the doorway and ran down the ramp. Laney hurried forward, catching Nyssa as she stumbled near the bottom of the ramp. Her hair flew forward, covering her face, but she just grinned up at Laney through the curls. "Back!"

"Yes, sweetheart. I'm back."

Tiger slunk out the door behind her. Laney's breath caught. Cleo. She missed her so much. Tears sprang to her eyes. She ducked her head down to keep her uncle from seeing them.

Nyssa wiped one tear away. "Don't cry."

Laney hugged Nyssa to her. "I'm working on it," she whispered. She stood with Nyssa in her arms as Cain joined them. She gave him a one-armed hug, Nyssa refusing to let go of her perch. "How are you?"

"I'm good." The skin on the edges of his blue eyes crinkled as he smiled. It was strange seeing Cain with normal eyes. But when the capstone energy had been released, he had been released from his punishment as well. From what they could tell, he was just a normal man now.

"Are you?"

"It feels wrong to say I am better than I have ever been when so many others are suffering, but I feel lighter than I ever have." He tweaked Nyssa's nose, who giggled in response before she hid her head in Laney's chest. "I have the life I always wanted."

"I'm glad." And she was. Right now, though, she did not feel the same. A life without Drake, without Cleo, was not what she wanted. And accepting that reality was a daily struggle. She handed Nyssa over to him. "You know, I think

I'm just going to go take a little nap. I'll come back for dinner."

"Before you go, you need to go see what Dom left for you." Cain nodded toward the back door.

"Uh, sure, okay." She headed up the ramp. Only Tiger followed her. She paused, looking back at the other three. "You guys aren't coming?"

"No. It's better if it's just you two."

Laney frowned but then shrugged and headed inside. Tiger padded past her, heading for the living room. Laney followed, stopping in the doorway, her eyes going wide. A cage sat in the middle of the room, a bright blue blanket inside, a small black shape curled up on it.

Moving forward on trembling legs, she dropped silently next to the cage. The small black jaguar yawned, stretching out its legs and arms, opening its mouth wide to reveal a perfectly pink tongue.

Tiger sat down next to her, and she stared at him in shock. "How?"

Cain spoke from behind her. She hadn't heard him follow them in. "Cleo was pregnant. Gina kept her on life support long enough to deliver the cub."

"Why— Why didn't she tell me?"

"She didn't want you to be heartbroken if the cub didn't make it. Cleo had been through so much, Gina wasn't sure what shape the cub would be in."

"But she's good? She's healthy?"

"She's perfect."

"Who's the father?"

Tiger nudged her.

Laney looked over at him and smiled, rubbing behind his ears. "Hey there, Daddy."

With trembling hands, Laney opened the cage.

"She's a little timid at first, but once she gets to know you, she's all right," Cain said.

The little cub opened her eyes, and as soon as she saw Laney, she let out a little cry and scurried toward her, climbing into her lap.

Laney wrapped her arms around her, nestling her to her. "Hello, little one."

Hello.

Laney blinked. No, she couldn't have heard that. Her powers were gone.

Missed you.

Laney pulled the cub away and stared at her. "Cleo?"

Tiger licked Laney's cheek. *Yes.*

Laney started to laugh, and then she started to sob, pulling the cub close. *Cleo.*

Chapter Ninety-Nine

AFTER MEETING THE CUB, Laney had spent the afternoon with her uncle and Cain. They had talked about everything that happened. Laney had explained all she'd been going through, all she'd been thinking. Getting it all out, it helped. She felt better sharing her pain. But mostly it was having Cleo back that filled up part of the emptiness inside of her.

Now Cleo lay curled up on Laney's lap as she sat on the couch in her cottage. Laney ran a hand through her fur. She couldn't believe she had Cleo again. She knew souls reincarnated. She was proof of that. Practically everyone she knew at this point was proof of that. But Cleo basically giving birth to herself, that seemed a bit much.

But then she remembered what she had read by a man named Brian Weiss. He claimed that souls were not assigned until just before birth. So once Cleo's soul had left her body, it was waiting for a new one. It just happened to be this cub.

Laney wasn't going to turn herself in knots trying to figure it out. She was just going to appreciate this small gift.

She looked up at the ceiling, not sure who she was talking to, and said, "Thank you."

Cleo rolled onto her back. Laney moved her to the couch beside her. She was dreaming, her little legs moving as if she was running, with small sounds coming from the back of her throat. Images of a field with a squirrel darting away through tall grass flashed through Laney's mind.

She could still understand the cats. And they could understand her. But Laney didn't know how that was possible. Of course, she hadn't actually tried to use any of her abilities since Egypt. There'd been no need. And with the hole consuming her, she hadn't even thought about it.

But now she had to wonder. Of course, the cats were not a natural construct. They had been created in a lab. Perhaps they were a loophole to the whole removal-of-powers incident. Maybe the connections forged through the communication over the years couldn't be severed.

Laney wasn't sure how it happened. She was just grateful it had. A soft knock sounded at the door. She looked down at Cleo, who grimaced. Carefully, she picked her up and placed her on the dog bed on the floor. With the way she was dreaming, she didn't want her rolling off the couch. She couldn't resist running her hand over her one more time.

The knock sounded again. Laney made her way to the front door and opened it. Molly McAdams stood there, a hesitant smile on her face, Zaria next to her. "Hi."

Laney smiled, opening the door wide. "Hi." She looked down at Zaria. *Hi, Zaria.*

Hello.

Laney smiled wider.

Molly held up a tray with tinfoil over it. "I thought

maybe you would like some dessert. It's lemon meringue pie."

Laney stepped back. "I would love some, as long as you eat it with me."

Molly stepped in shyly. "I'd love that. Um, did Dom leave you anything?"

Laney linked an arm through hers. "Come see."

Epilogue

One Year Later

THE CRICK in Laney's neck only grew worse as the long flight continued, but she hadn't wanted to move and disturb Nyssa, who had fallen asleep on her an hour ago. Cleo was curled into her other side. She glanced toward the back of the plane. Cain was reading quietly, the glasses he had picked up at the optometrist perched on the edge of his nose. She'd never known someone so happy to need reading glasses before. Patrick was asleep in the chair next to him, a novel face down on his lap. The McAdams kids were all sprawled out across the back of the plane. Jake and Mary Jane were talking quietly, their heads together. Henry and Jen were in the bedroom with Tori. Tori had been teething for weeks now, and all three of them were exhausted.

But they wouldn't miss this for anything. They were all going on vacation down to Luiz's ranch in Peru. Well, it was also a reunion. Mustafa was flying in with Gerard and Noriko. Yoni, Sascha, Max, Dov, and their daughter, Noel, had landed a few hours ahead of them. For one week, they were all going to take advantage of Luiz's hospitality.

An hour later, they were pulling onto Luiz's long drive. Laney smiled at the rubber trees that lined it. The scent of the vanilla orchids floated through the open windows. As they got closer to the main house, she could hear the sound of laughter. A group of kids was playing kickball in a field to the right of the house. Yoni's bald head shone like a beacon as he stood in the outfield and called out plays. David yelled back counter plays, and the kids ignored both of them and just did what they wanted.

Laney smiled as she stepped out of the van.

"They're here!"

Laney turned to the porch as Lou vaulted down the steps and wrapped her in a hug. Laney smiled, staring down at her. Her skin was glowing, her eyes bright, and she had some new freckles around the bridge of her nose. "I think Luiz's ranch suits you."

"This place is incredible! I'm so glad you made me come down here."

"I merely suggested that seeing how Rahim was running the refugee center might help you figure things out."

"It really has. Rahim's great."

"Yes, he is," Laney agreed as the man in question stepped out of the front door, a small child in his arms. He smiled at Laney as Lou took the child from him and disappeared back inside. He hugged Laney warmly. "How are you?" she asked.

"Very well, especially now that you are all here."

Rahim had put his skills with resettlement to work, aiding those who'd been uprooted by the war against the Fallen. With Luiz's blessing, he'd established a refuge on Luiz's ranch. It was supposed to be a halfway point, helping families get settled. But a lot of children had been left on their own when the dust had settled, so they'd established an orphanage as well, the sister school to the orphanage in Italy. Rahim ran it with David's help. Susan Jacobson had also moved down to the ranch. And to the surprise of everyone, she and Luiz had really hit it off. Susan waved as she walked in from the fields next to a man in shorts and a t-shirt. Laney's mouth dropped open when she realized it was Bruce Heller. She didn't think he owned anything but suits.

Behind her, the children at the kickball game squealed. Laney knew what had set them off. She turned to see Cleo and Tiger stepping out of the van.

Kids? Cleo asked.

Laney smiled. *Go ahead. But be gentle.*

I know. Cleo gave her an annoyed look before tossing her head and heading for the kids. Laney shook her head. Cleo's teenage angst had shown up two weeks ago. Laney would be very happy when they were past this stage.

"Would you like a tour? A lot has changed since you were last here."

Laney linked her arm through Rahim's. "I'd love one."

THAT NIGHT, Laney sat outside under the stars with everyone after dinner had been cleared away. Chinese lanterns had been strung over the outdoor patio, and Luiz's staff had set up tables and chairs and little sitting areas all throughout the space.

A small dance floor had been set up, and Yoni was showing the kids his dance moves, which was setting most of them off into peals of laughter. Sascha finally grabbed him, demanding her own dance. Nyssa danced around

Patrick's chair where he obligingly put out a hand for her to twirl under whenever she put up her own hand. Noriko and Gerard looked lost in their own world. The teenagers seemed to be having some sort of strange dance contest. It looked like Joe McAdams was winning.

Cain, Bruce, and Mustafa were chatting over a bottle of wine. Luiz and Susan were fixing something back in the kitchen.

Cleo was curled up on the sofa cushion next to Laney. *Nice.*

Yes, it is.

It was hard to believe how far they had all come. A year ago she never would have been able to imagine a night like this. A night where everyone was relaxed. Where no country was trying to track them down. Where they weren't waiting for Samyaza or one of her people to unleash holy hell on some part of the world. For a year, they had slowly shifted from always on edge to cautiously watchful. To normal lives. Laney had even thought about going back into academia. But in the end she knew that would not fulfill her, so she'd started a non-profit for at-risk teens.

She'd linked up with other programs and managed to create safe harbors for kids that offered them a place to stay, educational and psychological services, as well as drug treatment centers. She traveled the country with Cleo, overseeing the twelve different centers, and she had plans to create another twelve within the next two years. She loved it.

Everyone, in fact, was doing well. Jake had married Mary Jane last month in a small ceremony on the estate. They were now in newlywed bliss. Patrick had retired from the priesthood, and he and Cain were raising Nyssa. Yoni and Sascha had moved back to the estate with their kids. Jen and Henry were ensconced in their home. Danny had taken on more leadership roles. Lou and Rolly would be starting college in the fall. Even Dom, who'd been struggling for so long, was coming around, thanks to Gina.

It all made Laney feel good. And yet there was still that hole that Drake had left that had never closed up.

Cleo's head jolted up.

"Cleo?"

Cleo didn't respond. She just darted into the trees. Laney stood up with a groan.

Henry called over to her. "Everything okay?"

"Yeah. She probably just saw a monkey." She'd been obsessed with the creatures ever since they'd arrived. "I'll bring her back."

She slipped away from the crowd, following the path that led toward the school. Torches lit the way, flickering shadows across the path. *Cleo?*

No response.

She frowned, not sure if she should be worried or annoyed. Cleo had gotten into the habit of occasionally ignoring Laney when she called. Gina assured her it was a normal stage of adolescence that she would grow out of. As far as Laney was concerned, it couldn't happen soon enough.

Cleo appeared on the path ahead, stepping silently out of the bushes just before the path turned out of view.

Laney picked up her pace with a sigh.

"Hey there, furball."

Laney froze at the sound of the voice as Cleo disappeared around the bend. Then Laney jolted back into movement. She ran sprinting around the turn before coming to a screeching halt.

Drake's blue eyes met hers. "Hello, Ring Bearer."

Laney drank in the sight. His hair was tousled, his skin tanned, his clothes casually perfect. Everything around them completely disappeared.

At the same time, she recognized exactly what was happening. "You're not real, are you?"

He smiled. "Not exactly. You're the only one who can see me, although Furball here can sense me."

"Were you ever real? Or was Michael the real one?"

"No, he was the shadow. A man who never loved, who never laughed. You brought me to life Laney. In Egypt, those roles were written for us. But that was not me. That person, he no longer exists."

"But neither do you."

"I do, in your heart. Just as you live on in mine."

Laney looked away from him. It hurt to look at his face and not be able to touch him. "I miss you."

"You don't have to miss me, Laney. I am always with you."

Tears rolled down her cheeks. "Not the way I want you to be."

"And not the way I want to be either. That is not our lot in life, it seems."

"So what? A few more centuries and maybe we get another chance to love and lose?"

"No. You'll see me before then." He leaned over and kissed her forehead. Laney closed her eyes. It felt so real. "I love you, Delaney McPhearson. I have since the first moment I saw you fight off that group of brats trying to hurt that stray. I have loved you every moment since. And I will love you every day you live and even beyond that."

Tears flowed freely down her cheeks. "Please don't go."

"I am never far away," he said, even as his voice started

to fade. When Laney opened her eyes, she was once again alone.

Goodbye, Drake. I love you too.

IT HAD BEEN a great week at the ranch. Luiz had been an incredible host. Laney's legs had given out after she'd seen Drake. She'd sat there, letting the tears flow freely. But when she stood up, her heart felt lighter. He had loved her, and he loved her still. She hadn't realized how much she had doubted that. But that doubt was gone. And she was reminded that while life was fleeting, their love was eternal.

And for the first time, Laney was looking forward to what the future was going to bring her personally.

Now she sat watching as everyone milled around the dessert table. It was their last night. They would be leaving in the morning. Right now, she was so stuffed she couldn't possibly fit in another bite. Of course, if there was more of that homemade ice cream that Luiz served last night, she might see how she felt in an hour.

Max stepped away from the crowd, a giant cone in his hand. He licked the sides as he made his way over to her.

She patted the bench next to her. "Have a seat, my friend."

Max clambered up. He'd be eight in a few days. Maddox and Kati had been gone for nearly two years. It was hard to believe it had been that long.

He hadn't had a vision in the last year. Laney hoped that maybe with the Fallen issue resolved, he no longer would. "How's the ice cream?"

"Good." He tilted it toward Laney. "Want a lick?"

She quickly straightened his cone before he lost half of

it. "I'm good. I might go get my own cone in a little bit." She paused. "Are you happy, Max?"

He nodded. "Yeah. This ice cream's really good."

She sighed. That wasn't what she'd meant. But then again, being he was eight, it was a perfectly normal response. She draped her arm over his shoulders and squeezed him. "Good."

The two of them sat there in silence, just people-watching. Cleo snuck up on Yoni and nearly tripped him before disappearing into the trees.

Max laughed. Laney joined in. Then he went still, the ice cream toppling from his hands. The hair on Laney's arms rose. Max was no longer with her.

He stared straight ahead, an otherworldly quality to his voice. "All is not set. The future remains uncertain. The path of Giza is still unwinding. The forces of evil will not sleep. Another showdown will come."

"When?" Laney asked. "Is it the Fallen? Are they not gone?"

"They are gone, but there is one chance for them to regain their footing. The Giza prophesy will still come true. The final step will be taken. The path will be complete."

Max sat back, shaking his head. He looked around, confused, and then down at the ground. "No!"

Laney cleared her throat, struggling to keep her tone even. "It's all right, Max. Why don't you just go get yourself a new one?"

He sighed, climbing off the bench. "Okay."

Laney watched him go, but she barely saw him. The Giza Prophesy. She knew exactly what he was talking about: the timeline through the Great Pyramid that had identified all the major points in humanity's history were accounted for on the way to the apex. But that timeline didn't end last year. It continued until the year 2038. At which time, humanity would either evolve into who they were meant to be or devolve into destruction.

Laney sat back, staring at the people she loved, all of them oblivious to the danger years in the future, and wishing she could be one of them again. But she would make sure they had their peace. No one would be given this burden. She would bear it alone until she needed to bring the others in.

And then she would prepare them to fight again.

Also by R.D. Brady

vinci-books.com/alive

The government's secret alien project was supposed to save humanity. Instead, it might just be our extinction event.

Turn the page for a free preview…

A.L.I.V.E.: Chapter One

LOWRY AIR FORCE BASE, COLORADO

Seven Months Ago

Four medics ran along next to the stretcher bearing Devon Shantz.

"Make it stop!" Devon screamed, his skin pale despite his tan. Sweat and blood soaked through the blue Oxford he wore. Blood pooled on the stretcher, dripping over the side, leaving a trail to follow to the infirmary in spite of the bandages being used to stem the ever increasing flow.

Martin Drummond followed the blood trail as he walked behind the moving medical emergency. A black suit with a white shirt and black tie covered his tall, gaunt frame. His dark hair was long and pulled back behind his ears. He knew that the nickname Angel of Death had been attached to him back at Langley, in part due to his appearance but also his skills. But today as he followed Devon, the name was not hyperbole.

His aide would not survive those wounds. He'd seen the man's intestines through the rips in his skin and he knew they had ruptured as well. If he didn't die of blood loss, sepsis would undeniably set in and kill him.

Ahead, the doors to the medical unit at Lowry Air Force Base stood open, waiting for its newest patient. The medics hustled the stretcher into the unit and right to the waiting doctors, already gowned.

"Get him on the table," the female doctor ordered.

Martin stepped into the unit. A flurry of medical individuals in blue scrubs blocked Martin's view as they worked frantically to save Devon's life. Martin pulled a pack of cigarettes from his coat pocket and lit one up as he leaned against a wall. An older woman in a nurse's uniform pursed her lips and started to walk over, but she was intercepted by another nurse who spoke urgently to her after a quick nervous glance back at Martin.

The first nurse glanced at him again, this time with traces of fear before she headed out the other door.

Martin took a long, satisfying drag, his feet crossed at the ankles, picturing the attack on Devon. It had happened so fast. The guards with them had been stunned. Martin had his weapon cleared of its holster before they'd even begun to react. But even then, he'd known it was too late for Devon.

Dr. Hasan Verma, the head of the medical unit, walked into the room. He glanced over at the flurry of activity around Devon before making his way to Martin. "Mr. Drummond, are you all right?"

Martin took a slow drag of his cigarette and blew the smoke out. Most of it hit the doctor in his face. Dr. Verma pulled his head back with a grimace but said nothing.

"I'm fine, but I cannot say the same for my aide."

"We have the best medical staff here. They will do everything in their power—"

"He won't make it. You know that as well as I do."

Dr. Verma nodded. "Most likely. But were you hurt in any way?"

Martin shook his head. "No."

Dr. Verma's gaze flicked to the bottom of Martin's shirt. Martin followed his gaze and noticed for the first time the dark blue spot that had spread there. Surprise flashed through him. *I didn't realize it had gotten so close.*

He met the doctor's gaze. "Obviously *that* blood is not mine."

"A med unit was dispatched for the creature as well."

Martin raised an eyebrow. "Why?"

The doctor frowned. "To—to see if it could be saved."

Martin dropped the cigarette and smashed it under his shoe. "Then tell them to stop and make sure the thing is dead."

"But, sir—"

"Dead, Dr. Verma, tell them to make sure it is dead." With one last look at Devon, he strode for the doors, pulling out his phone, careful to make sure that no one saw him smile.

A.L.I.V.E.: Chapter Two

TODAY

Dayton, Ohio

The horse's hooves thundered across the field, her flank damp with sweat. Maeve Leander's fingers ached as she clutched the reins. Alejandra's dark mane flew behind her, as did Maeve's own hair. She'd pushed Alejandra hard and had nearly been thrown a few times. But she didn't dare slow down. Instead she silently begged—please, my friend, go faster.

She'd heard about the raiders when she had been in town. She'd crossed through Copper Canyon to avoid the roads and cut her time in half. But now the road was her only option. Caution dictated she slow down but fear wouldn't let her. She knew she had already pushed the old girl too hard. But she still urged Alejandra to go just a little bit faster. And the horse responded as if she too understood what was at stake.

As soon as the horse gained traction on the dirt road, her pace picked up. But not before Maeve saw that which she was dreading—hoof prints. Lots of them.

A.L.I.V.E.: Chapter Two

No, no, no. Terror slid over her. The reins became slick in her hands.

A waft of gray smoke drifted over the hill in the distance. Disbelief and fear fought inside of Maeve, each trying to gain the upper hand.

She leaned forward, keeping her focus on the hilltop, not letting herself think what the smoke meant. It can't be. It cannot be, she repeated to herself as Alejandra began the climb. She kept up the mantra as they ascended. Finally, she reached the peak, and her family's farm came into view.

Maeve reined Alejandra in sharply. Her breath left her body in a gasp just as sharp, and the fear she'd been shoving away broke free, threatening to swallow her whole.

A pyre of flames burned brightly in front of the barn, gray smoke wafting up angrily from the blaze. Even from this distance, she could make out the red shawl being engulfed by the flames, the body it still clung to already burning. Tears streamed down her cheeks and a hole developed in her chest, threatening to split her in two. "Mama."

No one else was in sight. Just her family's home and the barn, watching in silent horror as her mother left this world in ashes. Maeve wanted nothing more than to turn Alejandra around and flee. But she knew she needed to check.

She needed to be sure her mother was the only one they had found.

Maeve Leander's eyes flew open. *Mama.* She reached up and felt the tears on her cheek. She stared at the ceiling, her reality coming into focus as the dream faded. But the feelings of grief remained, raw and deep. She swiped at the tears on her cheeks, but new ones replaced the old. And this time it was for her own mother, not the girl in the dreams.

Alice Leander had died over a year ago from breast cancer, but at moments like these her death seemed like it had occurred just yesterday.

A vision from the dream returned, the red shawl

A.L.I.V.E.: Chapter Two

covering the body as it burned in the pyre. Maeve shivered at the memory. Her dreams had been so vivid lately. And they all revolved around the same place—Mexico. She'd never been to Mexico in her life, and she couldn't understand the source of the dreams. Her subconscious was obviously trying to tell her something. But what?

The alarm clock on her side table blared to life. Sitting up, Maeve fumbled for the button to switch it off.

She sat with her head in her hands for moment, her dark wavy hair tumbling over her shoulders. With an impatient gesture she pushed it back.

She's gone, but she would want you to be happy. She would want you to keep going.

She knew her affirmation was right, and she wasn't one who gave up. But sometimes she just missed her so much. She sat for a moment staring around the Spartan one-bedroom apartment. A delivery person had arrived last week with the bed and asked if she'd just moved in. Maeve had told him yes, even though she'd been here for five years. But her life was not spent here. Here was where she slept, occasionally ate, and showered. Her real life occurred at Wright-Patterson Air Force Base.

A small face appeared in her mind, chasing away her feelings of grief. She wasn't alone. And there was still someone counting on her.

Pushing herself from the bed, she crossed the short distance to her windows and pulled back the room's darkening curtains. Bright sunlight streamed in and Maeve blinked hard, taking a step back. She glanced at the clock. 4:02 pm.

Time to go to work.

A.L.I.V.E.: Chapter Three

Maeve sat near the front of the bus reading her book as she and twenty others who worked at Wright-Patterson Air Force Base were driven toward the base. Security on the base was incredibly strict, especially for the research divisions. As of three weeks ago, no personnel were allowed to drive in. They were bussed from a parking area set up outside the base perimeter. All bags were checked before entering the bus and before leaving the installation. And no unauthorized personnel were allowed within three miles of the base. They said it was for construction, but Maeve was pretty sure it was a new security measure.

From behind her, she felt a tap on her shoulder. She turned around.

Greg Schorn pushed the dark hair from his eyes, pushing his glasses up his nose. He nodded out the window. "What's that?"

Maeve looked up from her book with a frown. "What?"

Greg nudged his chin toward the front of the bus.

A.L.I.V.E.: Chapter Three

Maeve looked past the driver and saw the familiar fence of the base. But today there was something new—protestors.

"Never seen that before," Greg murmured. "I wonder how they managed it?"

Maeve was just as baffled.

Wooden sawhorses had been set up to keep the protestors from blocking the road. Military police lined up along the sawhorses as well.

"I don't get it. Why didn't security just run them off?" Greg asked.

Maeve read a few signs as they passed.

Stop Animal Abuse.

Animals Are Not Disposable.

The protestors ranged in age from college students to senior citizens and all raised their fists towards the bus. Some yelled, although the heavy glass windows made their words impossible to discern. *An animal rights demonstration?*

"I wonder which project they're protesting," Greg said.

She wanted to turn around and ask Greg if he knew anything about the protest but she didn't. One of the biggest rules of working at Wright-Patt's National Air and Space Intelligence Center (NASIC), formerly the Foreign Technology Division, was that you never asked questions about what was happening on base unless it was absolutely necessary. In fact, Maeve had ridden the bus with these same twenty people for the last three weeks but she had known their faces for much longer. But she didn't know what project a single one of them worked on—not even Greg, who she'd been friends with for years.

The departments were all completely separated. Maeve herself had top-secret clearance and she simply assumed no one else did. It was just easier that way. Who the others worked for and what their clearance was she didn't know

A.L.I.V.E.: Chapter Three

and simply couldn't risk finding out. Anyone who spoke with someone outside their project parameters about their research would be immediately dismissed.

Maeve knew of three people that had been dismissed for violating that rule. And Maeve had way too much at stake to break it.

But despite that precaution, she and Greg maintained the friendship they'd developed in college. In fact, Maeve was the reason Greg applied for the position at Wright-Patt. And Maeve enjoyed having a friendly face around, even if neither of them ever mentioned their work.

The bus pulled up in front of Hangar One, and three people got off. Wright-Patterson Air Force Base had been established back in 1948 with the merging of Wright and Patterson fields. In fact, the base had its origins with the fathers of aviation: the Wright Brothers Huffman Prairie Flying Field. In 1917, it was established as a military installation. Since that time, the US military had used that same piece of land as a testing site for aviation. Now it had grown to cover almost twelve square miles and employed over twenty-seven thousand people, both military and civilian.

Greg leaned forward. "Hey, did you do anything good this weekend?"

Maeve shook her head. "I was here."

Greg shook his head. "You know, I'm dedicated to my research and all, but you take it to a whole new level."

You have no idea, Maeve thought but just smiled as the bus pulled up to her stop. "Lunch this week?"

"Yeah. Let me know what's good for you."

"Will do," Maeve said as she headed for the door.

With a nod of thanks to the driver, Sam, she stepped out into the cool night air. Building 23 stood fifty feet away. It was a square brick building only three stories high, one wall

A.L.I.V.E.: Chapter Three

almost completely made of glass and dark metal framing. It looked completely unassuming and identical to another dozen buildings or so on the base.

Maeve moved quickly up the short path and placed her hand on the palm plate at the front door. The door popped open and she stepped into the vestibule. A guard sat at a desk at the back of the foyer with a thick wall behind him. A steel door stood to the guard's left, which led to the upper floors, and another one stood to the right, which housed another security detail. But even those guards weren't allowed into the building itself unless there was an emergency.

There were only two other doors in the entryway, one on either side of the hallway.

A quick nod at the guard and Maeve turned into the women's locker room on the right. Grabbing a pair of pale blue scrubs from the shelf on her right, she quickly stripped off her clothes. Donning the blue scrubs, she folded her clothes and put them in her locker, securing the lock.

She exited the locker room through the back. After sliding her ID through the scanner, the steel door by the guard slid open. Bypassing the elevator, she quickly made her way to the stairs. She jogged up the two flights to her lab, and at the landing of her floor, she waved her ID over another scanner. The door buzzed and she pushed through. Her floor had bright white walls with gray tile and was lined with eight doorways. To her left was a small lounge, the cafeteria, a med room, the security office, and two bathrooms. To her right was only one room: her lab.

She turned right. Another wave of her ID over yet another scanner and the light above her door bloomed green. She pushed through and pulled on a lab coat hanging by the door.

A.L.I.V.E.: Chapter Three

Her 'lab' actually consisted of five rooms with only one entrance. This part of the lab contained a large room with two large, long tables. Along the back wall was a couch and her desk. To the left was a large glass wall, beyond which was the control room, which housed a series of computers and monitors. Beyond that was another glass wall.

Maeve glanced over but the lights beyond the second glass wall were still dark. Inside that room were three doors leading to an additional three rooms—a medical suite, a physical therapy room, and a living space.

Maeve waved at Greta Schubert, who sat behind a console and a row of screens beyond the first glass wall. Greta had worked at the base for as long as Maeve could remember. Greta smiled, her brown hair, lined with only a few hints of gray, was pulled back in a bun. She wore a blue turtleneck that contrasted with her white lab coat and brought out the blue in her eyes. Greta gave her a quick wave before turning back to the console.

Maeve glanced at the clock and the still, dark room beyond Greta. *Good. I should have about an hour.*

She made her way to her desk, which was neat, just how she liked it. The only adornment was a picture of her with her mom and a small *E.T.* doll that Greta had picked up for her one birthday a few years back.

Maeve grabbed the reports that had been printed out by Greta during the day. She took a seat on the couch, flipping through them. EKG readings were normal, as were the sleep pattern readings. She frowned a little at the neurotransmitter levels. They were a little low, especially the dopamine, serotonin, and norepinephrine. She'd have to check that.

She hopped on her computer and quickly wrote up her views on the lab reports. She was just replying to an email from the head of NASIC when Greta called her through the intercom.

"He's waking up."

Grab your copy...
vinci-books.com/alive

Afterword

FACT OR FICTION?

As with all books in The Belial Series, facts play a large role in creating the story line. For this book in particular, I also wanted to go back to some of the basic facts that started the whole series. For me, my interest in alternate history began with the Giza plateau and the three pyramids. I knew that was where we needed to end up. And the fact that we had not discussed the Great Pyramid seemed a tragedy. So I knew I needed a mystery surrounding the Great Pyramid and the missing capstone is perhaps one of the greatest mysteries involving the Pyramid.

Now on to the facts!

Gnostic Prayer. In the prologue I included a prayer that Father Clementis was translating much to the anger of Constantine. That is an actual Gnostic Prayer. It is called *The Thunder, Perfect Mind*. It is part of the Nag Hammadi Library.

Constantine. The scenes involving Constantine are of course fictitious. However, he did have a huge influence on the structure and content of the Catholic faith. As explained in *The Belial Sacrifice*, Constantine had a vision of a cross in the sky during the Battle of Milvian Bridge, outside Rome. After consulting religious scholars, he interpreted it as a sign from God and converted to Catholicism. He was responsible for calling the Council of Nicaea which in turn determined which books would be included in the Bible. Although not mentioned in this novel, in previous books I have mentioned that the Book of Enoch, which had been incredibly popular, was one of the books that was discounted. In fact, all Gnostic books that were discounted.

The Pyramids. All the information on the dimensions of the pyramids and the history of the Giza Plateaus are accurate to the best of my ability. Much has been written about the Giza plateau. For those interested in more information, I encourage you to check out Graham Hancock's *Fingerprints of the Gods*.

A Void in the Great Pyramid. I thought that due to the age of the Pyramid and the interest it has generated for hundreds, if not thousands, of years, that every inch of it had been investigated. That is not true. They are constantly finding new aspects to the Great Pyramid. As mentioned in *The Belial Sacrifice*, a void large enough to hide the Statue of Liberty was found back in 2017. Prior to that time, they had no idea it was there.

Capstone for the Great Pyramid. There is no record of the Great Pyramid having a capstone. Each historical record that describes the Pyramid describes it without a capstone. Having said that, it does seem odd that this marvel and testament to precision is missing a capstone. In my search

Afterword

for any information about a capstone, I came across the Ra conversations from the Law of One Society. Similar to Edgar Cayce's trances, Ra was allegedly channeled through a trance and would answer questions about human nature. In one of these sessions, Ra said there had been two capstones, one gold and one granite. The gold was largely decorative but the granite was said to have energy conducing abilities.

Capstone for the New Century. There was actually a plan to create a capstone for the top of the Great Pyramid. Toward the end of the twentieth century and to celebrate the new century, the Egyptian government began to develop plans for a capstone to be created and placed on top of the Great Pyramid for the New Year's celebration. Then, in December 1999, just a few weeks shy of the New Year, the plans were scrapped. According to the Egyptian government the plans were scrapped due to concerns about a terrorist threat.

Gate of the Sun. The Gate of the Sun is real. It can be found in Tiwanaku, Bolivia. Tiwanaku is located near Lake Titicaca, where the legendary Viracocha is said to have lived. Some maintain that the gate is a calendar, representing 290 days. Others, however, argue that the gate is a doorway to the land of the gods and that certain blessed individuals were allowed access in the past.

War Debt. The numbers provided in *The Belial Sacrifice* for the cost of war are sadly true. $2.4 trillions dollars have been spent in Iraq and Afghanistan according to Reuters.

Afterword

Michael. Before I began writing The Belial Series, I thought I had a good basic understanding of the archangel Michael. Twelve years of Catholic schooling will give you that sense of knowledge. But as I began to research Michael, I realized I did not know nearly as much as I thought. Originally, at least within Christianity, Michael was viewed as a healer, not a warrior. The Book of Revelation, however, identifies Michael as the warrior of God in the Book of Revelation that ultimately defeats Satan's army. Constantine helped further this image with associating Michael with the slaying of a dragon. His archangel status was established in the fourth century.

Historical Sites and War. Sadly historical sites are not immune to the violence of war. The examples provided in *The Belial Sacrifice* are real. For me, the destruction of the giant Buddhas in Afghanistan by the Taliban, which had stood for nearly two thousand years, is the first image that comes to mind when I think of this callous disregard for history.

More recent attacks come in one of the oldest regions of the world: Iraq and Syria. Spearheaded by Isis, the latest attacks involve taking bulldozers and explosives to archeological sites, also thousands of years old. In 2015, ISIS destroyed multiple sites in the ancient city of Palmyra including a temple to the ancient god Baal and the 1900 year-old Temple of Baalshamin. Other attacks include the destruction with pick axes and sledgehammers the Mosul Museum, home of the artifacts from the ancient city of Nineveh, which flourish from 900 BC-600 BC.

Child Soldiers During the Civil War. Children were not legally allowed to fight in the Civil War. However, when the war was going badly for each side, recruiters would look the

Afterword

other way when obviously young boys lied about their age to enlist. Like Johnny Clem, who'd joined the Union army as a drummer boy at the age of eleven. He saw combat and was still actively serving until 1915 when he retired as a Brigadier General

Drake. I know a lot of people wanted Laney and Drake to end up together. I actually wrote an ending where that happened but then I decided to switch it.

About the Author

Author, Criminologist, Terrorism Expert, Jeet Kune Do Black Sash, Runner, Dog Lover.

Amazon best-selling author R.D. Brady writes supernatural and science fiction thrillers. Her thrillers include ancient mysteries, unusual facts, non-stop action, and fierce women with heart.

Prior to beginning her writing career, R.D. Brady was a criminologist who specialized in life-course criminology and international terrorism. She's lectured and written numerous academic articles on the genetic influence on criminal behavior, factors that influence terrorist ideology, and delinquent behavior formation.

After visiting counter-terrorism units in Israel, RD returned home with a sabbatical in front of her and decided to write that book she'd been thinking about. Four years later she left academia with the publication of her first book, *The Belial Stone*, and hasn't looked back.

Acknowledgments

I cannot thank you, the reader, strong enough. Your interest in The Belial Series changed my life. Thank you for staying with me through fourteen books. I hope you have found a little joy along the way.

Thank you to Crystal Wantanabe and your staff at Pikko's House. Your editing advice and time has been beyond helpful. I appreciate the time and diligence you have all taken. And I look forward to our future work together.

To the handful of people who have helped by reading or discussing aspects of the book I was struggling. Thank you for your input and your support.

To my kung fu family, thank you for always inspiring me and pushing me forward. And a special thanks for letting me bounce ideas off of you (and occasionally fists and sticks).

To my children. Life got better the moment you all showed up. It's hard to imagine my life before you were in it. Thank you for making sure I step away from the computer and have a little fun. You are a constant reminder of what is actually important in this world.

To my husband. I never would have been able to go down this road without your support and love. You didn't blink when I said I was going to write full-time. You simply asked what you could do to help. I am forever grateful for that and for having you in my life.

And finally, to my four furry writing companions: you are the best co-workers ever!